THE
SON
G OF D

SHARON LINDSAY

This Is My Son

THE SON OF GOD

Series: Book 2

TATE PUBLISHING
AND ENTERPRISES, LLC

Published by Tate Publishing & Enterprises, LLC
127 E. Trade Center Terrace | Mustang, Oklahoma 73064 USA
1.888.361.9473 | www.tatepublishing.com

Tate Publishing is committed to excellence in the publishing industry. The company reflects the philosophy established by the founders, based on Psalm 68:11,
"The Lord gave the word and great was the company of those who published it."

Book design copyright © 2015 by Tate Publishing, LLC. All rights reserved.
Cover design by Nino Carlo Suico
Interior design by Jomel Pepito

Published in the United States of America

ISBN: 978-1-68028-126-2
1. Fiction / Religious
2. Fiction / Historical
15.03.23

To my mother, Mary Cross
She read Bible stories to her children
every night before they went to bed.
She helped us memorize a Bible verse each week
and often played Bible games with us.
Many times I saw her praying
by her bed on her knees.
My mother, like the characters of the Bible,
faced many difficulties in her life
with strength from God.
Mom, I love you
and deeply appreciate you.

Contents

Introduction

This book continues the story of the life of Jesus that began in *The Son of God, Book 1*. Joseph and Mary, Toma and Kheti, Heli along with Jethro and Moshe continue to interact in the life of young Jesus. The story picks up when Jesus is eleven, before Luke's account of Jesus's visit to Jerusalem with his parents to celebrate the Passover.

This Passover experience is the only story from the childhood and adolescence of Jesus that is recorded in the Bible; therefore, it would seem that we know very little about this period in the life of our Messiah. But by carefully considering everything that is written about Jesus in Scripture, as well as researching the time and the culture in which he grew up, we can assume much about this period of his life without moving into a realm that contradicts Scripture.

This book is based on the following assumptions:

- ➢ Jesus was Jewish and lived by the laws of the Torah. (Matthew 1:1–17)

- ➢ He lived in a typical small Israeli town in the region of Galilee, and he participated in town life. (Matthew 2:19–23)

- ➢ It was an agricultural community and he worked with his father who was a carpenter. (Matthew 13:53–57)

- ➢ A number of his parables could have come from actual stories within his community and extended family.

- ➢ He had both immediate and extended family. (Matthew 13:53–57, Luke 1:36–80)

➢ During his ministry, he lived and worked in Capernaum. This was not an unfamiliar place. He had already made relationships there. (Matthew 4:13)

➢ The roots of many friendships and relationships are in his childhood or adolescence.

➢ First-century Jews were looking for a military and kingly messiah to free them from the Romans. There had been and still were those who claimed to fill that role. To the Romans and some upper-class segments of Jewish society, they were outlaws; to ordinary Jews they were heroes. (Acts 5:33-39)

➢ Within Judaism, there were three distinct theological streams—Pharisees, Sadducees, and Essenes—and within those three groups there were subgroups. During the ministry years of Jesus, his teachings sometimes addressed the doctrines of these groups. (Matthew 22: 15–45, 23:1–37)

➢ This was a period of preparation in the life of Jesus. From his earthly father, Joseph, he was learning how to become a man in Jewish society. From his Heavenly Father, he was learning who he was, who his enemy was, and what his purpose was. (Luke 2:41–52)

➢ During his ministry years, Jesus often referred to himself as the Son of Man. When Jesus left heaven, he put his divinity aside and confined himself to living as men live. Every miracle that he does is initiated by God and done through the power of the Holy Spirit. From his birth to his death and resurrection, he only does what his Father tells him to do. (John 5:19–30)

➢ The total scope of the miracles and words of Jesus are not recorded in the Bible. We only have a fraction. And the part that we have seems to indicate that for Jesus, these events were part of his normal life. He never indicates surprise when someone is healed, the dead are raised, food multiplies, he is visited by heavenly beings, God speaks to him, demons flee, and nature obeys. (John 21:25)

➢ Just as God moves us step by step into the fullness of our calling, so he moved Jesus into the fullness of his divine purpose. (Matthew 4:1–11)

➢ Any way that God has communicated with man, he would also use to communicate with Jesus while he is on Earth in human form. There are far too many texts to list in support of this assumption, so I will list a few obvious biblical characters who experienced unique personal communication with heaven: Adam, Enoch, Abraham, Jacob, Moses, Elijah, Elisha, Ezekiel, Daniel, Isaiah, Joseph the Earthly father of Jesus, Mary, Peter, John, Paul, and others.

➢ The Hebrew scriptures were an important source of divine revelation regarding his purpose. (John 5:39)

So now that I have laid a foundation, we can safely allow our imaginations to consider things that could have happened during the formative years of Jesus, the Son of God and the Son of Man.

Prologue

The First Family of Earth

In the beginning was the Word, and the Word was with God,
and the Word was God. He was with God in the beginning.
Through him all things were made; without him nothing was
made that has been made. In him was life, and that life was
the light of men.

—John 1:1–4

From heavenly Mount Zion, God the Father watched. His omnipotent gaze penetrated deep space and sliced through Earth's atmosphere. His eyes focused on the deserted Garden of Eden and then moved to a small patch of cultivated ground that Adam had wrestled from Earth's thorny soil.

Restlessly, the Holy Spirit flowed from one side of the throne room to the other. Like an undulating sea of molten lava, his spirit-being remained in constant motion while his eyes never left the family of Adam and Eve.

Adam and Eve, with two sons and two daughters, approached the altar Adam had erected not far from the beautiful garden that had been their first home.

"I can never forget what it was like to hold them in my arms," Yeshua sadly stated. He had also been watching, but now, for a moment, he turned away and looked at his empty hands. "As I created Adam my son and Eve, my daughter, I touched every organ in each of their bodies. My lips pressed against their lips, and I blew my life into their lungs."

"That is why we cannot forget them," Father God responded.

Yeshua nodded in agreement. "Together, we have created many living beings, but only in mankind did we put so much of ourselves. They are truly our children, the image of who we are."

As the seraphs and cherubim who constantly sang praises above and around the sapphire throne sensed the profound sadness of the Godhead, their praises ceased. Silence prevailed. God the Ruler of the Universe, Yeshua the Creator of All Things, and the Holy Spirit turned their entire attention on the first family of Earth.

Approaching the altar near the entrance to the beautiful garden, Adam led the way, with his two sons walking on either side. Eve followed. Her arms were linked with the arms of her two daughters. As the first family of Earth came over a small rise, Eve could see the flashing heavenly sword that faithfully guarded against any unauthorized return to that garden paradise. Gradually, she slowed her pace, dropping farther back behind Adam and the boys.

"It is so painful to remember," Eve whispered her regret. Tears flowed down her cheeks, a blessing that blurred her vision. "It breaks my heart to see the wonderful garden. It was my first home." Eve took a few more sorrowful steps, her daughters supporting her on either side. Then she collapsed in the dust, sobbing. "Forgive me!" With her fists, she beat the ground. "My children, forgive me! If I had not disobeyed, this garden would be your home. The Creator and all the heavenly beings would be your companions. You would not have to live in this wasteland with Satan and his demonic warriors."

"No, no, Mother," her oldest daughter protested. "We have the promise of a deliverer. He will come and fight Satan."

"Satan hid himself within the serpent, and he deceived you," her youngest daughter reasoned. "The Creator who lives in heaven understands. He will see to it that we are released from the domain of the Evil One. Do not despair!"

"No, Mother, do not despair." The twin sister of Cain tugged persistently at her mother, trying to pull her face up from the dust.

Slowly, the girls coaxed their distraught mother into a sitting position within their comforting arms. Together, they watched as Adam took their most precious lamb from his youngest son, Abel. Leaning heavily on the head of the lamb, he loudly proclaimed, "God, I have sinned. In the garden, I rejected your counsel and heeded the words of your enemy. Forgive me!" Pushing harder on the head of the mute animal, he cried out again, "I am now a prisoner in the land of Satan. My willful disregard of your commands gave that rebellious angel the right to steal my position as companion to the Creator and ruler of this planet."

The head of the lamb nearly touched the ground as Adam leaned with all his might into the animal, laying on that innocent animal the full weight of his transgression and remorse. The man who had once received dominion over Earth directly from the hands of Yeshua now trembled under the weight of his punishment. "Because I did not submit to your authority, my sons and their descendants have lost their God-given inheritance. Forgive me!" With tears streaming down his face, he nodded to each of his sons. "Place your hands on top of mine."

Abel, whose eyes were fixed on the ravaged face of his father, placed both of his adolescent hands on top of his father's work-callused ones, but Cain hung back and had to be told a second time. Then he reluctantly placed one hand on top of his brother's hands.

"Keep your promise, O Lord!" Adam looked imploringly toward heaven. "Remember me and my sons and all the generations that will follow. Send the Deliverer, who will release us from the curses we brought upon ourselves. Accept this sacrifice." He removed his right hand from beneath Abel's hands and picked up the knife.

With one clean thrust, he severed the juggler vein of the innocent animal, and the life of the lamb poured out onto the ground.

Tears streamed down Abel's smooth cheeks. Adam sobbed, but Cain showed no emotion. The young man's face, like a majestic rock, never changed. Once more, Eve sank to the ground, weeping into the dust. "It is my fault. It is my fault." This time, her daughters draped their bodies over hers and cried with her.

"Adam and Eve are truly repentant," Yeshua commented as tears streamed down his immortally majestic face. "My heart aches for them."

"They regret. We regret," God sorrowfully added.

"It is more than regret," Yeshua stated. "They miss being with us. They long to return to those days when we sat together in the garden, when we shared every moment in their lives." Yeshua sighed wistfully. "Adam and I created together. We made plans together…" His words trailed off, and one more crystal tear slowly slid down his beautiful face.

"Adam's children are also calling for the Deliverer," God observed as he watched young Abel assist his father in laying the lamb on the altar. "Adam's youngest boy never lived in the garden or visited with us, yet his heart is pure."

"But Cain!" The Holy Spirit flared momentarily as he spoke the name of Adam's eldest son. "His heart is fertile ground for our enemy. See how he turns away from the altar, how his lip curls in a derisive sneer."

"Our enemy!" Yeshua announced with alarm. "He is coming out of a cave on a nearby hill." The all-seeing eyes of the Godhead fixed on the dark angel who once supported the sapphire throne in their Holy Sanctuary.

"He has become ugly," the Spirit stated. "He no longer reflects the light of his Creator."

"Still, he retains enough light to fool those who have never experienced the brilliance of heaven," observed Yeshua.

"Deceiver!" Father God passionately muttered. "You have made yourself invisible. If Adam saw you, he would know there is no heavenly light in you."

"Look, Satan is approaching Cain. The boy has no defenses. He does not know his enemy!" Yeshua cried in alarm.

"Michael!" Yeshua called the angelic commander of the heavenly hosts. Instantly, the magnificent warring angel stood at his side. "I commission you to destroy Satan, the cherub I wish I had never created!" Yeshua announced as a glowing sword suddenly materialized in his hand.

"Wait! In the planning stages, when we gave the gift of choice to the beings we were going to create, we also established a plan to deal with rebellion in the kingdom." God moved between Yeshua and Michael, preventing Yeshua from placing the weapon in the commander's hand. "We studied serious questions involving cause and effect outcomes within the kingdom. Will the destruction of Satan result in bringing Cain to the place where he yearns for our companionship?" God restated a question from the planning phase of creation.

"He will only fear us," the Spirit answered.

"And what about the other heavenly beings, the ones who almost joined Satan as he took one-third of the heavenly hosts with him?" God continued his thought-provoking questions. "Will they continue their loyalty to us out of love, or will that love turn into fear?"

"Satan must be destroyed!" Yeshua insisted. "That was our final conclusion!"

Raising his right hand, God reaffirmed, "I have sworn to destroy him!" Like thunder, the words of the Ruler of the Universe rolled throughout heaven. "But I will not destroy the foundations of our kingdom in the process. Our violence will not conquer his violence. We cannot be like that evil cherub."

"We must never resort to deceit and disregard for life," the Holy Spirit spoke thoughtfully. "We even have to protect the life of our enemy until we can demonstrate the essential differences between us and him."

"We are love," Yeshua stated. "Satan is hate."

"We are truth," Father God added. "Satan is a liar."

"Satan is the destroyer," the Spirit growled. His words flew like fireballs around the throne room. "But we are the Creator and the rebuilder."

"We own eternal life," Yeshua announced. "And our enemy owns eternal death. I will take death, his most powerful weapon, away from him."

Stepping aside and looking pointedly at the sword in Yeshua's hand, God asked, "At this moment, what action will you take?"

Stepping past the Archangel Michael, Yeshua the Creator placed the sword in the hand of Eternal God. "You decide the time, the place, and the method of Satan's destruction, only let me do battle with him face-to-face. Let me carry out your final judgment on our enemy."

Nodding in agreement, God accepted the glowing sword. As he gripped the hilt with his right hand, the sword glowed and flashed.

"We cannot just leave them without assistance!" The Holy Spirit flared in alarm. "Look! Satan is speaking to Cain. He is planting thoughts in the boy's mind, and the boy is unaware that our enemy is the source of those thoughts."

"Go!" God and Yeshua spoke at once. "Be our voice. Counter Satan's words. Give the boy a clear choice and then let him choose."

Like a fiery comet, the Spirit of God soared out of the throne room, burning a path through space to the altar where Adam and his family lay facedown in the dust, waiting to see if the Eternal One would accept their sacrifice.

Annoyed, Cain lifted his head just enough to view the altar with one eye. How long would they lay in the dust before the great Triune Ruler showed approval by striking the altar with fire and consuming the offering in a blaze of flame and smoke?

Carefully, Cain turned his head to the other side. He could see the faces of his parents pressed flat to the ground. Their bodies still undulated with heartbroken sobs. His sisters also had their faces pressed to the ground, but they were not sobbing. His eyes lingered on his twin. He was drawn to her. Then his eyes strayed to his brother, Abel. The boy was sobbing as hard as his parents.

There was a voice in Cain's head. "When will your family come to their senses? When will they forget the garden and the memories attached to it? When will they move on and live?"

Its presence did not alarm him. Instead, the young man agreed with it and then entered into mental conversation with it. "It is time to begin my own life, time to take a wife and start my own family." He spoke to himself and to the voice within his head. Again his eyes roamed up and down the prone form of his sister. "You will be my wife. I will take you and leave this area. We will live in a place that is no longer under the shadow of the past."

"You know, your parents have chosen your younger sister to be your wife. They are going to give your twin sister to your brother, Abel." Satan leaned close and whispered information gleaned from lurking and eavesdropping on family conversations.

Resentment, like a slow-burning fire, smoldered in the back of Cain's mind.

Suddenly, there was a startlingly loud crack! A blazing ball of fire struck the carcass of the slain lamb on the altar. As the Holy Spirit touched the dead animal, he prophetically signaled to Satan. "The Eternal One plans to consume you in a lake of fire."

Instantly, Satan withdrew to the mouth of a nearby cave, pressing himself into a jagged black crevice. From the darkness, he observed.

The Holy Spirit stretched and spread himself like a shimmering mantle above the entire family. Gradually, gently, he lowered himself until the heat of his presence made their prone bodies glow.

"He is here," Adam called reassuringly to his wife as he stood up and lifted his arms toward heaven. "The Spirit of God has come to comfort us."

"I know," Eve responded as she also came to her feet and walked to her husband's side. "Remember, he used to come with the Creator. We always felt his presence like wonderful fire all over our bodies."

"Now it is only tingling warmth. Do you feel it, Abel?" Adam turned to his youngest son.

"Oh, yes, Father!" Abel's face glowed, and his young arms reached heavenward. "The Spirit is speaking to me in my head. He says I am loved!"

"And you, Cain?" Adam inquired.

"The lamb and the wood under it have been totally consumed," Cain responded by stating the obvious. "We have spent most of the day in this place. I am hungry and would like to return to our home."

"But don't you feel—" Eve pleaded.

Obviously annoyed, her oldest son cut her off, "I feel hungry. I will take my sisters back to our cave." Scornfully, he continued, "We will prepare a meal. When you have finished staring into the sky—"

Firmly, Adam interrupted, "When we have heard what the Spirit has to say, we will worship again and then return to the cave." With a nod of his head, he indicated that Cain and his sisters should leave.

Without hesitation, Cain turned away from his parents and his younger brother. Signaling his sisters to follow, he strode down the dirt path toward the cave where his family made their home.

Satan followed, keeping pace and then creeping forward until he walked unseen beside the eldest son of Adam. "In the valley below this mountain is a level fertile piece of ground," he whispered.

Cain pictured the place where he had recently laid out a new garden. He remembered a beautiful winding stream, a flat rockless meadow. He considered the possibility of taking mud from the stream and shaping it into bricks that would harden in the sun. Then with those bricks, he could build a home.

"No more cave living for you! You can build a home out of mud bricks," Satan said, encouraging Cain's dreams. "You do not have to live like your parents, afraid to move to any place that is not within walking distance of that garden where they used to live!" With a wave of his arm, Satan signaled one of his spirit warriors whom he had named Resentment. "Carry on for me," he ordered as he slipped away from Cain.

Resentment swooped in. Turning his spirit form into a wedge, he forced himself through the opening Satan had made in Cain's mind. "Your parents have no present and no future," the dark spirit whispered. "They only have a past that is tied to a vengeful God who requires regular blood sacrifices."

As the path widened, Cain's two sisters stepped up beside him. Cain glanced at his youngest sister. She looked like Abel. She had his dark hair and sharp features. "She reminds you too much of the brother you hate," Resentment spoke again. "Your parents cannot really expect you to marry her and continue to live in the cave with them!"

Cain considered and agreed with the voice in his head. Turning to his right, he smiled at his twin. The rays of the setting sun danced across her thick cascade of straight red hair. Possessively, Cain reached out and put his arm around her shoulders.

"You were meant to be together," Resentment urged. "Your parents don't understand. Your union was ordained from birth."

"Yes," Cain concurred with the voice in his head, "we are meant for each other."

"Do whatever you have to do," Resentment pressed. "Do not let your parents give your twin sister to your brother."

Chapter 1

MEET YOUR ENEMY

The Spirit of the LORD will rest upon him—the Spirit of
wisdom and of understanding, the Spirit of counsel and of
power, the Spirit of knowledge and of the fear of the LORD—
and he will delight in the fear of the LORD.

—Isaiah 11:2–3

"*Now Abel kept flocks, and Cain worked the soil.*" Heli bent over his grandson, Jesus, and tried to make his eyes follow the line of Hebrew characters as the boy carefully placed them from right to left on the new Torah scroll. The aging scribe was not worried about accuracy. This son of his daughter Mary had copied from one scriptural scroll to another with unbelievable perfection from the time he had first learned to write all the Hebrew characters.

Stiffly, Heli straightened up and stroked his beard as he tried to remember when he had taught Jesus the skills of a scribe. He smiled to himself as in his mind, he saw little Jesus, five or maybe six years old, standing at his elbow, intently watching while he carefully copied from one scroll to another. "Jesus?"

With his quill in midair, the boy looked up from studying the frayed scroll of the First Book of Moses.

"Do you remember the first time I put a quill in your hand?" Heli asked.

"Oh yes." Jesus gave a little laugh as he spoke. "I remember. I made the first Hebrew character so big that it nearly filled the whole scrap of parchment skin I was writing on. Then this gust of wind came out of nowhere. That little piece of stretched animal skin went flying. You jumped to catch it and knocked the ink flask over. All the ink spilled into my lap and ran down my legs."

Heli's thin lips broke into a big grin, and with a satisfied chuckle, he added, "Your mother scolded both of us!"

Ruefully, Jesus reminded his grandfather, "My legs were black for the entire month, even though my mother scrubbed them every day. I thought she was going to take my skin off!"

"Yes," Heli agreed, "we both had to pay a little price for that afternoon. That was the last of my ink, and I had to spend days making a new batch. But now, six years later, you are as good a scribe as I ever was!" Heli spoke with proud satisfaction. "Let's see?" The old man stepped to the side so the fall sunlight would more clearly illuminate the fresh script. He bent close and placed a thin pointer under the first character of the last line Jesus had penned.

Knowing his grandfather could no longer see the characters clearly, Jesus read for him, "*In the course of time, Cain brought some of the fruits of the soil as an offering to the* Lord."[1]

"That's good!" Heli approved the new copy as if he could see each jot and tittle, perfectly placed. The aging scribe patted the sturdy young shoulder of his grandson. "Blessed be the name of the Holy One," he whispered as he moved toward the bench next to his home. "You, God, provide for your people. You sent this boy to help me. Praise your holy name! How else could I keep my word and complete this last job? You have seen the need of your humble servant."

Sitting heavily on the bench, Heli then leaned against the stone wall of his home. He sighed and let the ancient stones take the full weight of his body. Slowly, his eyes closed, and he drifted into the sleep of an old man resting in the afternoon sunshine.

"*But Abel brought some fat portions from some of the firstborn of his flock.*" As he copied, Jesus tried to picture the scene in his mind: two young men—one still a teenager and the other in his twenties, one bringing a food offering and the other a meat offering to the Lord. Jesus knew about offerings. At the age of five, he, like the rest of the boys in the village of Nazareth, had entered the synagogue school to study the Third Book of Moses, which contained all the laws for sacrifices and living a life that would not be offensive to the God of Abraham.

Heli's light snoring drifted across the sunny courtyard as Jesus continued to copy. It was tedious work for a boy who preferred the physical labor of helping his father in the carpenter's shop.

"*The Lord looked with favor on Abel and his offering, but on Cain and his offering he did not look with favor*—" Suddenly, Jesus stopped writing. He carefully placed his quill on the edge of the table and then looked around. He felt like someone had been looking over his shoulder, but his grandfather was still sleeping, and no one else was around. Puzzled, he picked up his quill, dipped it again, and continued. "So *Cain was very angry, and his face was downcast.*"[2]

Stepping out of the shadows, Satan approached. He could see Michael, the great warring cherub who often stood by Yeshua, who was in a boy's body. Michael had stepped aside giving him permission to approach. Bending over the boy's left shoulder, Satan read, "*Then the Lord said to Cain, 'Why are you angry and why is your face downcast? If you do what is right, will you not be accepted? But if you do not do what is right, sin is crouching at your door; it desires to have you, but you must master it.*'"[3] Just as he read the last word Jesus had copied, Satan felt an extremely warm cosmic wind strike his back. Without turning, he knew the Spirit of God was aggressively making the fullness of his presence obvious.

The Evil One turned and angrily objected, "It is not you I want to face. It is the Deliverer. He is the one I am destined to battle and conquer!"

"At one time, you thought Cain was the Deliverer," the Spirit taunted.

"I made him my servant," Satan arrogantly responded.

"Then you thought Abel might be the Deliverer."

"Yes, and by manipulating Cain, I killed him!" Satan announced.

"Now do you know who the Deliverer is?" the Spirit of God inquired.

"Yeshua the Creator in the body of this boy," Satan sneered as he gestured toward the lad who sat conscientiously copying from one Torah scroll to another. "You keep him well protected!" Satan nodded toward Michael, who stood with flaming sword drawn, ready to defend his Creator.

"Father God has decided to give you some limited access."

As the Holy Spirit spoke the name of that part of the Godhead that kept all things in order, Satan snarled. Pure animal-like hatred emanated from his degraded spiritual body.

The Spirit ignored his response and continued, "When you see that I and the warring angels have stepped back, then you and your demonic spirits may approach without fear of being destroyed."

"Why can't Jesus just face me any time I choose to approach?" Satan resentfully argued. "He is Yeshua the Creator, even in the body of this boy!"

"He is equally a boy who must be allowed time to grow up," the Holy Spirit countered. "In his flesh, he must be as able as Adam to recognize you and choose where to place his allegiance."

"Man is easy to subdue," Satan sneered. "Every man has chosen me over you at sometime in his life."

"This boy has never chosen you," the Spirit pointed out.

"Only because you never let me get close enough," Satan asserted.

"At this moment, I am giving you an opportunity," the Spirit stated as both he and Michael withdrew.

Momentarily uncertain of his next move, Satan stood over Jesus, hating the boy's purity and considering the various temptations other children of Abraham had easily succumbed to.

Once more, Jesus paused, this time to stretch a little and work the cramps out of his fingers and shoulders. His body was not built for the work of a scribe. For his age, his muscles were thick, accustomed to heavy manual labor. Every evening, he loaded his father's cart with the building materials that would be needed the next morning. Three days each week, he spent the afternoon planing the sycamore beams his father used to construct buildings. That kind of work made him sweat and breathe deeply. He liked the way his body felt after a few hours of physical labor.

Satan could feel the burning gaze of the Holy Spirit on his back. A little smugly, he thought, I will show him how easy it is to bring this boy to choose my way of life. With a snap of his fingers, the evil cherub summoned two of his most devoted spirits, Resentment and Dishonesty. Then with a mocking bow, he stepped aside, giving them access to the boy.

"Your grandfather has no right to expect you to spend two afternoons each week fulfilling his commitments," Resentment whispered.

Startled, Jesus looked up from the word he was copying. There was a thought like a voice in his head. It had never been there before. Instantly, he responded, speaking in his mind, "Honor your father and your mother and their parents also, for this command is generational. Each generation must honor the previous generations all the way back to Eternal God, the ultimate parent of all mankind."

Rebuffed by scripture and the mature interpretation of God's word, Resentment backed off, allowing Dishonesty to search for a way to make a home in the mind of this boy.

"This is such an insignificant part of the scripture you are toiling over," Dishonesty asserted.

Bewildered, Jesus stopped copying and considered the thoughts that were entering his mind.

"This passage is read in the synagogue only once every three years. You could leave out a line here and there. Tell your grandfather you are finished. Then you would be free to run over to the blacksmith shop to see if your friend Simon also has some free time," Dishonesty suggested.

"I cannot be a false witness before God, who gave these sacred words to Moses!" Jesus countered. He spoke aloud, even though he did not know to whom he spoke. "How can I misrepresent my God, my grandfather, and myself? It is unthinkable!" the boy proclaimed. "Where have these thoughts come from?"

"You have asked a good question," the Spirit of God responded as he swept both demonic spirits aside while rushing back to the boy's side. "Reread the lines you have just copied."

"*Sin is crouching at your door; it desires to have you, but you must master it.*"[4] The words seemed to jump from the Torah scroll as Jesus reread them. He thought, Sin is crouching like a lion ready to steal a lamb or like a bandit on the road waiting for an unsuspecting traveler! Jesus pondered the scripture and then asked, "How can that be?"

"I will show you," the Spirit responded as he placed in the mind of Jesus precisely selected memories from the mind of Yeshua the Creator. Immediately, Jesus could see a scene from the past.

Sitting on a flat boulder near the entrance to a cave, a young man in his midtwenties scowled into the afternoon sun. Away from the sun, a teenager walked toward him.

Jesus responded to this revelation as he instantly recognized the characters in the scene, "Cain is on the rock and his brother, Abel, is coming toward him!"

With focused attention, Jesus watched, peering into the supernaturally revealed past. He heard a sneering voice and knew Cain heard the voice also, "Here he comes, the favorite son."

Curiously, Jesus studied the scene to find the source of the sneering voice.

"Look behind Cain, just inside the mouth of the cave," the Holy Spirit directed.

"There is a tall shadowy figure lurking in the darkness!" Jesus exclaimed. "His body seems to glow, but not with heavenly light."

"That is Satan, once an angel of light, now an enemy of God and all his creation," the Spirit informed.

"I see other shadowy figures creeping around Cain. Some seem to be lying in wait for an opportunity to attack," Jesus observed.

"Yes," the Spirit responded. "When Satan, who used to be called Lucifer, was cast out of heaven, he took with him one-third of the spiritual beings who had once served God."

"Demons!" Jesus stated as the reality of the term he had sometimes heard struck his young mind.

"That is the name men have given to these agents of Satan," the Holy Spirit affirmed as the scene continued while Jesus studied it intently.

"Cain!" Abel called as he came within hailing distance. "Father wants us to go together to the altar and sacrifice."

"Father wants us to go sacrifice," a dark mocking voice echoed. "You know what he really wants," the disembodied voice of evil continued. "He wants you to become like your disgustingly perfect brother, always eager to please, never willing to walk your own path in life."

"Satan!" Once more, Jesus identified the voice of the enemy of God. Jesus watched as the scowl on Cain's face deepened and his body became rigid. Unseen by Cain, the enemy of heaven stepped out of the cave. "His body is huge and powerful," Jesus exclaimed, "and he has four faces: a lion, an eagle, an ox, and a man! They are violent faces!"

"Once, he was a cherub who supported the sapphire throne of the Eternal God. When he lived in a state of heavenly purity, those faces were powerful and majestic, glowing with the reflected glory of his Creator."

Jesus nodded in agreement as the information the Spirit was giving him sparked his own heavenly memories. The story flowed without further prompting by the Spirit.

Moving closer, Satan crouched at the base of the boulder on which Cain sat. "If Abel was dead, your father, Adam, could no longer compare his two sons and express disappointment in you, his firstborn."

"Dead, like an animal on that disgusting altar," Cain muttered. "I would like to see Abel burned up and gone, never to torment me with his piousness again!"

"If Abel was no longer among the living," Satan further suggested, "then there would be no reason for your parents to require a marriage between you and your younger sister. You would be free to choose the one you desire. With your wife, you could go to another part of the Earth, away from those tedious stories of an ancient garden home."

As Abel approached, Satan slipped back into the shadows of the cave, placing some distance between himself and the boy whose spirit was so much like the spirit of those who lived in the kingdom of God.

"My brother?" Abel was now close enough to speak normally. "Do you have an offering?" A generous smile flashed across his smooth, beardless face.

Slumped over and glowering, Cain responded with a slight negative shake of his head. He hoped this response would end the efforts of his father and brother to make him participate in another of their frequent oblations to the invisible God somewhere in the heavens.

"I could find a lamb for you in my flock," Abel eagerly pressed. "I have several unblemished year-old males."

"A lamb! Another blood offering!" From a black crevice near the mouth of the cave, Satan flashed his taunting response into the mind of Adam's eldest son. "When you give a blood offering, you confess your sins. You grovel and whine and beg for forgiveness and mercy. Why are you expected to go through such humiliation when you have done nothing that needs to be forgiven? Let your father and your brother grovel. You do not need to humble yourself. Hold your head high," Satan suggested. "Give a thank offering instead of a sin offering."

"That is not according to the law as it is written in the Third Book of Moses!" Jesus immediately protested. "A sin offering must be given first to reconcile man to God, then a thank offering would be appropriate."

"Cain knows the protocol of offerings," the Holy Spirit responded. "When Adam and Eve were put out of their garden home, the Creator himself explained the procedure and the purpose for each offering. Adam has faithfully relayed that information to his sons."

"Then why?" Jesus began to ask.

The Spirit of God interrupted, "Keep watching."

And once more, Jesus turned his attention to the supernatural recounting of the scriptural story.

Begrudgingly, Cain gestured toward a basket of produce. "The first harvest of the growing season is the Lord's."

"There is a year-old lamb in a pen near my flock. I have been saving it for the Lord. Together, we can place our hands on the head of that lamb. It can be the sin offering for both of us." Abel responded. "Let's go now, before the sun sets."

Without a verbal response, Cain reluctantly rose to his feet and shouldered the basket of produce.

A big smile broke out on Abel's young face. "I'll get my lamb and meet you at the altar." He turned and ran toward the sheep pens not far from the cave.

As Cain walked, one by one, demonic spirits fell into step beside him.

"Cain is not alone!" Jesus observed.

"Many of Satan's spirits have attached themselves to him. There is Resentment." The Holy Spirit drew a glowing circle around the same spirit who had just tempted the boy, Jesus. "He focuses on making people believe they are too good to serve. He tries to make people believe God and everyone else are misusing them. He tells people they should not submit to the authority of God or to the earthly authorities God has established."

Jesus studied the scene the Spirit of God placed before him. "Resentment looks like a gray cloak hanging on Cain's back. What is the name of the spirit attached to his hand?" Jesus asked. "It is dark and shaped like the blade of an ax."

"Spirits can take on many shapes, depending on their current assignment," the Holy Spirit responded. "You have identified Murder. Wherever you find Murder, you will also find Bitterness, Anger, and Hatred."

Horrified, Jesus gasped. "Look at those ugly black birds. They are circling and pecking at Cain's head! Can't a son of Adam throw those spirits off?"

"He can only throw them off if he unites himself with the Eternal God, but as you can see, Cain has aligned himself against the Creator of his parents. In his heart, he has stepped out from under the protection of the authority of Father God, as well as the authority of his father, Adam."

In his mind, Jesus could see the sun was close to slipping behind the treetops as the brothers approached the altar. He listened to their exchange of words.

"It is late, my brother," Abel called as he arrived, a little out of breath from running. "We can sacrifice together. First, we will place our hands on the head of this lamb. You may slay it, and I will prepare it. Then after God receives it with fire from heaven, while it is still burning, you can arrange your first fruits around it," he suggested.

"I have had to share too much with you already," Cain angrily retorted. "I will not share this altar with you, and I do not want any part of your lamb!"

"But—" Abel tried to reason.

"Go build your own altar!" Cain shoved his younger brother hard. Abel fell to the ground, losing his grip on the lamb, which scampered away.

"Cain? Cain?"

Jesus recognized an eternal voice. "That is your voice," he spoke to the Spirit.

"Yes, I was sent from the heavenly throne room to reason with Cain, but he refused to respond. See how I call and call but he never stops arranging the wood or placing his produce on the altar? Now look at Abel."

"He is building his own place of worship, stacking nearby stones to make a small crude altar," Jesus responded.

"Cain is finished. The first fruits of his harvest are on the altar, and he is pacing back and forth, waiting impatiently for me to come and consume his offering," the Spirit of God continued as he moved the story along. "I will not do it!" he suddenly announced.

Jesus felt a warm blast of air as the Spirit spoke so emphatically. The faded brown and yellow leaves covering the ground under the oak tree close to his grandfather's courtyard gate unexpectedly flew into the air. They swirled and then slowly settled back down onto the dusty ground. At the same time, Jesus felt the Spirit of God like warm tingles all over his skin.

The Holy Spirit spoke again, "Abel my child has struggled so hard to please me. He has given his best lamb. He has built his own altar. And even in the face of his brother's abuse, he holds no animosity in his heart. That is why Satan hates the boy. Abel leaves no place for the Evil One or his spirits to attach themselves to his life."

Suddenly, there was a bright flash, and fire from heaven struck Abel's offering. In an instant, the animal, the wood, and the stones were consumed.

Awed by the powerful display, Jesus continued to be absorbed by the scenes that were being revealed to him. He saw Cain had stopped pacing. The eldest son of Adam looked at the smoldering ashes that had once been his brother's altar. Nearby, Abel was kneeling, bent over with his face touching the ground.

"Where is the fire for my sacrifice?" Cain ranted as he shook his fist toward the sky.

Jesus heard another voice and knew immediately that it came directly from the throne room of the Eternal. "Why are you so angry? Why is your face covered with an ugly scowl?"

"That is the voice of Father God!" Jesus stated with complete certainty. Then he focused on the communication from heaven to earth.

"If you do what is right, won't I accept your offering just as I accepted your brother's offering?" God asked.

"I brought the first fruits of my harvest to your altar," Cain retorted.

"But sin is stalking you, attaching itself to you," God warned. "Only blood can atone for sin. You are not coming to me with a heart submitted to my authority. Your heart is being taken over by my enemy. You must say no to the thoughts he is putting in your mind before he becomes your master."

"I will have no master," Cain retorted, "especially that boy!" He pointed to his brother, who was still kneeling, caught up in his own private communication with God.

Jesus watched.

Refusing to speak further with the Ruler of the Universe, Cain took hold of Resentment with both hands and wrapped the demonic spirit securely around himself.

"He should throw Resentment off!" Jesus observed.

"He believes Resentment is his friend and comforter," the Holy Spirit answered. "Man has been given free choice. He only has to give the tiniest indication that he wishes to be free from Satan's influence, and all the hosts of heaven are at his disposal, but until then, he lives with his demons."

"Jesus?"

The boy felt a hand on his shoulder and turned to see his grandfather standing behind him.

"Who were you speaking to?" Heli asked with a slightly puzzled, almost confused inflection in his shaky voice.

"The Spirit of God was speaking to me," Jesus replied with perfect candor. "He was showing me this story." Jesus pointed to the Hebrew text he had just copied.

"Yes," Heli responded, "the Holy Spirit often seems to whisper in my mind as I copy from one scroll to another, but I never speak aloud to it." The old man shook his head and scratched at his scraggly beard. "You are a strange child, but a good child," he muttered to himself as he returned to the bench by the wall of his home to complete his afternoon nap.

Brilliant sunlight bathed the white stone walls of the recently rebuilt city of Sepphoris. Joseph's cousin Toma held his hand above his eyes to lessen the glare. Then with a wave of his arm, he signaled the caravan forward toward the man-made pool and watering trough where water from Roman-built aqueducts was available. Turning his head, Toma looked back along the line of heavily loaded camels, trying to spot Kheti, his trading partner and coowner of this caravan. When he saw his Egyptian partner walking briskly toward the front of the caravan, he called, "We can water the camels and donkeys here and then push on to Nazareth. There will be good grazing not far from the home of Joseph and Mary, but the water supply there is limited to the one spring that sustains the village."

Kheti responded with a nod of his head. Then he relayed instructions to the drovers who managed the long strings of camels interspersed with donkeys.

Before Toma reached the next Roman mile marker, his partner caught up with him. "It will take some time to water the entire caravan," Kheti stated. "Why don't you and I go into the city and see what the prospects are for doing some business in their market?"

"Never!" Toma spat the word as he raised a work-hardened fist toward heaven. "I will never enter that heathen city!"

"Sepphoris is a Jewish city in the region of Galilee." Kheti scratched his wiry black beard as he tried to understand his partner. "You want to go to Petra, capital of the Nabataean kingdom, to take advantage of the new trade routes that have been opened by Herod Antipas, who recently married the daughter of King Aretas IV, but you will not enter this city in your own land?"

"Sepphoris is no longer a Jewish city," Toma responded. "It is a Roman taunt flung in the faces of all Jews, a city built on the graves of my people for the friends of Herod Antipas!"

"Your anger is talking again. Most of the time, you are a brilliant merchant, but when bitterness and anger rise up in you, there is no profit to be made." Kheti slowly shook his head from side to side. "What has it been? Ten or eleven years since the Romans marched into Bethlehem and killed your family? I thought time would eventually quench that flame of hatred."

"The death of Sarah my wife, Leah my mother, and my beautiful little son, Avrahm—" Toma choked on the familiar knot in his throat before continuing. "It pains me every day. But here"—Toma pointed to the walled city—"thousands of my people were killed. Like my family, they were put to the sword in their own homes just at the whim of a tyrant. Don't you know, forty years ago, when Herod the Great came to power, he slaughtered most of the population of this city? Then he built an arsenal and a palace for himself. Not long after the death of that wicked monarch, the famous Galilean, a self-proclaimed messiah, led a raid on the arsenal and the palace. As retribution for that act of rebellion, Varus, the Roman governor of Syria, razed the city again. He killed or enslaved every Jewish person inside these walls! That was just seven years ago. All who survived to be enslaved live every day with both the loss of their loved ones and the loss of their freedom!"

"Yes, I know about that tragedy. I also know the Galilean is still somewhere in these hills." Kheti's arm swept the rock-strewn landscape around Sepphoris. "Chances are very good it was a band from his camp that attacked our caravan just a few days ago."

"What choice do our enemies give them?" Toma gestured angrily toward a small group of Roman soldiers lounging beside the aqueduct.

"You need to be less angry and more calculating," Kheti advised. The dark-skinned Egyptian pointed to the Roman guards who were casually watching two slaves as they turned the giant waterwheel, continuously refilling the watering troughs. "You cannot physically harm these Roman soldiers without bringing more harm on yourself than you inflict on them, and you cannot get rid of every son of Herod."

"Jerusalem got rid of Archelaus!" Toma interrupted.

"Yes," Kheti agreed, "and Rome appointed a governor to oversee the region."

The caravan came to a halt near the watering troughs. Toma and Kheti turned to the task of unstringing and unloading the camels and then started to help the drovers lead the animals to the water. Between tasks, Kheti continued making his point. "Toma, listen to me! Do you think you are hurting Herod because you will not sell trade goods to his friends? You hurt them more when you get a good price for our goods. When you make a hefty profit, you injure their purses."

"It's blood money!" Toma emphatically retorted. "If I do business with them, I feel like I am betraying my son, my wife, and my mother. I am also giving my silent approval to the slaughter and enslavement of my people." As Toma talked, his gaze was drawn to the two strapping young men who were steadily turning the waterwheel. Instinctively, he knew they were Jewish. "In this city, my people are forced to do the work of animals! We should not have stopped to drink their water." In disgust, he turned away.

At the mouth of the aqueduct, the young slave Barabbas steadily pushed and then pulled on the wooden pole that protruded from the wooden waterwheel. Leather buckets of water splashed one after another into the watering trough at the side of the reservoir. His work-hardened muscles bulged, and a fine film of sweat soaked the ragged tunic covering his scarred and sun-browned back. This was mindless work, but his mind always worked on a way to escape. Several times over the past seven years, he had tried to run away, but each time, he had been recaptured.

With one eye on the ever-present but rarely watchful Roman guards, Barabbas gave the pole he was pushing another strong shake. It wiggled loosely in its wooden socket. Soon, it would break loose and become another tool of escape.

"Toma!" Kheti came up behind his friend and partner. "You have been an asset to my business. You encouraged me to expand, and then you became my partner. Look at our caravan! It is almost too big to manage! Remember when we were in Jerusalem? You refused to go with me to meet some wealthy Jews who were friends of the new Roman governor."

"Yes," Toma replied with a little irritation, "I stayed in the market and sold our goods."

"One of the friends of the governor is a man who is looking to buy rare and expensive jewels, and even pearls if we can find them. I'm sure we can find gems in Petra."

"What is your point?" Toma grunted as he hefted a basket containing bolts of fine Egyptian linen from its place on the side of a kneeling camel and carried it to a central area where all the goods were being guarded.

"There are wealthy Jews in Sepphoris, friends of Herod Antipas. I have a few names of men who also might want us to procure pearls and fine stones."

"Go!" Toma waved his hands toward the city in an exasperated motion. "You go. I'll stay with the caravan. You can catch up with us at Nazareth."

"You'll see!" Kheti called over his shoulder as he turned and began walking briskly toward the city gates. "You'll see. This is a very good city for business."

"Debir!" Toma turned his back on his partner and called the head drover to come over for instructions.

The Holy Spirit took advantage of the moments while Toma waited for the head drover to respond. "Toma?" the Spirit spoke into his thoughts. "Many have forgotten the innocent lives that were lost here and in Bethlehem, but I have not forgotten them. Their names are in my Book of Remembrance."

Angrily, Toma snarled back at the voice in his head. "The God of the Jews has surely forgotten and dismissed the entire nation! Look at the crosses where Romans hang Jewish men and look at these slaves!" Toma could see Debir was approaching. His eyes strayed from his camels and piled-up goods to the slaves who steadily turned the waterwheel like beasts of burden.

The Holy Spirit continued, "Many of my people have forgotten, and others have invented convenient excuses, but this is a Year of Jubilee. That means it is my time for debts to be canceled. You are no longer indebted to Kheti. He brought you under his wing during your time of bereavement, but now that debt has been paid. It is also time for farmers to rest and slaves to be freed."

"It is time for slaves to be freed," Toma muttered.

"I'm not a slave," Debir protested as he approached.

"No," Toma hastily agreed, "you are a valuable servant. I was not thinking about you when I made the comment about slaves." Toma continued his explanation, "I was remembering the ancient laws of my people regarding slaves. They are to be freed after seven years of service and at the beginning of each Year of Jubilee."

With his eyes, Debir followed Toma's line of vision to the waterwheel. Intuitively, he responded to Toma's thoughts, "I am an Egyptian, and I do not know all your customs. In this land, I am very uncertain about what I should and should not do, but one thing I am certain of, those two men are slaves of the

Roman army." He casually gestured toward the waterwheel as he continued, "The Roman army does not care about the laws of your people. Those men will be slaves until they die."

After a thoughtful pause, Toma pulled his thoughts back to the business of the caravan. "Assign eight men to water the animals and four to guard the merchandise."

Debir nodded an affirmative response.

"Work quickly," Toma added. "I want to get on the road to Nazareth as soon as possible."

With one strong twist of his massive arm, Barabbas freed the loosened pole from its wooden socket. It was a stout piece of wood, good for a club or a tool of diversion. Suddenly, Barabbas's attention was drawn to a commotion near the watering troughs.

"Stop! Thief!" Toma shouted the alarm as, with cattle prod in hand, he broke into a run, chasing the man who had slipped close enough to the baskets of merchandise to grab a wineskin.

Nearby drovers joined the chase. The Roman soldiers suddenly became alert. All but one moved toward the scene, but not before Toma and his drovers had apprehended the man.

Toma saw the soldiers approaching. Debir had a firm hold on the captured thief, so taking a steadying breath, Toma took several steps away from the commotion. The soldiers were within a few paces of the man who lay bloody and pleading for mercy. Toma caught Debir's eye and nodded for him to deal with the situation. Then Toma retreated further from the scene. He did not want to interact with Roman soldiers unless there were no other options.

At the waterwheel, Barabbas never broke his push-then-pull rhythm. He watched the drovers tackle the thief, throw him to the ground, and then begin to beat him unmercifully. He noticed that only one Roman soldier remained close to the waterwheel.

Ungodly Opportunity immediately whispered, "Jam the waterwheel. Get that one soldier within arm's reach and then do to him what Herod's soldiers did to your father."

Without considering the consequences, Barabbas pulled the wooden push-pole from its socket and jammed it into the mechanisms of the wheel. Water sloshed prematurely from the leather buckets as the wheel suddenly became unturnable. The other slave sank gratefully to the ground. Only Barabbas remained on his feet. "The wheel is jammed!" he called to the soldier who was focused on the chaotic scene near the trading caravan.

Annoyed that he was left alone to deal with this problem, the soldier removed his helmet and tossed it to the ground before striding meaningfully toward the immovable wheel.

Deliberately, Barabbas stood in front of the wheel, using his body to block the soldier's view of the jammed mechanism.

"Get out of my way!" With the butt of his whip, the soldier landed a heavy blow on the bare shoulder of the slave.

Barabbas didn't flinch. He had been beaten so many times in the past seven years, that it no longer mattered. Without emotion, he took a calculated step to the side, just enough to let the soldier get close and bend over for a better look.

"It's jammed! You did—"

The soldier never finished his accusation. With a quick snapping motion, Barabbas broke the neck of his military overseer, letting the man's body fall heavily into the mouth of the watering trough.

Toma had seen it all. Now he watched as the young slave looked quickly around, searching for an escape route. He glanced back at the thief, bloody, unable to walk, and supported between two Roman soldiers. Debir seemed to be ending his statements. Toma knew the soldiers were about to turn back toward the city, back toward the motionless waterwheel. Immediately, he hurried from his aloof vantage point and injected himself into Debir's conversation with the soldiers. "I am the owner of this caravan. What are you going to do with this man?" he demanded.

The explanations started again. Toma asked question after question for as long as he dared. When the soldiers finally turned toward the city, Toma could see that the waterwheel was still jammed and both slaves had disappeared.

Rocks and scrub brush, the land outside the walls of Sepphoris did not offer many hiding places for runaway slaves. Barabbas knew somehow he had to get away from the city and into the hills where there were caves. Furtively, he exchanged glances with the other runaway slave. Both seemed to instinctively know they would have a better chance alone. Without a verbal exchange, they separated. Barabbas ran toward the watering trough, straight to an ox-drawn wagon full of iron scraps and covered with a tarp. Quickly, he slipped under the tarp and pressed his body flat against the jagged chunks of scrap metal, hoping that the form of his body would not be outlined under the heavy fabric. Sharp points of broken implements gouged his skin, but he ignored the cutting pain. Protecting only his eyes by covering them with his hands, the rest of his body surrendered to innumerable superficial piercing wounds.

Unmeasured time passed. Through the tarp, the autumn sun raised his body temperature. Sweat mingled with blood. He listened. Outside the wagon sudden, alarmed shouts eclipsed the ordinary sounds of watering and hitching animals. The dead soldier had been found! Running feet, more shouts. Barabbas could tell the soldiers were fanning out and calling for assistance as they searched for both runaway slaves. The running, the shouted threats, the curses of the soldiers—it seemed to go on for an eternity. Stoically, he refused to respond to his physical pain and the prodding impulses of fear that urged him to throw off the tarp and flee. Barabbas focused on controlling his breathing so his body did not move the heavy fabric covering the wagon and its load. Time passed painfully, suffocatingly. To the seventeen-year-old boy, it seemed he lived a lifetime of misery before he felt the wagon move.

Chapter 2

Papa God

He said to me, "You are my Son; today,
I have become your Father."

—Psalm 2:7

In Nazareth, young Jesus looked at the sun; it was just about to touch the top of the hills that surrounded his village. "Grandfather," he called Heli from his third nap of the day. "It's time for me to go home and help James feed the animals."

"Oh yes!" Heli squinted as he also looked at the position of the sun.

"Next week, our family will be watching the village flock, so I will not be coming to copy Torah until the following week," Jesus reminded his grandfather. "James and I will be relieving Ahaz and Harim, the sons of Moshe the tanner."

"James has never spent nights out in the pastures surrounding the village, has he?" Heli asked.

"No, this is his first time." Jesus answered. "Every day, he has been practicing with the sling Father made him, and he has packed and repacked his shepherd's bag."

Heli chuckled. "I remember my first time out on the hills. Baruch, the old shepherd of Nazareth, was a very young man at that time. The town elders had just made an agreement with him to care for the village flocks and to train the young boys to assist him." Heli looked at Mary's oldest son as he recalled, "That week,

I was convinced a lion was stalking the flock. I flung stones into every bush that trembled with the slightest breeze. I wasn't very good with a sling, so some of my stones sent the sheep running for their lives and Baruch scrambling after them."

"I expect James will do the same thing." Jesus laughed as he thought about his active younger brother.

"And you?" Heli inquired.

"Well, I have been out with the flock many times. Baruch has trained me to use the sling and the rod accurately. I can keep the sheep safe."

"Baruch has been a very good, faithful shepherd for our little village. He was never blessed with sons, only daughters," Heli commented. "And like the rest of us, he is getting old."

"Now he no longer spends the nights with the flock," Jesus informed. "He goes to his home to sleep while the boys he has trained guard the animals. During lambing season, Baruch's daughters spend the nights with the flock until all the ewes have delivered their lambs."

"And you're one of those boys Baruch has trained," Heli stated with pride. "What do you do during those long star-filled nights?"

"I keep the fire going. I play my flute and sing."

"Just like your ancestor, David. Do you sing the Psalms of David?"

Jesus nodded. "And I recite scriptures I have memorized."

"That is good." As Heli began cleaning the quills and pouring the ink back into its storage container, he began quoting from the Psalms of David, "*How can a young man keep his way pure?*"

Jesus responded with the next line of the scripture, "*By living according to your word.*" He rolled up the woven mat he had been kneeling on and moved it next to the house.

Heli began rolling the worn and frayed First Book of Moses, and Jesus came over to assist. Then as they worked together, Heli continued with the next line of the passage, "*I seek you with all my heart; do not let me stray from your commands.*"

Jesus quickly completed the portion, "*I have hidden your word in my heart that I might not sin against you. Praise be to you, O LORD teach me your decrees.*"[1]

Heli held the scroll upright while Jesus secured it. Then looking around the scroll directly into the eyes of his grandson, Heli inquired, "And does God teach you his decrees?"

"All the time," Jesus replied. "For as long as I can remember, there has been a voice in my head that comments on the Torah and the prophets."

"Do you know—" Heli hesitated. "I mean, has this voice in your head ever told you—"

Heli's question was cut short by the childish voice of Mary's youngest son, Jose. "Jesus! Jesus! Toma has come, and Father needs you!"

"Toma's here!" Jesus repeated the exciting announcement as he started running to meet his brother and greet his favorite out-of-town relative.

Still pondering the question he wanted to ask Mary's son, Heli turned and carried the old scroll into his home. "Do you know, Jesus, that God sent an angel to your mother to announce your birth?" the old scribe muttered into his beard as he carefully placed the scroll of the First Book of Moses into one of the cubicles Joseph had constructed to hold the many scrolls he had accumulated during his lifetime. "Has God revealed himself as your father? Has he spoken of your destiny?" Heli ran his hand over the smoothly finished wood. Joseph is a fine craftsman, he silently acknowledged, but maybe he has made a mistake by not revealing to you, my grandson, the special circumstances of your birth. Returning to the low writing table in his yard, Heli carefully placed a tent-like covering over the new scroll so the ink could dry undisturbed. His hands trembled a little more than usual. "Youth and strength, where have you gone?" he wondered aloud.

Sandals pounding on the hard-packed dirt, Jesus quickly rounded the last twisty bend in the maze of narrow dusty streets that connected the homes in his village. At the edge of the village of Nazareth, near the road that entered the town, he saw his own home attached to his father's carpentry shop. Four camels knelt in the trampled dirt outside the shop. Jesus could see his father and Toma unloading and stacking broken camel saddles.

"Shalom, Toma!" Jesus called and waved as he continued to race toward the shop.

"Shalom!" Toma paused and looked up, beckoning with his hand as he returned the typical greeting. "Hurry and help us. There are more broken saddles on the last camel." Toma pointed as he spoke, and Jesus immediately ran to that camel, quickly untying the cords securing damaged wooden saddles to both sides of the shaggy animal.

"How did you damage so many saddles?" Jesus asked as he placed the last camel saddle on the floor next to ten other saddles.

"Bandits," Toma replied.

Joseph looked up from assessing the damage and calculating the amount of wood he would need. "What happened?"

"We sold our linen, salt, and Alexandrian imports in Damascus, then went straight to Caesarea Philippi. There we sold our wine, some spices, and more linen. At Magdela, we purchased large quantities of dried fish that we plan to sell in Petra..." Toma began the saga of their most recent trading venture.

"Petra?" Joseph echoed.

"I know it is a long journey." Toma held his hands up, indicating no more questions on the wisdom of such a venture. "But we are carrying goods people in the inland regions cannot produce themselves. We lost some of those goods." Toma shook his head in disgust. "Between Magdela and Sepphoris, we were attacked. About twenty men surprised us at dawn just as we were breaking camp. Our drovers fought them off but not without some injuries and some damage." He held up a badly broken saddle. "While we were busy fighting, a few more of their men sneaked in and grabbed some of the baskets that had not yet been loaded. That was the real purpose of the attack, a diversion so they could steal."

"I thought the new Roman governor promised to put an end to the problem of bandits," Joseph sarcastically commented.

"He creates more than he captures," Toma bitterly replied. "These were Jewish men forced into hiding, forced into bands of resistance. I know they need supplies to survive, and I would rather give them some merchandise to ensure our safe passage than be attacked."

"How can you do that?" Joseph looked his cousin in the eye. "You aren't going to join them, are you?"

"No, but I can connect with the main leaders in each area and arrange an exchange of goods for safe passage along the main roads," Toma answered.

"How will you find these bandit leaders?" Jesus suddenly interrupted the conversation he had been intently following.

Both men turned and looked at the boy, realizing that Jesus had possibly heard more than he should.

Joseph answered, "Son, there are men in every village who send supplies to loved ones who have been forced to flee their homes and live in the hills."

"Like Jethro the blacksmith?" Jesus innocently inquired.

"How do you know about Jethro?" Joseph quickly countered.

"Everyone knows about Jethro!" The reply to Joseph's question came from the open doorway that separated the shop from the family's living quarters. Hands on her hips and lips pursed, Mary stood in the doorway. "His property is adjacent to ours," she continued. "During the night, men come and go. They walk through our garden!" She threw her hands up in exasperation. "They trample my cucumbers! They steal my melons! And they endanger this entire village." She emphatically pointed her finger at her husband. "Joseph, you have to have a talk with our neighbor!

His affairs cannot become our affairs. We must divorce ourselves from that family, and Jesus should not associate with his son—"

"Mary, Mary," Joseph tried to calm his wife. "Jethro is an observant son of the covenant and a good friend. He and I have a working relationship. How can a carpenter make a living without nails from a blacksmith?"

"But the garden!"

"I will talk to him about the garden, and I will ask if his family needs some additional melons," Joseph added while sending the cryptic message that in his own quiet way, he also supported those men in the hills.

In response, Mary threw her hands in the air and turned her back on the men. Giving the door a hard slam, she closed it behind her.

"Mary is no longer the meek girl you married," Toma commented. "I think she has become more like her mother."

Joseph chuckled. "Not that bad. We have had three sons and one daughter, and I suspect another child may be on the way. Last year, Mary lost one child, and then her mother died. Life has changed all of us." In an effort to lighten the conversation, he pointed to his cousin. "Look at you! Who would have thought you would become a wealthy traveling merchant!"

Toma shook his head. "No, Joseph. You are the one with great wealth. Nothing is more valuable than your family. My life"—Toma threw his hands in the air as if tossing something away—"it is nothing more than a caravan of memories that will not allow me to settle in one place. Those memories own me. All I own is a burning hatred for our Roman oppressors!" He just shook his head and took a deep breath. "So tell me about Jethro."

"Jethro's brother-in-law is living in the hills. Several years ago, he became another fugitive, hunted and hiding. One afternoon, Roman soldiers marched into Nazareth, straight to his door, ready to take him to their place of crucifixion near the main highway that runs south to Jerusalem."

"Why?" Toma asked.

"He had taken a cartload of produce, just melons and goat cheese, to Sepphoris. All of his produce was purchased by the Roman garrison. Immediately after that, there was an outbreak of illness among the soldiers. A few even died."

Before Joseph could finish the story, Toma speculated, "They suspected him of poisoning the soldiers?"

"Yes." Joseph shook his head sadly. "Fortunately, Jethro received a warning, and there was enough time for his brother-in-law to escape."

"So, Jethro knows how to contact the resistance in this area?" Toma looked to Joseph for confirmation.

"He knows how to contact some of the men hiding in the hills of this area," Joseph answered. "I do not know whether those men are part of an organized resistance to the occupation of Rome, if they are just thieves, or if they are nothing more than unfortunate men separated from their families."

"I have heard the Galilean and his bands of men operate from caves in the nearby hills?" Toma turned his statement into a question.

Joseph responded, "I have heard the same, but I am uninvolved."

Once more, Jesus inserted himself into the conversation. "There are meetings late at night in Jethro's shop."

"How do you know about the meetings?" Joseph asked with a little alarm.

"Jethro's son, Simon," Jesus responded. "Sometimes, well after dark or in the early morning hours before sunup, men come to the shop. They make plans to do things, mostly to rich Jews who live like the Romans, but sometimes they steal from the soldiers."

"Simon knows these things for certain?" Joseph asked incredulously.

"He has been in the meetings," Jesus answered. "Jethro makes weapons for the men who hide in the hills."

"You have not been to any of these secret gatherings?" Joseph firmly questioned.

"No, Father." The eyes of the carpenter's son locked squarely and truly with the eyes of the carpenter.

"Good, stay away from such activities," Joseph admonished. "Never forget the man who chooses to live by the sword will die by the sword."

"But shouldn't Jesus begin to get involved?" Toma quietly protested in a voice that only Joseph could hear. "You once told me your son was the—"

Joseph cut Toma's words off. "Jesus, take Toma's camels to the pasture on the other side of the house and secure them for the night." As the boy left the shop to do his father's bidding, Joseph turned back to Toma. "The boy has not yet been told about the special circumstances of his birth."

"Why not?" Toma was incredulous.

"Mary wants to wait, to allow him to grow up naturally, to see what special abilities he will develop."

"And?" Toma prodded.

"This boy does not have the heart of a warrior. He is studious—"

Toma interrupted, "Some of our greatest freedom fighters have been famous teachers in Jerusalem. Remember the two scribes who led the young men to pull down the golden eagle of Rome that was mounted over the Temple gate?"

"Remember their fate?" Joseph pointedly asserted.

"I will never forget," Toma answered in a voice made hard with years of bitterness. "I was there."

"I think Mary is afraid for him," Joseph tried to explain. "The boy is very tenderhearted. He brings home injured wild animals: birds, a fox, and once, a mouse. Mary refused to let the mouse in the courtyard."

"So he is good with animals." Toma shrugged. "He is also very strong and well built for his age. Shouldn't he learn how to use a sword and how to fight with his hands?"

"I gave him a sword once, and he just set it down and walked away from it!" Joseph protested. "His brothers wrestle with each other, compete and contend, but Jesus never enters into such behavior."

"He is manly?" Toma pointedly inquired.

"Oh, yes," Joseph said, "that is exactly it. He is manly, but not typically boyish. I want you to know he is a reliable and meticulous apprentice." Joseph pointed to the piles of broken saddles. "Jesus will repair most of these, and they will be as good as new. I expect he will begin working tonight before I even ask."

"Maybe you should tell him that he is the Messiah," Toma suggested.

"We don't understand everything the angel said to Mary," Joseph answered. "All we know for sure is God sent angels to announce his birth."

"And God is his Father," Toma quickly asserted.

"Yes." Joseph nodded his head in agreement. "I think, in our hearts, Mary and I have been waiting for an angel to come to the boy, just like an angel came to us." Joseph shrugged. "It has not happened, so I will tell him before he becomes a man, before that first Sabbath after his thirteenth birthday, when he stands in the congregation and reads from the sacred scrolls, but I will only tell him what I know for sure. I will not use the word Messiah. I will not say anything the angel did not actually say."

Barabbas clamped his teeth together and refused to let even the slightest moan escape his lips. With each rock and sway of the oxen-pulled wagon, the sharp shards of scrap iron dug and cut into his flesh. It had been some time since he had last heard a Roman soldier shout, "Look over there!" Cautiously, he moved, causing fresh wounds and newly spilled red blood to run over the dark clots that already clung to his body hair. Slowly, he lifted the tarp just enough so he could see the wagon was in the countryside.

There were no houses. He moved the tarp a little more. There were no soldiers. The only person he could see was the drover walking beside the oxen with a prod in his hand. Ignoring the way the metal cut into his hands, Barabbas pushed himself up from under the tarp and over the edge of the wagon to land lightly on his feet. The runaway slave then slipped into the bushes that lined the road. The drover never looked back.

"Jethro! Jethro!"

Joseph and Toma ended their conversation as they stepped out of the carpentry shop and looked down the road that led into town. One of the young boys from the village was running ahead of an ox-drawn wagon.

"My friend Jethro has been waiting for a new supply of scrap iron. I think it has arrived, and I should help him unload it before complete darkness," Joseph stated.

"I will go with you," Toma offered. "I want to talk to the blacksmith of Nazareth about some swords for my drovers and…"

Joseph finished his sentence for him, "…some men hiding in the hills around here."

Toma nodded in the affirmative as he and Joseph stepped together onto the hard dirt road behind the cart filled with scrap iron.

Eager young footsteps pounded the dirt behind them. Joseph glanced back to see Jesus running to catch up, expecting to assist with the delivery. Usually, Joseph appreciated the boy's willingness, but maybe this time Jesus should stay home and not be privy to the conversation between Toma and Jethro.

"I saw the wagon," Jesus announced as he caught up with the men. "Simon told me they would need help when it arrived." Then he spoke to Toma, "Your camels are secured. They have food and will not wander away."

Toma nodded and smiled at the boy. Then as if he could read Joseph's mind, Toma looked challengingly into the eyes of his cousin.

Joseph easily read the questions in Toma's dark eyes. "Well, are you going to let the boy be a part of my conversation with Jethro? Are you going to let him begin the road to his messianic destiny? The Messiah has to free us from the Romans, doesn't he? Isn't it time? Isn't this part of what God wants you to teach your son?"

They were at the door to the blacksmith shop. Joseph listened for a voice in his head that would guide him, but there was no voice. The only response he had for Toma was a casual shrug of his massive shoulders and a slight step to the side that allowed Jesus to run past the men, calling, "Simon! Simon, I've come to help you and your father."

Even with their hands wrapped in sturdy rags, cuts could not be avoided. Broken knives and swords, jagged old plow blades and damaged farm implements, shattered nails and bent spikes— the three men unloaded and carried the used metal while the two boys sorted and stored it in the wooden bins at the back of the shop. The boys were still sorting when the men finished and stood together washing their hands, pouring old wine and fresh olive oil over the wounds of their labor.

Joseph spoke first, "My cousin Toma wants to place an order with you."

Jethro looked up from blotting his hands with a clean rag.

"I need seven swords," Toma stated as he eyed a pile of finished swords near the back of the shop.

"That's a large order," Jethro responded with raised eyebrow. His eyes followed Toma's gaze to the swords he had completed that were now waiting to be picked up.

"Bandits, thieves—it is an escalating problem," Toma answered. "My caravan is going all the way to Petra to buy spices, incense, and copper, even some precious stones if we can find them. I need to properly arm my drovers."

Over the pile of scrap metal, Jesus quietly supplied commentary for Simon, "Toma's caravan was attacked on the way to Sepphoris, and then just outside of Sepphoris, there was another attempt to take their goods."

"I could buy those swords now." Toma pointed to the stack of finished weapons.

"Those have already been sold." Jethro stepped over to the pile of swords and picked up one of the large flat-bladed weapons. He placed it in Toma's hand so the man could examine the workmanship.

"A fine weapon," Toma commented as he tested the point with his thumb and then swung the sword to feel the balance of the blade that was firmly secured in the hilt. "If the owners of these swords are willing, I will purchase them at a higher price than they are paying you, then you can make them new swords." Toma looked squarely into the eyes of the blacksmith as he made his offer.

"I can ask," Jethro responded.

"I would like to ask them in person," Toma countered. "I would like to meet the men who need such a large number of sturdy swords."

"Father made those swords for the Galilean," Simon whispered as he handed a broken plow blade to Jesus.

"The famous Zealot who is telling everyone not to be counted in the census and not to pay Roman taxes?" Jesus responded in hushed amazement.

"Yes, the same man who successfully raided the arsenal at Sepphoris seven years ago," Simon confirmed. "The whole Roman army is looking for him. He is coming here just before sunrise, and my Uncle Daveed will be with him."

Jesus let his breath out in a soft amazed whistle. "Such a dangerous man in your father's blacksmith shop! Is your father one of his men? Is he a Zealot?" Jesus asked as he looked over at the three men who were deep in conversation.

"That is a secret," Simon answered in hushed tones. "No one must know."

"Are you a Zealot too?" Jesus inquired. "I mean, do they let you—"

"I am at every meeting," Simon answered. "Sometimes, I deliver messages to people."

"Have you been to their hideout?" Jesus could hardly contain his eagerness to find out.

"Twice," Simon replied. "Once with my father, and—" He paused and glanced at the men who were still in animated discussion. "You cannot tell anyone." He looked Jesus in the eye.

"I give you my word," Jesus responded.

"Once, I went alone to deliver a message to my Uncle Daveed. I know the way."

It was almost dark when Barabbas spotted the little campfire burning near the mouth of a cave. Cautiously, he approached. After leaving the wagon, he had become acutely aware that his body needed both water and food. A small flock of sheep, along with a few goats, had been bedded down in a rustic sheepfold of rocks and tangled thorn branches. Not far from the flock, two young boys cooked their evening meal while an old man rummaged through a pile of supplies at the mouth of the cave. Barabbas watched until the old man gave a few parting instructions and then left the campsite.

It should not be difficult to approach the boys, Barabbas thought, to ask for a portion of their stew. The aroma of dried fish cooked with wild herbs nearly overpowered his senses. He had to have some food, but—

"You can't trust anyone," Rejection and Fear suddenly shouted in unison. "No one is going to just give you food. You have to take it by force."

In a soft reasonable voice, the Holy Spirit countered, "Remember the teaching of your mother and father, 'If you have a need, ask.'"

With great effort, Barabbas began to search his memories. It was difficult to remember the proper way to approach people. Those memories were deeply buried beneath seven years of Roman slavery. He had not been a part of polite Jewish society since the age of ten. The day when the Romans had demolished Sepphoris and killed his parents, they had ripped him from a world where he could request and receive. For a moment longer, he pondered and groped for the right word.

"Shalom." The Spirit plucked the word from the recesses of his memory and placed it on the tip of his tongue.

"Shalom!" Barabbas called as he stepped out of the foliage and into the firelight.

Ahaz and Harim, the sons of Moshe the tanner, looked up from their evening meal. Fear seized both boys. It gripped them firmly, refusing to release their thought processes.

Ahaz's eyes grew wide with fright. "Madman! Demoniac!" he screamed. Both boys dropped their wooden bowls and jumped to their feet.

"No!" Barabbas protested while raising his blood-encrusted hands in a gesture meant to calm the boys.

Reaching for his sling, Ahaz shouted to his younger brother, "Run to the village! Get Baruch! Get Father!"

Still screaming in terror, Harim dashed toward the path that led to the village of Nazareth.

Instinctively, Barabbas took a few quick steps, blocking the boy's escape route, and then scooping the terrified youngster up into his massively strong arms. He felt the sudden sting of a stone as it hit his shoulder. "Don't fling another stone!" he warned as he pulled the screaming boy around and held him like a flailing shield in front of his chest. "I won't hurt you." Barabbas took another step toward the fire.

"He will! He will hurt you!" Fear screamed his twisted response into the minds of both boys. "Look, that man is covered with blood!"

"A murderer!" Distorted Truth chimed in.

For a tense, uncertain moment, Ahaz and Barabbas locked eyes. Harim continued to scream and kick. Without warning, Ahaz suddenly picked up his shepherd's rod and ran directly toward the bloody, desperate man who held his brother.

"Stop!" The word flew from the mouth of the runaway slave. His massively strong arm clamped hard across the neck of the resisting child. There was an immediate snap. The boy in his arms went suddenly limp. Stunned, Barabbas allowed the boy's body to slip from his arms and fall to the ground.

At that moment Ahaz's wiry young body slammed into the runaway slave. Blindly, the boy pummeled the intruder with his rod.

Oblivious to the blows, Barabbas lifted the shepherd boy and tossed him aside into the dirt of the path. The runaway then stepped to the fire. He picked up a bowl of uneaten fish stew. Then with his free hand, he grabbed the shepherd's bag, which he knew would contain dried food. Glancing over his shoulder, he saw that both boys remained on the ground where he had tossed them. Satisfied that they could not immediately follow him, he disappeared into the dry overgrowth on the rocky hillside.

Stunned by the impact of being thrown onto the packed-dirt path, Ahaz slowly pulled himself up to a kneeling position and then to his feet. His head reeled as he staggered over to his younger brother who lay in an unnatural heap on the rocky ground.

By the light of the fire, he could see Harim was not moving, not breathing. He moved his brother, and the boy's head rolled as if it was not secured to the rest of his body.

"He's dead! He's dead!" Fear screamed while spirits of Premature Death and Murder continued to clamp their cold hands around the neck of the young shepherd boy. Through the limbs of Barabbas, they had applied pressure without mercy until the boy's vertebra had shattered and his windpipe had collapsed.

"My brother!" Ahaz cried out in sudden realization and terror. Desperately, he struggled to lift the deadweight of Harim's slight body into his thin arms, then with a staggering gait, he felt his way down the moonlit path to the village.

"My brother, my brother!" The plaintive cries of the shepherd boy cut through the rarely disturbed stillness of Nazareth.

Toma was the first to hear the high-pitched terrified wailing. Quickly, he picked up a lamp and hurried to the door; Joseph followed. As soon as the men saw Ahaz, Joseph rushed ahead, relieving the boy of his brother's body, taking Harim, small and limp, into his muscular arms.

"Oh God!" Joseph pressed his ear to the boy's chest, then his cheek to the boy's mouth and nostrils. "No! God! This cannot be!" he cried out to heaven as he carried the son of his friend Moshe through his courtyard gate and into his own sleeping area. Brokenheartedly, he laid the child on his own bed. Tears were streaming down his cheeks as he quickly examined the boy for any sign of life. When he looked up, he saw that the entrance to the small sleeping area that he shared with his wife was crowded. Most of his family was watching, horrified and deeply saddened. His eyes fell on his second son, James. "Go to the home of Moshe and bring him here," Joseph instructed. Then he broke a path through his own family members to reach the courtyard where he could breathe the night air and search his mind for words that would comfort his dear friend.

Toma was listening to Ahaz tell the story of a wild man, a blood-covered man, who had entered their camp. Jethro with his son, Simon, were the first of the villagers to burst through the courtyard gate.

Aware of the unexpected disturbance on the street and then in his own courtyard, Jesus slipped through the door that separated the carpentry shop from the living quarters. "What has happened?" He hurried over to hear Toma repeat the boy's story. How awful! How terrible! Jesus was stunned to hear the news. "Father?" He turned to Joseph. "Where is Harim? Where have you laid him?"

"On my bed, son." The deeply lined face of the carpenter was a map of grief.

Jesus looked up into the grim face of his father. "Is he really…" Jesus could not even say the word.

"Yes, son. He is dead."

A sob caught in Jesus's throat. Then he heard a familiar voice in his head, the voice that directed all his actions. "Yeshua, go into your parents' sleeping area. Go sit beside the body of your friend Harim."

Without delay, Jesus moved away from those who crowded around Ahaz and quietly slipped into the curtained area where his parents slept. Harim was there, so unnaturally still. Jesus reached out and touched the hand of his friend. It was cold, lifeless.

"Yeshua?" Jesus heard his Hebrew name. It was the name he heard in his head every time the Spirit of God spoke to him. "Yes," Jesus answered in a sobbing whisper.

"Look beyond your grief," the Holy Spirit gently admonished as, for the second time that day, he pulled aside the veil that separates the physical from the spiritual world.

"Murder!" Jesus exclaimed. "I see the spirit of Murder in this room, and his hands are crushing the bones in the neck of Harim, my friend. Death is also here, hovering over the bed and laughing."

"It was never the intention of God for your friend to die at such a young age. It was not the intention of the man who came into the shepherd's camp to snap this boy's neck. Those spirits you are seeing took advantage of a situation to do this evil deed. This is a life Satan is stealing. It is not too late. Speak to those evil spirits! Command them in the name of the Eternal God to release the child," the Holy Spirit instructed.

"In the name of God Almighty..." Jesus's voice faltered.

The demonic spirits sneered and mocked, "Who is this child, and what can he do to us?"

"He only has to speak the word, and I will enforce it!" the Holy Spirit announced.

"Yeshua! Speak with authority," the Spirit admonished. "Speak like you would speak to a dog caught in the act of stealing your chickens!"

"In the name of God Most Holy," Jesus sternly restated, "remove your evil hands from my friend and leave my home!"

Like a shower of sparks from a heavy log carelessly tossed into a cooking pit, Holy Fire suddenly burst across the room. The sparks flared and swirled and then united to form a blazing free-wielding sword.

A little startled cry left Jesus's lips as his eyes grew big with surprise. The brightly burning sword swiped over his head, followed by a swirling gust of warm wind that unexpectedly extinguished the oil lamp Joseph had left by the bed. Still, by the light of the glowing sword, Jesus could easily see the grotesque shapes of Murder and Death as they chaotically dashed from wall to wall, searching for an escape. The Sword of the Spirit pursued and threatened to destroy them.

With an angry shriek, both demons suddenly disappeared through the small opening between the top of the rock wall and the roof. The blazing sword also vanished, leaving Jesus in sudden darkness, all his senses keen for the next heavenly revelation.

"Now," the Spirit quietly instructed, "ask your Father to restore the boy."

Immediately, Jesus stood to obey. He did not think about the instructions. He moved quickly toward the curtain that separated the sleeping chamber from the rest of the house.

"Not your father, Joseph."

The Spirit's admonition brought Jesus to an abrupt halt. Somewhat confused, he stopped and stood still, waiting for clarification.

"Your Father, God, lives in heaven," the Spirit informed. "It is his desire that you call him Papa. Place your hand on Harim's neck, then call to your Papa in heaven. He can make Harim live again." Then without further explanation, the Holy Spirit once again closed the veil separating the physical and the spiritual worlds.

In the semidarkness of the lampless room, Jesus turned back toward the lifeless body on his father's bed. By the dim light that seeped through the roughly curtained partition, Jesus made his way back to the place where his father, Joseph, usually slept.

Pushing aside a torrent of questions, Jesus knelt by the bed and groped with his hands across the bedcovers until his fingertips found the body. Warm human flesh touched cold human flesh. The tips of his fingers, sensitive to the grains and seams of wood, easily identified a large flaccid vein in the boy's neck. At that moment, with certainty, Jesus knew his friend was dead. No human could change that fact. "Papa, my Father in heaven," he repeated the unnatural phrase. "Please, my friend Harim is dead. His father will be brokenhearted."

The tingling started at the top of Jesus's head, then flowed through his chest with ever-increasing strength until it surged like a rushing stream down his arm, pouring through his hand into the lifeless body that lay on his father's bed. These sensations did not alarm Jesus. On a few other occasions, he had experienced this flow of energy, but he had not really connected it with the miraculous healing that had followed.

Now under his burning fingertips, the large vein in his friend's neck began to pulse. Breaking into a small smile of understanding and giving a satisfied nod of his head, Jesus suddenly connected previous miraculous events with this sensation. Life was returning to Harim's body, and that life was somehow flowing through him!

He could feel the steady pulse, the increasing warmth of Harim's skin. Inquisitively, Jesus slipped his hand further around Harim's neck, feeling for displaced and broken bones. When his fingers found the broken vertebrae, Harim's neck immediately stiffened and then snapped from side to side as the fragments moved and fused. Jesus could feel the bones align and pop into place.

"Oh!" a gasp of amazement slipped from the lips of the carpenter's son. He knew the basics of construction, and what was now taking place was truly beyond human ability.

Removing his hands, Jesus sat back and studied his friend, wondering what would happen next. In the semidarkness, he could just make out the outline of Harim's body. There was still no obvious life.

"Papa?" Jesus asked again. In that one word, there were numerous questions. What are you going to do next? Why am I to call you Father in such a personal way? Will my friend really live again?

As if in response to those unspoken questions, Harim's chest abruptly rose then fell, then rose again. At that moment, Harim opened his eyes and sat up.

"How do you feel?" Jesus asked as he leaned forward and reached for his friend's hand. "Are you hurt anywhere?" He peered closely at his friend. Jesus could see nothing out of the ordinary.

"I'm fine." Harim looked around, puzzled. "Where am I? I was—"

"You were with the sheep," Jesus answered as he pulled his friend out of the bed and onto his feet.

Wails and screams suddenly filled the courtyard as Moshe, with his family, burst through the gate. Both boys took the few steps through the curtained partition. They just stood on the other side of the curtain, amazed at the number of distraught people who had packed themselves into the small house and courtyard.

It seemed like the entire town of Nazareth had come and was still coming.

Above the heads of the wailing townspeople, Jesus could see Joseph with Toma pushing people aside, leading Moshe toward the sleeping chamber. He could hear him saying, "Moshe, my heart breaks with yours. I am so sorry…"

Jesus stepped away from the curtain and tried to approach his father, but too many people were in the way. All he could do was watch as Moshe laid eyes on the son he thought was dead. The tanner let out a joyous whoop as he leaped toward the boy. "My son! My son! He is alive! Hiram is alive!"

"But—" Joseph did not know what to say. He looked at Toma, who was equally speechless.

Quickly, the news spread from person to person. A collective sigh of relief and rejoicing went up from the crowd as it quickly broke up. Returning to their homes, the villagers of Nazareth retold the story of a demoniac in the hills and a boy who was thought to be dead, but had only passed out from the stress of the moment.

After talking with Baruch and arranging for two men from the village to return to the village flock, Moshe, with his two sons, was the last to leave. He thanked Joseph profusely for caring for his son while Joseph only replied that he praised God because Harim lived.

When the gate closed, Joseph turned to face his whole family. He looked first at Mary, then at Jesus, then back at Mary.

Toma broke the silence. "That boy was dead! I checked him before you laid him on your bed."

"Children, prepare your beds for the night," Joseph suddenly ordered. "Jesus, come with me to the shop."

Obediently, Jesus opened the heavy wooden door and walked through the family entrance to the carpentry shop. Joseph, Mary, and Toma followed. Once in the shop, Joseph looked directly at his son and asked, "Were you behind the curtain with Harim?"

"Yes," Jesus answered. "I went in to sit beside his body and mourn."

"Then what happened?" Mary breathlessly asked.

"I heard someone call me by my Hebrew name, and I knew it was the Spirit of God. When the Spirit talks to me, he calls me Yeshua."

"And?" Joseph prompted.

"Remember, Joseph?" Mary interrupted. "I told you about the time when James was just a baby and so very ill. One minute, he was in his cradle, sick to the point of death, and the next minute in his brother's arms." She pointed to Jesus as she finished, "My second son was completely healthy. You thought it was my imagination and that the baby just got well by himself."

"When did he heal James?" Toma excitedly inquired.

"When we were living in Egypt," Mary answered.

With an impatient wave of his hand, Joseph motioned both his cousin and his wife to be silent, then he returned his attention to his eldest son. "Tell me, Jesus, what happened behind the curtain?"

"The Holy Spirit told me to speak firmly to the demons that were holding Harim by the neck. I was told to order them to remove their hands and leave this house. When I obeyed, the Holy Spirit became a flaming sword that chased the demonic spirits away. Then the Holy Spirit told me to ask Papa, who lives in heaven, to restore Harim to life."

In a soft reminiscing whisper, Mary began speaking to herself, *"The Holy Spirit will come upon you, and the power of the Most High will overshadow you. So the holy one to be born will be called the Son of God."*[2]

Toma and Joseph did not notice Mary. They were just intent on hearing the boy's account.

"It seemed strange to use the word Papa for anyone other than you." Jesus looked at his father, Joseph, as he spoke. "But"— he shrugged his shoulders—"everything was strange: demons holding my friend by his neck, a fiery sword flying through the room. I did not understand, but I knew I was hearing the Spirit of God, so I obeyed."

"Joseph!" Toma broke in. "Your son hears the Holy Spirit, and he just brought a boy back to life! He must be—"

"Be silent!" Joseph again held up a restraining hand.

"Look at how simply the boy told his story," Mary rushed to insert her thoughts. "He obviously does not understand the magnitude of this event."

"Or his special relationship with the Holy One," Joseph added.

"You have to tell him," Toma forcefully intruded once more into the family discussion.

"What do you need to tell me?" Jesus asked. He looked first at Toma, then Mary, his innocent eyes finally stopping and demanding an answer from Joseph, the only father he had known.

"Son, do you know that Harim was really dead and now he is alive?" Joseph asked.

"Yes," Jesus responded. "Isn't that a good thing?" He puzzled over the way the adults seemed so disturbed.

"Oh yes! Praise God! Yes, it is a wonderful thing," Joseph answered, "but you raised him from the dead, didn't you?"

"I don't know," Jesus answered. "I just obeyed the voice of God's Spirit in my head, and God did the rest."

"Do you know that the Spirit of God doesn't speak to the rest of us like that?" Once more, Toma inserted himself into the conversation. "We are not shown demons and fiery swords."

"Why not?" Jesus looked at each pair of eyes, waiting for someone to answer.

"Tell your son, Joseph," the Holy Spirit commanded. "Right now, tell him about the angel Gabriel who came to Zechariah and then to Mary."

"Son." Joseph hesitated and then inserted, "Oh, I love you." He reached out with both arms and brought Jesus to his chest. For a long moment, he hugged the boy he called his eldest son.

"Come"—Joseph pulled away from the embrace—"sit on the bench with me." He brushed a few wood shavings onto the floor and made a place for Jesus to sit beside him. Mary and Toma each pulled a stool close and made themselves comfortable, intent on how Joseph would explain.

Obediently, Jesus took his place beside his father. Looking up into Joseph's weathered face, he read both love and hesitation in his father's eyes.

"Jesus, you have always been a special child. While I was betrothed to your mother, before I brought her into my home to be my wife, the angel of the Lord visited her. He told her that even though she had never had sexual relations with a man, she would become pregnant with a son."

At that moment, Jesus turned and looked at his mother for confirmation.

"Yes," Mary confirmed. "The angel said that if I was willing, the Spirit of God would overshadow me." She smiled as she remembered. "I was willing, and it did. The Eternal God is your Father."

Amazed, a little stunned, Jesus turned back to Joseph. "How did you?"

"I almost didn't." Joseph shook his head as he remembered. "I did not believe your mother's story. I thought she had been unfaithful. I was going to divorce her, but God sent an angel to me in a dream. The angel instructed me to take your mother to be my wife and to take you to be my son."

"Angels came when you were born," Mary inserted. "They came to the Temple shepherds in the fields around Bethlehem and announced your birth."

"Then wealthy foreign emissaries came from the court of King Manu III of Edessa, which is a city-state in the Parthian Empire," Toma added.

"They said the stars had announced your birth. They brought us gifts." Joseph shook his head again. "I am still amazed when I remember their visit."

"But they had been to the court of Herod." Toma's voice became hard. "When those foreign ambassadors did not return to Herod with information that would lead him to you, Herod went on a rampage and had all the young boys of Bethlehem killed."

"That's when your boy died?" Jesus gently asked.

"And my wife and my mother," Toma added through clenched teeth.

"But I was not harmed?" Jesus looked to Joseph for the explanation.

"An angel," Joseph responded. "Once more, the angel of the Lord came to me in a dream and told me to take you and your mother to Egypt."

"I remember living in Egypt." Jesus responded. "And I remember the journey from Egypt back to the land." He turned to Toma. "You were with us." Turning back to his father, he asked seriously, "So what does all this mean?"

Joseph took a deep breath while everyone else held their breath. "It seems to us that you may be the Anointed One, the promised Messiah."

"But we do not know for sure," Mary quickly asserted. "I do know for sure that God in heaven is your Father, and obviously, he speaks to you and does amazing things through you. He will reveal his plans for you."

"If you are the Messiah, then you will be the one to run the Romans out of our land and set up a real Jewish government," Toma announced.

"Do not think of yourself as the Messiah," Joseph admonished. "Think of yourself as the son of God. He speaks to you. Do not do anything he does not tell you to do."

"But the Romans!" Toma started to object.

Joseph cut him off, "Many men have gathered armies and claimed to be the Messiah. They hide in the hills and attack passing caravans." Joseph nodded toward the pile of broken camel saddles on the floor of the carpentry shop. "They annoy the Romans until the day the Roman soldiers lay a trap and catch them."

"Every man who has ever claimed to be the Messiah has been killed," Mary added in a choked whisper.

"Simon says the Galilean is the messiah," Jesus asserted.

"The Galilean is just an angry man who was mistreated by the Romans," Mary firmly spoke her mind. "He has gathered other mistreated and angry men around him. He is telling everyone not to pay taxes to Rome. What do you think the Roman soldiers will do to the town of Nazareth if we do not pay taxes?" Mary looked squarely at her husband and raised a questioning eyebrow.

"Simon says his father, Jethro, is not going to pay the Roman tax," Jesus added his information to the conversation. "He says a lot of the men in the village have talked about it and they agree with the Galilean. 'Only God has a right to part of our income,' they say."

"Zealots!" Mary nearly spat the word. "Jethro and his friends call themselves Zealots because they believe they have zeal from God to use against the Romans."

"How do you know about this?" Toma asked.

"All of the wives know, and all of the wives talk at the well," Mary answered.

Turning to Jesus, Toma asked, "Does the Spirit of God ever talk to you about Zealots and Romans and taxes?"

Jesus shook his head from side to side, indicating he never heard about those things from God.

"What does the Spirit of God tell you?" Joseph asked.

"He explains the scriptures," Jesus answered, "and sometimes he shows me what to do to help people."

"That's all?" Toma asked incredulously.

"That's all," Jesus replied.

"And that's enough," Mary responded while Joseph nodded his head in agreement.

Chapter 3

CHOOSE MERCY

I will save my flock, and they will no longer be plundered.

—Ezekiel 34:22

"James!" Jesus gave a startled yell as a smooth round stone struck the boulder close to his left shoulder. "What are you aiming at?" Jesus took his eyes away from the town's flock of sheep and goats to watch his younger brother put another stone in his sling.

In response, James grinned toothlessly back at his older brother and then pointed to a small mound of twigs on top of a smooth flat rock. "Baruch told me I needed to practice."

"Well, don't try another stone until I show you how to hit your mark." Jesus jumped up and ran to James, who held the sling out for the offered demonstration. Casually, Jesus took the sling with a stone already in its leather pouch. "Accuracy depends on the point of release," Jesus explained as he began swinging the long braided ends of the sling round and round over his head. "You have to feel the velocity of the stone as it goes around faster and faster, and then when it is at a point almost directly opposite your target, release!" As he spoke, Jesus let the stone fly. It sailed cleanly across the top of the rock, wiping out the little mound of twigs he had been aiming for. "I'll set the twigs back up for you," Jesus then offered as he returned the sling to his brother.

"You will not have much longer to practice," Baruch called to the boys as he slowly made his way down the rocky hillside. A runt of a lamb was securely tucked in the folds of his cloak. "We will soon have to lead the flock to the quiet pools beside the stream that runs from the spring in the middle of town. Once there, I will show you how to keep the goats separated from the sheep so they do not compete for water or trample each other." Baruch then turned away, moving from ewe to ewe, using his experienced hands to judge the gestational progress of each animal that carried an unborn lamb.

Jesus looked into his younger brother's eyes to make sure he understood the instructions from the old shepherd. This was the first time James had stayed with the flock, and it was Jesus's responsibility to make sure he took his responsibilities seriously.

James nodded his understanding.

Jesus continued teaching his brother about the art of shepherding. "In four months, just as Passover season begins, the lambs will be born. Then Baruch's daughters and granddaughters will spend the nights in the fields with the flocks to help bring the lambs into the world. If you would like, we can also spend a few nights keeping the wild animals away."

"What about Passover?" James asked.

"Hopefully, before the tenth of Nissan, most of the lambs will have been born. After that date, Baruch's daughters and granddaughters usually stay here with the flock while the men go to Jerusalem," Jesus answered.

"That's good," James replied. "I wouldn't want you to have to spend your twelfth birthday out with the sheep." Then eager to perfect his skill with a sling, James turned away and began to scour the ground for more well-shaped stones.

After a quick count of the flock, Jesus returned to sit on the mossy knoll in the shade of the massive boulder that nearly blocked the shepherd's cave. This cave was one of many shallow caves in the hills around Nazareth that were used for shelter or storage at various seasons of the year.

Out of his shepherd's bag, Jesus pulled a wooden flute and began a lilting tune. It was one of the tunes often sung by his people as they traveled the roads that led to their Temple in Jerusalem. After playing the tune through a few times, Jesus set the flute on the ground and began to sing, "*God presides in the great assembly; he gives judgment among the "gods": How long will you defend the unjust and show partiality to the wicked?*"[1]

The familiar voice of the Spirit of God broke into his song. "Yeshua? It is a good question: How long will you, Oh God, defend the unjust and show partiality to the wicked?"

Jesus stopped singing and pondered the question. Finally, he responded with his own observations. "Several days ago, I went with Toma and father to the shop of Jethro, the blacksmith. It was two hours before dawn. There, we met men who have been banished from their homes, men who are hunted because they have offended the Romans who rule this land. They say we should refuse to pay the emperor's taxes. They claim that you want everyone to rise up and drive Romans into the sea. Is that true?"

God spoke directly into the mind of his son. "It seems to most humans that I am deliberately blind. Because I do not correct every difficult or unjust situation, people either blame me or set up scenarios that, in their minds, will force me to act.

"They do not understand. I see and know all, yet I have sworn an oath to allow all of my creation freedom to choose and to live with the results of those choices. From the very beginning, it has been so."

With one swipe of his fiery hand, the Holy Spirit once more pulled aside the veil separating the physical from the spiritual realms.

"I see Abel with his flock of sheep!" Jesus exclaimed. "He is shearing the wool from one of his ewes. I believe he was a humble, observant youth," Jesus commented.

"Yes," the Spirit of God responded. "Abel's heart was pure and submitted to his Creator. Who else do you see?"

"Cain! He is walking across the field toward his brother, and many demonic spirits are with him," Jesus answered. "He has a stout staff in his hand."

"And an evil plan in his heart," the Spirit commented.

"Can't you stop him?" Jesus implored.

The Holy Spirit replied, "I have begged Cain to reconsider. But *the fool says in his heart, 'There is no God.' They are corrupt, their deeds are vile; there is no one who does good. The LORD looks down from heaven on all mankind to see if there are any who understand, any who seek God.*[2] Cain has refused to hear my voice. He has chosen to heed the voice of my enemy, and I have to allow him that choice."

Once more, Jesus turned his attention to the scene playing across his mind like present reality.

"My brother!" The tone of Cain's voice was forceful and harsh.

Abel looked up from his task and smiled welcomingly.

"Come with me," Cain demanded. "In the field beyond the ravine, I have found a hive of bees. Together, we can smoke them out and gather the honey."

"He is lying! Cain is lying!" Jesus exclaimed.

"How can you tell?" the Spirit inquired.

"I can see the demonic spirits. They are telling him each thing to say. Cain is only repeating," Jesus stated.

"You have made a good observation," the Holy Spirit responded. "All demonic spirits are Lying spirits. Satan, their master, is the Father of Lies. Every word that proceeds from the mouth of a demonic spirit is either a lie or a twisted truth."

"But why? What is the purpose of so many untruths?" Jesus asked.

"*No one who practices deceit will dwell in my house; no one who speaks falsely will stand in my presence.*[3] It is the desire of my enemy to make it impossible for man to be restored to life as it was before Adam and Eve were put out of their garden home. If he can get a man or woman to believe his lies, to repeat his lies, to act on his lies, then he can rob me of the pleasure of their eternal companionship," God answered that question. His voice came directly from the throne room.

"Cain is repeating Satan's lie," Jesus stated as the supernatural drama continued to unfold before his spiritual eyes.

Abel quickly finished shearing the ewe and rose to his feet. "Which way do we go?" he eagerly asked his older brother.

Cain pointed eastward, and Abel began walking briskly in that direction.

"No, Abel!" Jesus warned. "No! Do not be so trusting. Do not go so easily to your own destruction."

As the two brothers traversed the ravine, Abel dropped his shepherd's club, and Cain retrieved it. There was an immediate flurry of demonic activity around Cain. Then suddenly, he dropped his staff and sprinted forward, as if trying to catch up with Abel who had already reached the level ground and was surveying the field for a fallen log or a clump of boulders where bees might make a hive. Quickly, Cain came up behind his younger brother. He raised Abel's shepherd's club above his head, poised to strike.

Jesus covered his physical eyes, but with his spiritual eyes, he still viewed the bloody work of Satan and his demonic forces.

Murder held Cain's hand as the club smashed against Abel's head, bringing the boy to the ground with the first blow.

"My brother!" Abel cried out in pain and surprise. "What have I done?"

"You have been righteous!" Cain snarled as he hit him again. "You have made Father despise me." Cain swung the club again, smashing his brother's left shoulder. "You have agreed with our father that my twin should become your wife. She is mine!" Cain laid another crashing blow on his brother's head.

Instinctively, Abel raised his right arm to protect himself as he tried to roll away from the next blow, but Cain was swift, and he was gaining strength from the demonic forces that now possessed him. The next crashing blows broke Abel's arm, then his nose.

"I hate you!" Cain screamed as he tossed the club aside and picked up a rock the size of a melon.

"No," Abel moaned as his brother towered over him ready to inflict the final crushing blows.

"Our father promised my twin would be your wife. But now she will become my wife!" Cain taunted as, without hesitation, he smashed his brother's head into the ground again and again until the earth would no longer absorb the blood and fragments of skull were exposed to the afternoon sun.

"Many times I have read the story of Cain and Abel, but to see it makes me ill." Shaking with the horror of what he had witnessed, Jesus remained crouched against the rock, his eyes still covered with his hands.

"You were equally aghast and overwrought in the heavenly throne room of the Eternal God. There, your tears mingled with the tears of God the Eternal Father and the Holy Spirit."

"My tears?" Jesus repeated incredulously.

"Yes, your tears," the Holy Spirit confirmed. "What I am showing you is actually your own memory. You were a witness."

"I am remembering!" Jesus stated in amazement. Then from his own memory, he recalled, "When Cain and the demonic spirits who had engineered the murder saw Abel dead on the ground, all those evil spirits except Fear fled."

"Yes," the Spirit of God confirmed. "They expected immediate retribution from God."

Jesus continued telling the story as he supernaturally recalled the events. "Looking down at the bloody body of his brother, Cain was overwhelmed while Fear screamed at him, 'Look at what you have done! Adam, your father, will do the same to you! Your mother, Eve, will declare you were never her son.' Fear gloated and danced around the pitiful man who sobbed and shook. 'You will be alone, cast away from your family or destroyed.'

"'They cannot know. My family must think that some animal has done this.' Cain talked to himself like he had lost his reasoning. In blind desperation, he began dragging the body back to the ravine. There he saw a deep crevice, and with an audible sigh of relief, he threw Abel's broken body into it."

Jesus stopped telling the story. He just watched and recalled.

"*Where is your brother, Abel?*"[4] From the sapphire throne of the Eternal Ruler, God challenged Cain.

"*I don't know,*" Cain replied. "*Am I my brother's keeper?*"[5]

God persisted, "*What have you done? Listen! Your brother's blood cries out to me from the ground.*"[6] There was a sudden and unexpected groaning that seemed to come from beneath the earth, then a trembling and a heaving.

In panic, Cain screamed, "No, Lord, Creator of my parents! I did not mean to kill my brother. It was an accident!"

But there was no response from the throne room of the universe. Instead, the earth heaved and rolled more violently. Then without warning, the ground quaked and cracked and then unexpectedly tossed Abel's broken body back up onto level ground at Cain's feet.

"I did not create the earth to accept the blood of innocent people. Do not lie to me, Cain! I saw you kill your brother. *Now you are under a curse and driven from the ground, which opened its mouth to receive your brother's blood from your hand. When you work the ground, it will no longer yield its crops for you. You will be a restless wanderer on the earth.*"[7]

"That is my own voice!" Jesus suddenly exclaimed.

"Yes," the Holy Spirit confirmed. "In your heavenly role, before you were born into a human household, you were Yeshua the Creator."

"How? Why?" Jesus tried to formulate a question.

Understanding the unspoken questions and the immaturity of the boy's human mind, the Spirit of God answered as simply and clearly as possible, "Even before the creation of this Earth, in omnipotent wisdom, a plan was made to remove the curses that would come from disobedience. At that time, you volunteered to come to Earth to reverse those curses. At this moment in the history of mankind, you were so heartbroken over what had become of your creation that you again announced your resolve to come to Earth and put an end to the curses man had brought upon himself."

"I do not know what to do or what is expected of me!" Jesus felt overwhelmed.

"I will teach you," the Spirit quickly assured, "to see the curses that Satan has placed on my people, and I will show you over time how to set the people free."

Once more, the Spirit of God swept open the veil that separates the physical from the spiritual realm, and Jesus viewed Cain bent over and sobbing, his tears falling on his brother's blood. *"My punishment is more than I can bear. Today you are driving me from the land, and I will be hidden from your presence; I will be a restless wanderer on the Earth, and whoever finds me will kill me."*[8]

"You were deeply moved by his brokenhearted humility," the Holy Spirit commented.

"Not so." Jesus heard his own heavenly voice from the beginning of Earth's history. *"If anyone kills you, Cain, he will suffer my vengeance seven times over."*[9]

Then Jesus watched as what was once his own hand reached out and touched the temple on the right side of Cain's head. Immediately there was a mark, like a large purple handprint. Then with that same hand, Yeshua the Creator beckoned a demonic spirit to approach. It obeyed. "You are Guilt," Yeshua addressed the spirit, "and you will remain with this man until the day when he chooses to repent and submit to my authority."

Immediately, that spirit of Guilt entered Cain and became part of his genetic pattern.

"Can you see the spirit of Guilt in him?" the Holy Spirit questioned Jesus.

"Yes," Jesus answered. "I can see it when I look into his eyes. It stares malevolently back at me."

"When you look into the eyes, you can see whether I or a spirit of Satan dwells in the soul of a man." The Holy Spirit continued his instruction. "*So Cain went out from the* LORD'S *presence and lived in the land of Nod, east of Eden.*[10] He took with him his twin sister, and she became his wife.] *Cain lay with his wife and she became pregnant and gave birth to Enoch. Cain was then building a city, and he named it after his son Enoch.*[11] And Enoch had sons and daughters, and so began a line of sin-filled men and women, for the sin of Cain became a curse that passed his violence and rebellion on from generation to generation. Because of the command of God, Guilt was free to torment those who lived in rebellion so they would never forget there was another choice to be made."

Barabbas looked at his own reflection in the still waters of the shepherd's pool at the base of the hill. "It is no wonder the shepherd boys thought I was a madman," he muttered to himself. With his right hand, he scooped up water and splashed it on his chest while with his left hand, he worked at washing away the dried blood that still clung to some of his body hair.

"You killed that shepherd boy!" Guilt screamed in his head. "He was one of your people. You are no better than the Romans who killed your parents."

Barabbas scrubbed harder. Ineffectively splashing water on the tatters of his blood-soaked tunic and digging at his chest with his fingernails, he attempted to scrape away all the dried blood that seemed to stubbornly cling to his body. The voice in his head continued to scream, "You are guilty, guilty of innocent blood." Almost frantically, Barabbas continued to wash. "You killed the shepherd boy! Now there is no place for you to run and no place for you to live with your countrymen!"

At that moment, he heard the lilting sound of a shepherd's flute. Looking up from his bath, he saw an old shepherd accompanied by two shepherd boys. They were coming over the hill, leading their small flock of sheep and goats. Instinctively, Barabbas hid, slipping away from the pool behind the boulders and drought-brown bushes to the place where he had been hiding for several days.

From there, he studied the old man and the boys. The old man, he remembered, but these boys he had not seen before. Unlike the two wiry brothers he had previously encountered, these boys were both stocky and sturdily built, one obviously older than the other. The shepherd appeared to be so old that he seemed as ancient as the boulders on the craggy hillside.

Hungrily, the runaway slave turned his attention to the approaching flock. After days of scouring the hillside for a few edible roots, the idea that meat could be his made him salivate like a predatory animal. Covetously, he watched the flock, trying to pick out a lamb or a kid he could easily steal, one small enough to tuck under his arm as he dashed away. Oh, he was ravenous! It had been days since he had eaten anything substantial. He moved and felt a little light-headed, then he wondered if he had the strength to snatch a lamb and run.

As the flock neared the pools of water, the old shepherd called, "James, use your staff and firmly push each goat to the left, away from the sheep. Push them toward the lower pool."

Barabbas watched as the smaller boy responded by using his staff to prod two of the large headstrong goats toward the pool where the runaway slave had just been washing.

"Watch out for old Jehosophat!" the experienced shepherd warned just as the largest goat skirted the staff, turned, and came from behind with head lowered. The younger shepherd boy tried to move out of the way, but he was not fast enough. The old goat dashed forward and butted with his head, sending the young shepherd flying.

"You're a mean old animal!" the taller shepherd boy scolded the goat as he helped the smaller boy to his feet. Then while the younger shepherd watched, the older one efficiently used his staff to separate the sheep from the goats, sending each to separate pools of water.

From his hiding place, Barabbas observed the goats. There was one small kid standing near its mother and drinking from the pool of still water. He glanced back at the shepherds. Both boys were holding down one of the ewes while the old shepherd removed insects from her ears. This was his chance! Quickly, but not quietly enough, Barabbas darted out from behind the bushes.

Immediately, Jesus looked up from applying oil to the insect-infested ear of the ewe. His eyes went straight to the man who was emerging from the bushes and reaching for the young goat. "The demoniac!" Jesus exclaimed while quickly jumping to his feet. The ewe bolted away from the shepherds who now focused on the desperate man near the goats.

James had a stone in his sling and was swinging the weapon over his head before Baruch could shout.

"Stop!" the old shepherd firmly ordered.

Without hesitation, James let the stone sail from his sling. It went wide and landed in the pool, scaring and scattering the other goats.

Amid the confusion of scattering animals, Barabbas snatched the kid and began to run.

"Catch him!" Baruch ordered.

Instantly, Jesus leapt into swift pursuit.

"Don't let the rest of the animals scatter," Baruch called to James as he also took up the chase, but the ground was rocky, and the thief fled uphill, making pursuit difficult for the old shepherd. Pausing to catch his breath, the old shepherd judged the distance while removing his rod, a short nail-studded club, from his belt. Planting his feet, he threw it with deadly accuracy.

The small club hit between the shoulder blades of the fleeing man. It knocked the breath from his lungs and brought him face-first to the hard ground. The kid easily scampered away from his captor.

A few swift strides brought Jesus to the man who was struggling to recover from the blow, flailing his limbs ineffectively in an effort to rise to his feet and flee once again into the hills around Nazareth.

"Don't move." Jesus placed his hand heavily on the shoulder of the struggling man.

With an almost inhuman snarl followed by a vile curse, Barabbas looked up into the face of the boy whose hand seemed as heavy as a Roman shackle. He took a deep breath, gathering his physical resources to wrench himself free and bolt for the hills.

At that decisive moment, Jesus locked eyes with the eyes of the desperate man. Guilt, Fear, Bitterness, and Hopelessness stared back at him. "Be still!" It was a Spirit-powered command that flew from the lips of Jesus, immobilizing every demonic spirit within the man.

Stunned at the sudden loss of power, the young man collapsed.

In those brief moments while he waited for Baruch to arrive, Jesus studied the blood-encrusted rag that served as the man's tunic and the partially exposed crisscross of scars on his back. Compassion, then an unexpected rush of tears, briefly washed through his youthful body. At that moment, he felt this young man's emotional pain, his demonic torment, his helpless desperation.

"Papa?" Jesus looked to heaven and cried for the man who cowered helplessly at his feet.

"Your son is pleading for this man," the Holy Spirit, omnipresent in heaven and on Earth, spoke to God, who sat on his throne.

"That is the reason Yeshua came to Earth, to experience the plight of men and plead their case before my throne. His response to this man pleases me."

Angry and breathless, Baruch arrived to viciously strike the man with his staff as he shouted, "You're the man who accosted the sons of Moshe the tanner."

"He is no threat to us!" Jesus held out his hand to intervene before Baruch could strike again.

"Tie his hands," Baruch instructed as he tossed a leather thong onto the dirt beside the thief.

Jesus quickly obeyed, securing the man's hands behind his back.

Then with a nod of his head, Baruch signaled Jesus to help the man up from the ground into a kneeling position.

"I was just hungry," Barabbas protested.

Baruch turned away from the pleading man and retrieved his rod.

"I needed food. I did not mean to injure the boys."

"Who are you?" The old shepherd turned back to the thief. The rod in his hand was ready in case the young man tried to make an escape.

"Barabbas of Sepphoris," the thief answered.

"Son of Papa," Jesus said, easily deriving the literal meaning from the Hebrew roots in the name.

"Is your father the devil?" Baruch sarcastically responded.

In the spirit realm, the demonic spirits chorused, "He is a son of Satan, and we are his masters."

"No!" the Spirit of God countered. "This young man was not born to belong to my enemy. Other evil men brought him to this circumstance. He has been badly mistreated, and that mistreatment has allowed the spirits of Satan to attach themselves to him. They are not really his masters. They live with him. They advise him, but they do not control him."

Jesus's eyes grew wide in amazement at what he heard. Quickly, he glanced at Baruch in an attempt to judge his reaction, but it appeared the old shepherd was just disgusted because the thief only stared sullenly at him, refusing to speak.

"What are we going to do?" Jesus quickly asked. It was a question for both the old shepherd and Father God.

Baruch answered, "The town council will know what to do with him. He will have to answer their questions. They will be his judge. Stand up!" Baruch kicked at the young man with the toe of his sandal.

Immediately, Jesus reached out to help the man to his feet.

"Jesus, you come with me. I would not want this rascal to think he can overpower or outrun me. James can stay with the flock."

"We can take him to the blacksmith's shop," Jesus suggested. "It is close to the road."

"Yes, Jethro will have fetters that can hold a man like this," Baruch agreed as he nudged Barabbas forward with the sharp points of his rod. "I've killed many a wild animal with this rod," Baruch threatened. "If you run, all the men of the town will have to do is bury your body."

In the shop of Jethro, the blacksmith of Nazareth, the men of the town gathered to see the madman that the sons of Moshe had encountered. The elders of the town stood together: Heli, the scribe; Zerah, the head elder and teacher of the synagogue school; and Salmon, who owned the largest olive orchard in the vicinity. They had finished questioning Baruch, Ahaz, and Harim. Now they turned their attention to the accused.

Zerah spoke first, "You have heard the charges that are being brought against you. What is your response?"

"God *defends the cause of the fatherless*,"[12] the Holy Spirit whispered into the heart of the accused. "Explain your circumstances and allow these men to be merciful."

"You have been a slave for seven years," Bitterness countered, "and not once have your countrymen attempted to free you. Why should you appeal to their Jewish mercy now?"

In the blacksmith's shop, there was an expectant silence. All eyes were fixed on the sullen young man in the center of the room. Near the bins of scrap iron, Jesus stood beside his father, Joseph. In his heart, Jesus sensed that God, his heavenly Father, was also observing the scene.

"*I raised and brought up children, but they rebelled against me.*"[13] From his throne room, God spoke into the mind of the boy Jesus. "There is not one man in this room who would have responded differently to the circumstances of this young man's life. So my counsel for the men of Nazareth is *to act justly and to love mercy and to walk humbly.*[14] Now *speak up for those who cannot speak for themselves, for the rights of all who are destitute. Speak up.* Tell Joseph, your father, my counsel in this situation is to *judge fairly; defend the rights of the poor and needy.*"[15]

Obediently, Jesus tugged at his father's tunic until the carpenter turned his attention from the accused to his son. Bending down, he allowed Jesus to whisper in his ear.

"Father God does not desire punishment for this man. He desires that he be restored."

For a moment, Joseph's eyes met the eyes of his son. Then he spoke to the men in the blacksmith's shop, "We should all be aware none of the flock are missing and neither boy is injured." Joseph pointed to Moshe's sons as he spoke. "Obviously, this man has felt the Roman whip." He then pointed to the crisscrossing scars visible through the torn tunic that hung loosely from the runaway slave's back. "We should listen to the circumstances of his life with an open mind."

The Holy Spirit immediately empowered the words of Joseph so they offered a measure of acceptance and understanding rather than total rejection and immediate condemnation.

Suddenly, Barabbas felt encouraged to speak for himself. "I am a Jew without an inheritance. After the most recent Roman raid on Sepphoris, I was left orphaned and enslaved." As he spoke, Barabbas looked around at the Jewish men who had crowded into the shop. Would they be merciful, or would they return him to the Roman army?

"Speak for this man!" With a fiery finger, the Spirit of God lightly tapped Jethro.

Unwittingly responding to the heavenly summons, Jethro immediately stepped forward and passionately proclaimed, "Is it not the desire of God to restore to each man his inheritance? A Jewish man can only be enslaved for seven years. In addition, every fiftieth year, all slaves are released, and at the same time, the land must be returned to its God-given owners. *Who is like the* L*ord our God, the One who sits enthroned on high, who stoops down to look on the heavens and the earth. He raises the poor from the dust and lifts the needy from the ash heap.*[16] Has not God seen, and does he not know *what has happened to us*; does he not *look, and see our disgrace? Our inheritance has been turned over to aliens, our homes to foreigners. We have become orphans and fatherless, our mothers like widows.*"[17]

"Spoken like a true Zealot," Spirits of Fear and Hatred disdainfully commented.

Their words were repeated by Samuel, son of Ezra.

"The Romans aren't interested in our ancient laws," Moshe said, adding another note of caution, "and you can be sure they are not returning any land to its rightful owners, especially in Sepphoris!"

"This man has broken Roman law." Influenced by hate-filled spirits, Ezra, son of Samuel stepped forward again and became the spokesman for all who were infected by the spirit of Fear. "If we give this runaway any assistance, we are also guilty of breaking Roman law! We cannot harbor a runaway slave without expecting to be caught and punished. The Romans could enslave every person in this village, and it would be lawful retribution."

"I have called you, Joseph, to be a protector: first for Mary, then for Jesus, and for all who are unable to stand up for themselves. This is the mission that was proclaimed over your life at the moment you were conceived." The voice of the Holy Spirit roused within Joseph his heavenly calling.

"The prophets command us to *seek justice; defend the oppressed. Take up the cause of the fatherless.*" Joseph's emphatic words abruptly drowned out Samuel's fear-filled rhetoric.

"Come now, let us settle the matter," says the LORD. *"Though your sins are like scarlet, they shall be as white as snow,"*[18] Heli said, finishing the scripture Joseph had started, and then he added his thoughts. "We are not to be concerned with Roman law above God's law. We are not even to be concerned with whether or not this man has broken the law that was given on Mount Sinai by attempting to steal from our flock. Has not God said he can turn sin into righteousness?"

"Sepphoris was burned, and all the people were slaughtered or enslaved. That was seven years ago," Salmon added a little factual information.

"Seven years! This man's slavery should end," the Holy Spirit whispered to each man who had not allowed demonic voices to close their spiritual ears.

Thoughtfully, Jesus studied the face of the man Baruch and he had brought before the council. It contorted, as though a struggle was taking place.

The Holy Spirit whispered, "Listen, Yeshua, and you will hear what happens over and over in the minds of men."

"Do not speak to these men! They have no mercy for you," Fear and Rejection insistently shouted.

"There is understanding and forgiveness in the hearts of the men who hear my voice," the Holy Spirit countered. "Seek their understanding and their forgiveness for attempting to steal from the flock."

"I-I was desperately hungry," Barabbas haltingly began his apology. "Please…"

"Don't beg! Don't beg!" Pride tried to assert himself.

Barabbas stumbled over his words. "Sorry. I was wrong. I should not have tried to take the kid, but I had tried approaching the boys, asking for a bite of food. They thought I was a madman. I didn't mean to injure them. It was all a misunderstanding."

"How did you come to be a slave?" Salmon abruptly asked.

"I was ten when the soldiers broke down the door of my home. They killed both my mother and my father on the threshold of our home," Barabbas responded to Salmon's question. "I have been a Roman slave ever since, but now I have escaped." Purposefully, Barabbas raised his shoulders and leveled a defiant gaze at Samuel, son of Ezra, who seemed to be the spokesman for those who were opposed to giving him any assistance.

"We can't help an escaped Roman slave!" Samuel forcefully repeated his objection. Then turning from side to side, he began to urge those closest to him to join in promoting the idea of returning the runaway slave to the Roman authorities at Sepphoris.

"Lunge for one of those swords," Murder advised as he directed Barabbas to look at the new swords leaning against the wall of the shop. "Fight your way out of this room."

"Wait!" the Holy Spirit countered. "Trust in the mercy of men who try to live by the Torah."

Joseph stepped forward. "My cousin Toma told me about a slave who turned the waterwheel at Sepphoris. This man killed his Roman guard and escaped. Are you that man?"

"Answer honestly," the Spirit of God advised.

"Lie!" chorused every evil spirit that had attached itself to this young man.

"Turning the waterwheel at Sepphoris was one of my tasks," Barabbas carefully replied.

"We cannot protect a runaway slave and a murderer!" Samuel increased the volume of his protest. "Nazareth will become like Sepphoris!"

Heli interrupted, "Once there were cities of refuge—"

"And the law of the kinsman avenger," Salmon inserted. "It allowed a close relative to avenge the murder of a family member."

Heli continued, "We must base our decision on the Torah, not the law of Rome."

"Torah demands a life for a life," Zerah asserted. "*Whoever kills a man must be put to death.*"[19]

"Not in all cases," Heli responded. "When our ancestors were camped in the wilderness and a sin that was an abomination to the Lord was taking place, Phinehas, the grandson of Aaron, ran a man and a woman through with a spear. It was a righteous act."

"Is it not a righteous act to end unjust slavery?" Jethro raised the question.

"And to take the life of an enemy of Israel?"

All the men looked up to see that another man had entered the blacksmith's shop.

"Daveed!" Jethro acknowledged his brother-in-law, a follower of the infamous Galilean some called the new messiah because of his many successful raids on the Romans.

"I came to pick up the swords you promised. Darkness has fallen, and by this time, your shop is usually empty." The fugitive Zealot glared at the men who filled the blacksmith's shop.

Those who secretly considered themselves to be Zealots squirmed uncomfortably.

"Who is this young Jewish man you have put on trial?" Daveed demanded.

"Barabbas of Sepphoris," Jethro answered.

"He was stealing from the flock," Zerah responded to Daveed's inferred accusation.

"I will cover the loss." Daveed pulled a pouch of coins from his belt.

"Actually," Heli spoke up, "there is no loss. The kid was recovered."

"Then he should be free to go," Daveed asserted.

"No!" Samuel, son of Ezra pushed forward. "This man is a runaway slave, a Roman slave, maybe even a murderer. We cannot assist him in any way or we will be—"

Jethro cut into Samuel's protest as he moved close to the thief. "If these fetters on his feet were to unexpectedly come off—" There was an unmistakable clanking as Jethro easily unfastened the iron fetters.

"And the man was suddenly to have a weapon." Daveed thrust a sword into Barabbas's hand.

"Then we could not stop him," Jethro finished as Daveed quickly led Barabbas out the backdoor of the shop and into the night.

"There was nothing we could do," Zerah announced with a satisfied smirk. Heli and Salmon nodded their agreement.

As the crowd began to break up, Jesus heard his father say to Baruch, "I will go with Jesus back to the flock, and I will spend the night there with the boys."

The path to the pasture near the shepherd's cave was deeply shadowed. The half-moon and distant constellations offered enough light so Jesus with his father walked quickly and confidently. All of nature seemed to be sleeping. There was not even a breeze to rustle the dry branches.

Jesus broke the silence. "Father, did we break the law, tonight?"

"Which law?" Joseph responded. "The Roman law? Yes, I'm sure we broke the law of our occupiers."

"Will our town be attacked and burned to the ground?" Jesus asked.

"Only if someone talks, and that is unlikely," Joseph answered.

"Samuel, son of Ezra?" Jesus asked a whole question with one name.

"He is a good Jewish man, but he will not actively resist Rome. Neither will he go out of his way to speak of these things," Joseph assured his son.

"Is it God's desire for us to take up arms and drive the Romans from our land, or is it his desire that we continue to live under their authority?" Jesus continued, pressing for answers that would clarify the events of the evening.

"We, as God's chosen people, are to *be very strong, and careful to obey all that is written in the Book of the Law of Moses, without turning to the right or to the left.*[20] Mercy is the predominate theme of the Torah. We are to be especially merciful to the orphan and those who are being mistreated." Joseph answered.

"If he had been returned to the Romans," Jesus asked, "what would have happened to him?"

"Crucifixion," Joseph answered. "It is the penalty for killing a Roman soldier."

"Oh," Jesus thoughtfully responded as he continued to walk with his father. After a prolonged silence, Jesus spoke to Joseph again. "Toma told me the Messiah is supposed to be a descendent of King David who will conquer the Roman army and set up a Jewish government that will be in compliance with the Torah. How is that possible?"

"It is not humanly possible," Joseph answered, "but God is a great warrior. He will have to fight for us."

"King David is our ancestor, isn't he?" Jesus asked.

"Yes," Joseph responded, "but history has taught us that deliverers who move against our enemies on their own always fail. Only those who wait for specific directives from the Lord experience success."

Ahead, they could see the campfire. James had going, a blaze as big as the signal fires men built on the mountain tops to announce the beginning of each new month.

"I don't think any wild animals will come near the flock tonight," Joseph commented as they approached. Then to conclude their conversation, he added, "God will have to show me a sign as big as that fire before I pick up a sword against

Rome. Until then, I am sympathetic and quietly supportive for those who have been forced to live their lives on the run."

Jesus responded with a nod of understanding before calling, "James, we're coming into camp."

The young shepherd came running to meet them, loaded slingshot in hand. "I saw a lion," the boy breathlessly announced.

"Are you sure?" Joseph asked with a little grin.

"Oh yes, but I scared him off," James asserted.

"The first time I stayed with the sheep, I think I saw a lion also," Joseph responded with a little chuckle. "But that was in Bethlehem." He turned to Jesus. "Let's count the sheep and make sure they are all in the fold. Then we can get some sleep." Joseph moved over to the stone enclosure where the sheep were bedded for the night while James hurried off to throw a few more pieces of wood on the fire.

Not far from the perimeter of the shepherd's camp, a magnificent lion prowled. Angry and agitated, Satan turned his lion face toward the campsite where Joseph with his two sons prepared for sleep. The fallen angel shook his golden mane, then snarled as he stood up to study the youthful Jesus. Like every shepherd boy in the land, he spread his woolen cloak on the ground and placed a shepherd's bag for a pillow. The fire still blazed as Joseph and both of his sons lay down to sleep.

Slowly, the Evil Cherub turned his lion face from side to side, searching for signs of Michael and his warring angels. As far as he could see, the spiritual landscape seemed empty. With a muffled growl of satisfaction, he cautiously approached the campsite.

The simplest solutions are often the best, Satan mused. How many times since man had been put out of the Garden of Eden had a sleeping child rolled into a cooking fire? The enemy of God could not count all the times he had enjoyed their screams of pain, their deaths. It would only take one quick nudge with his powerful arm.

For a tiny moment in time, Satan stood over young Jesus, the embodiment of the Godhead. "I never dreamed it could be so easy," he spoke softly over the sleeping boy as he moved closer.

Suddenly, two glowing swords crossed his chest! Their fire seared the surface of the energy field that was his body. "Your hand will not touch the body of your Creator."

Satan looked into the faces of Michael the archangel commander of the angelic hosts and Ophaniel, the beautiful seraph who had watched over Jesus since his birth.

With a resentful snarl, the evil opponent of God drew back. "There are many ways to destroy the Creator!" he roared as he backed away. "The sons and daughters of Adam will destroy him. I do not need to raise my hand!" Then the Evil One bounded away into the blackness of night.

Chapter 4

Feast of Dedication

Good and upright is the Lord; therefore he instructs sinners
in his ways. He guides the humble in what is right and
teaches them his way.

—Psalm 25:8

Mary lightly hummed a psalm of thanksgiving as she, along with her daughter Ruth, cleaned and prepared all the oil lamps for the evening festivities. She was a mature married woman now, a woman with all the responsibilities of a growing household.

As she moved about her home taking each clay lamp from its niche, she thought about the size of her family and all the things each person required. There was food to prepare daily. Grain had to be ground into flour, the flour kneaded into dough, and finally, that dough had to rise and bake. Her eyes paused appreciatively on the three stacks of flat, round loaves that had come from her oven before noon. Setting a few more lamps on the floor beside Ruth, she briefly paused to look out the window and up into the cloudless sky.

Very soon, gray clouds would be moving across the land, leaving their precious moisture to soften the sun-baked soil. As soon as the winter rains began and had fallen sufficiently to soak the earth, Joseph would sow their barley, and she would prepare the ground for the family garden. Mary looked forward to that time.

She enjoyed working with the earth and the plants it produced. Until then, there was a basket in the corner. She scowled at it, and it stared mockingly back at her. It was heaped with wool that nagged at her and reminded her daily that it needed to be spun into thread, woven into cloth, and finally, cut and then shaped into warm clothing for the winter months. That basket seemed to shout, "Both Jose and Jesus are growing out of their cloaks!"

For this season, Mary turned her back on that basket of responsibilities. Bless the God of Abraham, tradition dictated women were not required to work by the light of the festival lamps, so that task could be delayed until the end of the eight-day Feast of Dedication.

Through the heavy wooden door that separated their living quarters from the carpenter's shop, she could hear Joseph hammering iron nails into a piece of furniture. Plucking the last of her clay lamps from the window ledge, she moved to sit down heavily on one of the woven mats that covered the floor. "This is the last one." She added one more lamp to the array of gray clay lamps that surrounded her daughter. Then she sighed and leaned back against the cool stone wall.

In that moment of rest and quiet introspection, Mary lightly rubbed her hand across her protruding belly. Another child was on the way. Maybe it would be another daughter. Daughters were such a help around the house. She glanced at seven-year-old Ruth, who was sitting on the floor not far from her side and diligently rubbing the smudges of charcoal from one of her oldest lamps. Yes, she did hope for another daughter.

Even as she rested, she knew she could not afford to remain idle. Pulling herself away from the wall and reaching across the low table, she slid a basket of shelled almonds over to her side of the table. Deftly, she poured a small heap of the light brown nuts into her mortar and began pounding, crushing, mashing them into a paste. As her hands worked, her mind leaped ahead to plans for this evening, this first night of the Feast of Lights. A little smile played at the corners of her mouth, and she began to sing another psalm.

> *I lift up my eyes to the mountains—*
> *where does my help come from?*
> *My help comes from the Lord,*
> *the Maker of heaven and earth.*
> *He will not let your foot slip—*
> *he who watches over you will not slumber;*
> *Indeed, he who watches over Israel*
> *will neither slumber nor sleep.[1]*

Mary paused in her singing to get up and fetch the heavy jar of honey, along with another wooden mixing bowl. Returning to her place at the table, she poured the mashed almonds along with some honey into the bowl and stirred it together, then she began to spread the gooey mixture on the round, flat barley cakes she had baked that morning.

Tradition, especially family tradition, was so important. She scooped a little of the sweet almond spread onto her index finger and then licked it clean, savoring the sweetness, looking forward to the evening. Every year, when her family gathered to celebrate the Feast of Lights, she made this sweet treat, and every year, she remembered with a little sadness that on one of the nights during this season when the rededication of the temple was remembered, she and Joseph had escaped Bethlehem. Friends and family members had lost their lives while her own little family lived to make a temporary home in Egypt. She began to sing again.

> *The Lord watches over you—*
> *the Lord is your shade at your right hand;*
> *The sun will not harm you by day,*
> *nor the moon by night.*
> *The Lord will keep you from all harm—*
> *he will watch over your life;*
> *The Lord will watch over your coming*
> *and going both now and forevermore.[2]*

One more glance out the window to judge the distance of the sun from the western horizon brought Mary to her feet, ready to set her household in motion. "Ruth, fill those lamps with oil and set the wicks, one for each member of the family. We will carry them to your grandfather's house."

Mary opened the wooden door to the carpentry shop. "Joseph?" She leaned into the shop to make sure he heard her instructions. "You have just enough time to wash and change your clothing."

Then with a swish of her robes, she turned to exit the front door and hurry to the back of the house. "Jesus! James! Jose!" Mary stepped into the animal shed where the boys were feeding the donkey and cleaning its stall. "Don't waste time," she admonished. "Your grandfather expects us at sunset. And"—she paused at the entrance to the animal shed—"don't forget to wash and put on clean clothes. I don't want any of you smelling like this stable."

Laughingly, Jesus responded, "I'll scrub both of them myself."

"No, you won't scrub me!" Jose made a dash to exit the small animal shed, but Jesus was faster. He caught the rebellious four-year-old with one arm. Without ever letting the boy's feet touch the ground, he determinedly carried his little brother to the large jars of water that sat in a corner of the courtyard.

"I can get away!" Jose taunted when his feet finally touched the packed-earth floor.

"No, you will not go anywhere!" Joseph firmly announced as he stepped up to the water jars and began stripping down to his loincloth.

With a little resigned sigh, Jose stopped struggling and allowed Jesus to remove his tunic and begin pouring tepid water over his energetic body.

"Papa?" Jesus spoke to his father, but did not take his eyes or hands from the task of washing his little brother. "I have been thinking about what you told me, that God is my Father."

"Yes?" Joseph stopped washing and looked directly at Jesus, waiting for his question.

"I don't know what that means." Jesus hesitated and then said, "I don't know what I am supposed to do. Toma has told me several times I will force the Romans out of the land."

"Don't listen to Toma," Joseph cautioned. "He holds the Romans responsible for every evil." Recognizing that the boy's confusion mirrored his own, he reached out and put his wet arm around the boy's shoulders. In that moment of closeness, he noticed Jesus seemed much taller than he had remembered.

God spoke into the mind of his faithful servant from his heavenly throne. "Your son is growing into manhood. Joseph, you have done a fine job, but now I must instruct him."

"A lot of men believe the test of messiahship will be the establishment of a Jewish nation, completely free from the authority of any other nation." Jesus looked searchingly into his father's face as he continued, "This morning, I heard Jethro—"

Joseph cut into the thought Jesus was expressing. "What have you heard from your Father who lives in heaven?"

"Explanations of the scriptures and warnings to be aware of demonic deceptions," Jesus answered.

"Has he told you the ideas of men are often full of demonic deceptions?" Joseph asked.

"Yes," Jesus answered.

"Then do not consider deeply words that come from men. Consider and act on the counsel of your Father in heaven. Jesus, as much as I love you, never forget your Father is God. He is the one you are to listen to and obey. You are a special boy. God works through you in ways that he does not work through other boys."

Jesus nodded. Then he glanced away from his father, Joseph, to notice James had arrived at the water jars and Jose was standing unusually still. Both boys stared at Jesus and Joseph with puzzled expressions on their faces.

The puzzled expression on James's face quickly turned into a resentful scowl as he complained, "Jesus left me to finish cleaning out the stable."

"Your mother needed his help," Joseph calmly responded as he turned to look sternly at James. "You did finish the job, didn't you?"

"Yes," James sullenly replied.

Resentment leaped from the corner where he often lurked. In this busy household, there were often opportunities to fan the flames of discontentment, and this was a golden moment. "Your parents think Jesus is so special," the satanic spirit whispered directly into the mind of James. "In their eyes, your older brother can do no wrong. Have you noticed he never receives even a deserved rebuke, but you often are the object of their displeasure? Look at your father, Joseph. He is still smiling at Jesus, but just wait. The next thing he will say to you will not be said with a smile."

As Joseph pulled his clean tunic over his head, he turned and noticed James, unwashed, still dressed in his dirty work clothes. "James!" Deep-set wrinkles formed as his dark eyebrows came together in a hard scowl. "Move quickly! Wash! Change your clothes and be at the gate in less time than it takes a bird to flee the nest!"

Rebellion, a companion spirit to Resentment, rose to the occasion. "Drag your feet, James. Spill the water as you dip it from the clay jar. Make sure Jesus gets wet when you let the brass dipper slip from your hand and don't let him help you. You know he is going to offer!"

Responding to the spirit of Rebellion, James slowly pulled his dirty tunic over his head, and then gave it a little toss. It landed on the lip of the family water jar. With a careless jump, he reached to retrieve it.

"James!" Warning and alarm flew from both Jesus and Joseph at the same time.

Joseph moved, but Jesus caught the water jar before it tipped over. Tepid water sloshed over the rim and soaked the clean tunic Jesus had just put on.

"James!" Joseph's voice was like a storm. "Clean up the spilled water while I get my robe." As he walked toward the basket where Mary kept his best robes, Joseph had an additional word for his second son. "There is not time for your carelessness, so watch what you are doing!"

Jesus protested at the way his brother was stirring the water into the packed-earth floor. "James, you are turning the floor into mud. Blot it! Just lay your dirty tunic on the puddle and allow the fabric to soak up the water," Jesus instructed.

From a far corner of the house, Joseph asserted his authority, "James! Listen to your brother. He always does his tasks correctly."

"He always does his tasks correctly," the spirit of Resentment mocked. "Despise your brother. He is deliberately causing you problems."

Responding to the verbal exchange near the water jars, Mary stepped quickly into the courtyard carrying a linen tunic for Jose and one that Jesus had outgrown for James. One glance in the direction of the water jars caused Mary to adamantly exclaim, "No!"

But it was too late. James had already flung the muddy fabric into a corner of the courtyard. As the fabric flew, mud splattered everything in the area. "Look at the mess you have made," Mary scolded her second son, "and you have not even washed!"

"You have gotten mud on these clean clothes!" Mary moaned. "Now Jose will have to wear the tunic that is a little too small. And, Jesus, you will have to wash again! Your hair has clumps of mud in it!"

Growling like an irritated lion, Joseph came up behind his wife. "Just leave the tunic for James with me," Joseph told Mary as he stepped around her and took James in hand, quickly scrubbing him from head to toe with a rough wet cloth. Not one word did

Joseph have for James, but his silence screamed condemnation and displeasure.

"Jesus?" Joseph looked up from dressing James to see that Jesus had already dressed his youngest brother and had also cleaned himself.

"Blessed are you, O Lord our God, King of the Universe, who has sanctified us by your laws and has commanded us to kindle these seasonal lights." At the courtyard gate, Mary chanted the traditional prayer and gave a tight-lipped smile to each member of her household. Moving from person to person, she lit each lamp and steadied each hand.

Normally at this point, Mary would begin a song and lead her family down the road, but this festive evening, preparations had been fraught with discord and chaos. For the moment, her joy had been stolen.

"You've done well," Raziel, the once-glorious seraph of the heavenly throne room, made his presence known to the lurking demons. "Satan congratulates you for planting seeds of dissatisfaction and resentment in the household of Mary and Joseph."

Resentment and Rebellion responded with satisfied snickers. Praise from their Evil Prince was rare.

"You have managed to disrupt the peace of every person in this household except Jesus," Raziel continued. "Your assignment is to disrupt the peace of that boy, to make him say a thoughtless, destructive word. You are to make his parents displeased with him and find opportunities to plant seeds of resentment and rebellion so he will dishonor his parents and be unfaithful to the Law of Moses."

Solemnly, the spirits of evil nodded their agreement. Raziel then disappeared in a blaze of diminished glory. Dutifully,

Resentment and Rebellion continued to shadow the family, moving with them out of the courtyard down the narrow packed-dirt road. They were waiting for a word or a gesture that would signal another opportunity.

"Hold your lamp carefully," Mary admonished Jose.

Before the little boy could tip his lamp, Jesus quickly reached out and steadied his brother's hand. "We will carry these lamps to Grandfather's house and light up his windows." Jesus smiled at his brother while he checked to make sure there was not too much oil in the little boy's lamp. "Then later, we will bring them back home and place them in our own windows. Hold your lamp with both hands," he advised.

As Jesus looked at the glowing lamps held by each member of his family, a song suddenly flowed from heart.

> *The precepts of the LORD are right,*
> *giving joy to the heart.*
> *The commands of the LORD are radiant,*
> *giving light to the eyes.*

The family joined in.

> *The fear of the LORD is pure,*
> *enduring forever.*
> *The decrees of the LORD are firm,*
> *and all of them are righteous.*[3]

With a damp rag, Mary wiped the sticky almond-honey paste from the chin of her busy four-year-old, then she settled back to look at the flickering lamps and hear the traditional story that made this evening possible. She looked at her father. The Scroll of Maccabee was spread on the table in front of him. It brought back so many memories of years gone by. Out of habit, her eyes strayed to the corner of the room, to the place her mother had always occupied during these holiday readings. It was empty. Mary brushed a tear from the corner of her eye.

"Jesus?" Heli looked up from studying the historic scroll. "I think I have found the right place, but by this lamplight, I cannot be sure."

Immediately, Jesus was on his feet and at his grandfather's side locating the beginning of the passage with the pointer.

"You read." Heli nodded toward Jesus, who obediently began, "Out of the generations of the ruling sons of Alexander came a totally wicked son of Satan. Antiochus Epiphanes was his name. In those days, men of Israel who did not fear the Holy One sought to follow the godless ways of the Greeks. They built in Jerusalem an exercise place. They sewed animal skin on their bodies to cover their circumcision. Without fear of God, they rejected the sacrifices and the authority of the priesthood, seeking instead to welcome the government of Greek infidels into Jerusalem."

"Oh, how our people were deceived," Heli inserted.

And every person in the room responded with low moans.

"Continue." Heli nodded toward Jesus, who remained poised over the historic scroll.

"After Antiochus had brought Egypt into submission, he marched his troops on to Jerusalem, the city God has chosen. There, he made a great massacre. The blood of all who opposed him ran in the streets. Without regard for God, he proudly entered the Temple grounds, even entering the sanctuary of the Most Holy. Every piece of gold, every treasure dedicated to the Lord of heaven and Earth, he carried away back to his heathen homeland."

Again, Mary, Joseph, Heli, and the children groaned their response.

"Throughout the land, there was great mourning," Jesus read.

"For two years, the remaining priests and those loyal to God kept the laws of Moses, but they were opposed by their own people who wanted to live the life of the heathen in the shadow of the Temple," Joseph added.

"Laws were made forbidding the worship of God," Heli asserted. He then moved over to the scroll and took the pointer from Jesus's hand, moving it to another section. Squinting, staring hard at the Hebrew script, he showed Jesus where to continue reading.

"On the fifteenth day of the month of Kislev, Antiochus returned to Jerusalem, the city of God, and in the Temple, he erected an idol, Zeus."

"It had been prophesied," Heli stated. "*His armed forces will rise up to desecrate the temple fortress and will abolish the daily sacrifice. Then they will set up the abomination that causes desolation.*"[4]

"Pigs were sacrificed on the altar of burnt offering," Jesus added. "Through that act, the Evil One intended to show he could alter the commands of God at will."

"The entire Temple complex was turned into an armed camp, a place where Syrian soldiers would slaughter pigs and Jewish men who refused to participate in those defiling sacrifices," Heli supplied more information. "*With flattery*, Antiochus, along with his soldiers, *corrupted those who had violated the covenant, but the people who knew their God staunchly resisted him. Those who were wise instructed many, though for a time they fell by the sword or were burned or were captured or were plundered.*"[5]

In response, another collective groan went up from the listeners.

"Our Jewish people are strong people," Joseph enthusiastically pushed the story forward. "We continued to teach our children from the Torah. They learned as they played clever games, and we continued to circumcise our sons."

"For that act, some mothers, along with their babes, were brutally put to the sword," Mary quietly added.

"But each death and each hardship did not pass unnoticed," Jesus quietly commented. Father God has a Book of Remembrance. Every faithful and heroic deed is recorded and will be rewarded."

As he spoke, Jesus stepped away from the scroll from which he had been reading and walked toward the center of the room. The flickering fire from a room filled with oil lamps illuminated his young face. Every adult felt compelled to lean toward him, to strain to hear the next thing he would say.

"In the synagogue school, Zerah taught us that on the twenty-fifth of Kislev, Moses completed the Tabernacle in the wilderness. On that day, the fire on the altar of burnt offering was kindled, and it was never to be extinguished. The fire on that altar was symbolic of the work of God's Spirit, consuming the flesh and allowing the spirit to be reunited with God."

Heli added, "Many times during the history of our people, that flame has been extinguished, the altar and the Temple deserted."

"It was on the twenty-fifth of Kislev that Nehemiah rekindled the holy flame in the second Temple," Jesus continued.

"And it was in the month of Kislev that Antiochus desecrated the Temple," Heli countered.

"But exactly three years later, Judah Maccabee broke through the gates of the Temple," Joseph excitedly asserted. "A battle was fought right in the Temple courts and righteousness prevailed."

"And again, in the month of Kislev, the Temple was purified, the fire on the altar was kindled, and with only a little oil, the seven-branched lampstand was lit. Angels fought beside our brave Jewish ancestors, and the Spirit of God guarded the flames that were lit in the name of the Eternal God!" Jesus finished the story.

At that moment, Mary reached over and squeezed her husband's hand. Joseph bent his head to hear what Mary had to say.

"When Jesus speaks of heavenly things and historic events, it seems like he has been there and seen it with his own eyes," Mary whispered.

"I know," Joseph responded as he nodded his head, acknowledging the proud moment he shared with his wife.

The moment was not lost on James. He looked at both parents and noted the way they turned almost simultaneously to stare with admiration at his older brother.

In the dark corners of the room, there was a sudden evil stirring as lurking spirits responded to the observations that James was making.

"Jesus isn't as wonderful as they think," a Lying spirit seized the moment. Speaking into the mind of Jesus's younger brother, he added, "You wait. He will disappoint your parents."

"Yeshua?"

The boy Jesus sat straight up in his bed. He could see nothing but the darkness in the sleeping area he shared with his brothers, James and Jose. Listening hard, he could hear both boys breathing slowly and softly, and he knew they were sleeping soundly. "Speak, Spirit of God," Jesus whispered his response.

"Since birth, I have whispered your name and spoken to you. The voice that has always been in your head is the voice of your Father God." It is my voice also because we are the same person." Resting his chin in his hand, Jesus carefully considered the information that the Spirit of God had just given him. It raised questions in his mind.

In response to the questions in Jesus's mind, the Holy Spirit responded, "You are also one with us. There are three parts to the person of God. Each part has its own role. Each part can function independently, cooperatively, and in complete unity with the other two. To humans, so far removed from intimate communication with us, this is a puzzle, but Adam and Eve understood. They interacted with us in all our forms and roles."

"I want to know you as Adam knew you," Jesus replied.

"Once, you ruled and created in union with us," the Holy Spirit informed as, with a fiery hand, he ripped open the heavens.

The roof of the little home in Nazareth seemed to disappear. The night sky was also gone. Without moving from his sleeping mat, Jesus looked up into the glorious brilliance of heaven.

Suddenly, the angelic chorus sang,

Who has gone up to heaven and come down?

Above the sapphire throne, Ophaniel responded with a voice clear as a trumpet, "Yeshua the Creator has left his throne and has gone down to live among men!"

Again a small angelic chorus posed a musical question,

Whose hands have gathered up the wind?

Ophaniel raised his hand, and on the downbeat, the entire heavenly chorus antiphonally responded, "Yeshua our Creator has made all things with his own holy hands!"

Ophaniel sang,

Who has wrapped up the waters in a cloak?

The angels sang the name of their Creator over and over. "Yeshua! Yeshua!"

Jesus was amazed, but at the same time, he supernaturally remembered the throne room and the angels above the throne. In the flesh, he was sitting in a dark, cramped alcove within the stone walls of a very ordinary home on the outskirts of Nazareth. His brothers were sleeping beside him, yet his spirit was with heavenly beings. The experience was overwhelmingly wonderful.

The Holy Spirit hovered close, embracing young Jesus while God asked a final set of questions. "*Who established all the ends of the earth? What is his name and what is the name of his son? Surely you know!*"[6]

Ophaniel supplied the answer, singing, "God, who reigns supreme, has sent that part of himself known as Yeshua the Creator to unite with the flesh of humanity."

The angel chorus responded,

Yeshua is Lord!
Yeshua has become a son of Adam!

For God so loved the world
that he gave his one and only Son,
that whoever believes in him shall
not perish but have eternal life.[7]

Yeshua is Lord!
Yeshua is the Son of God and the Son of Adam!

The open portal into the sensory glories of heaven suddenly closed, but the heavy presence of holiness remained in the room. In the darkness of his sleeping chamber, Jesus shivered with the thrill of the nearness of the Eternal.

"Yeshua?"

Once more, Jesus heard his name, like rushing water, and he knew it was the combined voices of the Holy Spirit and Father God.

"I am your Father who lives in heaven. It was my divine genetic seed that united with your mother's human seed so you could be born. I want you to understand that from this union, you hold within your body both heavenly and earthly qualities."

"Man and God," Jesus whispered to himself as he tried to understand.

"Like Joseph loves you, I also love you. The same way you share in Joseph's life, I desire for you to share in my life. Talk to me often, Yeshua, like you talk to Joseph. Respect and obey me like you have faithfully respected and obeyed Joseph. Just as

Joseph is training you to work in his carpentry shop, so I am training you to do my work on Earth."

"Yes, Papa," Jesus humbly replied. He did not fully understand, but he trusted that in God's time, he would possess sufficient understanding.

"This is the time of your preparation for manhood. It is also the preparation time for your divinely assigned role," God continued.

"Father God," Jesus whispered into the darkness, "what is my role? At times, my mind whirls with questions." For a moment, Jesus hesitated, and then in one breath, he asked directly, "Am I the Anointed One, the promised Messiah? Toma says I am destined to fight the Romans. But Father says I am a special child and I should wait until it is revealed what I am to do."

The question seemed to hang in the silent darkness, waiting.

Then Father God answered, "You are the seed, the offspring of the woman. In the scriptures, you have read, *I will put enmity between you and the woman, and between your offspring and hers; he will crush your head and you will strike his heel.*"[8]

I recently copied that scripture, Jesus silently recalled. In his sharp mind, he could see the Hebrew text like a scroll that had been opened in front of him. "Father, in that scripture, you were speaking to the serpent, the Evil One, who deceived Adam and Eve."

"Yes," God replied. That one word was filled with confirmation and affirmation for all the hours Jesus had spent copying, reading, and contemplating the sacred scrolls. That one word went out as a blessing for Heli, who first introduced Jesus to the scriptures, and for Zerah, the teacher at the synagogue school in Nazareth. So much was accomplished when God spoke one affirmative word.

In his spirit, Jesus sensed the blessing of his Father. In his mind, he waited for a more complete explanation, but there was only darkness and the sound of his brothers sleeping in the room with him.

Thoughtfully, Jesus began to work with the scripture God had given him. My heavenly Father, God, will put hatred between the Evil One and a chosen woman and between the sons of the Evil One and me. I, Jesus, will crush the Evil One's head, and the Evil One will strike my heel.

"Father God? Who is the Evil One?" Jesus whispered his question into the blackness of the lampless room.

"I have shown you the Evil One. He is Satan."

"The fallen angel along with his demonic forces!" Jesus exclaimed so loudly that Jose sat up and looked bewilderedly from side to side before laying back down to continue his sleep.

At that moment, the Spirit of God opened his memory, and Jesus saw the dazzlingly beautiful angel called Lucifer as he fell from the golden walls that surround the City of God, like a signal fire pushed over a rocky cliff. Myriads of smaller lights, like shooting stars, also fell from the golden walls, tumbling with their rebellious leader into the blackness that would be their new home.

"Yes, our enemy is a master of disguise and deceit, but I have already begun to reveal him to you, so you will learn to recognize him and his patterns of behavior," God answered.

"Are the Romans part of Satan's demonic forces?" Jesus asked.

"Only indirectly," God quickly replied. "Satan can easily manipulate mankind to do some of his demonic work, but these men are not your enemies. They are only enslaved captives who need to be freed."

"Like Barabbas, the runaway slave?" Jesus asked.

"Exactly," God confirmed. "Throughout the history of your people, Satan has tried to bring an end to the hereditary line that would eventually birth the Deliverer of all mankind. There were times when everything rested on just one person making a difficult choice."

"Like Esther?" Jesus asked.

"On the day after the Fast of Esther, take sweet cakes to your grandfather, Heli, and ask him to show you the scroll of your mother's lineage for that is your human heritage. You must understand both your divine and human heritage so you will be able to stand against the Evil One." Then God spoke no more, but his holiness lingered.

Settling back on his mat, Jesus lay awake, staring into the darkness, waiting, wondering if his Father in heaven would have more to say, but there was only that sweet, lingering holiness in the lampless room. Jesus was still awake when dusky morning light woke the sleeping birds and their chirps announced the beginning of another workday.

Chapter 5

MARY'S GENEALOGY

Who has done this and carried it through, calling forth the
generations from the beginning? I, the LORD—with the first
of them and with the last—I am he.

—Isaiah 41:4

Jesus watched as Zerah, the teacher and ruler of the synagogue
in Nazareth, directed a tall white-robed stranger up to the
bema to read from the scroll of Esther. As the visitor began to
read, there were appreciative nods among the small group of men
who lived and worked in the town. The story was being read in
the everyday Aramaic instead of ancient Hebrew, and it was easy
to understand.

"Then Esther sent this reply to Mordecai: '*Go, gather all the*
Jews who are in Susa and fast for me. Do not eat or drink for three
days, night or day... When this is done, I will go to the king, even
though it is against the law. And if I perish, I perish.'[1]"

Sitting on a wooden bench next to his father Joseph, Jesus
listened as the visiting teacher read the heroic story for this festive
season. Occasionally, he would stop and comment or pause as the
men responded with cheers for the heroes or jeers for the villains.
Glancing through the narrow windows, Jesus could see the first
three stars of the evening. A new day was beginning. It was a day
to celebrate after three days of fasting. It was a day to remember

a time when God had supplied a deliverer. Jesus felt his empty stomach growl.

Joseph heard the ruminating noises and glanced over at his eldest son. "You did not need to fast for three days," he gently admonished. "Fasting is not a requirement for those who have not reached the age of manhood. Neither is this time of fasting a command of God that is written in the Torah. It is only tradition, and even tradition has shortened the fast to only one day."

Grinning back at his father, Jesus whispered, "I want to identify with my historic people." His stomach growled again, and Jesus, responding to his father's inquiring eyes, softly explained, "After three days without food or water, my flesh complains, but I must put that aside so I can fully understand the desperation of God's people during this period of persecution and deliverance."

Moving into the room and warmly embracing Jesus, the Holy Spirit broke into his thoughts, "At this historic time, my enemy, through his servant Haman, was poised to annihilate the people I had established to be the lineage of the Deliverer of all mankind. Everything rested on the willingness of one young woman to put herself in a position of almost certain execution. She was a type of the Deliverer that was yet to come." The Spirit paused, allowing Jesus to refocus on the ancient narrative as it was being read from the scroll.

"*On the third day, Esther put on her royal robes and stood in the inner court of the palace, in front of the king's hall... When the king saw Queen Esther standing in the court, he was pleased with her and held out to her the golden scepter that was in his hand... Then the king asked,... 'What is your request? Even up to half of the kingdom, it will be given you.'*"[2]

Sweeping the present aside, the Spirit of God visually presented the Court of Xerxes to Jesus.

In the mind of Jesus, the story unfolded: a beautiful dark-haired woman draped in shimmering Persian robes gracefully stepped forward to touch the scepter that was extended to her.

She did not look to the left or to the right. Her eyes were fixed on the king. On either side of her path, guards stood ready with spears and swords. It was obvious if for one moment, the king changed his mind and lowered his scepter, her body would be immediately chopped into pieces.

Once more the Spirit spoke into Jesus's thoughts, "In her mind, Esther has already laid all concern for her own life aside. Her heart is fixed on saving her people. That is why she can fearlessly approach the king. When the Deliverer, the promised seed of the woman, has considered the things men can do to him, he will submit to death, but it will only be a temporary visit to the Place of the Dead because after three days, his life will be restored. Then he will approach God, the King of the Universe. Like Esther, he will be graciously received."

As the Holy Spirit spoke, a memory from the mind of Yeshua the Creator was released into the preadolescent mind of Jesus. He saw the throne room of the Eternal. The sapphire throne, the emerald bow, the transparent gold—it all seemed comfortably familiar.

"Eternal God will extend his scepter. Not half but all of the kingdom will belong to the Deliverer, and then he will sit at the right hand of God, ruling with the King of the Universe."

When Jesus returned in his thoughts to the small synagogue in Nazareth, the teacher was closing the scroll. The men of the town were standing, exchanging small talk, preparing to return to their homes and to the festive meals that were waiting for them.

"Come, Jesus." Joseph nudged his shoulder. "It's time to go home and break the fast."

"My stomach has stopped protesting," Jesus replied. "I do not feel hungry anymore!"

Joseph, looking surprised and slightly puzzled, responded, "For the sake of your starving father who has not eaten since this time yesterday, let's hurry home."

"The teacher from the Essene community spent this last week in my home," Zerah, the rabbi of the small synagogue school in Nazareth, began a conversation with his old friend Heli. In the late afternoon, both men sat on woven mats under the gnarly bare branches of an ancient oak that grew near Heli's home.

"I was impressed with his reading," Heli responded. "Not only did he read correctly without hesitation, but he had passion."

"Yes, last night, I was more moved by the courage of Queen Esther than I have ever been before," Zerah agreed. "My guest left this morning. He is returning to Qumran to study with his brothers."

"The Essene community is very admirable. They are a pious group of men," Heli commented. "I understand they have devoted themselves to preserving the scriptures in addition to many other religious and historic writings. I purchased the historic scroll of Maccabee as well as the Book of Enoch from them. Both scrolls are excellent copies."

"More significant than their collections of scrolls is their life of piety," Zerah asserted. "They are maintaining the original calendar of feasts, and they want nothing to do with the pollution that is now controlling the Temple and its services."

"Do the men of the Essene communities think because they have chosen a peculiar way of life that they are better than the Pharisees? Does purification by bathing three times a day and remaining aloof from the Temple services help the nation?" Heli questioned.

"They are sending out teachers," Zerah responded a little indirectly. "Throughout the land, many people are becoming convinced that the Essenes have the correct interpretation of scripture. You know, a large section of Jerusalem has become an Essene community. In addition, there are several cloistered Essene communities in the desert regions not far from Jerusalem. Throughout the land, many of the ordinary priests identify themselves with the Essenes."

"Last Passover, I found out that my wife's relative, a priest who once lived in Carem, has moved from his village to the Essene community in Jerusalem," Heli admitted. "But he did not make the move because he has aligned his religious philosophy with theirs. He made the move because his wife, Elizabeth, has died, and he still has a son to bring into manhood. The Essene brotherhood holds all things in common, and they make sure everyone is provided for."

With a resigned shrug of his shoulders, Zerah admitted, "Everyone knows the wealth of the Temple goes to the high priest's family and friends. The ordinary village priest is fortunate to get a few coins and some animal skins from the Temple sacrifices. That is not enough to live on."

"The ordinary priests, like my wife's relative, Zechariah, who served in the Temple for only a few weeks each year, have no influence with the Temple authorities, and neither do the members of the Essene communities," Heli emphatically added. "The Essenes are not actively influencing either the Temple or the Roman government. It is nothing more than a religious philosophy and a benevolent lifestyle. Their only tangible contribution to the interests of our nation is their production of excellent sacred scrolls."

"That's because the time has not yet come," Zerah asserted.

"The time?" Heli echoed.

"The Messiah!" Zerah made his point by jabbing his index finger toward heaven. "The Essenes have studied the writings of the prophet Daniel, and they have determined that the Messiah will come in about another fifty years. We have to wait until then because that is the time for the hosts of heaven to fight with us." Zerah lowered his voice to a whisper. "They have written an entire war plan, but that is a secret. That scroll is hidden. The instructions for the final battle with the enemies of God are not to be followed until the appointed time, but"—Zerah sighed—"you and I, we will be in the grave by then. Nevertheless, our grandchildren will see it." As he spoke, Zerah pointed down the road toward Heli's grandson, Jesus, who was walking briskly toward them.

"It is believed by those with the same philosophy as the Pharisees that when the Messiah comes, he will raise the righteous from their graves. On that point," Heli asserted, "I concur with the Pharisees, especially those from the school of Hillel."

"I have wavered back and forth on the subject," Zerah admitted. "When I was young, I agreed with the Sadducees that the dead are in an eternal sleep, never to return to this life. Now that I am older and closer to that eternal sleep, I like the idea that God will bring this old body back from the grave with renewed vigor, able to pick up a sword and support the Messiah as he takes over the kingdom. I want to see the coronation of the Son of David." Zerah glanced up as Jesus stepped off the road and ran toward them. Then the small-town synagogue teacher returned to expressing his thoughts. "The kingdom of the Messiah cannot just be for one generation of youngsters." Zerah shook his head at the absurdity of all the previous generations being left out of such an important event.

At that point, Jesus stepped under the leafless limbs of the winter oak, his intrusion unintentionally disrupting the conversation. Both Heli and the synagogue teacher gave the boy welcoming smiles as Jesus placed a basket of his mother's sweet cakes on the mat between them. "My mother sends you this gift to help you celebrate the Feast of Esther," Jesus offered.

"Heli, this young man is my brightest, my best scholar, better than those Jerusalem city boys," Zerah announced. "In another year, he is going to come up to the bema in the synagogue to read the scripture he has chosen for his thirteenth birthday."

"Then he will be a man in the congregation." Heli beamed with pride as he spoke.

"Responsible before God for all his choices," Zerah added while Heli extended his hand, indicating that Jesus should sit and join them.

After giving a respectful bow to both of his elders, Jesus took a place on the mat. He spoke first to his grandfather, "I have come to learn about my heritage through my mother."

"See what a diligent student this young man is!" Zerah exclaimed. "I require all the boys in the synagogue to research their heritage through their father's line. No one ever asks about the maternal line unless they are of priestly lineage. But Jesus, he understands he is the product of two parents."

"Yes, I like to think that the good parts of me are part of him," Heli responded as he slowly pulled himself up from the mat. "In the house, I have several short scrolls. I even have a copy of my wife's lineage. Her grandfather was a priest."

"That's the reason that my cousin John is a Levite while I am from the tribe of Judah," Jesus commented.

Heli picked up the basket of sweets as he turned to his friend. "Stay, Zerah, you might know a few things about my ancestors that I have forgotten."

Zerah and Jesus followed Heli into the house.

"I knew your father Matthat, and his father, Levi, taught in the synagogue school when I was very young," Zerah reminisced. "Levi terrified me into learning. He scratched the Hebrew characters into the dirt with a stick, and if I could not copy them correctly, he used that same stick to encourage me to pay attention!"

"I was in that class with you," Heli responded. "He was just as hard on me as he was on you."

Heli carried several small scrolls out and unrolled one on the low table in front of the house. "Here." He pointed with a thin stick. "Jesus, the clouds have diminished the sunlight, so you will have to read."

"*Heli, the son of Matthat, the son of Levi,*"[3] Jesus read the text as his grandfather moved the pointer from right to left.

Heli placed a hand on Jesus's shoulder, and the boy paused. "It was when Levi was a young man that Herod the Great marched into Jerusalem. Within a very short time, the high priest had no more civil authority, and the governing of Judah was then in the hands of a non-Jew."

"And at that point, we began to look for the fulfillment of Jacob's prophetic blessing for his son Judah," Zerah added. "In the blessing, Jacob stated that the Messiah would come when we were no longer ruled by a descendant from the hereditary line of Judah."

"The line of Herod comes from Abraham through Esau and his descendants," Jesus repeated some thoughts from Zerah's lessons. "The Herodian family does not come from Abraham's anointed seed, through Isaac and his son Judah."

Zerah nodded proudly as he listened to his best pupil.

"You were born during the reign of Herod the Great." Heli gave his grandson's shoulder a little squeeze as he placed the pointer in the boy's hand.

Quickly, Jesus found his place on the scroll and continued reading, "*The son of Melki, the son of Jannai, the son of Joseph*[4]—"

"There!" Zerah suddenly interrupted. "It was during the lifetime of Joseph that the Romans first came to our land. That was the beginning of the end of our self-rule."

"A judgment on the nation because of the corruption of its leaders," the Spirit of God whispered into the mind of Jesus.

"The Roman general Pompey marched into Jerusalem," Heli added.

"It wasn't difficult," Zerah retorted. "The gates of the city were opened for him."

Heli continued his commentary. "But the Temple gates were closed and barred. He had to batter them down, and then he massacred everyone inside and desecrated the sanctuary of the Most Holy One."

The Holy Spirit commented again, "Your ancestor Joseph was a noble man. He loved to worship in my Temple. After the Romans withdrew from the Temple complex, he, along with many others, entered to clean and purify the area so it would once more be a suitable place for my presence." At that moment, the Spirit of God opened the past, and Jesus could see the old second Temple. In the Court of the Priests, worship had ceased, and men were on their knees adding tears and sweat to the water they were using to scrub the blood of their countrymen from the floor stones. "That part of your ancestor Joseph, who cared deeply about the purity of the Temple, has been passed on to you," the Spirit proclaimed.

"Keep reading." Zerah nudged Jesus out of what appeared to be a little daydream.

Jesus read, "*The son of Mattathias, the son of Amos, the son of Nahum, the son of Esli[5]—*"

"Esli," Heli repeated the name that Jesus had just read. "He fought with Judah Maccabee. He was a warrior for righteousness."

"Warriors die." Jesus heard a sadistic warning.

Jesus looked around. He saw nothing unusual, but he did recognize the voice. Satan was also making commentary on his lineage.

"Did Esli take part in restoring the Temple at that time?" Jesus asked. "Did he help to rebuild the altar of the Lord?"

"No," Heli answered. "Esli died in the battle for the Temple fortress, but his son Nahum was there. For our family, he witnessed the rekindling of holy fire on the newly dedicated altar."

"Esli died," Satan repeated. "Warriors for righteousness die."

Jesus ignored the evil voice and turned his attention back to the scriptures. "*The son of Naggai, the son of Maath, the son of*

Mattathias, the son of Semein, the son of Josech, the son of Joda."[6] Jesus moved the pointer as he read.

"Right here, our line would have ended if it had not been for Esther and Mordecai," Heli announced as he placed his finger under the name of Joda.

"Now continue," Heli directed.

And Jesus read, "*The son of Joanan, the son of Rhesa, the son of Zerubbabel*—"

"The builders of the second Temple!" Zerah suddenly exclaimed. "It took nearly one hundred years and great leaders like Zerubbabel, then Ezra, and finally, Nehemiah to complete the second Temple and rebuild the walls."

"And you, my son, will build temples in the hearts of men, places where my law will be written and kept on tablets of flesh. You will make for me a dwelling place in the heart of each man, woman, and child who is willing." While Heli and Zerah debated the trivia of genealogy, God spoke directly into the mind of Jesus.

With the words of his heavenly Father still ringing in his heart, Jesus watched Heli and Zerah as they tried to outdo each other with the vast amount of historical trivia each mind retained. When silence finally took control of the space between the old scribe and the old teacher, Jesus continued to read, "*The son of Shealtiel, the son of Neri, the son of Melki, the son of Addi, the son of Cosam, the son of Elmadam, the son of Er, the son of Joshua*[8]—"

"Those names, Jesus, are the men of the Babylonian captivity," Heli interrupted.

"Joshua and Er probably experienced the final siege of Jerusalem," Zerah added.

"Such tragedy and horror, people reduced to eating the flesh off the numerous unburied corpses that littered the streets," Heli commented.

"And the Temple, Solomon's beautiful Temple, destroyed," Zerah added.

"That is when Jeremiah hid the ark of the Lord," Jesus stated.

The Spirit of God, at that moment, opened a memory in the mind of Yeshua: Linen-clad priests led by Jeremiah hurried through dark underground chambers. Without speaking, they turned abruptly, squeezing into a side passage that opened into a small stone chamber. There, they left the ark and as many of the sacred implements of worship as they had been able to carry. Upon exiting the chamber, they filled the entryway with rubble and left no mark to identify the place.

In his mind, Yeshua saw his own hand place a glowing eternal seal over the stone-filled entry.

"Yes, Jeremiah remained in the land," Zerah commented.

"Both Daniel and Ezekiel were already captives in Babylon," Heli added.

Zerah plucked the pointer from Jesus's hand. He moved it under the line, prodding Jesus to focus on the Hebrew script and continue reading, "*The son of Eliezer, the son of Jorim*⁹—"

"Eliezer and Jorim lived under the righteous rein of the great King Hezekiah." Once more, Zerah interrupted the flow of names.

"Both were scribes and acquainted with the great prophet Isaiah," Heli added. "Now continue here." Heli plucked the pointer back from Zerah's hand and placed it back in the hand of his grandson, at the same time guiding the point to the top of the next column of characters.

Jesus continued to read, "*The son of Matthat, the son of Levi, the son of Simeon, the son of Judah, the son of Joseph, the son of Jonam, the son of Eliakim, the son of Melea, the son of Menna, the son of Mattatha, the son of Nathan, the son of David*¹⁰—"

"There!" Heli exclaimed. "Nathan is Solomon's brother, also David's son by Bathsheba! Jesus, you are a direct descendant of King David!"

"Not everyone can make that claim!" Zerah added.

"I copied this lineage from the Temple archives before Herod had them destroyed," Heli asserted. "They are accurate!" From memory, Heli began to quote, "*Now David is the son of Jesse, the son of Obed, the son of Boaz*[11]—"

"Who married Ruth, the righteous widow and daughter-in-law of Naomi from the land of Moab," Jesus commented.

"You were listening when I told that story," Zerah stated with satisfaction. "Now tell me, what do you know about Salmon, the father of Boaz?"

"He was one of the spies Joshua sent across the Jordan to scout out the city of Jericho. There he met Rahab, the harlot."

"A woman of legendary courage and beauty," Heli softly added.

"He gave her the red cord to tie in her window and returned to rescue her and her entire family," Jesus continued to recite the story.

"Salmon also married Rahab, the harlot from Jericho, and from that time, she has been known as a righteous woman in Israel," Zerah completed the mini history lesson.

Again Jesus placed the pointer and read, "*The son of Salmon, the son of Nahson, the son of Amminadab, the son of Ram, the son of Hezron, the son of Perez.*"[12] Then he stopped reading and looked up at his grandfather and teacher.

"If Salmon was one of the men who crossed the Jordan with Joshua, then Nahson and Amminadab and possibly Ram died in the wilderness. Most likely, Ram and Amminadab went through the Red Sea and witnessed the defeat of Pharaoh."

"Ram and Amminadab danced around my golden calf!" Satan triumphantly announced.

Suddenly, Jesus could see it! In his mind, frantic half-naked men leaped and shouted before a small gold calf while behind and above that idol, Satan stood, his ox face glowing from the adoration of misguided men.

For a moment, that burnished ox-like face turned and looked directly at the boy who sat under the winter oak studying a scroll with his grandfather and his teacher. Amazingly, he opened his mouth and announced, "One day, you will also worship me!"

A little shiver ran through Jesus's body, and he quickly glanced first at his grandfather and then at his teacher to see if they sensed anything unusual. They seemed unaffected.

"Hezron the son of Perez, his grandson Ram, and Amminadab all lived at least a portion of their lives in slavery," Zerah continued his commentary. "Perez was a twin, born to Tamar—" Suddenly, Zerah stopped talking and looked up at the sky.

Big heavy raindrops began falling, splattering on the scroll. Jesus quickly picked up the open scroll, and shielding it with his body, he hurriedly carried it into his grandfather's house.

"That is enough for today." Heli took the scroll and carefully blotted a few water spots before rolling the skin and securing it with a thin piece of leather. "Jesus, you had better hurry home before your mother starts to worry."

Joseph bent his head back, and by the sputtering light from a handheld oil lamp, he studied the packed sod-and-thatch ceiling of the room where Jesus, Jose, and James slept. With a practiced hand, he reached up and tested a few spots for dampness and sagging.

Beside him, Jesus also looked up at the ceiling, trying to see what the experienced eye of his father saw. "The roof will hold," Jesus confidently stated.

"How do you know?" Joseph asked as he glanced down into the serious face of his oldest son. "The rain has not let up for six days, and this roof is very new. Grass has not yet taken root, so there are no roots to hold the sod firmly in place."

"We built a good a roof," Jesus responded. "I helped you tear off the old roof and put on this new roof. We made a sturdy framework, and I carefully overlapped each bundle of thatch, so there are no holes. The sod you packed over the thatch will not wash through, and after this rain, grass will grow on the roof, more firmly securing the sod."

"I can always count on your work, Jesus. You're right. We did everything as we should." Joseph set the lamp in one of the little niches in the wall where the white limestone intensified the light from the sputtering flame. "It is early, but it is already dark, so let's go to bed," Joseph announced to all three boys. "Your mother and your sister have already gone to sleep."

"A story?" Jose requested as he unrolled his sleeping mat and spread his covers.

"We're ready!" Jesus and James called from their hastily laid-out sleeping mats. All three mats were spread side by side, each boy sitting on his own jumble of covers.

Joseph chuckled as he squatted down on his heels, level with his sons. "All this rain reminds me of a man I once knew in the city of Capernaum."

"Did he work for Uncle Zebedee?" James asked.

"Yes, he was one of the fishermen who worked for Zebedee," Joseph answered.

"The man wanted me to build him a house close to the lake's shore. When I looked at the spot he had chosen, there were no rocks for a foundation, only sand. I told the man, 'This is not a good place to build. Storms will come. Waves will soak the sand, and your house will sink.'" Slowly, Joseph shook his head from side to side. "That man would not listen. He begged, even insisted that I build his house on the exact spot he had chosen. Finally, with one last warning, I gave in and did as he requested. During the winter months, the rains came and soaked the sand. The winds whipped the waves on the lake. Those waves rolled across the sand and splashed against the sides of the house."

"It collapsed!" James and Jose shouted.

"How did you know?" Joseph asked.

"You told us this story before!" The boys laughingly answered.

"He should have built his house on a rock, high above the waterline," Jesus seriously commented.

"You're going to be a good carpenter and a fine builder," Joseph complimented his son.

"Then the man went to live with Uncle Zebedee until the rains ended," James and Jose continued telling the story. "Uncle Zebedee yelled at him every day and told him he was a foolish, foolish man."

"The man told me it was like living in a thunderstorm that never ended!" Joseph chuckled over the memories.

"Tell us about Uncle Zebedee's house!" Jose demanded.

"Uncle Zebedee has a sturdy house," Joseph replied. "I built it for him four years ago. It is anchored on a large flat rock that overlooks his fishing spot on the Sea of Galilee."

"When are we going to see Uncle Zebedee again?" James asked.

"After the plowing and planting, when the barley is nearly ripe, it will be Passover and the Feast of Unleavened Bread. Then we will meet Uncle Zebedee on the road to Jerusalem," Joseph answered with assurance. "I don't know if Aunt Salome will come, but you can be sure that Zebedee will come and he will bring your cousins, James and John."

The boys suddenly started giggling and excitedly exchanging plans for a week of adventures in Jerusalem with their cousins.

Joseph stood up. For a moment, he just stood there watching his three sons. They were all good boys, boys that a father could be proud of. Briefly, he thought of Mary. Her time to deliver another child would probably come soon after Passover. Maybe she would give him another son. With that thought in mind, he reached over the heads of his laughing sons and retrieved the sputtering oil lamp from its niche in the wall. He carried it with him as he moved into the main living area of his home, leaving his sons to talk themselves out and then fall asleep.

Darkness gently pressed the sons of Joseph flat onto their sleeping mats. It closed their eyes and wrapped them in oblivion. Fragments of their day wove themselves into the unfathomable patterns of dreams. In moments of restless sleep, Jose rolled first onto Jesus's mat and then over onto the mat where James was sleeping.

"Yeshua?"

Unexpectedly, in the midst of a contorted, meaningless dream, there was sudden order and clarity. Jesus heard his Father call his name.

Remaining in his dreamy state, he responded, "I am here."

Then amazingly, he seemed to be suddenly transported onto the road to Jerusalem, and there, above the road, he saw a house—a house brilliantly illuminated with the burning lamps of the Feast of Dedication.

"My son, you are like a house secured on the rock of my righteous generations, rooted in my revelations to your ancestors." The warm flowing words of Father God filled the mind of Jesus. "Yeshua, you will light the land with the words I have spoken to each generation. Through you, all my words will be established. By the light you shed on this land, men will read and understand my laws."

Coming out of his dream-filled sleep, Jesus rolled over onto his side. In the quiet blackness of his sleeping chamber, he considered the words of his Father, "You are like a house secured on the rock of my righteous generations, rooted in my revelations to your ancestors."

My ancestors—the generations of my mother. Jesus began to run through his mind the names that Heli had shown him. He could list them in order. In his mind, the scroll of his maternal ancestry opened before him, and one name seemed to leap from the carefully prepared animal skin.

"The son of Judah," the Holy Spirit announced as he continued revealing to Jesus the foundation that had been laid in preparation for his birth.

"*What will we gain if we kill our brother and cover up his blood?*"[13] A swarthy bearded man stood with his back to a gaping hole in the ground.

From that hole, a desperate young voice called, "Judah, don't let them kill me."

"Be quiet!" With an irritated glance over his shoulder, Judah ordered his half brother, Joseph, to be silent. Then he turned back to face his nine agitated and angry brothers. "I am asking you again. *What will we gain if we kill our brother and cover up his blood?*"[14]

"Not the birthright!" One brother exclaimed. "If this son of Rachel does not live to inherit, then our father's blessing and his wealth will go to her other son."

"The sons of Leah have been passed over!" Ruben, who was Isaac and Leah's eldest, voiced the obvious.

"I never expected to inherit," Dan, the son of Rachel's maidservant, spoke up.

"Neither did I expect to be ordered about by a mere boy like I was a slave and he the master," Dan's full brother, Naphtali, complained.

Judah tried again. "I know Father has been unfair and Joseph has been as irritating as a splinter in the hand, but *come. Let's sell him to the Ishmaelites and not lay our hands on him; after all, he is our brother, our own flesh and blood.*"[15]

"I chose your ancestor, Judah, to produce the royal line because he had a greater capacity for compassion than any of Jacob's other sons," the Spirit of God commented.

"Compassion?" In the midst of his revelation, Jesus questioned the Holy Spirit. "He sold his brother into slavery!"

"Joseph's brothers were the tools of my will. Events that I set into motion cannot be stopped. In the scriptures, you have read how Joseph, the favorite son of Jacob, was first loved and honored by his father. Then he was despised and sold by his brothers. For a portion of his life, he received an unjust punishment. Honor, power, and authority did not come to him until after his time of enduring. So it is with all those whom I have chosen to be deliverers. In various ways, every deliverer I have sent to my people has been a type of the perfect Messiah.

"Think about your ancestor, King David. As a young man, he was chosen and anointed. Then before he could take the throne, he was forced from his home into the caves and barren regions. To human eyes, it appeared his battle was with King Saul, but in reality, he fled from and fought with the spirits of Jealousy and Murder. The kingdom of Satan has always been and still is intent on destroying the messianic line.

"Even Moses, so revered by the rabbis, had to endure unreasonable persecution until I called him at the burning bush to return to Egypt and deliver his people. In infancy, my enemy attempted to take his life. As a youth in Pharaoh's palace, Satan offered Moses the riches and power of Egypt. Finally, in the strength of his manhood, Moses was defeated by Anger and Murder. Fear chased him into the wilderness to the place I had chosen. There, in the barren regions of Arabia, I sheltered and prepared him to become a deliverer for my people.

"The learned men of this land who sit in the porches of the Temple focus only on the triumphant ruling Messiah. They do not see that first, my Anointed One must struggle, and even seem to be completely defeated. All mankind struggles against an enemy it does not understand. My Anointed One is both man and God, so he struggles, but he knows who it is that he struggles against.

"The great teachers of the land imagine the Messiah is coming to do their bidding, to attain the goals they have set for him, but I tell you, my Anointed One has come only to do the bidding of Father God." After speaking so much into the mind of Jesus, the Spirit of God withdrew and allowed Satan to approach.

"Jacob, the son of Isaac." The enemy of God tried to make it seem that the Spirit of God was still speaking. "Never forget. You are both the son of God and the son of Mary. All the inherited traits from Mary's ancestors are part of your physical body. Therefore, because Jacob was a deceiver, you can expect to sometimes lie and even deceive people. Remember, Isaac, the son of Abraham, as well as Abraham, the great father of all Jews, did not trust God to protect their families. They both went to Egypt and became subject to the pharaohs of that land. They put their wives in danger because they were overcome by Fear.

"Always remember, your forefathers climbed to the tops of the ziggurats to worship the sun and the moon. *Terah, the son of Nahor, the son of Serug, the son of Reu*[16]—they all worshipped household idols."

"My faithful servant, Abraham, buried the household idols when he buried his father Terah," the Holy Spirit interrupted Satan. "Willingly, he left them in the cave with his father's body. Even before I proclaimed my possessive love on Mount Sinai, Abraham understood, '*You shall have no other gods before me.*'[17]"

In the twilight of nearly sleeping, Jesus suddenly saw a giant step pyramid, The Tower of Babel. Its baked-brick walls rose from the earth layer upon layer until they disappeared in a fog of clouds. The top could not be seen. All that could be seen were line upon line of carved stairways, zigzagging and crawling with construction workers.

"Peleg, the son of Eber." The Spirit of God suddenly focused on two men standing at the base of the tower watching the misguided efforts of their friends and relatives. "Both Peleg and Eber watched as the tower was built, but they did not participate because they remembered the warnings of Shem, the son of Noah. They knew this construction was an affront to the rainbow covenant I had made with all mankind."

Suddenly, Jesus saw a bolt of lightning strike the top of the tower. Men dropped their baskets of mortar. The entire structure quaked and cracked. Those builders who were on the tower fell facedown, clinging to the clay steps to keep from falling to the levels below. When the quaking ceased, men began unintelligible shouting, and Jesus saw terrified looks of confusion on the faces of the laborers. In his mind, Jesus could see spirits of Panic, like giant birds of prey, swoop in with talons ready to capture every man on the tower. Screaming, leaping, and trampling each other, the workers on the tower fled to the security of solid earth.

Another bolt of lightning struck. It seemed to hang and glow above the tower, burning away the fog that had covered the topmost layer of the ziggurat. There stood a dazzling white angel, announcing, "*Give thanks to the LORD, call on his name: make known among the nations what he has done. Sing to him, sing praise to him: tell of his wonderful acts. Glory in his holy name; let the hearts of those who seek the LORD rejoice. Look to the LORD and his strength; seek his face always. Remember the wonders he has done, his miracles, and the judgments he pronounced.*"[18]

"I, the Lord, confused their language and *scattered them from there over all the earth, and they stopped building.*[19] Peleg, with his clan, went to live between the two great rivers, Tigris and Euphrates."

The angel that still hovered over the top of the unfinished Tower of Babel continued the genealogy of Mary the mother of Jesus. "*The son of Shelah, the son of Cainan, the son of Arphaxad, the son of Shem, the son of Noah.*"[20] Like a clap of thunder, each name rolled across the flat Plain of Shinar until the baked clay ziggurat disappeared. There on the plain sat an enormous wooden structure, a giant ship!

"Japheth! Help Shem hoist those anchors to the top deck. Ham, tie the doors open. The animals are coming!"

In his dream, Jesus watched as a wild-haired old man bellowed orders to three strapping young men who were working at a mammoth ship construction site. Two men used a rope and pulley system to raise gray stone anchors, cut and carved boulders, up to the flat surface of the box-shaped upper deck.

Then a noise like a stampede caught Jesus's attention. On the horizon of the treeless plain, a cloud of brown dust rose into the air. Above it, a vast variety of birds, both great and tiny, soared directly toward the massive wooden ship that sat on the dry grass, no water in sight.

"They're coming! They're coming!" The old man jumped up and down, waving his arms in excited gestures that resembled the flapping wings of a bird. "Wife! Daughters! Open the stalls. Prepare to receive those animals chosen by the Lord."

"Do you see the angels?" the Spirit asked.

"Yes," Jesus replied in a sleepy whisper, "they are leading and following the animals. I have never seen animals like some I see in this herd!"

"Yes, in your life as the son of Mary and Joseph, you have only seen the domestic animals of your land, but as Yeshua the Creator, you imagined and spoke into existence every kind of bird and beast you are now seeing."

Awestruck, Jesus watched as the herd thundered to a halt not far from the giant rectangular boat. Then guided by angelic drovers, they formed an orderly line of pairs and groups of seven. In that manner, they tamely walked up the ramp and allowed themselves to be led into the various stalls that had been built in the giant ship. When the last animal had entered and been secured in a stall, Noah and his sons followed. Immediately, an angel soared to the massive double doors, the only entrance to the ship. With one mighty movement, he swung both doors shut.

Thunder then rolled across the early morning sky. It startled Jesus into complete wakefulness. He sat up in his bed. On either side, his brothers continued to sleep. Outside, rain fell in torrents. Through the open doorway, Jesus could see his father Joseph approaching, oil lamp in hand.

"Jesus, I'm glad you are awake. Baruch's oldest daughter has been out in this storm looking for her father. Your mother is drying and warming her now. We must join the men of the town to continue the search."

Immediately, Jesus was on his feet, rolling up his sleeping mat, lacing up his sandals, preparing to go with his father and the other men to look for the faithful old shepherd of Nazareth.

"Baruch! Baruch!" Jesus called.

"Baruch! Baruch!" Some distance away, Jethro also called the name of the missing shepherd. The early morning downpour had diminished into an uncomfortable drizzle as the men of Nazareth along with their older sons scoured the hills and ravines around the town.

"There is a cave near the top of this hill." Joseph pointed as he directed Jesus. "Run up there and look inside."

Before his father completed the request, Jesus was sprinting up the slippery hill. He knew the cave his father had mentioned. He also knew that from the mouth of that cave, one could see far down into the narrow valley that cut between twin hills.

Upon reaching the summit, Jesus first entered the cave. "Baruch!" His voice bounced off the limestone walls and echoed back at him. Then he turned and looked out. His young eyes scoured the steep sides of the opposite hill and then moved down toward the rock-strewn floor where new grass was sprouting from the soggy soil. "Baruch!" Jesus called again as he made his eyes sweep back and forth, studying each shrub and unusual rock formation. For a moment, he paused and looked heavenward. "Father God? Where is Baruch?"

"There is a piece of gray fabric on top of that large boulder," the Holy Spirit said, directing Jesus to look at a large rock that jutted out near the foot of the hill. "That is Baruch's mantle. He hung it there to prevent the rain from driving into his shelter."

Looking closely, Jesus could just make out what had appeared to be a darker part of the rock. Now his discerning eyes could see that the dark area was actually a piece of woolen fabric held in place by several melon-size rocks.

"Father! Jethro!" Jesus called for assistance as he slipped and slid down the muddy sides of the steep hill to the place where the shepherd's cloak lay. Upon reaching the rock, Jesus did not wait for his father, Joseph. He quickly dropped to his belly and lowered himself over the side of the boulder. Baruch was underneath, curled into a tight lifeless ball, as if he had died trying to keep himself warm. An injured ewe lay trembling beside him.

Before Jesus could drop to his knees beside the old shepherd, Joseph was there, moving him aside, checking for signs of life. Joseph stated what Jesus already seemed to know. "I'm afraid Baruch is dead."

"Why?" Jesus choked out the one-word question as his tears began to fall.

"Baruch was old." Joseph put his sturdy arm around the shoulders of his son. "He was older than your grandfather, Heli. Last night was cold and wet. Most likely, he went searching for this ewe and found her." Joseph dropped to his knees and began to examine the injured ewe. "A lion had this animal. See?" He pointed to the wounds on the animal's neck. "That's where the lion grabbed her and tried to carry her off. Baruch probably fought the beast." Joseph picked up the shepherd's rod that lay nearby. He held it up to the early morning light. It was bloody, and small tufts of matted fur clung to the iron studs. "Baruch was a good shepherd." Once more, Joseph moved over to the body of his friend. Without saying anything, he pointed to the arms of the old shepherd.

Jesus saw the claw marks, evidence of a struggle for the life of this one sheep. "He loved each animal in the flock," Jesus acknowledged through his tears.

"Did you see the lion's tracks?"

Jesus looked up to see that Jethro and his son, Simon, had arrived.

Without speaking, Joseph held up the shepherd's rod, then pointed to the deep scratches on the shepherd's arms. The wounds along with the bloody weapon told the story.

Jethro responded with a sad shake of his head, and then he picked up the shepherd's staff and handed it to his son.

Joseph put the rod in Jesus's hand. "Take the ewe back to the flock. Move slowly with her. She is badly shaken and may collapse on you." There was a raspy quality to Joseph's voice as he sent the boys away. "On your way, tell the men who are still searching that Baruch has been found."

"And, boys," Jethro called after them. "That lion may be nearby, hungry and injured; so be careful!"

Leaving Jethro and Joseph to bring the body back to town, the boys began to pick a safe trail for the traumatized animal. Simon led the way, and Jesus walked behind, urging the ewe to keep moving. As they walked, a torrent of questions rushed through his mind. "Father God? Will Baruch live again?"

"A day will come when the archangel Michael will blow the shofar and the bodies of all the faithful will be released from their graves. They will live with us forever. My faithful servant Baruch will be called back to life," the Spirit of God answered. "Remember the words of my long-suffering servant Job, *'I know that my Redeemer lives and that in the end he will stand upon the Earth. And after my skin has been destroyed, yet in my flesh will I see God.* [21]"

"His family will mourn, and the town will be without a shepherd," Jesus responded with deeply felt empathy.

"I chose Baruch to be the shepherd of Nazareth. He taught you many things about the sheep. Remember those things and remember the faithful shepherd of Nazareth."

Leading the way, Simon suddenly stopped and looked around. "Jesus, do you know where the flock is?"

"No," Jesus replied as with his eyes he scanned the low rolling hills that extended to the foot of the craggy, steep side of a massive hill. "Let me stay here with the ewe," Jesus suggested. "We should not stress her by wandering back and forth. You go look for the flock and return to me. Then we can take her to the flock by a short and direct route."

Simon nodded his agreement and immediately set off in a direction that would take him south of the town. Jesus slowly lowered himself onto a flat rock. For a while, he watched the ewe as it lay on the grass, still trembling, not even attempting to stand and graze.

For a long time, Jesus sat on the rock. After a while, he noticed black clouds rolling across the sky again. He began to look around for a shelter where he along with the ewe could find protection from the elements.

"Yeshua," the Holy Spirit warned. "Satan has been given opportunity to approach."

From behind thornbushes that concealed the mouth of a cave, Satan called to the boy Jesus, "There is shelter in this cave." Then for a moment, he allowed himself to enjoy the sleek beauty of the lion that rested on the stone floor of the cave, nursing the wounds Baruch had inflicted.

Immediately, the Holy Spirit rushed forward and faced the enemy of God. "Do you think you can easily destroy Yeshua?"

"Your servant Daniel was safe enough in the lion's den," Satan sneeringly responded. "Why shouldn't your special boy take shelter there?"

"He is more than a special boy. He is God. He is your Creator and master in human flesh," the Spirit of God announced. "You can be sure Yeshua in this fleshly body will not be deceived into going to his death!"

"That boy is not part of the Eternal Godhead!" Satan angrily protested. "He is not my Creator or my master! More easily than I brought Adam and Eve into heeding and obeying my voice will I bring this child into submission!"

"Look, Jesus," Satan called to the boy who kept one eye on the ewe and another eye on the fast-moving storm clouds. "My son, look behind the bush. In Abraham's time of need, he found a ram in the bush. Now that the storm is bearing down on you, you need to find shelter in the cave behind this bush."

Before Jesus could respond to Satan's deception, the Holy Spirit warned again, "Yeshua, do you recognize the voice you just heard? Was it the firm and loving voice of your Father God? Were those the soul-burning words of God's Spirit? Yeshua, I tell you, do not believe every voice in your head, *but test the spirits to see whether they are from God.*[22] Ask this spirit to affirm the truth of your mission."

"Spirit who speaks to me," Jesus said, "Can you affirm that Yeshua the Messiah has come from God to Earth in human flesh?"

"Never!" Satan shouted. "On Earth, all are sons of men. Not one human is a son of God. They are all flesh, and the Spirit of God does not dwell in any of them!"

"Speak no more to me," Jesus firmly responded, "for it is clear you are the enemy of my Father."

Lightning suddenly shot across the sky, and a peal of thunder echoed across the hills. In his mind, Jesus saw the angel again continuing to announce the genealogy of Mary. *"The son of Lamech, the son of Methuselah, the son of Enoch, the son of Jared, the son of Mahalalel, the son of Kenan, the son of Enosh, the son of Seth, the son of Adam, the son of God."*[23]

"Yeshua," the Spirit of God spoke with authority. "Know that you are both the son of Adam, a representative for all mankind, and the Son of God, part of the Eternal Godhead. In your humanness, you will stand in the place of Adam against Satan, the enemy of all mankind. *Be self-controlled and alert, your enemy, the devil prowls around like a roaring lion looking for someone to devour. Resist him, standing firm*[24] on the law and the prophets for Satan fears every word that has ever been uttered by the mouth of God."

"Jesus! Jesus!"

Jesus could see Simon running toward him.

"I found the flock. They are on the other side of this hill near the shepherd's caves. Harim and Ahaz are moving the sheep into the shelter of the caves." Before Simon could say more, Jesus was urging the ewe to her feet, nudging her to move forward and follow Simon to safety.

"Plowing will soon begin." Joseph made the announcement as the family broke bread together at the beginning of the day.

"How many yoke of oxen will we be using this year?" Jesus asked.

"In the town, there are four yoke of oxen," Joseph answered. "We will begin with the field of Ezra, son of Samuel, and continue moving the oxen to each field in the vicinity of Nazareth until all the fields have been plowed and the seed sown. But before we can begin turning the earth, each pair of oxen needs a new yoke. That is our contribution to the preparation of the fields around Nazareth." Turning to Jesus, Joseph added, "Son, I want you to go to the willows near Moshe's vineyard. Find sturdy yet pliable branches that can be shaped to form the underpinnings of the yokes."

"I will, Father." Jesus was on his feet and walking out the door when he heard his father say, "James, you and Jose are to go to our field and remove as many rocks as you can."

A picture of the stone-strewn barley field behind Joseph's carpentry shop suddenly filled the mind of James. "It is backbreaking work to pick up and move all those stones," Resentment shouted. "Jesus should be helping you, not taking a leisurely stroll through the willows. Resist this mistreatment!" Resentment ordered.

"Oh, Father," James complained. "Jesus always gets the easy jobs. Why can't he pick up rocks and pile them at the edge of the field? I will go find the willow branches."

"Jesus knows how to select smooth, sturdy branches that will not chafe the animals or break under the strain of the job," Joseph replied. "Now go and pick up every rock that is smaller than a melon!"

Reluctantly, James rose from the low table. Motioning for Jose to follow, he resentfully headed for the field where his family planted their barley.

In the willows near the small vineyard that belonged to Moshe the tanner, Jesus began moving from tree to tree, examining various branches, from time to time cutting a branch and laying it aside. He was so involved in his work that at first he did not notice he was not alone.

"Jesus?"

Jesus looked up to see Harim, Moshe's youngest son, high in the branches of the tree where he had been cutting. "What are you doing up there?" Jesus called as he peered up through the leafless branches.

"Nothing," Harim responded.

"Nothing?" Jesus echoed incredulously. "It's almost plowing time, and everyone is busy! Stones have to be removed from the fields, our mothers are digging up their gardens with pointed sticks, and the vines in the vineyards have to be cut back. The daughters and granddaughters of Baruch have to stay in the pastures with the sheep because every man and boy is needed to plow and plant the fields. Harim, don't you know how much work needs to be done?"

"And the stone walls that support the terraces of the vineyards need to be repaired," Harim interjected in a rebellious tone. "Father told me to repair the terraces, and I told him I didn't want to do it today."

"Harim!" Jesus was aghast. "You can't mean that you told your father you wouldn't do the job? He is counting on you!"

"That's what I told him," Harim triumphantly answered.

"The law—" Jesus began.

Harim interrupted, "Don't lecture me like you're my elder. Don't tell me about the law that states we are to honor and obey our parents. At least I did not bear false witness like Ahaz."

"What do you mean?" Jesus asked in alarm.

"My father told both of us to work in the vineyard today. Ahaz assured him that he would do the work, but he is not working! He has gone to see the sights of Sepphoris."

"No!" Jesus gasped. "When your father finds out, he will take a rod to him."

"My father is too busy to come out to the family vineyard. We only have a few grapevines on a terraced hillside. Ahaz and I are supposed to care for them."

"Then you should care for those vines," Jesus admonished his friend. "A good harvest of grapes means grape honey and sweet wine for your family. Don't you know God gave you life instead of death when that runaway slave attacked you?" Jesus asked. "Do you think God allowed you to remain in the world of the living so you could dishonor your father and allow your family to be deprived of bounty from the land?"

"No," Harim groaned his response as he slowly made his way down from the tree. "You have taken all the fun out of my day. I don't feel like climbing trees anymore."

"Isn't there a voice in your head telling you to go and do as your father has asked?" Jesus inquired.

"Yes," Harim responded with a sigh as he made the last little jump from a low branch to the ground. "But that voice is not as loud and insistent as your voice," Harim complained. "Now there is nothing else to do. I guess I will have to go and rebuild the terrace walls." Slowly, Harim shuffled down the narrow path toward his family vineyard.

Jesus turned back to his task, checking branches with his eye and then with his hands before making a selection.

"Yeshua?"

Jesus stopped working and waited for Father God to speak.

"Yeshua? Do you love me?"

"Papa, you know I love you."

"I will know you love me when I see you doing the tasks I give you to do. Which son of Moshe really loves his father? Ahaz, who said that he would work in the vineyard and did not, or Harim, who said he would not work in the vineyard but had a change of heart and is now repairing the terraces?"

"Harim loves his father," Jesus answered.

"Remember this incident," God said with finality.

As Jesus, along with James, approached the freshly plowed field that belonged to Ezra, son of Samuel, Jesus could see the men resting under a small stand of almond trees. His sharp eyes studied the tangled bare branches silhouetted against the late afternoon sky. He could see the little bumps that indicated the trees were just beginning to bud, just beginning to shout their promise of spring. "James, look!" Jesus pointed to the trees. "When the almond branches are covered with pink and white blossoms, then it will be time to go to Jerusalem for Passover."

"Then will we see all our cousins?" James asked as he shifted the basket full of food he carried.

Jesus freed one hand from the load he carried and helped James with the basket as he nodded in the affirmative.

"What about Toma? Will he be there?"

"I don't think so," Jesus answered. "He avoids Jerusalem during the feasts. Father says he is angry at God and at the Romans."

"He is supposed to go," James said.

"I know." Jesus glanced at his younger brother as he answered, "But not everyone does everything they should."

Jesus, with his brother, James, carried the lunch Mary had sent for the workers: mashed lentils, flat bread, goat cheese, and olives. As he approached, he could see Ezra's wife, Abigail, moving from man to man with her water jar and clay cups. Jesus quickened his pace. He knew the men would want to eat and then return to the field to scatter the seed. Stepping onto the new grass where the men sat, he handed the baskets of food to Abigail, who began to lay the food out for the men.

"Jesus?" Joseph beckoned to his oldest son as he called his name.

Jesus moved quickly to respond while James wandered over to examine the four teams of oxen, free from their yokes, grazing on freshly sprouted grass.

"Is our field ready for the teams to plow tomorrow?" Joseph asked.

"It will be," Jesus carefully answered.

"Will be?" Joseph growled as he softly echoed Jesus's words. "I put James and Jose to work in that field a week ago. There should not be a stone anywhere!"

"All this morning, I have been working on it," Jesus responded. "I think some stones were a little large for them, and some stones they did not move completely off the field onto the stone wall."

"James?" Joseph bellowed his second son's name.

The boy came running, excited about the yearly plowing. "Father, can I help yoke the oxen? Can I walk behind the plow?"

"Can you do the one job I have asked you to do correctly?" Joseph replied.

James quickly glanced at Jesus and then back at his father, Joseph. For him, the joy of the planting season immediately wilted under the stern glare of his father's displeasure.

Always watchfully lurking, ready to respond to every opportunity, Resentment swooped in. "Your brother brought a bad report to your father," the demonic spirit eagerly informed James. "He did it just so you would look bad and he would look good."

Jesus saw the evil spirit. He heard its accusation, but he did not respond or attempt to defend himself. Instead, he turned to his father, Joseph, and offered, "James and I will have the field ready before sunset."

Still directing his stern admonitions to James, Joseph said, "Son, a worthy laborer is one who completes a task so that no man can find a flaw in the work. You have asked to help with the plowing, but *no one who puts his hand to the plow and looks back is fit*[25] to do the job."

"Listen, my son," God spoke into the mind of Jesus as he stood beside his brother, "*no one who puts his hand to the plow,* to work the soil of my kingdom, *and looks back* desiring an easier field to plow or a day to rest, *is fit for service in the kingdom of God.*[26] Remember this time and this teaching from your father, Joseph, and from your Father who lives in heaven."

Chapter 6

John, Son of Zechariah

And you, my child, will be called a prophet of the Most High;
for you will go on before the Lord to prepare the way for him,
to give his people the knowledge of salvation through the
forgiveness of their sins.

—Luke 1:76–77

John looked up from loading the last of twelve clay jars of honey into the back of the cart. His aged and nearly blind father, Zechariah, was unsteadily trying to find the right grip along with a secure foothold so he could climb up onto the seat of the cart.

"Father, wait! I will help you!" With his waist-length hair flying wildly around his young face, John ran to the front of the cart. It didn't take much to settle his father on the wooden seat behind the donkey.

"Bless Ephriam for loaning you this cart and donkey." Zechariah's voice was gravelly and soft as he spoke to his son who had moved forward to check the donkey's harness and halter.

"The loan is only for one day," John reminded his father. "We'll have to sell all our wild honey and nuts today."

"This is the Passover market," Zechariah stated with confidence. "For the entire month before this feast, people are planning and purchasing for Passover. Wise housewives buy their nuts and honey for the sweet Passover dip early. Then they purchase extra honey to eat with their unleavened bread. You cannot eat unleavened bread all week without honey."

"I know," John replied as he prodded the donkey so she moved at a slow but steady pace. "I gathered all the honey I could find over the summer and into the fall months. I sold as little as possible over the winter because this is the best market. This is when we will get the best price."

"And you gathered the nuts that fell from every nut-bearing tree along the edges of the fields," Zechariah stated approvingly. "You are an industrious son. I could not survive without you."

"And we, like so many other priestly families, could not survive without the Essene brotherhood. If they did not share with us—"

"And we with them," Zechariah interrupted his son's complaint.

"The Temple treasuries are going to be emptied. All the priests in the land are to be paid." John's voice was hopeful.

"There is never enough for the active priests to get a fair portion," Zechariah cautioned John against fruitless dreams. "Those of us who are too old and infirmed cannot expect—"

"But you were born a priest, and you are a priest for life," John interrupted his father. "Specific offerings in the Temple are set aside to provide for you."

"After the high priest and his associates provide for themselves," Zechariah responded with realistic cynicism.

"Palaces in the Upper City! Bribes to obtain important positions!" John protested. "Geber, the teacher from Qumran, says we should have nothing to do with the Temple and its services because the high priest and his subordinates are so corrupt. He even insists we are not observing Passover on the correct day."

"I know," Zechariah said. "I have heard all the discussions about the calendar that Moses gave us and how it was changed when the family of Maccabee came into power." He sighed. Discussions over which day was originally designated for each feast wearied him. Hoping to change the subject, the old priest commented, "The market should be nearby." He squinted in an effort to see a little bit of the crooked Jerusalem road that led to the people's market not far from the Essene Gate.

"Father? You have not answered me." John then asked directly, "Three weeks from now, it will be Passover week. Should we be observing Passover on the fourth day or the fifth day of that week?"

After a thoughtful pause, the old priest responded to his son. "I am aware of corruption and injustice at the highest levels in the Temple, and I do understand there are differences in the ancient calendar of Moses and the calendar we use today, but I cannot break away from the Temple calendar and its services. For too many years, I have served before the Lord in that Temple. Has God totally abandoned the Temple? I think not! His angel appeared to me as I was officiating before the veil. His angel announced your birth and your destiny."

"You have told me that story many times," John responded, "and you have also told me about the miraculous birth of my cousin, Jesus. I believe all of it, but those prophecies are for the future. Right now, someone should make the Temple authorities do what is right! Three times each year, the Temple treasuries are emptied, and each time, you are supposed to get paid. You did not get paid at the Feast of Tabernacles."

"I was too ill to go to the Temple," Zechariah protested. "And Joram said they refused to release my pay to him because he was not a family member."

"This year, I will go to collect your wages," John determinedly announced.

"Our friend Joram is a priest! The officer of the treasury would not listen to him. Do you think the officer of the treasury will listen to a boy who has not even entered manhood?"

"I will make him listen," John insisted.

"Be cautious, my son. Choose your words carefully when you approach the keeper of the treasury. You do not want your name associated with insubordination. Insubordination in the face of a Temple officer is a punishable offense."

"Father." John's voice betrayed his youthful impatience. "You are always cautioning me, but I must speak the truth. The truth is you did not receive your wages the last time the treasury was emptied and you should receive them now, along with what is currently due! I promise not to mention all the other times you were not paid or were paid at a reduced rate."

"*A good name is more desirable than great riches; to be esteemed is better than silver or gold,*"[1] Zechariah admonished.

"I will remember," John promised.

"Also," Zechariah continued with his admonitions, "*A prudent man sees danger and takes refuge, but the simple keep going and suffer for it. Humility and the fear of the LORD bring wealth and honor and life.*"[2]

"Father!" This time, John's voice reeked with exasperation. "I will speak politely to the officers of the Temple. I will be careful to observe all the Temple regulations. I know I must show respect for the offices these men hold, even if the men are unworthy of their positions."

"I am afraid Geber and the other men of the Essene community where we now reside have spoken far too freely and far too critically," Zechariah responded. "Temple officials and ordinary citizens of Jerusalem, *rich and poor have this in common: The LORD is the Maker of them all,*[3] and he is their judge."

"*I am God, and there is no other; I am God and there is none like me. I make known the end from the beginning, from ancient times, what is still to come!*" In the spiritual realm, the Holy Spirit, like a glowing torch, processed ahead of John, announcing the role he was learning to fill even at this young age, "*I say: My purpose will stand, and I will do as I please...I summon... a man to fulfill my purpose. Listen to me, you stubborn-hearted, who are far from righteousness. I am bringing my righteousness near. It is not far away.*"[4]

Within his heart, John felt his determination solidify. He would get both his father's back and current wages from the treasurer of the Temple. In his young heart, it seemed to be a righteous act—to make clear this injustice and see it corrected.

"The market is just ahead," Zechariah announced.

"How can you tell?" John asked. "Can you see it?"

"No, I can hear it. I can hear the shrill voices of haggling women. I can smell the herbs and spices."

John slowed and then stopped the donkey as he looked for a place to display the clay pots filled with wild honey and the baskets heaped with nuts.

"Stop the cart near the spice merchants," Zechariah directed. "The aroma of the spices will draw shoppers to our honey and nuts."

A refreshing Mediterranean breeze wafted across the dusty coastal caravan route from Caesarea to Ashkelon. "I'm looking forward to Ashkelon," Kheti said, making light conversation with his trading partner, Toma, the cousin of Joseph.

Toma raised an eyebrow before responding, "I believe what you are really saying is you are anticipating the pleasures of the bathhouse you visited the last time we were in Ashkelon!"

"I am in need of a bath," the Egyptian merchant asserted as he pretended to smell himself.

"I imagine you also are in need of the services the women of the bathhouse offer?" Toma suggested with a hint of disdain.

"I have not had the opportunity to wash and have my needs met since we left Petra," Kheti protested the inferred condemnation. "Your Jewish towns do not offer such establishments." The Egyptian merchant shook his head in bewilderment. "It is rumored along the caravan routes when Jewish men have the foreskin of their offspring removed, they also diminish their sex drive."

"Nonsense!" Toma responded with undisguised offense. "We follow the laws of Moses. Those laws require cleanliness and fidelity to a marriage partner."

"Where is your marriage partner?" Kheti quickly retorted.

"You know," Toma growled.

"I know your wife was killed more than ten years ago. It is now time for you to get a new wife," Kheti urged. "It is not healthy for a man to be without the services of a woman. It makes him hard to live with and difficult to work with."

"Marriages are arranged," Toma argued. "I have no time for those negotiations, and where would my bride live? You do not understand the Jewish way of doing these things."

"Do not underestimate my knowledge of your culture," Kheti retorted. "I am a very broad-minded man. I can do business with every people group in this region without offending or being offended. When we are back in your land, among your people, I can negotiate a Jewish wife for you."

Toma laughed. "Do not trouble yourself. I am satisfied with my solitary life. Tonight, while you are cavorting with the town prostitutes, I will take pleasure in solitude. I plan to wash in the Great Sea, dry myself by a campfire of camel dung, and then sleep on the sand."

"You!" Kheti lightly jabbed Toma in the chest with his finger. "You, I do not understand! Today, you flaunt your Jewish code of purity as if it is the law you live by, and because of that, you seem to see yourself as better than all the men in this caravan. But in a few weeks, it will be your Jewish Passover, a day when you are supposed to be in Jerusalem keeping a holy feast. Then you will flaunt your right to turn your back on your God and your heritage. It is not good to live such a divided life."

For the next Roman mile, Toma's response to his trading partner was stony silence.

Kheti finally broke that silence. "Ahead! I see the walls of Ashkelon! We will set up camp for the night and then go to the market early in the morning."

"Since we both have plans for this evening, Debir, our head drover, will have to oversee the camp tonight," Toma stated.

"That will be satisfactory," Kheti agreed. Then he asked again, "Are you sure you don't want to come with me? The water is heated. The women will scrub your back."

"I will wash in the Great Sea, thank you," Toma responded.

"You know," Kheti suggested again, "what you need is a wife, a good Jewish wife. It has been too many years since you enjoyed the pleasures of marriage."

"Stop!" Toma insisted. "Stop all this talk of marriage and family. I am now a man of the road with nothing to tie me to a single place called home."

By the light of a nearly full moon, Toma picked his way from the caravan campsite to the Mediterranean shore. On his back, he carried a basket containing his clean clothes and a few carefully wrapped pieces of dried camel dung. To be certain of the route, he followed the city sewer line, a stone-lined trench filled with the refuse of the city, waiting for the next rain that would wash its odoriferous contents into the Great Sea. The smell nearly gagged him. As soon as he reached the sandy shore, he turned northward, away from the sewer, walking until he reached a place a good distance from the mouth of the sewer. He found a spot where a crooked finger of land jutted out into the sea forming a small cove of quiet water. There, on the beach, he built a fire, removed his dirty garments, and then he walked into the wavelets to wash.

"Have mercy on me, O God, according to your unfailing love; according to your great compassion blot out my transgressions,"[5] the Spirit of God began to intercede for Toma, urging him to join in

petitioning the throne where God, the Faithful Judge and Ruler of the Universe, heard the pleas of all men.

"*Wash away all my iniquity and cleanse me from my sins.*" Toma found the words of his ancestor, David running through his mind. "*For I know my transgressions, and my sin is always before me.*[6] Three weeks from today, in the city of Jerusalem, the Passover lambs will be slain, and I, a son of the covenant, have deliberately chosen to travel south of Jerusalem, into a foreign land." Toma felt the pull of the Spirit to return to a life that was governed by the Laws of Moses and submitted to God, the author of that law. He ducked completely under the softly rolling waves, completely submerging himself like Passover pilgrims going through their ceremonial cleansing in the pools near the Temple.

"You should be in Jerusalem!" The Holy Spirit was insistent. "You are a son of the covenant. God is calling you back into fellowship with him, back into fellowship with your countrymen."

Toma could not shake the urging he felt to return to his God and his people. It demanded a response—"*Against you, you only have I sinned and done what is evil in your sight.*"[7] As the waves gently washed over him, Toma began to speak the words out into the night and up toward the heavens, "*Surely you desire truth in the inner most parts; you teach me wisdom in the inmost place. Cleanse me with hyssop, and I will be clean; wash me and I will be whiter than snow. Let me hear joy and gladness; let the bones you have crushed rejoice.*"[8]

In that introspective space of time when Toma instinctively waited for a divine response, he felt the water gently lift him off his feet. At the same time, there was an immediate and unusual lightness in his soul as, for a few moments before he found solid footing again, he floated, as if resting in the arms of God. "This year, I will go to Jerusalem," Toma promised. He looked up into the night sky, trying to see beyond the stars. "I will go to my hometown of Bethlehem and then return to the city with Uncle Shaul."

Refreshed and feeling better than he had felt in years, Toma walked out of the water. He picked up his garments. With the corner of his cloak, he dried the salty water from his face. Tears or waves? He did not know which. All he knew was for the first time since the death of his family, a great weight had been lifted. By the warmth of the fire, he dried and then lay down to sleep.

First, the birds began to sing. Then the gray light of predawn called Toma to wakefulness. Quickly, he cleaned up his campsite, then made his way down the beach back toward the sewer and the Syrian city of Ashkelon. With adequate morning light, Toma did not need to walk so close to the sewer. From a distance, he could see it and pick a parallel path back to his caravan.

"Ahhhh!" An unusual quivering wail pierced the normal sounds of the seaside morning. "Ahhhh!" The wailing was insistent, dominating every natural sound. It brought Toma to a halt, causing him to look around and determine that the sound was coming from within the sewer.

"Go! Investigate," the Holy Spirit urged. "Do not pass by."

Pushing aside underbrush and shrubs, Toma hurried to the stone lined sewer, to the point where the sound seemed the loudest. He noticed the bathhouse where Kheti had spent the night. It was not far away.

Scrambling onto a fallen log, he peered down into the reeking trench. Gasping and gagging at the same time, he could not believe what his eyes saw—babies, dead newborn babes in various states of decay. Instinctively, he turned his head away. But his eyes had already seen, and his mind instantly recalled the small mutilated bodies in the dusty streets of Bethlehem. Without warning, his stomach churned and he dry heaved his own gastric juices.

"Ahhhh!" The cries were still coming, insistent and demanding.

"There is a baby, a newborn. It is alive in that sewer of death and dismemberment!" The Spirit's voice was filled with urgency, and it compelled Toma to act.

Once more, he turned back to carefully study the twisted decaying bodies to find the one little body that was moving, that was crying out. He saw it—a newborn, unwashed, with a long fresh umbilical cord wrapped around its body and still attached to a bloody placenta.

"Take this child, the son of a bathhouse prostitute. Adopt him. Let him be your son," the Spirit of God urged. "Look at this living babe just abandoned on this rotting heap of death and then remember your own son, Avrahm, fresh from his mother's womb."

Toma no longer noticed the stench. He was on his knees, bending over the side of the trough, reaching down into the garbage and decaying flesh. His eyes were fixed on that newborn, the baby boy who flailed his arms and trembled each time he wailed. "Live, little one," Toma whispered as he drew the child out of the muck and brought him close to his chest. "Live and be my son." Toma's heart had never felt so full as when he lifted the infant out of the sewer. He only paused a few moments, just long enough to wrap the unwashed babe along with the umbilical and placenta in his own garments. Then he ran back to the caravan camp, back to the place where he could safely cut the cord, bathe the child with warm water, and find a way to feed it.

"What is this?" Kheti stood over Toma, who cradled the newborn in one arm and held a leather bag of camel's milk in the other so the infant could suck on the corner where a few small holes had been pierced through the leather.

"I didn't know where to find a wet nurse, and we had no goats." Toma looked up at Kheti. His eyes were filled with concern for the survival of this child.

"The wandering tribes of the desert feed their little ones camel's milk," Kheti offered. "They grow up healthy and strong."

"That is what Debir told me, so I followed his advice, but it is not lawful," Toma stated with a resigned sigh.

"It is an extreme situation," Kheti asserted. "The child must eat or die." The wise merchant then sat down beside the fire and watched as Toma finished feeding the baby and then laid him down to sleep. "Is this a business investment?" Kheti carefully asked. "Are you going to raise this child, and then will you sell him in the slave market?"

"No!" Toma was horrified. "I have taken him to be my own son." Turning away from Kheti, Toma looked down at the sleeping infant. How a man and a baby could bond so quickly he did not understand, but he loved this child with all the love he had had for his own son. With his index finger, he lightly touched the soft skin of the little hand and stared in amazement as the tiny fingers curled around his own callused finger. "*On the day you were born your cord was not cut, nor were you washed with water to make you clean, nor were you rubbed with salt or wrapped in cloths,*" Toma spoke softly to his new son. "*No one looked on you with pity or had compassion enough to do any of these things for you. Rather, you were thrown out*[9]—"

"I believe one of the women in the bathhouse delivered a baby last night," Kheti interrupted Toma. "In their business, children are a liability. Unless the owner of the house wants to raise the child and train it to work in the bathhouse, it must be abandoned."

"How barbaric! How utterly evil!" Toma declared.

"In every land, unwanted infants are left in the fields," Kheti reasoned.

"Or the sewers?" Toma retorted. "It does not happen in every land. My people do not abandon their newborns. They value every child. Every child is a gift from God."

At that moment, the infant began to stir and whimper.

Toma picked the baby up. The once-abandoned newborn opened his eyes and looked into the eyes of the man who was now his father. His little lips moved in sweet suckling movements as Toma spoke softly and directly, "*I heard your cries as I passed by and saw you kicking about in your blood, and as you lay there in your blood I said to you, 'Live! … grow like a plant of the field* and be my son.'"[10]

At that moment in the heavenlies, the Spirit of God spoke, "For more than ten years, I have seen you in your own mind believing you were abandoned by Father God. I saw you kicking about in your emotional and spiritual pain, but now I say to you, Toma, live! Learn to love and be loved again. *Weeping may remain for a night, but rejoicing comes in the morning.*"[11]

"When we get to Jerusalem or maybe your hometown of Bethlehem, I'm sure you will be able to find a woman to care for the child," Kheti suggested.

Absentmindedly, Toma nodded his agreement. He was so absorbed in watching his little one sleep that he hardly noticed the young man who stepped up to the tent he shared with Kheti.

"Debir said you wanted to see me?"

Kheti turned his attention from the new baby to the new drover he had just hired on. "I see my men found you some clothing. Have you eaten?"

"Yes," the young man replied. "It was the best food I have eaten in months."

"Better than the corncobs you were gnawing on in that swine shelter behind the bathhouse?" Kheti gave a little chuckle as he considered the great understatement he had just made.

Toma looked away from the sleeping infant into the face of the newcomer. Instinctively, he knew, but he asked, "You're Jewish?"

"Yes," the young man replied, "but I have been away from my homeland, traveling in foreign lands for several years. Now I am returning." The young man's voice quivered a little. His last sentence ended with an uncertain inflection.

"I have taken him on to help with the camels," Kheti asserted.

Toma raised a quizzical eyebrow. "Did we need additional help with the camels?"

Kheti gestured toward the young man as he spoke. "Nodab was without funds and needed to continue his journey back to…"

The Egyptian caravanner hesitated as he tried to remember the name of Nodab's hometown.

"Bethany, just east of Jerusalem," Nodab filled in the missing information.

"I know the area," Toma stated. "It is not far from my hometown of Bethlehem. I plan to return to Bethlehem straightaway in hopes of locating a wet nurse for this little one."

"Bethlehem is a town of small land owners and shepherds. Those families may not be willing to take in another child, even for a fee," Nodab offered. "On my family's estate, there are many tenant farmers. Always, there are some wives that are able and willing to nurse another child for a fee," he suggested.

"Could you take me there? Introduce me? Ask your father—" Toma did not get to finish his request.

"It would be better if you made your inquiries without me." Nodab hung his head as he continued, "I am returning in disgrace. The only request I am fit to make is to live and work as a servant on my family's estate."

"And if your father will not accept you back, even as a servant?" Kheti asked.

"Then I will work where I can." Nodab's eyes quickly swept the length of the caravan camp.

"You would not be the first Jewish man to make this caravan his home," Kheti responded.

"We will be in Jerusalem in less than two weeks," Toma stated, "From there, I will travel to Bethlehem and you can walk on to Bethany."

"Thank you for your kindness," Nodab replied. "Up to this point, it has been a hard journey, a journey that has taken nearly a year."

"You will sleep with the camels," Kheti said. "I am hiring you to guard them at night, to make sure none are stolen or wander away."

"I will do my job," Nodab answered.

As young John entered the Court of the Gentiles through the double-arched Hulda Gate, he could hear silver trumpets announcing the opening of the thirteen chests of coins that usually lined one of the colonnaded sides in the Court of the Women. He knew that within the treasury room of the Temple, they would be emptying several more chests of coins, Temple taxes and offerings from the Jewish communities in Babylon, Egypt, and other distant places. Totaled, it was a staggering sum. In his mind, there was not a number large enough for the wealth that accumulated and was then distributed in this holy place three times each year.

Three times each year, every priest in the land was to come to the Temple to serve and to receive a full week's wages. John walked briskly past the barrier that separated the Court of the Gentiles from the Court of the Women. Zechariah had not been paid at the Feast of Trumpets. Now it was Passover. The Temple owed Zechariah two week's worth of pay. John calculated and recalculated as he stepped into the line of priests and Levites queued up and waiting to approach the officer in charge of dispersal.

It was a long line. John looked around. The Temple police were present, along with many priests and Levites standing guard. He did not see one recognizable face. All the priests seemed so much younger than his father. As he waited and observed, he realized most of his father's generation had passed away or were, like his father, too enfeebled to come.

The sun had reached its zenith, and John was now only a few paces from the treasurer's table when he felt a hand on his shoulder. Turning, he looked up.

"You're Zechariah's son, aren't you?"

John smiled as he recognized Joram, a priest in his father's division from their hometown of Carem. He was one of the priestly guards for the day.

"Yes, I am the son of Zechariah, the priest from Carem," John responded.

"I will approach the officer of the treasury with you," Joram offered. Before he could explain further, a sudden scream of pain disrupted the normal noise of human conversations, then another scream.

All conversations ceased, and the count could be heard. "Nine!"

A wrenching human groan sent shivers along John's spine.

"Twelve!" No one in the crowd was speaking, so the three leather thongs of the whip were easily heard as they cut through the air and then struck the bare back of a man tied and laid flat on the stones of the Temple courtyard.

"No more! No—"

John could hear the man pleading, but he could not see. Joram's body blocked his view.

"Fifteen!" The count continued in multiples of three. Now above the soul-searing cries of the man under punishment, everyone could hear the Torah reading that always accompanied Temple beatings. "*If you do not carefully follow all the words of this law, which are written in this book…*"[12]

John reached up and touched Joram on his back, getting him to turn his head and look down at him.

John could see Joram's face was grim. He could feel the tension radiating from Joram and from every other man in the line. "What did he do?" John's voice was an alarmed whisper.

"He tried to steal from the treasury," Joram answered. "He took the name of a deceased priest and presented himself to claim those wages."

"Twenty-seven!"

John could hear how the lash struck the breath out of its victim. The man could no longer cry loudly.

The scriptural reprimand continued. "*The LORD will send fearful plagues on you and your descendants, harsh and prolonged disasters, and severe and lingering illnesses.*"[13]

"How many more?" John trembled as he asked.

Joram held up four fingers. "Each blow is three lashes," he mouthed.

John nodded his head, relieved that this torture would be ending soon.

"Thirty-nine!"

A collective sigh of relief went up from the waiting priests and others throughout the Court of the Women.

"Bless the Lord!" The scripture of reconciliation was being read over the man who had just received thirty-nine stripes. *"Their hearts were not loyal to him, they were not faithful to his covenant. Yet he was merciful; he forgave their iniquities and did not destroy them."*[14]

For a moment, Joram stepped away to have a word with another priest, then John could see the Temple guard lifting the beaten man up from the floor. Horrified, John watched as several of the guards carried the man along the line of waiting priests. On his back, there was not one piece of unshredded flesh. After they had passed, a trail of blood remained on the dusty stones, and the entire line of priests stepped away from it, pressing themselves almost flat against the outer wall to make sure they did not become defiled.

"Next?" The dispersing officer for the Temple treasury did not look up. He continued to carefully record the amount he had dispersed to the last priest.

John, a little surprised that the man did not even bother to make eye contact with him, began speaking, "I am John, son of Zechariah, priest of Carem of the Division of Abijah. I have come to collect the wages that were due to be paid to my father at the Feast of Tabernacles and now at this Passover season." Completing his request, John took a deep and determined breath. Then he waited.

"Division of Abijah," the officer spoke to one of several scribes who sat at tables where scrolls containing the Temple records were spread.

"Zechariah of Carem last served before the death of King Herod," the scribe announced, "and he was fifty years old at that time."

The treasury official immediately looked up from the scroll that was spread before him, fixing John with a hard stare. "Two times in one day, someone comes before me and attempts to steal from the treasury of the Most High God?"

Joram quickly stepped forward. "This is the son of Zechariah, the priest of Carem."

"This boy is entirely too young to be the son of that priest!" the official exclaimed. "Does everyone think I am a fool?"

"A fool?" A mocking but extremely confident voice echoed the treasurer's words.

All discussions in the vicinity of the treasurer's table ceased. Every eye turned and fixed on the approach of an elderly Pharisee and the young men who followed him. The Temple treasurer stood and gave a small but polite bow. John glanced at the treasurer, who seemed to have forgotten him, and then at Joram, hoping for an explanation.

"The great teacher, Hillel," Joram whispered to John.

"President of the Sanhedrin," John heard another man say.

The renowned teacher projected his accusation, "From where I was teaching, I saw a man receive thirty-nine stripes without a trial." Hillel turned to his retinue of disciples. "Did anyone call me to sit on this man's trial?"

"No," they responded.

"So I did not teach through the trial?"

"No," they again responded.

"Neither did I sleep the sleep of an old man through the trial or attend to my bodily functions in the passages beneath this stone floor?" the famous teacher and jurist rhetorically asked.

His disciples snickered and then responded again, "No, Rabbi."

"Then am I correct in assuming a man was beaten in this Temple without a trial?" With his hand, he gestured toward the trail of dried blood on the courtyard stones, and his voice rose as he stepped into confrontational proximity to the officer of the treasury.

"The Law of Moses as it is written does not demand a trial for every offense," the officer responded.

"But the written rules of conduct for this Temple complex do require that a man be officially sentenced by a sitting legal body before he is to receive forty stripes less one!" Hillel protested.

"Annas, our new high priest, has instructed that anyone attempting to receive funds from the treasury by fraud is to receive a full thirty-nine stripes," the treasurer answered.

"So our new high priest thinks himself both priest and council of judges for the land! He has yet to sit and receive the counsel of the Pharisees. For a full week before the Day of Atonement, we will instruct him. I will make sure that instruction includes Temple protocol and justice. As for you"—Hillel pointed directly at the treasurer's chest—"be reminded it is legal for the people to rise up and stone any priest or official who abuses their position, and that punishment does not require a trial!" As he spoke, he casually gestured toward a pile of ruble beside a repair site.

Hillel's disciples chortled among themselves as they watched their teacher put one of the officials of the Sadducee Party in a position of public disgrace.

The treasury official took a deep breath and said, "If a trial is what you must have before a man or boy is punished"—he glanced back at John—"then have a trial for this boy! He claims to be the son of a priest who most likely died of old age before he was born!"

"No! No!" Joram protested. "A trial is not necessary. I am a witness for this boy. He is the son of Zechariah, the priest of Carem."

"Two witnesses are needed," Hillel responded.

"Let the Temple records be a second witness," Joram countered. "In the annals of the Temple, it was recorded about thirteen years ago that on the last day that Zechariah served in this Temple, he stood before the veil at the altar of incense, and there he received a messenger from heaven."

Hillel pointed to one of the scribes assisting with the treasury records. "Go to the Temple archives and find what is recorded about Zechariah the priest."

While they waited, John felt everyone's eyes on him. It seemed each person in that massive courtyard had stopped and fixed their gaze on him. John felt the pressure of their attention and then something stirred deep inside.

"The men of this Temple have wearied me with their words," the Spirit of God bitterly announced. "*They say, 'All who do evil are good in the eyes of the LORD and he is pleased with them.'*[15] But I tell you, God is not pleased."

John looked Hillel straight in the eye. "The words of God burn in my heart. I am to say to you and to all who will listen, "*Suddenly the LORD you are seeking will come to his Temple; the messenger of the covenant, whom you desire, will come!*[16] Be sharp-eyed! He comes, maybe at this Passover season." Turning his head slightly so his gaze included the treasury official, John continued, "*He will purify the Levites and refine them like gold and silver.*"[17]

"Those are powerful words for such a young man," Hillel counseled. "Are those the words of the heavenly messenger that spoke to your father?"

"No," John replied. "The messenger said, '*Do not be afraid, Zechariah, your prayer has been heard. Your wife Elizabeth will bear you a son, and you are to give him the name John. He will be a joy and delight to you and many will rejoice because of his birth for he will be great in the sight of the Lord. He is never to take wine or other fermented drink.*'[18]" At that point, John paused and pulled his turban from his head. His long black hair, which he had carefully coiled so it would be held and hidden by his head covering, tumbled to its full length.

"A Nazirite!" Astonished gasps flew from every lip. "That young boy is a Nazirite!"

"He is the only child of Zechariah and Elizabeth," Joram insisted. "He was conceived in their old age soon after the heavenly visitation. Since his birth, he has been a child filled with the Spirit of God, filled with the desire to see righteousness in all situations."

"Here is the scroll!" One of the scribes came hurrying forward. "Here is the account as Zechariah wrote it! He wrote it in his own hand because after the visitation, he could no longer speak." The small scroll was opened and spread out on the treasurer's table. One of the scribes began to read, "As I was about to pour the incense over the burning coals, there suddenly appeared at the right side of the golden altar, a man—dazzling white and much taller than the seven-branched lampstand. He said, '*I am Gabriel. I stand in the presence of God, and I have been sent to speak to you and to tell you this good news.*[19] *Many of the people of Israel will your son bring back to the Lord their God. And he will go on before the Lord, in the spirit and power of Elijah… to make ready a people prepared for the Lord.*[20]"

"That is quite a prophecy, quite a heritage to grow into!" Hillel commented.

John responded by squaring his shoulders and saying, "I understand it is my duty to speak truth and to demand righteous actions." He turned to the treasurer and, in a commanding voice, said, "The faces of the poor, the widowed, and the infirmed are always before the Most Holy God. Through his prophet Malachi, he says, '*I will come to put you on trial. I will be quick to testify against… those who defraud laborers of their wages.*[21]"

Hillel placed a hand on John's shoulder.

John paused and waited respectfully for the rabbi to speak.

"The Sadducees are not persuaded by the prophets. They insist that only the five books of Moses contain the laws we are to live by." Turning back to the treasury official, Hillel said, "It is written in the commands given from Sinai, '*You shall not steal.*'²²"

All eyes then focused on the treasury official.

"Why doesn't your father come in person?" the official begrudgingly asked John.

"My father, Zechariah, is old and almost totally blind," John politely answered. "He does not have the strength to climb the stairs or to stand in this line. I am his representative, and I have come to collect his wages."

Behind him, someone whispered, "The boy is fearless!"

"He speaks with amazing authority," another offered.

"And look!" the priest just behind John announced. "The boy is receiving full payment for his father!"

John accepted a handful of coins and then turned to leave.

Hillel stopped him. "You have not taken your place as a man in the synagogue, yet you speak with such authority. Do you study with a teacher?"

"Before my father's eyes dimmed, we read the scriptures together," John answered. "Now I study with Geber, a visiting teacher from the Essene community at Qumran."

"An Essene! He studies with the fanatics of the desert!" John could hear Hillel's disciples mocking his straightforward answer. He felt his face turn red as anger smoldered, threatening to escape. Impudent words of rebuke were on his tongue, almost spoken.

The great teacher must have sensed the anger rising in the youth who stood before him because he held up one hand and his students became silent.

"I know Geber, the Essene teacher. Years ago, he sat at my feet and received instruction. Would you like to study with me?" Hillel asked. "You could be one of my disciples." With his arm, he gave an inclusive gesture that seemed to unite John with the men who stood behind their rabbi glaring enviously at the boy who had captured their teacher's admiration.

"You are free," the Spirit of God advised as he placed within John's mind a picture of Hillel's disciples chained to the columns of the Temple and weighed down by the awesomely heavy shadow of their teacher. "Speak from your heart."

"The trees are flowering," John candidly answered. "The bees are going from blossom to blossom, and I must gather their honey. That is how my father and I provide for ourselves. You would not be satisfied with the little time I could spare to sit and listen to you teach."

"But you must have a teacher," Hillel protested. "I see your potential. One day you could become a great rabbi."

With simple sincerity, John responded, "In the morning, at first light, I read a short scripture. Then I go out to find the wild bee's nest. While I am searching, the Spirit of God talks to me about the scripture I have read. It is like having a teacher by my side all day. I am satisfied."

Nonplused, Hillel had no response. He seemed at a loss for words.

"Remove the boy from this situation," the Holy Spirit spoke insistently to Joram. "Remove him before Hillel takes offense, before he allows his disciples to mock my messenger."

Immediately, Joram responded, stepping forward and propelling John away from the famous teacher and those who worshipped his shadow.

Chapter 7

THE PRODIGAL RETURNS

I will set out and go back to my father and say to him: Father,
I have sinned against heaven and against you. I am no longer
worthy to be called your son; make me like one of your hired
men.' So he got up and went to his father. But while he was
still a long way off, his father saw him and was filled with
compassion for him; he ran to his son, threw his arms
around him and kissed him.

—Luke 15:18–20

Toma tossed a soiled piece of Egyptian linen into the campfire. He washed his new son and then got out a flint knife. With Nodab, the only other Jew in the caravan, holding his adopted son, Toma quickly sliced off the baby's foreskin. "I will call you Seth, son of Toma, because God has given me another son in place of the one that the soldiers of Herod killed.

Standing nearby, Kheti unwittingly made a shield for his own genitals by protectively crossing his hands in front of them. "This is a barbaric practice that only Jews do to their sons!" he commented.

Debir, another reluctant witness, cringed and nodded in agreement.

"It is a blood covenant we make with our God," Nodab informed.

"It is the sign we carry on our bodies to remind us that we are a people set apart to keep the laws of God," Toma added. Then he casually stated, "I will not be going with you to Petra this time. I am going to Bethlehem, and then I will spend Passover week in Jerusalem."

"Yes," Kheti agreed. "If you are going to pass your heritage on to this boy, you will have to live it. Debir and I can take the wine to our Jerusalem buyers. You go straightaway to your family and find a good woman to nurse this little one."

"Nodab has told me his father breeds and sells caravan animals: camels, donkeys, oxen, even a few horses. While you begin the journey to Petra, I will go to Bethany and look at his livestock. We need to replace a few animals," Toma informed his partner. "I can follow with the new animals. Just wait for me in Petra."

"A good idea," Kheti agreed. Then he nodded toward Nodab as he suggested, "And, Toma, while you are negotiating the price of camels, you can see how the reunion between father and son has fared."

"You are too kind. My father will have to forgive my stupidity and my extravagance. I thought I could buy and sell and make a fortune, so I begged him for my inheritance. I said it would be an investment. He gave it to me. Instead of arranging for a wife, he gave me half the land, half the oxen, half the camels, half of his donkeys, and two horses. I sold everything but one horse, and as if I was an extremely wealthy merchant, I rode away on that horse. I was seventeen and so confident. I left in search of precious gemstones. I thought I knew—"

"You were tricked, weren't you?" Kheti cut in. "It takes many years to learn how to recognize a stone of real value."

"I bought worthless rocks," Nodab admitted. "I made friends with men who used me, even stole from me. I tried to recover my losses, but all I did was lose more until I did not even have enough money for a meal. Before I started on this venture, my father tried to tell me, but I would not listen. Just because I had made a few shrewd sales at the animal markets, I thought I knew everything there was to know about buying and selling." Nodab shook his head remorsefully.

"Are you the eldest son?" Kheti asked.

"No, I have a brother, Lazarus, who is two years older. He will inherit what is left of the estate. My part of the estate, I have totally squandered. I also have two younger sisters, Martha and Mary. But"—he sighed—"five years have passed. By now, they may be married or promised in marriage. I do not know how my family is, and they do not know how I have fared."

"Your father will remember when he held you in his arms," Toma assured as he rocked and comforted his own son.

"Nodab, come help me!" Toma called. "Move this calf away from its mother so I can get this animal to kneel."

Nodab hurried over. With both arms, he tugged the eagerly nursing baby camel away from its mother. Then with considerable effort, he held the young animal back while Toma tugged on the leather strap attached to the peg in the nose of the mature animal. Obediently, it knelt, and Toma threw a protective rug and then the Egyptian style saddle over its furry hump. After so many years on the caravan routes, he saddled and loaded animals more efficiently than most people laced their sandals and dressed for the day. "I'll need two bolts of linen," Toma called to Debir as he passed by.

"It's a good thing you own half of the goods we carry," Debir commented. "That baby's bottom has used most of your linen profits for this trip."

"Egyptian mothers use rags, and they wash them every day," Kheti said, stepping into the conversation. Baby Seth was in his arms. He held the infant out toward Toma. "Your son is in need of fresh linen."

Toma turned from packing the baskets he had hung on either side of the female camel. With the point of his knife, he sliced a small length of fabric from one of the bolts of linen that Debir had added to his pile of supplies.

"Top-quality imported Egyptian linen soiled once and then tossed in the fire!" Kheti could not restrain his comment. "Not even the emperor of Rome knows such luxury!"

A little miffed, Toma responded, "We are on the road. Do I have a choice?"

"No, but when you find a wet nurse, buy her some low-grade domestic linen, the kind she can wash and reuse," Kheti advised.

Toma nodded his agreement as he completed cleaning and reswaddling his new son. He then carefully placed the baby in a bed in one of the baskets that hung from the pegs of the camel's saddle.

"Are you ready to go?" Kheti asked as he handed Toma two small leather pouches. "I boiled these this morning and put new holes in their corners."

"Thank you." Toma accepted the feeding bags. "After Passover, I will meet you in Petra and add the new animals to our caravan."

Kheti leaned forward and grasped Toma by the shoulders, quickly kissing him on each cheek. "May your God smile on you and your son today," he pronounced a parting blessing. "And Nodab"—he turned to the young Jewish man—"as Toma and I have traveled together, he has taught me some of the wise sayings of your famous King Solomon. This nugget of wisdom is for you. *When pride comes, then comes disgrace, but with humility comes wisdom.*[1] I believe your father will see you have attained the wisdom that accompanies the difficulties young men can bring upon themselves. May there be peace between you and your father, but if things do not go well, find Toma before he leaves for Petra. We can always use another man who knows camels."

Without further discussion, Nodab quickly attached the baby camel to its mother with a long leather strap. Toma grabbed the adult animal's halter, and the two men set off ahead of the caravan on the road from Emmaus to Jerusalem.

It was a more time-consuming trip than the men had expected. Twice before they saw the walls of Jerusalem, they had to stop, milk the camel, and feed the baby. When they finally arrived at the Upper Pool, little Seth needed to be washed and fed again. Around the outer walls, Toma and Nodab headed for the southernmost point of the city. There, where the road split going south and west of the city, both men paused to look deeply into each other's eyes, to silently recognize that each was heading down a road that would lead to a drastically changed life. Encouragingly, they put their hands on each other's shoulders, kissing cheeks in the Eastern fashion reserved for special greetings and partings.

"Do you have food for the rest of the journey?" Toma asked as they ended their formal parting.

Nodab brushed off his need for food. "My father's estate is less than a half day's journey from here."

"It will be better if you do not face your family on an empty stomach," Toma advised as he moved to one of the baskets that hung from the side of the camel and pulled out a cake of dried figs, along with some roasted grain. "Take this and be nourished as you journey home."

Hovering over the parting, the Spirit of God blew. Flames flew from his mouth, forming two brilliant torches: the heavenly spirits of Hope and Comfort. "Go," the Spirit directed. "Go and confront the demonic spirit of Discouragement that walks with each man. With your light, drive out his darkness and shine on their futures."

Once again, the Holy Spirit blew, and a shimmering mist swirled, then separated into four distinct streams. "Humility and Acceptance," the Holy Spirit spoke to his beautiful spirits, "pour yourself out on Nodab so he can repent and accept responsibility for all his actions." Then the Spirit of God issued commands to the two remaining spirits, Courage and Compassion, "Surround and join yourselves to Toma so he can face his loss and reach out to others who have endured the loss of their loved ones."

With one backward glance and a casual wave of his hand, Toma stepped onto the road to Bethlehem while Nodab continued on the road that followed the outer walls of the city.

Above both men, the Spirit of God still hovered, announcing for the entire spirit realm to hear, "No longer will you be defeated men, wanderers without a home. I have already placed you in families, and I have given you new names. Nodab the Headstrong, who vows to have his own way, I have heard your desire to change and start again. Now in the courts of the kingdom of God, you will be called Repentant, Tenderhearted, and Concerned with the Welfare of Others. And, Toma, my wounded and pessimistic son, I have brought joy into your life, and I am pouring out healing balm for your soul. In my kingdom, you will be called the Man Who Rejoices Again and Again." Then the Spirit kissed each man on the top of his head, like a father sealing the blessing he has just spoken over each child.

Bethlehem never changes, Toma thought to himself. He stopped at the well in the center of town so the camel could drink, the calf could nurse, and the baby could be fed. It was late afternoon, almost evening. He could see a few women leaving their homes, approaching with water jars balanced on their shoulders. Here at the well, he would begin his inquiries, his search for a wet nurse.

Toma watched as the first woman arrived. She set her jar on the stone wall that surrounded the well. With one hand, she grasped the rope with a weighted waterskin attached. Carefully, she began to let the rope out, lowering the leather bag into the water. Toma noticed she worked efficiently in spite of the fact that she only used one hand. Her other hand remained under the folds of her robe.

"Shalom," Toma approached.

"Shalom," the woman responded as she looked up from her task.

Their eyes met, and suddenly, Toma remembered looking down from the roof of Jabek's barn and seeing a Roman soldier running from Jabek's home. Jabek's one-year-old son, bloody and limp, dangled from his hand. Jabek's wife followed, screaming, clawing, struggling to save her son. Without warning, Toma felt the bile rise in his throat. A wave of nausea swept through him, and he felt beads of sweat quickly form on his forehead. Unsteadily, he lowed himself to sit on the stone wall that surrounded the well. He closed his eyes, but he could not shut out the memories: the sword caught the sunlight just before the soldier brought it down, slicing through the forearm of Jabek's wife.

"Toma? You are Toma, aren't you? Do you need a drink of water?"

Toma heard his name, like a voice calling him to come back to the present and leave the past. He opened his eyes and looked squarely into a face from his past, a concerned, inquiring, and beautiful face. After a moment of a silence that was pregnant with unasked and unanswered questions, Toma finally managed to speak. "Are you Jabek's wife?"

"I am Elesheva, Jabek's widow," the woman responded in a soft and assuring tone.

"Jabek died?" Toma repeated almost stupidly. Then he managed to add, "I am sorry for your loss."

"He became ill," Elesheva offered the information Toma did not know how to eact, then she changed the subject. "Is this your child?" She reached out with one hand and lightly brushed the baby's cheek.

"Yes," Toma responded, relieved to shake off the deaths of the past and focus on the new life in his arms. "I found him in a sewer, and I am in need of a wet nurse."

"A wet nurse? Let me think. Who has had a child?" Elesheva paused and then turned to another woman who was approaching the well. "Didn't Salma, the wife of Obal, recently deliver a baby?"

"Oh yes," the woman replied as she glanced curiously at Toma.

"Do you remember Toma?" Elesheva responded to her friend's unspoken question. "He lived in Bethlehem before the babies were slaughtered."

"Yes." The woman dropped her eyes as she softly said, "I remember your wife Sarah and your mother, Leah. Everything that happened that day was too horrible for words."

"Toma saved my life," Elesheva said.

As she spoke, her eyes met Toma's eyes. He noticed that Elesheva's eyes were a curious light brown with flecks of green. Those fascinating eyes penetrated the physical barriers of his body and cried to Toma's soul, "I know your anguish. I know what it is like to bury a child. But it was the will of God that we both lived, so today, we meet again."

"You were putting a new roof on our barn."

Toma suddenly realized that Elesheva was speaking to him.

"When you saw what the soldier had done, you leaped from the ladder and ran to me. You bound up my arm and stopped the bleeding."

"I wish I could have saved the life of your son," Toma genuinely responded.

"In the whole town of Bethlehem, not one male child under the age of two survived," Elesheva offered. "Only the Holy One could have saved the children."

"He saved one," Toma shared. "He saved the son of Joseph and Mary."

"I remember," Elesheva exclaimed. "About six or seven years ago, they came through Bethlehem. They were returning from Egypt! Joseph told me he had had a dream, and from that dream, he knew they had to leave immediately. It was so amazing! Only their little son survived. I cannot remember his name."

"Jesus," Toma offered.

"And what did you name your son?" Elesheva turned her attention back to the infant in Toma's arms.

"His name is Seth."

"I'm sure your wife would like to meet Salma," Elesheva offered.

"I never remarried," Toma stated.

"It has been three years since the death of my husband, and I have not remarried either," Elesheva informed Toma. Then she quickly added, "I will leave my water jar here and take you to Salma. Her husband is one of the Temple shepherds. They live on the outskirts of town."

Gratefully, Toma accepted her offer. Placing the baby in the basket and picking up the camel's leather halter, he quickly followed Elesheva to the edge of town. As they approached the unassuming home, Toma haltingly asked, "Should I speak to the woman or to the man of the house first?"

"I will approach Salma," Elesheva offered. "Then if she is willing, you should speak to her husband."

Toma nodded. "I am willing to leave both this female camel and her calf as payment," he informed.

"That is very generous payment," Elesheva commented as she stepped away from the road and approached the courtyard gate. "Shalom!"

From the road, Toma watched Elesheva. For the first time since the death of his wife, Toma felt desire stir in his heart.

At that moment, the Spirit of God announced, "*For this reason a man will leave his father and mother and be united to his wife, and they will become one flesh.*[2] God has declared it is not good for a man to be alone. Therefore, it is his will for all men and women to live in family groups. For Toma of Bethlehem, he has chosen Elesheva, the widow of Jabek."

"Father?"

Bohan heard his eldest son call his name, but he did not turn his head or respond. He could not deal with running his estate at the moment. A lone traveler was coming down the road. He wanted to watch until the man got close enough so that he could see his face clearly.

"Father?"

Bohan felt his son's hand on his shoulder and knew it demanded a response. Reluctantly, he turned to see what concerned his eldest son.

"It is time to tithe the herds and the other animals on the estate." Lazarus held the leather scroll that contained the inventories of the family estate. He offered it to his father.

Distractedly, Bohan glanced back at the road before he responded, "You and the servants can tithe the animals. I'm not needed for that task." He waved the scroll away and turned his attention back to the road.

"Father? After the tithed animals have been separated, do you want the servants to take them directly to Jerusalem before the roads become totally clogged with Passover pilgrims?"

"Son, you do not need to ask me." Bohan stepped out into the road as he spoke. "Do what you think is best." He could not keep his mind on the increase of his livestock and the tithe for the Temple. His eyes were drawn to the traveler. The way that man walked reminded him so much of his youngest son, the son he had not seen in five years, the one he worried about day and night.

Bohan took a few indecisive steps down the road. He sensed Lazarus, his eldest son, had gone. He was confident his eldest son would spend the rest of the day in the fields with the servants preparing the tithe that was due at Passover.

Bohan took a few cautious steps down the road so he could better see the shape of the young man's face and the slight build of his body. As Bohan watched, he found himself walking faster. At first, he cautioned himself, Maintain your dignity. But he could see the features of the young man's face. It was an older face, a more experienced face. Nodab's face?

Bohan hurried forward, raising his hand in greeting while he studied the young man. He had black eyes and straight brows.

Those were his mother's eyes, and he had a scar on his right cheek. When Nodab was just a little boy, he had fallen on a jagged terrace wall. "Nodab! Nodab!" Bohan heard himself calling his son's name even before his mind had consciously analyzed all the evidence. Bohan broke into a stumbling run.

At the entrance to the camel pens, Lazarus turned, and from a distance, he saw his father running down the road. It was not the first time his father had made a fool of himself, running up to perfect strangers. Lazarus turned back to the task at hand.

"When will your father stop looking for your ungrateful brother and notice that you have faithfully served him?" Resentment asked. "When will he stop mourning for a boy who cares nothing for his family or his responsibilities? When will he bless you? When will he thank you? It's through your diligence that the animals your brother sold have now been replaced. Because of your shrewd negotiating, the land your brother sold is just now being repurchased. Soon the family estate will be completely restored."

Dutifully, Lazarus shut off the accusations that ran around in his mind like the young camels cavorting in the pen. Calling a servant to assist him, he counted the number of recently born camels, recorded it, and then moved on to the pastures where cows grazed while their calves nursed.

Nodab knew he was walking the road that ran through his father's estate, but he kept his eyes on the hard-packed dirt. He did not want to see the grassy pastures to his right or the free-roaming herd of oxen that now belonged to someone else. Every blade of grass, every animal reminded him of his own stupidity. To the left were the lands his father retained. Shame did not allow him to look that way either. He could not bear to lift his eyes and recognize a servant. If he could not bear to raise his eyes to a servant, how could he speak to his father? With his shoulders bent and his head bowed, he studied the ruts in the road. How would he approach his father? How would he convey his extreme repentance? He would drop to his knees, prostrate himself in the dust—

"Nodab? Nodab?"

It was his father's voice. Startled, Nodab looked up to see his father running toward him.

"Nodab! I thought you were dead, but no! Here you are alive!" Bohan threw his arms around his son. "And you are in my arms again."

That wonderful embrace reminded Nodab of childhood, of every time he had fallen and his father had picked him up. It reminded him of the day his mother had passed away and the day he had departed so cocky and sure of himself.

He began to cry, then he pushed himself away and dropped to his knees in the dust. With both hands, he scooped dirt from the road, quickly pouring it over himself as he brokenly sobbed. *"Father, I have sinned against heaven and against you. I am no longer worthy to be called your son; make me like one of your hired servants.*[3] A day's wage is more than I am worthy to receive. I will take less and work far into the night, only let me return—"

"No, no, you are my son!" Bohan spoke with unwavering assurance. "Now stand! You are the son of the master of this great estate." As he spoke, Bohan removed his own richly woven coat. He threw it over the trembling shoulders of his son, covering the dirt that declared his brokenness. Then he lifted Nodab to his feet, and with his arm protectively anchoring the boy close to his chest, he walked him to the main house.

As the two approached the door, Bohan called out to the house servants, *"Quick! Bring the best robe and put it on him. Put a ring on his finger and sandals on his feet.*"[4]

The massive double doors of brass and wood opened before Nodab's tear-filled eyes. Joyfully, Bohan pulled his son into the lavish courtyard where the boy had spent the happiest days of his childhood.

To Nodab, it was like a dream, a dream that he had had over and over when his life had been worth less than the life of a pig. He was back in the home where he had grown up. Nothing had changed. He looked around the courtyard. Water flowed from a pipe in the wall into a shallow tiled pool; plants provided shade and color. The stone benches, the patterns of imported tiles that covered the floor—it was all dazzlingly beautiful. He had never appreciated it like he should. Servants were scurrying. His dirty clothes were being removed; he was being washed. His father was giving orders. *"Bring the fattened calf and kill it. Let's have a feast and celebrate."*[5]

Nodab felt his father put his arms around him again and heard him say to the servants, "Every one of you, stop for a moment and look!"

Dressed in a clean white tunic and wearing new sandals, Nodab sat on the bench by the pool. All the household servants gathered around and in their presence. Bohan put one of the family signet rings on his son's finger. "I want you to have no doubt about the position of my son Nodab in this household. He has been away, but now he has returned. Today I am a happy man, for it was like *this son of mine was dead and is alive again; he was lost and is found.*[6] So run to the homes of my neighbors. Call them to come this evening and celebrate with me!"

In the barnyard, Lazarus looked up from recording the number of donkeys that had been born that spring and the numbers from that increase that were required for the tithe. The servant who managed the donkeys approached. "We have done well, master."

"Yes," Lazarus agreed, "every female dropped a foal, and one even had twins. You have managed this herd wisely. I will tell my father about your faithfulness and productivity."

"I don't think he will want to talk about donkeys tonight," the servant replied. "Your house is full of friends. It is lit up like the Feast of Dedication."

"What?" Lazarus looked puzzled. "What are you talking about?"

"You will have to hurry home and see," the servant replied. "The fattened calf has been killed—"

"The calf we were saving for the first night of Unleavened Bread?" Lazarus incredulously inquired.

"Yes, it is in the fire pit now," the servant responded.

Without further conversation, Lazarus turned and strode toward the house. As he walked through the pastures, past the herds that were being corralled for the night, he used a corner of his lightweight cloak to wipe the sweat from his brow and some of the dirt from his hands. "Shalom," Lazarus greeted one of his father's hired shepherds as he walked past the enclosure where the goats were entering and being counted under the shepherd's rod.

From the top of the next hill, he could see the main house of the estate. He had been correctly informed: lamps were burning in every window. And he heard music, even laughter, as if a wedding feast had suddenly occurred! Curious and concerned, he hurried down the hill. Why hadn't his father mentioned plans for a celebration? And why would anyone have a celebration so close to Passover? This was a time to prepare: to inventory and tithe the increase; to remove the leaven; and to clean the house, the stalls, the animal pens, and the food bins. Lazarus saw one of the house servants bringing several wineskins from the storage cave in the hillside behind the house. He stopped him. "What is happening? Why have all these people come to our home? And what is the reason for this celebration?"

"Your brother has come back."

"Nodab! That good-for-nothing selfish boy?" Lazarus exclaimed. "Is he wealthy? Has he returned to flaunt his fortune?"

"No, my master. He has returned in poverty, but your father loves him, so *your father has killed the fattened calf because he has him back safe and sound.*"[7]

"My brother has come back a pauper! What did he do with half of this estate turned into gold and silver coins?" Lazarus raged. "Did he eat and drink and gamble? Or did he just throw it into the Great Sea while I worked beside the servants and hired helpers every day just to rebuild this estate! I work, and my father does not even notice. I work, and my father watches the road!" Lazarus felt Anger ignite in his mind.

"Don't let that insufferable excuse of a brother get away with this!" Resentment and Jealousy kept adding fuel to the fire that burned in every cell of Lazarus's body. "You know he has returned to take what you have earned. Right now, he is manipulating your father."

With one angry motion, Lazarus snatched one of the wineskins from the surprised servant. "I'm going to the barn!" Lazarus abruptly turned on his heel, leaving the servant to watch his heated retreat.

In the barn with the cows that had not yet dropped their calves, Lazarus slumped dejectedly onto a pile of hay. He took a long swallow of wine as he tried to digest this unexpected turn of events.

"Nodab has always been the favorite son," Resentment emphatically stated what he had frequently whispered. "Your father prefers him over you. Most likely, your brother has returned to lure your father into giving him the inheritance that belongs to you, the elder son! All of your work, all of your sweat, all of your devotion—it counts for nothing!"

"Lazarus! Lazarus!"

Lazarus looked up to see his two young sisters running into the barn. They both had braided gold crowns holding their linen mantles securely on their heads. Martha, who had recently married, wore the gold coins of her dowry across her forehead, and Mary just glowed with excitement.

"Nodab has returned!" Mary exclaimed.

"And you should hear the stories he is telling!" Martha added. "He has been across the Great Sea!"

"Is he telling what became of the family fortune? He took it with him, you know." Lazarus sarcastically responded.

"No," Mary answered. "Father will not let him speak about it. He deflects every question about Nodab's business ventures by announcing to everyone that this celebration is about the return of his youngest son who has come home to help run the estate."

Lazarus took another long drink from the wineskin.

Bitterness, like a weed with a thousand roots, firmly embedded itself in his soul.

"Father must think I need Nodab to sell off half of the estate one more time so I can repurchase it again piece by piece!" Lazarus spit his words through clinched teeth.

The girls drew back. They had never seen their older brother so filled with anger and resentment.

"Father sent us to ask you to come in to greet your brother and to be a host to our guests," Martha timidly but dutifully relayed the message.

"Tell Father this is one banquet I will miss!" Lazarus stood up, wineskin in hand. "I'm going to spend the night with the shepherds!"

"Son?" Bohan stepped through the entrance to the barn. "There is no need for you to be angry. I don't want you to go sit at the shepherds' fire and talk about the mistakes your brother has made. Those mistakes are forgiven."

"His mistakes cannot just be forgotten!" Lazarus retorted. "I cannot forget how I labored to rebuild this estate. I have not even taken a wife because I have not had time to build her a proper house! Look at this barn. I built it, and it is full of cattle waiting to drop their calves. Look at the inventory of your estate." Lazarus picked up the scroll where he had been recording the number of animals in each herd. He held it out to his father. "*Look! All these years I've been slaving for you and never disobeyed your orders. Yet you never gave me even a young goat so I could celebrate with my friends. But when this son of yours who has squandered your property with prostitutes comes home, you kill the fattened calf for him!*[8] I am angry, and it is a righteous anger!"

"Yes! It is a righteous anger," Resentment and Jealousy chorused.

"Son." Bohan stepped forward and tried to put a hand on the shoulder of his eldest son.

Lazarus shook it off.

But Bohan continued to plead, "Don't you *know you are always with me, and everything I have is yours. But we had to celebrate and be glad, because this brother of yours was dead and is alive again; he was lost and is found.*"[9]

Resentment countered, "Your father sees nothing but Nodab! He does not see you. He does not see your faithfulness and the profit you have brought him. He only has eyes for his worthless son!"

Lazarus felt like he was going to burst into flames, like a signal fire doused with oil. "Let me go!" He pushed past his father, muttering, "The shepherds appreciate the wages I give them. They respect me and the work I have done on this estate!"

Shaken by their brother's outburst, Mary and Martha ran to their father, who put an arm around each. Together, they stood in the doorway watching Lazarus as he strode off into the evening.

Satisfied that he had found a competent woman to feed and care for little Seth, Toma stretched out on the bed he had spread on Uncle Shaul's packed-dirt roof. He was looking forward to a full night's sleep, a night when he would not be awakened by the numerous needs of a newborn. For a brief moment, his mind went back to Sarah. He remembered how selflessly she had cared for their son day and night. God must have given women a greater capacity for nights without sleep than he gave to men, Toma mused. Stars filled the night sky. The smell of spring and new growth was heavy on the night air. Toma yawned and stretched, then he closed his eyes.

He didn't hear the light tread of footsteps on the stairs that led from the back of the house to the roof. The flicker of a handheld oil lamp did not disturb the deepness of his sleep. Toma did not even stir when someone uncovered his feet and lay down on the packed earth with her own garment spread over his feet.

Before the early grayness of dawn kissed the Bethlehem hills, before the first birds began to chirp, Toma stirred. His foot nudged something warm and alive! Startled, he sat up. Elesheva lay at his feet. She was not asleep. When he moved, she responded by propping her head up on her one good hand and looking him squarely in the eyes.

For the second time that day, her eyes locked with his. Those beautiful light brown eyes, he could see them in the flickering light of the oil lamp that burned nearby. With her lips, Elesheva did not say a word, but her eyes cried out, "We are kinsmen in our anguish and in our ancestry. I am begging you, be my redeemer."

Toma sat up. Moved, he had not felt such tenderness, such desire since his wedding night. With both hands, he reached for Elesheva, gently bringing her up to a sitting position. With both of his work-hardened hands, he cradled her only hand, possessing it, not releasing it. "You have come to me like Ruth to Boaz," Toma stated, "but I am a man of the caravan routes. I have no home to offer you."

"You have no need to offer me a home or property. All that belonged to my deceased husband passes to my kinsman redeemer," Elesheva responded.

"It is my desire to be your redeemer"—Toma gave her hand a little squeeze as he spoke—"but there must be others who have a better legal claim than I."

"My husband has one living brother, Caleb of Jerusalem. He is a potter and lives near the Street of the Potters. Immediately after the death of my husband, we spoke. At that time, he was in poor health and unable to take on the responsibilities of a wife and property." Elesheva hesitated, then she dropped her eyes before adding, "He told me directly he did not need a wife with only one hand. He needed someone to help in the pottery shop. A one-handed woman would not do."

"I do not need your assistance in my trade," Toma assured. "I only need your companionship and for you to love and care for the son I have adopted."

Elesheva looked up again. Once more, her light brown eyes met his. "I can do as you request." Her voice was firm and confident. She then added. "The next in line to be my kinsman redeemer is Caleb's cousin, your Uncle Shaul."

"I do not think Uncle Shaul wants—"Toma hesitated. He did not know. Uncle Shaul was a widower. Elesheva was a beautiful woman, the most beautiful woman he had ever seen. Just the thought of someone else having the right to make her his wife made Toma's heart ache with anticipated loss. "I will speak to Uncle Shaul today." Toma hoped his voice offered Elesheva assurance and that it did not reveal his own fear that another relative might step forward and snatch her from him.

Elesheva responded with a slight nod of her head. Her eyes communicated such a depth of understanding that words were not necessary.

The stars were fading. The fiery rim of the morning sun was pushing up behind the Bethlehem hills, coloring the edges of dawn. "You must leave." Toma stood and reached to grasp both of her arms and help her to her feet.

Elesheva gasped, "Oh, no!" and started to pull away.

"There is no shame in having only one hand," Toma spoke softly but with unwavering certainty. "I understand your loss." With one hand, he held her hand, and with the other, he cradled her stub.

One by one, unexpected tears began to fall from Elesheva's eyes.

"We both know the heartbreak of losing a son," Toma said, choking on his words as unexpected sorrow wrenched at his heart.

"You lost so much,"Elesheva whispered her tender and heartfelt response. "Your wife, your mother, and your beautiful Avhram."

The fiery rim of the sun touched the hills that surrounded Bethlehem. It streaked the sky with gold and purple. It shimmered in the tear-filled eyes of Toma and Elesheva, those eyes that looked deeply into each other's souls and shared the anguish of each other's loss.

"I will make the necessary inquiries," Toma assured as he composed himself and took control of the moment. "Return to your home. Do not let anyone see you. I will send a message to you when I have an answer. Shalom."

"Shalom." Elesheva turned. Pulling her mantle so it covered most of her face, she stepped gracefully down the stairs and then took the paths that ran behind the homes of Bethlehem back to her own home.

Toma rolled up his sleeping mat, and then he hurried down the stairs, looking about to see if Uncle Shaul had begun his day. He found his uncle milking the goats. "Uncle? May I milk those goats for you?" Toma inquired.

Uncle Shaul looked up from his task, a quizzical expression on his face. "You have never offered to milk my goats before."

"I know, but while I am here, I must contribute to your household," Toma insisted.

A little stiffly, Uncle Shaul rose from the milking stool and, with a simple gesture, indicated that Toma could take his place.

Toma slid into Uncle Shaul's place and began pulling on the teats of the nearest female goat.

"I think something important is on your mind?" Uncle Shaul spoke with an inquiring inflection.

"Elesheva, the widow of Jabek, is on my mind." Toma stopped milking and looked at Uncle Shaul. "I want to be her kinsman redeemer."

"There are closer relatives that have the legal right."

"I know," Toma responded. "You are one of those relatives." Holding his breath, studying his uncle's body language, Toma waited for a response.

"I do not need more land to plant and harvest," Uncle Shaul began. "I am not as strong as I used to be. I expect to hire help for the barley harvest. And I have no desire for a wife, especially one that might be limited in her capacity to do the necessary chores." He looked curiously at his nephew before asking, "Do you really want her?"

"With all my heart," Toma answered.

"Then at Passover, we will find Caleb, the potter, in Jerusalem. Be prepared to give him your shoe."

Chapter 8

PASSOVER IN JERUSALEM

You must not sacrifice the Passover in any town the LORD
your God gives you except in the place he will choose as a
dwelling for his Name. There you must sacrifice the Passover
in the evening, when the sun goes down, on the anniversary
of your departure from Egypt… For six days eat unleavened
bread and on the seventh day hold an assembly to the LORD
your God and do no work.

—Deuteronomy 16:5–8

The jovial crowd of pilgrims from Nazareth chatted and danced sang and shouted their way from the green hills of northern Israel to the dusty mountain where Abraham had offered his son, Isaac. It was the fourth day of walking, and their destination was nearly in sight.

"Jose! Jose! Stop running through the crowd," Mary called to her youngest son, who seemed not to hear a word she said. "Joseph?" Mary's voice caught the attention of her husband and drew him away from casual male conversation with his strolling companions. "Jose is running in and out of the people walking along this road. He is like a little wild man! Look! He made Salome's little Benjamin fall and bloody his knee, and just now, that old man had to grab his wife to keep from falling. Put our son on your shoulders please."

Joseph responded by first watching four-year-old Jose as he speedily wove back and forth through the groups of Passover pilgrims, then the carpenter executed an intersecting move. With one muscular arm, he swooped the running child up into the air, bringing his impish little face into direct alignment with his own no-nonsense face. "It's time to slow down," Joseph sternly announced. "People are tripping over you and falling to their knees!" Without further elaboration, Joseph swung the child up onto his broad shoulders.

Heaving a little sigh of relief, Mary quickened her pace and fell into step beside her husband.

As they walked together, Joseph glanced down at his wife and her obviously pregnant belly. "Are you sure it was wise for you to come to Passover this year?"

"I haven't missed a Passover since we returned from Egypt," Mary answered. "Besides, it's not time for this child to be born, and even if labor begins, I have learned children can be born anywhere!"

"Anywhere?" Joseph repeated his wife's last word.

"There are a lot of stables between here and Jerusalem," Mary commented as if she knew what was on her husband's mind.

"I think one birth in a stable is sufficient for a lifetime," Joseph replied as he remembered that frantic night twelve years earlier when Jesus had been born in an animal shed attached to the home of Shammah and Zepporah.

"I have had three sons and a daughter," Mary responded. "Each birth has had its difficulties and its precious moments, but the birth of Jesus holds more treasured memories than all the others put together, especially the memory of you staying right by my side through the entire process, even assisting!"

Joseph quickly glanced from side to side, trying to see if any of his male friends who were walking nearby had overheard Mary's last remark. With lowered voice, he replied, "There are now plenty of good Jewish women in your life, and they can deal with whatever is necessary when your time comes."

"In Egypt, when James was born—" Mary began.

But Joseph cut in, "I don't know what got into me! I argued with a trained midwife and insisted that I should remain. Never again! What would the men of Nazareth think?"

"And what would the women say!" Mary chuckled as she imagined the gossip and the envy that would possess the women of her little town.

"Your sister, Salome, is coming back to Nazareth to stay with you until after the baby is born," Joseph said.

"How did you know?" Mary asked, knowing she had yet to mention it.

"Her husband, Zebedee, has been complaining. He will have to endure the cooking of his sisters until your season of confinement has ended."

"Zebedee is always complaining about something!" Mary commented. "His life is a constant rumble of thunder. It will be good for Salome to spend time in a peaceful home. I'm sure she needs the rest as much as I need her to assist me."

"James! John!"

Mary and Joseph looked up as they heard their brother-in-law's harsh voice rolling through the lighthearted pilgrims on the road to Jerusalem like a peal of thunder.

"Boys! I told you to watch your brother, Benjamin. Now look at him!"

Mary and Joseph watched as James and John, the two oldest sons of Zebedee and Salome, stopped walking and turned to face their father. Jesus and James had been walking with their cousins, and they stopped also.

"Why does Zebedee have to make such a scene over one little skinned knee?" Mary whispered to Joseph. "John is only six, and he looks so scared. He is practically shaking."

At that moment, Salome came running up. Mary could see the embarrassed blush on her sister's face and hear her placating tone. "Zebedee, it is just a little scrape. Here"—she reached out her arms for Benjamin—"I'll carry him."

"No." Jesus stepped forward, his sturdy twelve-year-old arms reaching his little cousin first. "Let me carry Benjamin on my shoulders. We'll take turns either holding his hand or carrying him on our shoulders." He glanced at his brother and his cousins who stood on either side of him to make sure there were no objections. "Uncle Zebedee, you won't have to even think about Benjamin until we arrive at Jerusalem. Then I will bring him to you," Jesus assured.

"Zebedee!" Jethro from Nazareth called his name.

Mary and Joseph observed Zebedee nod his acceptance of the offer Jesus had made and then turn away from the boys to greet Jethro. Jethro's son, Simon, ran ahead to join Jesus and the other boys.

"What act of sedition is Jethro promoting today?" Mary asked her husband in a hushed tone.

"Mary, what makes you always think Jethro is involved in some anti-Roman plot?" Joseph countered in an equally subdued voice.

"Because he is," Mary firmly replied. "Every time there is an incident in the region of Nazareth or Sepphoris, I hear the name Jethro the Zealot connected with that incident."

"Where do you hear such things?" Joseph questioned.

"At the well," Mary responded. "The men talk. Their wives hear and then repeat the tales when they bring their water jugs to the well. After each incident, Jethro's wife won't even come to the well for at least a week. She sends her daughter. She doesn't want to be asked any questions. Look at them!" Mary pointed to Jethro her husband's friend and Zebedee, her brother-in-law. "See how they are huddled together as they walk. It is obvious to me that secret plans are being made, and I don't want you involved!"

"You're right," Joseph admitted. "It amazes me how you figure out these things."

"Oh, Joseph," Mary blurted out. "It is my biggest fear that one day I will have to watch you die on a cross because of your relationship with Jethro!"

"Don't worry, I am not joining Jethro and his Zealot friends. The word has gone out. During this Passover season, Zealots from all over the land are gathering in clandestine meetings. They are planning an uprising that is to take place during the Feast of Weeks."

"No matter how many men gather to make a stand against Rome, it will not be enough!" Mary raised her arms in a gesture of exasperation.

"The Galilean is behind this," Joseph elaborated on what he knew. "Jethro believes this man is the promised messiah. He is certain when the actual battle comes, heavenly warriors will fight with the men of Israel."

"Where were those heavenly warriors when Herod killed all the infant sons of Bethlehem?" Mary retorted. "We received a warning and instructions to flee, but no heavenly beings drew swords to slay our enemies."

"I know," Joseph agreed. "In addition, most of those who maintain the Temple are working in concert with the Romans. They will not support any type of uprising. When Caesar agreed to dethrone Archelaus, the son of Herod, and only leave a governor to represent him, then the Temple authorities made a pact with Rome. They agreed to quell every hint of resistance to the authority of Rome, to keep that infamous worldwide peace Rome boasts about. Make no mistake. They will cause Jewish blood to be shed before they jeopardize the power Rome has given them."

"The evil involved in that alliance makes me shiver," Mary stated as a little chill ran up her spine. "I'm just glad we live in Nazareth, far removed from the politics of Jerusalem and Rome.

For the most part, no one cares about Nazareth. They ignore us, and I want to keep it that way!"

"I have to agree," Joseph said. "I really want nothing more than to work my trade and see to it that my family lives by the laws of the Torah. That's why I refuse to become actively involved with Jethro and the Zealots." Joseph looked down at his wife, locking her eyes with his own. "You know, Mary, I do not come to Jerusalem three times each year because I desire any involvement with the various factions that vie for power in this land. I come because I am drawn to the Temple and the God we worship."

"You have always been a faithful man of the Torah," Mary agreed, "and that fact reassures my heart."

"The city!" someone shouted.

The men who were leading the band of pilgrims from the area of Galilee began to sing a psalm.

> *Great is the LORD and most worthy of praise,*
> *in the city of our God, his holy mountain.*

The women sang the next line.

> *It is beautiful in its loftiness, the joy of the whole earth.*

The melody soared and resonated off the surrounding hills.

> *Like the utmost heights of Zaphon is Mount Zion, the city of*
> *the Great King.*[1]

At that moment, the sun appeared to focus its rays directly on the white limestone walls of the city, and they seemed to glow. "It is a beautiful sight," Mary commented.

"*The city of the Great King. God is in her citadels,*"[2] Joseph agreed. Then as if to reassure his wife, he repeated, "God is in her citadels. No matter what happens, Mary, no matter who is ruling, this is the city of God, the place where he dwells on Earth. It will always be that way. God has willed it."

Jesus and his companions sang with the men and tried to make their voices reach the deep valleys of manhood. Their voices strained and then cracked, but they continued singing.

> *The God of Abraham is our strong defense.*
> *Jerusalem is his city.*
> *When the kings joined forces,*
> *when they advanced together,*
> *they saw the city of God and were astounded;*
> *they fled in terror.*[3]

Standing on the wall of the city, the archangel Michael raised his glistening shofar and blew a staccato salute. Golden chariots with angelic drivers responded by swooping down on the wall, magnificently reining their fiery mounts to attention. Warrior angels stationed above the gate raised their swords in silent salute.

Satan, who lurked in the rocky shadows not far from the city, saw the angelic host come to attention. The power radiating from each heavenly being was almost overwhelming. He trembled and then cautiously gave the order for his demonic horde to fall back, retreating to the distant hills. Then from the barren hills that surrounded Zion, he continued to scan the throngs of worshipers, his evil eyes alert for that boy, Jesus, along with his family and his friends. The action of God's angelic warriors had signaled. The boy must be approaching.

"Can't you see it?" Jesus shouted excitedly to his brother and his cousins. "Can't you see the angels of the Lord moving along the walls of the city? They have shofars, and they carry burning swords. It is like what was written by the prophet, Isaiah—*I have posted watchmen on your walls, O Jerusalem; they will never be silent day or night.*"[4]

The boys walking on either side of Jesus glanced sideways at him.

"There he is!" Satan identified Jesus walking with his brother, his cousins, and his friend. Keeping one cautious eye on Michael with his angelic army and the other eye on the boy, Satan moved with his demonic entourage to the side of the crowded road, waiting, watchful for an opportunity. It came.

Feeling the pressure of his cousins' glances, James, the brother of Jesus, moved close and whispered, "Don't, Jesus! Don't talk about the strange things you see." He glanced back at Simon and his cousins. "It's embarrassing to hear you talk about seeing angels when no one else sees angels."

"It's all right," Simon pushed his opinion into the not-so-gentle admonition James was giving his elder brother. "I know Jesus is just seeing by faith. My father has said many times that the angelic watchmen on the walls are just waiting for us to engage the enemy that now occupies the city. Jesus, I can tell you sense God's urgent call for us to rise up and act. My father quotes the prophets every day. *You who call on the* LORD, *give yourselves no rest, and give him no rest till he establishes Jerusalem and makes her a praise in the earth.*[5] We cannot allow the Roman occupation to continue. We cannot rest until we have reestablished Jerusalem as God's city."

With a note of caution in his voice, Jesus admonished, "My father often says that *all who draw the sword will die by the sword.*"[6]

"I can see the gates!" John pointed as he shouted, and Jesus lifted little Benjamin up off his shoulders, holding him high above his head so he could see the masses of people streaming into the gates of the beautiful city of David.

Pass through, Pass through the gates!
Prepare the way for the people.[7]

The warrior host of heaven who stood on either side of each Jerusalem gate began to sing.

The Lord has made a proclamation to the ends of the earth:
"Say to the Daughter of Zion, 'See, your Savior comes!
See, his reward is with him,
and his recompense accompanies him.'"[8]

Then those angels that hovered over the city, along with those who held their fiery chariots in a pose of regal attention on the top of the walls, sang out.

The people who dwell in this city will one day be called the
Holy People, the Redeemed of the LORD;
and you, Jerusalem, will be called Sought After,
the City No Longer Deserted.[9]

"Beautiful!" Jesus exclaimed. "Wonderful, the plans that God has for this city! They are plans of peace and prosperity. He wants to bless and remove from the people the curse that sin has brought upon them."

"I don't know exactly what you are talking about," Simon responded to Jesus's excited exclamations, "but I can tell you that the curse of the Romans is about to be removed from Jerusalem." Digging deep into the folds of his linen girdle, the eldest son of Jethro the Zealot pulled out a small flat stone. On it was engraved the image of a shofar.

"What are you showing us?" James, the brother of Jesus, asked as the boys stepped off the road and stopped walking. They gathered around and peered curiously at the stone in Simon's hand.

"It is the pass," Simon answered. "With this engraved stone in my hand, I will be admitted to the secret meetings that are going to take place during this Feast of Unleavened Bread."

"What secret meetings?" John queried.

"From all over the land, the zealous sons of the covenant are gathering to plan the overthrow of Rome and the establishment of God's government," Simon answered. "The Galilean will lead us to victory."

"Are you sure?" Jesus asked in a quiet and serious tone. "I mean, is God directing this like he directed Gideon? God gave Gideon a specific battle strategy. Or is this just the idea of bands of men who call themselves Zealots and have chosen the Galilean to be their leader?"

"Of course God is directing," Simon exclaimed. "Jesus, you have studied the scriptures more than any of us! You above all people should know that God has called us to *blow the trumpet in Zion; sound the alarm on my holy hill.* It is the command of God," Simon began chanting the battle song of the Zealots.

"Listen to the words you are singing," Jesus urged. "*Let all who live in the land tremble, for the day of the* LORD *is coming. It is close at hand—a day of darkness and gloom, a day of clouds and blackness.*[10] Does that sound like human victory? No, you are singing about judgment and disaster. That is what happens when the trumpet of the prophet Joel sounds. Heed the words of the Psalmist: *I am still confident of this: I will see the goodness of the* LORD *in the land of the living. Wait for the* LORD*: be strong and take heart and wait for the* LORD.*"[11]

"Wait?" Simon retorted. "Waiting is for the weak and fearful!"

"No," Jesus quietly responded. "Waiting is for those who fear God more than man. The Roman army is not the enemy God wants to destroy. There is another enemy, an invisible enemy."

As Satan studied the body language and conversation of the boys, he kept one cautious eye on the angelic warriors gathered at the gate of the city. From experience, he knew that an attack on Yeshua-as-a-boy would be swiftly quelled, so he focused his attention on the boys who walked with Jesus.

"There is no other enemy," Satan said, pressing his deception into Simon's young mind. "Rebuke your friend before he convinces the others to ignore you and the just cause God has laid on your heart."

"Jesus, you're insane!" Simon suddenly shouted his accusation.

"Good, you have done the right thing." Satan encouraged. "Now turn your back on the son of Joseph. Jesus is a coward and a traitor. He does not deserve your friendship."

Spirits of Anger and False Pride suddenly flew from Satan's side and engulfed Simon. First, they enveloped him, then they found places to attach themselves so they moved as he moved.

Anger suddenly rushed through Simon's body; resentfully, he thrust his stone back into the folds of his belt. Then he looked at the faces of the other boys around him. "Those who want to be part of the liberation of Jerusalem and the land can walk with me." With a decisive step, he quickly moved back onto the road. The sons of Zebedee immediately followed him, easily falling into step while they eagerly pressed for more information. A few paces down the road, Simon abruptly stopped and turned to face Jesus, who still held Benjamin on his shoulders. James remained beside his brother. "If you are fearful, do not return for the Feast of Weeks." He shot the warning like an accusatory dart aimed for the heart of his friend.

The pain of rejection rolled through young Jesus. It hurt to be judged and found unworthy of friendship.

"Are you just going to stand by the side of the road until the sun sets?" James blurted out in an accusatory tone.

"I was just trying to figure out what I said, what I did?" Jesus groped for words.

"You were weird," James coldly responded. "You are always weird. First you see angels and then you reject the scriptural idea that the Messiah will lead our nation to victory over the Romans.

I've heard Mother and Father talk about you. They think you are some kind of gift from God. I've even heard Father use the word Messiah. Ha! You've really got them fooled. You're nothing but a well-read coward." As the last word left his lips, James began running to catch up with Simon and his cousins, leaving Jesus alone to carry Benjamin into the city as he had promised.

At the side of the road, fearful to further approach the well-guarded city, Satan nodded in satisfaction. He knew every time he spoke pain and rejection into the heart of Jesus through family and friends, he planted seeds that could grow into brambles of self-doubt and condemnation with roots of bitterness. The human heredity of Jesus, that half of his genetic code that came from Mary, was as susceptible to emotional and spiritual wounding as any other human. Satan gave one more satisfied nod as he assured himself it would be just a matter of time before one of these emotional wounds created a crack in the soul of this perfect son of man. And through that crack, he and his demonic spirits would build a stronghold in the life of Jesus.

With a wave of his hand, he beckoned the spirits of Self-Doubt and Rejection. "Follow him." Satan pointed to Jesus. "Taunt him! Give him no rest. Make him believe the words of his friend and his brother!"

"Insane! Weird! Coward!" Self-Doubt and Rejection began their mantra of accusations. Over and over, they repeated their lies.

Aching with the pain of rejection, Jesus stepped back onto the road. He easily matched his pace to the pace of those walking beside him. "Papa?" In his mind, he called his heavenly Father. "Why don't the others understand? Why am I left out?"

Before he heard an answer, his grandfather, Heli, called from behind, "Jesus, wait. I want to talk to you."

Jesus slowed. Then he stepped off the road just long enough to allow his grandfather to catch up. He began walking again, this time with Heli at his side.

"Jesus, while we are in Jerusalem, I want you to hear some of the great teachers who sit on the porches of the Temple and explain the Torah. I especially want you to hear the great Hillel. He is old now, and I do not know how much longer he will teach."

"You have spoken of him many times," Jesus responded.

"He is a good and gracious man," Heli affirmed. "And I want you to meet him. It could be," Heli mused aloud. "He might take you on as one of his students."

"I would have to speak to my Father first," Jesus replied.

"Joseph is a very cautious man who does not push himself or his children into the torchlight of important positions," Heli asserted. "I will ask him for you. I will ask him if you can accompany me to hear the great Hillel teach. I'm sure it will be all right. After all, what other plans does he have for you?"

"My Father God usually prefers that I read the scriptures and then wait for his commentary. He has never directed me to seek out teachers. I am to be ready to hear him anytime he speaks." Jesus looked seriously into his grandfather's face as he spoke.

"So you know?" Heli responded. A curious smile teased the corners of his lips as he asked, "What is it like when God speaks to you?"

"Sometimes, it is just a voice in my head," Jesus answered, "and other times, I see things in the spirit realm. He shows me what has happened, things recorded in the scriptures. It is just as if I had been there."

"It sounds exciting," Heli responded enthusiastically.

"Sometimes it is," Jesus answered as he recalled seeing the Holy Spirit like a flaming sword forcing Death and Murder out of the room. "But often, the Spirit of God just wakes me during the night when there are no other distractions. That's when he explains the scriptures I have recently read. It is just a quiet conversation."

"Well, let me know if God tells you to go hear the great Hillel. I will take you, and even introduce you," Heli offered.

"I will ask," Jesus answered with genuine willingness.

"So what are your other plans?" Heli asked.

"We do plan to see my cousin John and his father, Zechariah the priest. They are living in Jerusalem now," Jesus answered. "We will be eating the Passover meal in their home."

"Blessed are you, O Lord our God, King of the Universe, who has sanctified us by your Torah and commanded us to remove both the leaven in our homes and the sin that works like leaven in our lives," Zechariah chanted the traditional blessing while Joseph, with an oil lamp in one hand and a feather in the other, swept the corners of the cooking area and the food storage areas. Symbolically, Joseph was removing the last fine crumbs of leavened bread from the home where Zechariah lived with his son John.

In respectful silence, Jesus stood with his cousin John. Mary, along with James, Jose, and Ruth, followed Joseph as he moved around the home, peering with the lamp, sweeping with the feather.

Jesus, standing next to his cousin John, sensed the weighty presence of the Holy Spirit in the room. He knew the Spirit of God, like an additional member of the family, had entered the home. In his heart, he silently welcomed the presence of God on Earth and invited him to remain and be a part of the evening.

"Step away," the Holy Spirit whispered. "I want to speak to you about this Passover week."

Quietly, Jesus stepped away from John and bowed his head, focusing on the Spirit of his Father and the message that burned in his mind.

"At this Passover, my son, I will introduce you to an important battleground. It was built to be my dwelling place on Earth, but Satan has enlisted his powerful spirits of Religion and Arrogance, along with Corruption and Pride, to firmly establish their presence in that place. Every year, Passover pilgrims fill the city and the courts of the Temple. They come hoping to meet me. Instead, they are greeted by Pride and Corruption. Religion and Arrogance are so overwhelmingly present that one could easily miss those few humble rabbis who expound under my anointing on Solomon's Porch.

"I have placed the sword of the scriptures in your hand. During this Passover season, go and hear the men who teach in the Temple courts. My Spirit of discernment will be with you. You will speak the words that I will give you at the appointed times."

Nodding his head in silent agreement, Jesus considered the battle imagery of a sword in his hand. He knew that sword was the word of God as it was written in the Torah and the prophets. The battle imagery and the idea of possessing a sword brought back the pain of the rejection he had experienced earlier in the day. What about the Zealots? he silently questioned. Should I have anything to do with their plans for an uprising?

"Jerusalem is my city," the Spirit of God instantly responded to the question Jesus voiced only with his thoughts. "When I directed Abraham to build an altar on this mountain and offer his only son Isaac there, I proclaimed throughout the spirit realm, 'This is the property of the Eternal God!' At that moment, the mountain of the Lord became a battleground, a place where Satan has constantly challenged my ownership.

"The Zealots, the Romans, they are like animals unequally yoked. Each one struggles to pull away from the other, and my enemy holds their reins. The blade of the plow they pull is destined to gouge and tear up the soil of my city. At this moment, in secret meeting places, seeds of destruction are being sown by my enemy. Jerusalem, this plowed field sown with Satanic seed, will be watered many times with the tears of my people. Then when Satan's crop is ripe, a bloody and horrible harvest will ensue, and my Temple, that place where both the holy and the profane dwell, will be destroyed. Not one stone will be left atop another."

Jesus looked up. He could see everyone but John had moved to the food storage bins at the far end of the courtyard. For a few moments, he watched his father moving the empty food containers and sweeping behind them. The light from the lamp in Joseph's hand threw larger-than-life shadows on the white stone walls.

"The Spirit of God is here," John whispered to Jesus.

Jesus turned to see his cousin staring wide-eyed at him.

"I can feel his presence in this room. He is very close, but he is not talking to me, so he must be talking to you?"

"Yes," Jesus answered. Then he added, "Most people do not know when the Holy Spirit is revealing his presence. Very few have heard him speak."

"I have heard him speak," John assured.

"We will talk," Jesus promised as joy welled up inside. There was someone his age who understood! By the dancing reflections from the lamp in Joseph's hand, Jesus could see the face of his cousin John, and he could tell that John was equally excited and relieved. At last, someone else understood.

"John!"

Instantly, John bowed his head and stepped away from Jesus. Jesus watched and knew the Spirit now spoke to his cousin.

"See how Joseph searches for leaven? A time is coming when *I will search Jerusalem with lamps and punish those who are complacent, who are like wine left on its dregs, who think the LORD will do nothing either good or bad. Their wealth will be plundered, their houses demolished.*[12] *I will stretch out my hand... against all who live in Jerusalem. I will cut off from this place every remnant of... those who bow down and swear by the LORD and who also swear by*[13] my enemy, Satan."

It was then that Jesus heard the most beautiful music. He knew it was the angels singing.

Be silent before the Sovereign LORD,
for the day of the LORD is near.
The LORD has prepared a sacrifice;
he has consecrated those he has invited.[14]

Jesus glanced over at his cousin John and instinctively he knew his cousin was hearing the music also.

"Angels have accompanied the Spirit of God," Jesus whispered to John.

John grinned and whispered his excited response, "Sometimes I see them. They stand on the walls of the city."

A weight suddenly lifted from Jesus's heart, and out of the corner of his spiritual eye, he saw something quickly move, disappearing under the closed door.

"It was an Accusing spirit," John quietly informed his cousin. "I think it has been near you all day."

"Shouting a lie," Jesus responded with sudden insight as he recalled that moment earlier in the day when he his own brother had insultingly shouted, "You're weird!"

"That evil spirit spoke through my brother, my friend, and my cousins!" Jesus exclaimed.

"Then it followed you and kept repeating the lie," John asserted.

Lamplight suddenly illuminated each boy's face as the family returned to the center of the courtyard.

"We didn't find any crumbs!" Jose announced.

"That's because my father and I haven't cooked in here in a long time," John commented. "Our neighbors give us bread each time they bake, and we like to sit outside near the fig tree to eat."

"Yes." Zechariah chuckled. "Even a blind man could clean our cooking area."

Everyone laughed. Then Joseph spoke up, "Jesus, John, get your cloaks. We are spending the night on the Mount of Olives. I want to be at the animal market soon after dawn. If we don't spend the night there, the crowds will become massive, and we will not make it back to the Temple for the first or even the second group that is admitted into the Court of the Israelites."

"It is better to be in the first group," Zechariah knowingly commented. "The floor is still clean. By the time the third group enters to slay and skin their lambs…" He shook his head, remembering all the years he had served as a priest, the thousands of lambs that had been slain each year in three shifts and then the cleanup.

"Zechariah knows!" Joseph announced. "You boys hurry!" Joseph waved them into action with his hands, and then he turned to Mary. "We will be sleeping in the olive grove near the animal market. After we get the lamb, I will send John back to the house so he can build a fire in the oven behind the house and assist Zechariah."

"I will take care of the rest of the meal," Mary assured.

Laughing and eager, the boys came hurrying back, cloaks in their hands.

"Be safe," Mary added as Joseph, with Jesus and John, turned and walked out the courtyard gate.

On the Mount of Olives, near the entrance to a cave that housed an olive oil press, a campfire crackled and threw golden sparks into the night air. Barabbas tossed a few more olive branches into the fire and then positioned himself between the fire and the entrance to the cave. Dressed in robes supplied by the Galilean, he made his tough young body a barricade that separated the casual Passover campers from the small intense group of men inside the cave just beyond the fire.

From his position near the fire, the former slave scanned the crowded mountainside. So many people had come for Passover and so many were spending the night on this mountain that he wondered if there was room for every person to lay down. The wind shifted and smoke from the campfire blew into his face. He moved to the other side of the fire and stepped into the shadow of a boulder near the newly constructed animal pens. In the shadow of the rock, with his back to the fire and his arms folded menacingly across his muscular chest, he continued to study the crowd and anticipate the movements of each man who seemed to approach. He had assured both Daveed and the Galilean any man who approached the campfire would have to walk around him, and that would not be accomplished unless the man could show a stone with a shofar carved on its flat surface.

Barabbas took pride in the fact that he remembered almost every face he had ever seen. It was an important survival technique. On previous occasions, he had seen most of the men who now gathered at this meeting. He knew their faces, and he could name them. There was Jethro the blacksmith from Nazareth and Zebedee, a fisherman from Capernaum. From Sepphoris, there were the bakers who supplied bread to the Roman troops and kept the Galilean abreast of their movements. Several farmers, a tanner, a tent maker—most of the men at this gathering were from the region of Galilee, and most supplied the Galilean and his men with both information and the necessities of life. Jared, the owner of the olive press, walked by, and Barabbas stepped out of the shadows, nodding his permission to pass. Quickly, the ex-slave returned to the shadows and his ruminating thoughts. There was one man that Barabbas had expected—Toma the caravan trader. For a moment, Barabbas considered what might have kept him away, but then he turned his attention to the voices in the cave behind him.

Daveed, one of the Galilean's trusted followers, was leading the meeting. Barabbas could hear him explaining the strategy.

"At the Feast of Weeks, just fifty days from now, we will run every Roman out of this city. We will start by setting fires in these strategic locations." Barabbas heard a scratching sound and assumed Daveed had drawn some kind of map on the dirt. "The Temple is here. We will set fires along this wall."

"The Fortress of Antonia?" Zebedee asked.

"Yes," Daveed responded. "We will start several fires along the northern wall. As the soldiers hurry to put out the fire, we will pick them off with slings and arrows."

"They are not going to let us just pick them off," Jethro countered.

"I know," Daveed answered. "We plan to set more fires further out. We will not begin the attack until the soldiers have fanned out to fight the blaze, then we will set fires behind them so there will be no escape route."

As Barabbas listened, he agreed in his heart. The plan was good, and the cause was just. A man accompanied by two boys walked by. From the shadowed spot where he stood, Barabbas studied the man's face. It was Joseph, the carpenter of Nazareth. Barabbas recognized him, but he was unsure about the man's loyalty. As Joseph and the boys with him turned and seemed to walk directly toward the fire and the gathering of zealous men, Barabbas stepped out, ready to intercept them. But it was an unnecessary move. He watched as the trio turned and approached the lambs, which were penned and waiting for the morning sales.

The boys pointed out several lambs, and Barabbas could hear Joseph explaining, "The lamb must be a male, at least eight days old but not more than one year old. It must provide the exact amount of meat we can consume during the Passover meal."

"I won't be eating any meat, but I think we will need a pretty big lamb," John offered.

"We will have three adults, Jesus, then three more children." Joseph replied. "A three- or four-month-old lamb will be sufficient."

"How do we check to see if it is healthy and acceptable?" Jesus asked.

Before Joseph could answer, John spoke, "My father taught me to check for infestations of insects, to look for clear eyes, to observe the way the animal walks, and to look at its hooves and teeth. That is how the priests check the animals in the Temple."

"I have heard that sometimes, if the sale of Temple animals is slow, they reject perfectly healthy animals and force the people to buy from the Temple market." Joseph made his statement a question for John.

"That is true," John answered. "Both Joram and my father have told me about those situations, but it never happens at Passover. There are too many lambs to be slain between the evening sacrifice and sundown. There is not enough time for the priests to check the lambs closely."

Barabbas continued to watch. There was something compelling about the way Joseph interacted with the boys. It made him try to remember his own father, but his memories had faded, and all that was left was his anger and a hollowness that begged to be filled. After a short time, Barabbas saw them move on to a level spot beneath a gnarled olive tree. They spread their cloaks on the ground and curled up close together, huddled against the rough bark of the tree, away from the feet of milling people. As Barabbas watched, he saw Joseph put an arm around each boy, pulling both of them into the security and comfort of his own chest. In that position, they seemed to fall asleep quickly. For a long time, Barabbas could not pull his eyes away. A father with his arms around his sons—it tugged and pulled at his heart.

"Barabbas," the Spirit of God spoke into the hurting heart of the runaway who had given his allegiance to the current social messiah. "*I am a father to the fatherless… I set the lonely in families, I lead forth the prisoners with singing; but the rebellious live in a sun-scorched land.*[15] Do not hope the Galilean or any of his officers will be a father to you. God is your only hope."

The ex-slave focused on the unusual thoughts and feelings that were surfacing from some place within. It was a struggle to understand how these ideas and emotions fit into his life. Unexpectedly, Barabbas felt a hand on his shoulder. Tightening his fist, he quickly turned, ready to strike. "Daveed!" Barabbas slowly exhaled and forced his muscles to relax as he recognized his coconspirator.

"The men are with us," Daveed stated in hushed tones. "Each man has committed to recruiting ten more men, who will in turn recruit ten more." Daveed paused and looked at the crowded mountainside. "In just fifty days, most of these men will pick up a sword or even stones against the Romans. Come, it is time to report back to the Galilean."

> *Praise the LORD, you his servants;*
> *praise the name of the LORD.* [16]

The beautifully resonant tones of the Levitical choir rolled over the wall and through the closed gates that separated the Court of the Israelites from the Court of the Women.

"Hallelujah!" The deeply masculine response of more than a thousand worshipers seemed to shake the massively tall gate that had been shut behind the first group of men to arrive at the Temple with their Passover lambs.

> *Let the name of the LORD be praised,*
> *both now and forevermore.*[17]

Jesus looked up at the closed gate in front of him, and then he looked down at the restless lamb in his arms. "Father?"

Joseph looked down at his son.

"Will it be long before our division of worshipers is allowed to enter?" Jesus asked.

In response, Joseph shrugged before adding, "Longer than I would like. So many were in front of us! I think they must have slept with their lambs on the steps of the Temple."

Curiously, Jesus looked around at all the men standing shoulder to shoulder, each pair with a lamb between them. "How can all these lambs, as well as the lambs in the last division waiting behind us, be slain before the sun goes down? Jesus asked.

"You will see," Joseph confidently responded. "They have a very efficient system."

"Yeshua, you will see men doing without understanding, reenacting without remembering," God spoke into the mind of his son.

To Jesus, the crowded confines of the Temple court, the animal smell, even the presence of his father, seemed to disappear as he was swept into silent conversation with his heavenly Father.

"Remember?"

In his mind, Jesus was suddenly seeing a land he vaguely remembered from early childhood—Egypt. Without audible words, Jesus answered his Father. "I remember. That is the Nile River."

"And what do you see along the river?" God asked.

"Slaves, hundreds of slaves. They are making bricks. I do not remember so many people making bricks along the Nile."

"That is because you are now seeing the Nile during the reign of the satanically inspired pharaoh who decreed that all male infants must be thrown into the Nile. My enemy, Satan, has always demanded human sacrifice. His desire to destroy my most noble creation, man, has always been insatiable."

"Look!" Jesus suddenly exclaimed.

Joseph looked over at him curiously, and Jesus realized he had spoken aloud what he meant to say to his heavenly Father in his mind.

Giving Joseph a little sheepish grin, he said, "I didn't mean to speak out."

"Is this one of those times when God is talking in your head?" Joseph asked.

"Yes," Jesus replied.

"Then do not let me interrupt." Joseph reached out, exchanging the lamb in Jesus's arms for the staff of pomegranate wood he had been leaning on. "Now you will not need to think about the animal."

"Thank you," God whispered his appreciation to Joseph.

Joseph felt an unexplainable satisfaction sweep over him. Once more, he glanced at Jesus, and he could tell by the look on his son's face that Jesus was seriously concentrating on something.

"Something is floating on the river," Jesus announced to Father God. "It is a reed basket. An angel is guiding it. And on either side of the river, I see shadowy forms restrained yet straining to capture the basket as it floats by. A crocodile just entered the water."

Jesus shuddered and remembered that one time in Egypt he had seen that wicked-looking water lizard.

In his mind, he watched as the dangerous animal continued its powerful glide toward the basket. Unexpectedly, a baby cried, and immediately, Jesus realized the cries came from the basket. Instinctively, he held his breath, hoping he would not see one of countless newborn sacrifices to the evil god of the Nile.

Alarmed shouts pulled his attention to the shore, where an Egyptian princess bathed. Her servants had also seen the monster of the river. With spears in hand, they hurried out in their reed boat ready to do battle, but the crocodile, warned by their shouts, abruptly turned. And with a swish of its powerful tail, it dove beneath the muddy water.

"Look at this basket!" one of the servants exclaimed.

"It must be a gift from the god of the Nile to our princess," another responded as he leaned over the boat and captured the basket.

Demanding wails came through the tightly woven cover of the basket. "This gift from the Nile must be alive and hungry," the first servant asserted as he removed the cover of the basket.

"Moses!" Jesus exclaimed in his mind.

"A deliverer, a type of the Anointed One to come," God informed. "He was born in dangerous times. Satan sought to end his life before he was weaned. When his mother placed him in the river, it was to her as if he had died, but now look."

"He has been returned to her! Her child who was as good as dead now lives in her arms," Jesus responded as he watched the Egyptian princess place the baby back into the arms of his own mother.

"Meditate on the former things, the lives of the great men who have received my anointing to bring temporary deliverance to Israel. In their lives, you will find the foreshadowing events that will take place in of the life of my Anointed One, who brings eternal deliverance to both Israel and the nations." Then God paused, allowing Jesus to move back into the Passover ceremonies.

"Jesus?"

"Yes, Father."

"The gates are opening." Joseph nudged Jesus to begin moving with the mass of men carrying their lambs. Up the steps, through the tall bronze gates, Jesus looked around, taking in as many sights as possible. The massive altar of burnt offering occupied a large space in the Court of the Israelites. The rising smoke and the aroma of burning meat indicated the evening sacrifice was still burning.

A double line of priests stretched from wall to wall like endless evenly spaced columns. Silently and orderly, the men began lining up, each pair of men with their lamb finding a place in front of a priest. Each priest solemnly held a golden basin, and within that basin lay a sharp knife.

Three trumpet blasts split the silence, and as one, more than a thousand men picked up the knives and with one upward thrust slit the throat of their nonresisting lamb. Immediately, each priest leaned forward, catching the spurting blood in the golden basin.

With his hands supporting the lamb, Jesus felt the involuntary quiver of the animal as Joseph sliced through its flesh. He could feel the life draining out through the jagged slit in its neck until his own young arms completely supported the dead animal.

Once more, the voice of God filled his mind. "I spoke through Moses to the whole community of Israel. *Each man is to take a lamb for his family, one for each household… All of the community of Israel must slaughter them at twilight.*"[18]

The resonant tones of the Levitical choir filled the Court of the Israelites.

Not to us, O LORD, not to us but to your name be the glory.[19]

The priest who was assisting passed the gold basin full of blood down the line and placed a silver basin on the floor near the head of the dead animal. Without verbal instruction, Jesus helped Joseph lift the lifeless lamb up and hang it on one of the many hooks attached to the walls of the Temple just for this purpose. For a short space of time, the blood continued to drain into the silver basin.

The choir sang,

O house of Israel, trust in the
LORD—he is their help and shield.[20]

The men, all busy preparing their lambs, answered. "Hallelujah!"

More than a thousand men, all working like one man, pushed their staffs of pomegranate wood through the digestive tract of the lamb, entering and exiting the animal without breaking a bone.

The choir continued to sing.

The LORD remembers us and he will bless us.

"Hallelujah!" Without pausing in the preparation of their lambs, the men responded again.

He will bless his people Israel,
he will bless the house of Aaron.[21]

"Hallelujah!" Jesus sang the response with his father Joseph as he helped lift the lamb by the wooden pole that protruded from either end of the dead animal. Once again, they hung the lamb from the hooks on the wall of the Temple.

Fascinated, Jesus paused to look around. There was not enough wall space or hooks for all the men to use. Many men worked in groups of four: two men holding two lambs with the wooden poles over their shoulders while the other two men began the process of removing the whole skin. At the same time, the gold and silver basins filled with blood were still being passed from priest to priest until, at the altar of burnt offering, the blood was thrown with one swift jerk of the basin into the cavernous opening at the bottom of the altar. Jesus watched. Basin after basin, there was no way to count the number of blood-filled basins that were used. And from each basin, before it was emptied, a small amount of blood was flicked on the side of the altar.

God spoke again, "When I see the blood, I always remember my promise to spare the lives of those who believe my words and act on them. In the writings of Moses, you read about the first Passover. *Then they were to take some of the blood and put it on the sides and tops of the doorframes of the houses.*[22] The blood was a sign for them on the houses where they lived, the homes where they ate their lambs. When I saw the blood, I passed over them. No destructive plague touched my people while I struck down all the firstborn of Egypt."

Once again, Jesus turned his attention to the body of the lamb. Joseph, with an experienced hand, was removing the skin, separating it from the meat of the animal, discarding the fat and the kidneys into another basin provided by the assisting priest. There was so much to consider. Jesus recalled the scriptures he had studied in the synagogue school relating to the ordinances of God regarding sacrifices. *Then take all the fat around the inner parts, the covering of the liver, and both kidneys with the fat on them, and burn them on the altar.*[23] Jesus looked down into the basin. It was full. The assisting priest noticed that Joseph had completed the skinning and cleaning of the lamb. He took the basin and passed it down the row of priests. When it arrived at the altar, its contents would be tossed on the coals to be consumed by the fire that was never allowed to be extinguished.

The Levitical choir continued to sing.

I love the LORD, for he heard my voice;
he heard my cry for mercy.[24]

"Hallelujah!" the men continued to respond to each phrase. The smell of burning fat permeated the court. The smoke rose in a never-ending vertical column from the altar, and always the choir sang and the men responded.

Jesus helped his father take the lamb down from the hooks and cover the raw meat with the skin Joseph had removed from the lamb. Then they stood, waiting for the rest of the men to complete the process of preparing their animals so they all could exit the court together and make room for the next group of men with their animals.

The Levitical choir was now about half way through the traditional Passover psalms.

The cords of death entangled me,
the anguish of the grave came upon me;
I was overcome by trouble and sorrow.
Then I called on the name of the LORD:
'O LORD, save me!'[25]

"Hallelujah!" both Jesus and Joseph responded with all the men.

God continued his instruction, "When you see the body of the lamb your father is holding, it is easy to believe death is final, that there is nothing after the grave. But I am assuring you today, for any man who calls, '*O Lord, save me!*'[26] there is life with me for eternity. Do not be alarmed. My Anointed One must, like this lamb, submit to death. But after three days, he will live again."

Jesus looked at the lamb under his father's arm. Four raw legs and an almost unidentifiable head protruded from the bloodstained skin wrapped around the dead animal.

The Levitical choir was still singing the many verses of the traditional psalms for the Passover season. Jesus began to sing with the choir.

> *Precious in the sight of the Lord is the death of his saints.*
> *O Lord, truly I am your servant; I am your servant,*
> *the son of your maidservant; you have freed me from my chains.*
> *I will sacrifice a thank offering to you.*[27]

The massive gates on the sides of the court were slowly opened. Still singing, still responding with deep baritone hallelujahs, the men, with their lambs tucked under their arms, exited the Temple.

Chapter 9

THE PASSOVER MEAL

*The LORD's Passover begins at twilight on the fourteenth
day of the first month. On the fifteenth day of that month the
LORD's Festival of Unleavened Bread begins; for seven days
you must eat bread made without yeast.*

—Leviticus 23:5–6

The heady smell of seared meat filled the massive courtyard.
Three lambs roasted in clay-lined pits behind the opulent
home that belonged to a prominent Levitical family. Within
that Temple connected family, secret formulas for compounding
incense and aromatic oils were passed from father to son. On this
festive evening in that extended household, all but one disgraced
son were busy preparing to enjoy the traditional Passover meal.

Sitting on a woven mat with his shriveled and deformed legs
hidden by the folds of his garment, Ichabod, the youngest son of
the head perfumer, could only watch and bitterly imagine what
it would be like to walk briskly across the courtyard. He could
only imagine the satisfaction of working with his brothers to
compound the secret blend of fragrant spices that were added to
the anointing oil.

"Unclean!" The Condemning spirit that had attached itself at
birth reminded the cripple of his unworthiness. "No man with a
deformity in his body can touch those things that are holy unto
the Lord."

"Were the Passover pilgrims generous today?"

Ichabod looked up from his self-debasing contemplation to see one of his father's servants bending over to speak to him, bending over to estimate the value of the coins in his beggar's pot. "A lamb urinated on my robe," Ichabod bitterly complained, "and a man stepped on my hand. I spent the entire day by the Beautiful Gate harassed by the crowds. There are not enough coins in the entire city of Jerusalem to pay for my misery."

"Your mother has asked me to wash and dress you for the meal," the servant gave a polite bow as he spoke.

With a sigh of resignation, Ichabod agreed. He did long to remove his soiled and smelly clothes, to put on a fresh garment.

The servant bent over and lifted the young man easily. In the privacy of his sleeping chamber, his soiled clothing was removed, his body sponged, and then the servant carried him to the enclosed pool near the courtyard. Thin-boned and shriveled, Ichabod was easily carried down the stone steps into the clear water. The servant ducked under the water, and Ichabod felt refreshing coolness as his entire body was briefly submerged.

"The lamps are lit. The meal will soon be served. We must hurry," the servant said as he dried his master's son and pulled a fresh tunic over his head.

"You will eat with your family?" Ichabod casually asked.

"Yes, your father has graciously provided two lambs to feed all the servants and their families."

"My father and my brothers will dine together," Ichabod ruefully stated. "My mother and my sisters will laugh and feast while I eat alone because no one wants to remember that a cripple, only good for begging, was born into this family. For that reason, my father named me Ichabod, the glory has departed."

"Do not forget," the slave quietly admonished, "you are the most blessed of all the beggars in this city. Because of your father's position in the Temple, a space is reserved just for you beside the Beautiful Gate. Other beggars struggle for a well-trafficked spot.

They crawl on their hands and knees while you are carried on a litter. Yes, at birth you received an irreversible curse, but in life you have been blessed."

"What impudence!" the spirit of Bitterness exclaimed. "Your father's servant forgets he is just a servant in this house. He cannot say, 'Remember the blessings!'"

"Remember the blessings," the Spirit of God countered. "You have seen the beggars of this city wearing tattered clothing and sitting in their own waste. You know they are kicked and taunted every day, but you, because you were born into a unique family of Temple workmen, are the most honored beggar in the city."

Condemnation tried to cast aside the blessing. "Worthless! You are worthless!"

"On the day you were born, I looked at you and said, 'Live and be blessed,'" the Spirit of God shouted over the demonic clamor of Condemnation and Bitterness. "And today, I say it again. Live and be blessed!"

Coarse oaths as well as a sharp rebuke were on the tip of Ichabod's tongue. He swallowed his words. Instead of unleashing his Bitterness and Anger, Ichabod just muttered, "I do not want to hear it! Take me to my solitary table and do not dilute my wine with water."

When the first three stars could be seen in the evening sky, it was the beginning of Passover. By flickering lamplight, Mary arranged the cushions and set the tables for the festive meal: a table for the men and boys of the family, a separate table for John, and a small table near the cooking area where she and Ruth might enjoy their portions after serving the men. Around each table, she made sure there was enough space for each person to recline. On each table, she placed dishes of crushed bitterroots, fresh spring greens, a sweet fig and honey paste, boiled eggs, and unleavened bread. Near the head of the table for the men and boys, she placed a large jar of wine mixed with water. A small pitcher of diluted wine remained in the cooking area to be shared with Ruth. On John's separate table, she placed an earthen jar of water sweetened with date honey. Behind the house, she could hear Joseph, Zechariah, John, and Jesus. They were removing the lamb from the clay oven where it had been roasting.

"Blessed are you, O Lord, our God, who has provided a lamb for the salvation of his people," James and Jose excitedly chanted as they marched ahead of the roasted lamb that Joseph carried in and placed on a large wooden platter in the center of the serving table.

Behind the house, Jesus quickly raked the coals in the oven, piling them safely in the center of the baked clay floor so they would remain hot and available to his mother for heating water in the morning. He could hear his brothers chanting, and he felt the excitement of the evening.

"Yeshua?" Jesus heard his Hebrew name with his spiritual ears.

"Yes, Father." Jesus straightened up and looked heavenward, waiting to hear the words of God.

"Blessed are you, O Lord our God, who has provided a lamb for the salvation of his people," Father God repeated the traditional blessing James and Jose were chanting. Then he took Jesus back into his heavenly memory, to Mount Moriah before the streets and houses of Jerusalem covered its rugged terrain.

"What do you see?" God asked.

"An old man accompanied by a much younger man," Jesus answered. Then he continued to observe the supernaturally revealed scene. Walking toward the scrub bush–covered summit, the older man carried live coals in a covered bronze dish suspended from a stick while the younger man with a load of firewood strapped to his back strode companionably beside him.

"That is my friend Abraham, with his son, Isaac," Jesus voiced his supernaturally revealed recollection and then waited for Father God to affirm it.

"Yes," God answered. Then he added, "Do you see my enemy?"

"Yes," Jesus responded. "He is silently following them. I find his silence unusual."

"He is confused. Until this moment, Satan has believed Isaac is the seed of the woman, the promised Deliverer. He knows I have told Abraham to sacrifice his only son, Isaac, on the altar, but he does not know whether to encourage Isaac to flee and escape or to encourage Abraham to end his son's life with one swift thrust."

Suddenly, the Spirit moved Jesus into the scene, close enough to hear the conversation.

"Father?"

"Yes, my son?" Abraham replied.

"The fire and the wood are here," Isaac said, *"but where is the lamb for the burnt offering?"*

Abraham answered, "God himself will provide the lamb for the burnt offering, my son."[1]

Jesus watched as the two of them went on together. *When they reached the place God had told him about, Abraham built an altar.* One by one, with the help of Isaac, he hauled and stacked twelve good-sized stones on a level spot near the summit.

"Father, where is the lamb?" Isaac asked again.

"The Lord our Creator has given me specific instructions regarding this sacrifice," Abraham replied with a quivering voice.

"His heart is breaking," Jesus spoke to his Father.

"My heart breaks each time I see a lamb on the altar because I understand the full symbolic meaning of each sacrifice in a way you cannot yet comprehend," God responded. "Keep watching."

Deeply engrossed in the revelation, Jesus sat down cross-legged beside the warm oven. His mind focused on the crudely constructed altar. Together, Abraham and Isaac arranged the wood. Then Abraham turned and took both of his son's strong hands in his weaker, trembling hands. "God has commanded that you be the sacrifice, but he has also promised that through you,

I will be the father of a great nation. God cannot break his own promise."Tears rolled down the weathered cheeks of the old man, but his eyes never left the eyes of his son. "I have been assured in my heart that God is stronger than death. Even though I slay you, I know you will live to fulfill God's promise to me."

"No! No!" Jesus could hear that Satan was no longer silent. "Death is mine. Sheol is my kingdom, and no one who enters the Place of the Dead will ever return to the world of the living!"

"Abraham is not listening to Satan," Jesus commented.

"My friend has trained himself to only respond to my voice," God answered.

Fascinated, Jesus watched as Abraham *bound his son Isaac and laid him on the altar on top of the wood. Then he reached out his hand and took the knife to slay his son.*[2]

Jesus held his breath. It was a moment when he could see Michael, the glorious warring angel of the Lord, in hand-to-hand combat with Satan, the dark angel of the pit. Above the altar, each struggled to control the situation. In the midst of that heart-stopping struggle, he heard his own heavenly voice.

"Abraham! Abraham!"

In that moment, when Evil was startled by the Creator's commanding voice, Michael threw his opponent to the far hills.

"Here I am," Abraham immediately replied.

"Do not lay a hand on the boy," Yeshua said. *"Do not do anything to him. Now I know that you fear God because you have not withheld from me your son, your only son."*[3]

"My son who was dead has been returned to me," Abraham announced as he sliced through the ropes.

Abraham looked up, and there, in a thicket he saw a ram caught by his horns. He went over and took the ram and sacrificed it as a burnt offering instead of his son.

"So Abraham called that place the LORD Will Provide," God announced with unmistakable satisfaction. *"And to this day it*

is said, '*On the mountain of the* Lord *it will be provided.*'[4] My sacrifice will be made on that same mountain, in that exact spot."

"Jesus?" John bent over his cousin, placing his hand on his shoulder.

Slightly disoriented, Jesus looked up into the face of his older cousin and said, "Did you know God is preparing a blood offering and all the lambs placed on the altar in the Temple are merely symbols of the sacrifice God is going to provide?"

"I have been studying the writings of the prophet Isaiah with Geber, the Essene teacher. Isaiah speaks of a suffering Messiah who is *led like a lamb to the slaughter.*[5] But *after the suffering of his soul, he will see the light of life and be satisfied,*"[6] John responded.

"Yes, God has been speaking to me about those things." Taking his cousin's offered hand, he stood up. "It's time to eat, isn't it?"

"Your father sent me to get you," John answered.

"I want to hear Rabbi Geber," Jesus said.

John chuckled a little as he replied, "Don't call him rabbi. He despises the Temple establishment, with all its pride and pompous titles. Still, he goes there to teach. He says there should always be one clear voice speaking truth in the house of God. Tomorrow, we will go to Solomon's porch. I will introduce you to him."

"Blessed are you, O Lord our God, who on the first day of creation said, 'Let there be light.' In his holy name, we light these Passover lights." With head bowed and covered, Elesheva chanted the blessing over the two burning lamps she had just placed on the table where Toma sat with his Uncle Shaul and Obal, the husband of the wet nurse he had obtained for his new son.

Even though Elesheva's head was reverently bowed, Toma could see the lamplight reflected in her beautiful light brown eyes, and he could not pull his own eyes away. Her late husband's brother had passed to Toma the right of the kinsman redeemer, so a betrothal feast was to be held after the Feast of Weeks.

With his eyes, Toma followed Elesheva's every movement. She moved so gracefully from one man to the next, pouring the wine, working with only one hand. Toma was amazed. When she stopped at his side, he held up his cup, and she filled it. His eyes met hers, and she blessed him with a warm smile. He felt his heart race like a thirsty animal getting the scent of fresh water.

The Holy Spirit then spoke sweet affirmation over the couple. "Toma, you have returned to your hometown to become the kinsman redeemer for Elesheva. In the same way, Yeshua has come to earth to become the kinsman redeemer for my precious people, Israel and all the descendants of Adam."

From his reclining position at the head of the table, Uncle Shaul began to read from the Order of the Passover scroll. "The great and Holy One *said to Moses, 'I am the* LORD*... I have heard the groaning of the Israelites, whom the Egyptians are enslaving, and I have remembered my covenant... I will bring you out from under the yoke of the Egyptians.'* [7] Let us drink the first cup." Uncle Shaul raised his cup of wine for all to see. "This is the cup that brings us into relationship, man with God. Our God is a holy God who made a promise to his people and kept it!"

The three men at the table, along with Obal's three sons, drank deeply from their cups. By the serving table, Elesheva and Salma sipped from their cups. Toma, with eyes only for Elesheva, vowed in his heart, "I will keep my promise to be your husband and provider."

In the banquet hall of a luxurious home, the Levitical family of perfumers had gathered. At the head of the table, Ichabod's father reclined on a pile of enormous cushions. With one bent elbow, he supported his upper body so he could read the required scriptures and chants from a small scroll that lay open beside him. "*Who may ascend the hill of the* LORD*? Who may stand in his holy place? He who has clean hands and a pure heart.*"[8]

Ichabod watched as his father, in a disinterested monotone, chanted the blessing over the hand-washing ceremony. No one in the family paused to listen. The jovial chatter of his brothers continued while his mother, with one of his sisters, moved efficiently from person to person. One held a bronze basin while the other poured tepid water over the fingers of each man at the table. At the same time, the wives of his brothers moved with another basin from foot to foot, removing sandals, washing and drying each pair of feet at the main table. Everyone seemed so enamored with themselves, with their frivolous anecdotes. They laughed and chatted, ignoring the solemnity of the event they were celebrating.

Relegated to a solitary table, Ichabod, like a rodent that he saw staring at the family from a dark corner of the room, watched his brothers and sisters, his father and mother. He was not included in the conversations. His brother's wife dropped an empty basin, and the rodent scurried away. More than ever, Ichabod wished he could just get up and walk out. But his legs were so withered from disuse that he could barely crawl. Instead, he shifted his body so he had a clear view of the open window and the star-filled sky.

"Everyone is washing, but no one in this family has dirty fingers or dirty feet," Bitterness sneered. "These are the fingers that crush and blend imported spices to make incense and anointing oil for the Temple. These fingers never touch the cripple in the family. Servants are usually assigned to that task, but tonight, all the servants are having their own Passover meals."

Ichabod looked up. His sister was holding the basin, and his mother was ready to pour the water, but their eyes were averted. He was his mother's shame, a curse of unknown origin. What evil had she done? What sin had he committed while still in her womb? The unanswered question of who was to blame always hung between them. Without comment, Ichabod held out his hands, going through the time-honored motions. No one approached his table to care for his feet. He had not expected they would.

"The Israelites groaned in their slavery and cried out, and their cry for help because of their slavery went up to God."[9] In a modest home in the Essene quarter of Jerusalem, Zechariah held up a bowl of saltwater. "These are the tears of my people. They ate wild greens gathered after a day of working under the whip. It was a scavenger's meal, and it was seasoned with tears." The old priest dipped some spring greens into the saltwater, then he passed the bowl around the table. Each person dipped their greens and ate.

Sitting apart from the rest of the family with their cups of wine, John dipped his greens in his own little dish of saltwater. After swallowing, John announced, "Every year, my father has asked the traditional questions, and I, being an only son, have had to answer, but this year, Jose is the youngest."

"Yes!" Jesus and James both applauded with John while Joseph indicated that his youngest son should stand and be ready to answer the traditional Passover questions.

"Why is this night different from all other nights?" Zechariah asked.

A little bewildered and unsure, Jose stood, mentally searching for the right answer.

Jesus got up from his recumbent position and quickly moved to his little brother's side. He whispered into his brother's ear, "On a night like this, our ancestors were brought out of Egypt by the hand of God Almighty."

Flashing his brother a quick grateful grin, Jose carefully repeated the answer Jesus had given him.

"On all other nights, we eat bread that has been made with yeast and baked in the oven, but why, on this night, do we eat bread that is flat and made without yeast?" Joseph asked the second question.

Again Jesus whispered the answer in his four-year-old brother's ear. "Through Moses, God Almighty instructed our ancestors to be ready to leave immediately, so there was no time for yeast to be added to the flour to make the bread rise."

With a little prompting, Jose was able to repeat the correct response.

Zechariah asked the next question. "On all other nights, we eat a variety of vegetables, but why, on this night, do we only eat bitter herbs?"

"Life left a bad taste in the mouths of the slaves," Jose answered on his own, "just like these bitter herbs leave a bad taste in my mouth." He pointed to the dish of crushed horseradish.

Everyone in the room laughed at the youthful frankness of the boy's response.

"The Roman occupation of our land is leaving a bitter taste in many mouths today," Zechariah commented. "I may be blind, but I am not deaf. In the marketplace, I have heard talk of a rebellious uprising."

"Not tonight!" Mary spoke up from her place near the serving table. "Let's just remember the joy of that ancient deliverance when only the blood of lambs was shed."

"Mary worries. She fears someone she loves might get caught up in the bloody retribution that always follows even the slightest hint of rebellion against the Romans," Joseph explained. Then he added, "She is right."

From his private table, John spoke up, "May I ask the next question?"

"Go ahead," Joseph quickly responded as everyone shifted back into the comfort of tradition.

"Now, Jose, I want to warn you. I always ask the hardest questions," John baited the little boy.

Everyone laughed as they watched Jose squirm in anticipation.

"I'm here," Jesus assured his youngest brother.

John began, "On all other nights, we do not dip our vegetables or our bread, but why on this night, do we dip our vegetables in the saltwater and our bread in the bitter herbs?"

"I know! I know!" Jose exclaimed. "We must never forget the hardships of our ancestors."

"Yes!" Zechariah responded. "Their tears are our tears."

"Now for the last question," Joseph said, trying to move the ceremonies of the evening along. "On all other nights, we eat our meals while sitting at a low table, but why, on this night, do we recline on cushions?"

For a moment, Jose looked at the cushions and then back at his father, then he answered seriously, "This meal is very late at night. When we are through eating, we can just go to sleep."

Everyone laughed. The logic of the four-year-old was precious.

"James," Joseph called on his second son, "tell me, why are we reclining?"

James quickly answered, "Because we are no longer slaves. It is our privilege to rest."

As James gave the correct answer, Jesus got up from his reclining position. "As an Israelite who has been freed from slavery, I am able both to recline and to choose where to recline." He picked up his cushions and carried them over to the table where John, faithful to his lifelong Nazirite vow, sat apart from those who were drinking wine and eating meat. "I will share your sweetened water," he said to his cousin as he lay down beside him with one elbow on the low table.

Elesheva placed a cloth-covered plate holding three large pieces of unleavened bread in front of Uncle Shaul. Reaching under the cloth, Uncle Shaul took the middle piece. He held it up for all to see. "This is the bread of affliction, the bread of our forefathers. They left Egypt in haste and ate it for eight days. After walking day and night and then crossing the Red Sea, they were finally able to stop and cook again. Then they moved on to the mountain of the Lord." Breaking the bread, he said, "Blessed are you, O Lord our God, who gives us bread from the earth."

The Spirit of God bent over Toma and pronounced another prophetic blessing. "You have eaten the bread of affliction, and now I am giving you the Bread of Life—my son, Yeshua-Jesus, the adopted son of your cousin Joseph. His words will be life to you and to your descendants after you."

Toma took a bite of the unleavened bread. It was sweet in his mouth. Then he dipped into the ground horseradish. The bitter herbs stung his tongue and caused his eyes to water. But there was satisfaction in that experience, like the satisfaction of accomplishing a difficult task. Elesheva brought the sweet raisin and honey paste to him. He dipped again, this time into delicious sweetness. Life as a son of the covenant was good.

"Tell the story!"

Ichabod looked up from studying the pattern of piercings and stripes that had been baked into his piece of unleavened bread. His brothers were urging his father to hurry the traditional retelling of the history of Israel.

From her place near the serving table, Ichabod's mother testily restated their pleas. "My husband, tell the story quickly so we can have the second cup and then eat."

Ichabod heard his father reply, "Do not fear. I am not a long-winded Pharisee. I understand brevity and will only mention those things that are recorded in the books of Moses." He cleared his throat before continuing, "God is a maker of covenants. He made a covenant with Abraham the father of all Jews and with Abraham's son, Isaac, then with Abraham's grandson, Jacob. When the sons of Jacob moved to Egypt and after a number of years found themselves enslaved, God remembered the promises he had made to Abraham, Isaac, and Jacob…"

On this holy evening of remembrance, the Spirit of God entered every home in the region of Jerusalem and sat at each table. In the home of the Temple perfumers, he passed by the table where men mocked their duty to recall the victories of God and sat with the crippled man whose heart was breaking.

"I am the God of your father, the God of Abraham, the God of Isaac, and the God of Jacob," Quietly, gently, the Spirit of God began to speak his covenant of comfort and blessing over the crippled son of one of the most influential men in the Temple complex. "*I have indeed seen your misery... and I am concerned about your suffering.*[10] So tonight, I am making a promise to you. I have sent my son, Yeshua, down to Earth to rescue you from the torment of demons and the miserable condition of your body. Be assured, he will heal your infirmities and turn your sorrow into joy. To accomplish this, he will allow himself to be pierced, paying the price for your transgressions. By the wounds he receives, you will be restored in this life and in the life to come."

At his solitary table, Ichabod had been studying the patterns of imported tiles that decorated the wall behind the main table. In front of the beautiful designs, his brothers were rolling their eyes and gesturing for their father to hurry through the tedious historical details. He could hear that the sketchy retelling of the birth of his nation was almost complete.

Running his finger down one of the columns of print on the Passover scroll, Ichabod's father skipped over the story of Moses at the burning bush and then read, "And God, through Moses, brought plagues on the Egyptians. He sent a man and not an angel!"

"Because there are no angels!" one of Ichabod's brothers exclaimed.

"And those dreadfully dull Pharisees need to stop arguing that there are angels," another brother asserted.

"There were ten plagues," Ichabod's father projected over his sons as they jumped into the hotly debated topic of the existence of angels. "Blood!" he announced the first plague, and the brothers dipped their fingers into their silver wine cups, flicking the juice into the air as they continued their heated opposition to the opinions of the Pharisees.

The father raised his voice over the discussion. "Frogs!"

All the brothers at the main table flicked a little wine again, this time they flicked it at each other as they responded, "The Pharisees are like frogs. They hop to all the wrong conclusions!"

The third plague was announced. "Lice!"

Responsible men acting like irreverent children repeated, "Lice! The Pharisees are everywhere, like lice. The Temple is infested with them!" And again they flicked little drops of wine at each other as they laughed at their own cleverness.

"Flies!" The head of the family choked out the name of the next plague as he tried to swallow his own laughter and maintain some decorum. He too found their caricatures of the pests of the Temple amusing.

"Flies!" the boys raucously repeated. They flicked more wine and swatted at make-believe flies as they called out, "I got Hillel! And I got Shammai!"

"Cattle disease!"

"Their endless minutia is like cattle disease!"

"Boils!"

"Shammai is a boil on the backside of the high priest!" one brother exclaimed as he flicked a drop of wine.

"What about that Essene, Geber, who teaches in the Temple every day? He's a boil ready to spread infection to the entire population!"

Disgusted, the Spirit of God removed his presence from the home of the Temple perfumers while allowing himself to be more fully felt in the homes where faithful Jews recited his marvelous deeds with reverence and awe.

"*On that day, God displayed his miraculous signs in Egypt, his wonders in the region of Zoan.*"[11] Zechariah held up his cup of wine as he quoted the scriptures from memory, "*He turned their rivers to blood; they could not drink from their streams.*"[12]

"*Their rivers to blood,*"[13] everyone solemnly repeated. Each person dipped a finger into their cup of wine and placed a drop on their plate.

At John's table, both Jesus and John dipped their fingers into the honey-water. Then each allowed one drop to fall to their plates. Immediately, John licked his finger.

"*Taste and see that the LORD is good,*"[14] Jesus lightly commented.

"*Blessed is the man who takes refuge in him.*"[15] John completed the scripture.

"*He sent swarms of flies that devoured them,*"[16] Zechariah continued reciting the glorious vengeance of the Lord.

"*Swarms of flies,*"[17] everyone repeated.

"*And swarms of frogs that devastated them.*"[18] Zechariah's voice became stronger as he recited the powerful demonstrations of the Almighty.

"I am here, and I was there!" the Spirit of God triumphantly shouted. "I am God! Satan and his demonic forces were compelled to surrender then, and they will surrender to me again!"

"*He gave their crops to grasshoppers, their produce to the locusts!*"[19] Zechariah clapped for joy.

And everyone shouted, "Grasshoppers and locusts!" as they dipped into their cups once again.

"*He destroyed their vines with hail and their sycamore-figs with sleet. He gave over their cattle to hail, their livestock to bolts of lightning. He unleashed against them his hot anger, his wrath, indignation and hostility—a band of destroying angels.*"[20]

Suddenly moved by the presence of the Spirit, John stood and proclaimed, "God is a mighty warrior who builds great storehouses for hail and snow in the heavens. These he reserves to assault his enemies, to turn the tide of battle and win the war. He knows the *way to the place where the lightning is dispersed* and... *where the east winds are scattered all over the earth.* He *cuts a channel for the torrents of rain, and a path for the thunderstorm.*"[21]

"We are unworthy," Zechariah responded, "unworthy to speak your holy name, unworthy to look upon your face." With his aging hands, the old priest covered his mouth as he bowed his head.

Warmly, willingly, the Spirit of God made his presence known in greater measure to each person in the room.

Even little Jose stopped squirming and just stared briefly at each person as they lay on their cushions, too overcome by the Spirit to continue conversing. Curiously, Jose continued to visually search the room for that extra person he knew was present.

The stillness was broken by Zechariah, who stood and, without seeing, walked over to John. Placing both hands on John's head, he began to prophetically bless his son, "*And you, my child, will be called a prophet of the Most High; for you will go on before the* Lord *to prepare the way for him, to give his people the knowledge of salvation through the forgiveness of sins, because of the tender mercy of our God.*"[22]

Mary bent over and whispered to Ruth, "When John was just eight days old, Zechariah said those same prophetic words over him. I remember that day, and the presence of Holiness in that room was just like it is at this moment."

"*I will send my messenger, who will prepare the way before me.*" To Mary's surprise, Jesus was standing over John with his arm outstretched. The look on his face was amazingly mature and confident.

Through Jesus, the Holy Spirit continued to speak, "*Then suddenly the* Lord *you are seeking will come to his temple: the messenger of the covenant, whom you desire, will come.*[23] *He will be like a refiner's fire or a launderer's soap.* You can be sure that *he will purify the Levites. . .* who desecrate my Temple and mock my words. *Then the* Lord *will have men who will bring offerings in righteousness and the offerings of Judah and Jerusalem will be acceptable to the* Lord, *as in days gone by, as in former years."*[24]

Suddenly, an angel was seen flying swiftly through the spirit realm calling in a loud voice, "The mantle! God sends the mantle of Elijah the prophet!"

The Spirit of God looked up to see a worn cloak of camel hair falling from the angel's outstretched hands. Carried by spiritual winds, it drifted to Earth. With fiery hands, the Spirit caught the cloak and placed it upon the shoulders of John. *"Remember the law of my servant Moses, the decrees and laws I gave him at Horeb for all Israel. See, I will send you, like the prophet Elijah before that great and terrible day of the* Lord *comes."*[25]

In the room, everyone focused on John and the breathtaking words that had been prophetically spoken over him. For a moment, Zechariah seemed to tremble. Jesus and Joseph quickly moved to support him. Then still standing with his hands firmly planted on the head of his son, Zechariah spoke again, "Just as the Holy One of Israel called, first, Moses and then all of Israel into the desert to be instructed in his perfect law, so he is calling you to withdraw into the desert regions. Soon, I will close my eyes, and they will not open again until, after resting with the righteous, the Creator will call my name. When my soul departs, you, my son, are to also depart. You are to live in the desert regions until the time when God appears to you and calls you into the fulfillment of your prophetic destiny." Bending over John, Zechariah placed a long and tender kiss on the top of his head. The sweet tears of the presence of God's anointing fell from the eyes of the old priest onto the uncut hair of his only son.

Near the serving table, both Mary and Ruth quietly sobbed. Solidly, Joseph and Jesus stood on either side of Zechariah, physically supporting the old priest. Their faces were also dripping with tears. Jose and James remained on their cushions, silent, awed by the holy moment but not mature enough to fully comprehend all that was said.

After a time, Joseph helped Zechariah back down onto his cushions, and the meal continued.

Uncle Shaul passed the Passover Scroll over to Toma, who read, *"At midnight the Lord struck down all the firstborn of Egypt, from the first born of Pharaoh, who sat on the throne, to the firstborn of the prisoner, who was in the dungeon, and the firstborn of all the livestock as well."*[26] Relaxing by the serving table, Elesheva looked over at baby Seth, who was sleeping on a cushion next to the table. He was a beautiful child. His straight dark hair made her think of her own son, Kefa. Her mind refocused on the scripture Toma was reading.

"And there was loud wailing in Egypt, for there was not a house without someone dead."[27]

She knew Toma was reading about Egypt and an event that had taken place generations earlier, but in her mind, it seemed like Toma had said, "Not long ago, in every home in the village of Bethlehem, there was loud wailing." In a corner of her memory, she could hear the wails. She could still see the little mutilated bodies. Slowly, she moved her arm from under the folds of her garment and looked at the place where a hand had once been—a physical reminder of a tragedy she would never forget.

In her mind, she went back to that dreadful day when Roman soldiers had appeared to be marching through Bethlehem. Without warning, they had broken ranks and run into the village homes.

She had been spinning wool into thread while keeping an eye on one-year-old Kefa as, with one hand on the edge of a low table, he practiced sweet shaky toddler steps. Suddenly, the door to their courtyard had burst from its leather hinges, and two burly soldiers charged into the living quarters of the home she shared with her husband. Immediately, they saw her son. Before she could react, one soldier had roughly grabbed the child.

The rest of the memories were fragmented, like the broken timbers of the courtyard door. She remembered Kefa's startled cry, her own screams. At some point, she had jumped on the back of the soldier who dangled and shook her child like a crumb-filled cloth. With both hands, she had tried to strangle the man, but the other soldier had pulled her off. Kefa was still screaming when they ran out the door with him. She remembered when the screams stopped, when she attacked again, and when the soldier cut off her hand.

"Elesheva? Elesheva?" Salma put a comforting hand on her shoulder. "Here"—she pressed a clean cloth into Elesheva's hand—"wipe your eyes."

From the main table, Toma looked at Elesheva with concern. He knew she was remembering because he was also remembering. Who could forget the death of their firstborn son? Forgetting the timeless Eastern protocol that made a distinction between men's and women's places at formal occasions, Toma rose from his reclining position and moved quickly over to where Elesheva sat with Salma comforting her. "Elesheva?" He knelt in front of the woman he expected to take as his wife. "The firstborn of Egypt died a long time ago."

"I know," Elesheva answered with a quivering voice. "And God is merciful. Those babies died in their mother's arms. My son died in the dirt outside of our courtyard."

"God is merciful," Salma repeated Elesheva's words as she pushed herself between Toma and Elesheva. She held baby Seth in her arms. "God has returned to you, Toma, and to Elesheva what the Evil One has taken." Deliberately, she placed the baby in Elesheva's arms. "I know your betrothal is not yet official, but before these witnesses, promises can be made. The celebration can come at a later date."

"You know I have purchased the right to be your kinsman redeemer." Toma looked into Elesheva's eyes as he spoke.

From the table, Uncle Shaul called out, "The price was substantial! You are dear to this man!"

"Tonight, you have my promise. Together, we will rebuild our family and our lives. We will share the joy of having a son again." Toma took Elesheva's hand and looked into her light brown eyes.

"I accept you," Elesheva responded.

Ever helpful, ever involved, Salma quickly dabbed at Elesheva's tear-filled eyes.

Everyone laughed a little.

And Salma, blushing, explained, "She didn't have a free hand. Someone had to wipe those tears away so she could smile!"

"Let's eat the lamb," Obal suggested, "then we can seal this betrothal with the third cup."

"The cup of redemption," Uncle Shaul announced, "and tonight, it is not only a cup to remember the redemption of Israel but also the redemption of two shattered lives."

Immediately, Salma began to move to the serving table. Elesheva blessed Toma with her genuine smile as she placed little Seth in his arms. She watched as he laid the child, still sleeping, down onto a cushion.

"We have finished this lamb," Mary announced as she gave the last pieces of meat to Joseph.

"Then it is time for the third cup," Joseph announced. He filled his own cup with wine and then proceeded to refill the cups of all those reclining at the main table.

Jesus, resting next to John with only honey and water in his cup, said, "Every word that proceeds from the mouth of the Holy

One is sweet, but the sweetest words are those covenant promises of restoration—*I will redeem you with an outstretched arm!*"[28]

"Drink. Swallow in great gulps the promises of God," Zechariah announced. "They will bring refreshment when life is dry and hope when all is lost."

"Never forget the outstretched arm of the Lord!" John added, "*Burst into songs of joy together, you ruins of Jerusalem, for the LORD has comforted his people, he has redeemed Jerusalem. The LORD will lay bare his holy arm in the sight of all the nations, and all the ends of the earth will see the salvation of our God.*"[29]

"One more cup," Joseph announced as he refilled the cups for the last time. "It is a cup of praise!"

Before anyone drank, John began to sing.

> *To him who struck down the firstborn of Egypt.*

Everyone at the tables responded,

> *His love endures forever.*

John continued the psalm of praise.

> *And brought Israel out from among them...*
> *with a mighty hand and outstretched arm.*
> *His love endures forever.*
> *To him who divided the Red Sea asunder...*
> *and brought Israel through the midst of it...*
> *but swept Pharaoh and his army into the Red Sea,*
> *His love endures forever.*[30]

When the song ended, the cups were emptied.

"It will not be long before the sun comes up again," Mary commented.

Then Joseph got up and picked up little Jose, who had fallen asleep on his cushions. Mary rearranged his cushions next to the wall, and after Joseph laid Jose back down for the night, she covered him.

Jesus and John remained at their low table in quiet meditation until they heard Zechariah begin to move. Both boys immediately rose and assisted the old priest to his sleeping chamber. Then they went up on the roof to sleep under the stars.

Chapter 10

TEACHING IN THE TEMPLE

*When he was twelve years old, they went up to the Feast
according to their custom. After the Feast was over, while his
parents were returning home, the boy Jesus stayed behind in
Jerusalem, but they were unaware of it.*

—Luke 2:42–43

"Jesus!" John shook the shoulder of his sleeping cousin.
Stirring in his sleep and then rousing, Jesus opened his
eyes. The earthen rooftop where he had been sleeping was damp
with predawn dew. The sky was still dark. Only a slight hint of
gray edged the eastern hills.

"The Temple gates will open soon. Geber always teaches in
the morning. If we want to hear him, we must first bring water
from the Pool of Siloam, then care for the goats and chickens,"
John urged. "After that, we will be free,"

Responding to his cousin's prodding, Jesus quickly sat up.
Grabbing the cloak that had been his cover for the night, he stood
and gave it a good shake before throwing it over his shoulders
and following John down the stairs that led to ground level at the
back of the house.

It was a short walk to the Pool of Siloam, where water from
the Gihon Spring flowed through Hezekiah's tunnel, filling the
rectangular stone reservoir. Before filling the water jars they
carried, both boys quickly stripped and stepped into the cool dark

waters of the pool. The water only came to the top of their knees. Silently, almost reverently, each boy knelt and then stretched out on the hewn-stone floor of the pool. For a few moments, they were completely immersed beneath the gently moving water; it was their Jewish custom. As they stepped out of the pool back onto the smooth stones that surrounded the pool, they noticed a few other men had arrived to bathe.

"The tall man in white garments is Geber." John pointed as he spoke. "Those men accompanying him are his disciples."

As both boys dressed, they watched Geber enter the water and stretch himself out prone beneath the surface three separate times. When he stepped out of the water, his disciples entered the water. Following the example of their teacher, they also laid their bodies beneath the water on the stones that King Hezekiah had commanded to be placed at the construction of the pool. Three times, the men completely immersed, cleansing themselves both physically and spiritually.

"God's Spirit speaks to Geber like it does to you and me," John commented.

"Are you going to become one of his disciples?" Jesus asked John.

"Maybe for a time," John answered. He sat on a rock and bent over to lace his sandals as he continued, "But for now, I need to speak to him about—"

"What do you need to speak to me about?"

John looked up to see that Geber had come over and was standing beside him. Immediately, John started to stand, but Geber casually motioned for him to remain seated while he sat down on another large stone.

"Last night, my father gave me his final blessing," John stated.

"Was it Spirit-filled?" Geber asked. "Or was it just the words of men?"

"It was Spirit-filled," Jesus affirmed. "The words of Zechariah were anointed and placed on his lips by the Spirit of God."

A little surprised that another lad, an obviously younger lad, had responded to his question, Geber looked inquisitively at Jesus.

"This is my cousin, Jesus of Nazareth," John responded to Geber's nonverbal question. "He was present, and he also had prophetic words for me."

"It must have been a very special Passover meal," Geber commented. Then prompted by the Holy Spirit, Geber asked, "And now what troubles you about your father's blessing?"

"My father expects that he will die soon."

"*All men are like grass, and all their glory is like the flowers of the field. The grass withers and the flowers fall, because the breath of the* LORD *blows on them. Surely*[1] your father feels the breath of the Lord and knows that his days are numbered. Does that surprise you?"

"No, but it saddens me," John answered. "When he passes on to Place of the Dead, I am to go into the desert regions to be instructed by God, and I am to remain there until God calls me into the work he has prepared for me."

"When Zechariah closes his eyes for the final time, come to me," Geber responded. "I will take you to my Essene brothers at Qumran. There, you will find time to study and meditate on the books of Moses and the prophets. There will be nothing to distract you from hearing the words of God for you."

"Not even possessions." One of Geber's disciples joined the conversation. "Everything you own must be turned over to the leadership, and you will live your life by the rules of the community."

"My father is an ordinary priest," John responded. "We do not even own the house we live in."

"There are many priests who have become part of the Qumran community," Geber asserted.

"Because of my lifelong Nazirite vow, I will never become a priest," John informed. "And because of that vow, I must be allowed to remove myself from specific circumstances. I cannot even bury my own father because I must not come into contact with a dead body."

"The brotherhood at Qumran will respect your vow," Geber assured. "And now—" He stood. "I must go and take my place on Solomon's Porch. If I am not early, the powerful men of the Temple try to make sure there are no unoccupied spaces for an itinerant Essene teacher named Geber."

"After we have cared for the animals, we will find you there," John responded as he also stood, preparing to leave.

"If I am not on Solomon's porch, look for me on the steps of the Beautiful Gate," Geber called over his shoulder as he turned away and began walking with his disciples up the stone steps, away from the pool and into the early-morning Jerusalem streets.

Ichabod used his arms to push down on the stone step and briefly lift his hips away from its hard surface. All those who stood around him had no comprehension of his daily pain. They did not know that beneath his robe, there were scab-covered sores, where, day after day, the bony protrusions of his skeletal frame painfully pressed his flesh against the unforgiving stone steps. After a few moments' respite, he lowered himself back into his typical awkward position, one hip taking most of his slight weight while his legs crossed at odd angles.

"Denarii?" Ichabod lifted his beggar's bowl as he caught the eye of Joseph of Arimathea. From conversations overhead near the Beautiful Gate, Ichabod knew he was one of the new young elders in the Sanhedrin and one of the wealthiest men in the city. It was rumored that even though he was one of the Sadducees, he was a good and generous man who stood in opposition to many of the politically motivated schemers in that judicial body.

The metallic clinking of coins assured the beggar the young councilman had added several coins to those already in his pot.

"Thank you, Honorable One," Ichabod called after the councilman. Then with his eyes, he scanned the crowded steps again. He was a professional beggar, and he knew the value of building relationships and making eye contact. "Denarii? Denarii?" Ichabod caught the eye of a tall man dressed in white, pacing back and forth on the steps as if he were waiting for someone.

In response to Ichabod's nonverbal communication, Geber stopped beside the beggar. "If I had possessions, silver or gold, I would share them with you. All I have, I offer you now—the word of the Lord through the prophet Isaiah, *Be strong, and do not fear; your God will come.*"[2]

"I hear Geber," John announced to Jesus as he turned this way and that looking for a tall man dressed in flowing white garments. "There!" John nudged his cousin and then pointed. "He is by the Beautiful Gate. Some of his disciples are with him. Let's hurry. People are stopping on the steps to hear what he is saying."

"*He will come to save you.*" Geber looked directly into the hurt-filled eyes of the beggar. He did not acknowledge the men who were stopping on the steps, drawn by the Spirit to listen. His words were a direct communication from heaven to this hopeless man. "*Then will the eyes of the blind be opened and the ears of the deaf unstopped. Then will the lame leap like a deer, and the mute tongue shout for joy.* [3] It is the promise of the Creator of all mankind for you. Hold fast to this prophetic promise, but until then"—Geber turned to the men who stood waiting to hear him expound on the words from Isaiah—"the eyes of the Lord are always on the poor, the lame, and the fatherless among us. His heart of mercy commands that we be merciful and generous, so bless this man today." Geber stepped aside so the men could press forward and fill the beggar's pot.

Ichabod did not know what to think about the teacher's prophetic words. He knew his family would consider them nonsense—the very idea that Ichabod would ever walk! In his mind, the mocking laughter of his brothers seemed to bounce off the ornate gate at his back. Still, he did know how to feel appreciation for the flood of giving the teacher's words had prompted. Money was still pouring into his beggar's pot. It was the one thing that allowed him to hold his head up in his home; he did make a substantial contribution to the family treasury. And upon the death of his parents, he would not have to depend on the charity of his brothers.

Jesus and John hurried to that section of the steps where they could see Geber standing beside a beggar. The steps were filled with men and a few women waiting to hear the famous Essene teacher.

"Is the Galilean the Messiah?" someone called up to Geber.

Another shouted, "How will we know which messiah to follow?"

Jesus and John pressed into the crowd, listening for Geber's response.

"You will know the Messiah has come," Geber responded, "when you see lame men walk"—he pointed to Ichabod—"when you see blind men open their eyes and break into uncontrollable laughter because they see the amazed looks on your faces. The signs of Moses will accompany God's Anointed One: food and drink in desolate places, not a feeble Israelite in his company. He will say, *'Purify yourselves and change your clothes. Then come… let us go up and build an altar to God.'*[4] *He will purify the altar by making atonement for it.*[5] *The messenger of the covenant whom you desire will come.*[6] *He will purify the Levites and refine them like gold and silver.*"[7]

Daveed, accompanied by Barabbas, pushed his way past the crowd that was gathering on the steps at the entrance to the Temple known as the Beautiful Gate. "Talk, talk, talk," Daveed muttered. "These teachers stand on the steps in the courts of the Temple. They have words and more words. It's time for action." The two men broke free of the crowd as they stepped through the gate and into the Court of the Gentiles. Around the colonnaded periphery of the court, they strode with deliberate nonchalance. Near the northern wall, both men paused to look up at the Roman Antonia Fortress. All along the top of that northern wall, Roman soldiers stood at their posts peering with unholy eyes into the heart of all that was Jewish and sacred in the land. One surly fellow caught Daveed's eye as he let a wad of spittle fly from his mouth down into the Temple court.

"Let him come down here and do that," Barabbas threatened under his breath. "I'll break his neck and then hide his body in one of the many tunnels under this place."

Without responding, Daveed led the way, slipping into a stairway that descended beneath the Temple complex to the men's cleansing pools. Pointing to one of several large enclosed pools, he said, "On the first day of the Feast of Weeks, your men can gather here. The Romans do not enter this area where Jewish men immerse themselves before entering the sacred Temple courts, and the Temple guard will not consider a gathering of Jewish men unusual. Those who are going to ambush the soldiers as they move away from the fortress to extinguish the fires can purify themselves and then pick up their weapons." Daveed led Barabbas through a narrow stone arch and down a dark passage. "Jethro will have weapons waiting here—slings, bows with arrows, darts, and small daggers. You will disperse weapons to each man who shows you the sign of the shofar."

"It will be done," Barabbas said with such fierce determination that a shiver ran along Daveed's spine.

"God will have to protect the Levite who wanders this passage unaware," Daveed muttered. He knew the young man who followed him would not allow premature word of the uprising to leave the underground passages of the Temple on the lips of any unauthorized person, and only dead men did not speak.

Leaning heavily on the arm of one of his disciples, Hillel slowly climbed the steps to the Beautiful Gate. Ichabod the beggar sat in his usual place. "Give the man a coin while I rest a moment," Hillel instructed his disciple.

He stopped on the steps, surveying the crowds, anticipating a week filled with celebration. At sundown, the first day of Unleavened Bread would begin. Then after a high Sabbath, the ceremonial harvesting of the first fruits would take place in a nearby barley field. Throughout the night, the first grain offering of the year would be prepared and then brought before the Lord. Hillel nodded with satisfaction. It was one of his favorite times of the year.

"*Surly the arm of the* Lord *is not too short to save* us from those who now occupy our land, *nor his ear too dull to hear. But your iniquities have separated you from your God; your sins have hidden his face from you, so that he will not hear.*"[8]

Hillel looked up to see Geber, the Essene teacher, expounding on the words of Isaiah. "Geber?" the aging and most prominent rabbi called. "Wasn't there a place on Solomon's Porch for you today?"

Geber stopped his teaching and responded to the president of the Sanhedrin. "Shammai's disciples had too many rocks tucked in their robes this morning. They were waiting when I arrived, eager to pelt us with stones and run us off. I took my disciples and left before they could get the satisfaction of inflicting injuries."

"Shammai, Shammai, so intolerant! And his disciples, sometimes they are more like thugs than scholars. I will speak to the captain of the Temple guard. If I ask him, he will reserve a place for you to teach."

"Thank you," Geber responded. "I treasure those times when I sat under your instruction."

"Then come after the Sabbath," Hillel replied. "Bring your disciples. I will be teaching while the first fruits of the barley harvest are being threshed and ground into flour."

"Will Shammai and his disciples be there?" Geber inquired.

"I am sure they will be there. They never miss an opportunity to refute my teachings, but there will be no stone throwing! I guarantee it!"

"Then maybe we will come," Geber replied as he gave a respectful bow to his former teacher.

Once more, Hillel supported himself by leaning on his disciple as he continued climbing the steps.

"That is the rabbi my grandfather wants me to hear," Jesus whispered to John.

"He is the most famous and important teacher in the Temple," John responded. "He has more than eighty disciples who sit at his feet and then go out and teach. They even teach Gentiles!"

"Geber?" Jesus asked.

"At one time, Geber was one of his disciples. As you can see, both men have great respect for each other," John answered.

"And Shammai?" Jesus inquired.

"He is another famous Pharisee who teaches in the Temple and has many disciples, but he is a hard man and a powerful man. Joram, the priest from Carem who is now overseeing the wood supply for the Temple, has told me when Hillel dies, Shammai and his disciples will take over the Sanhedrin. Then everyone who does not meet his inflexible standard of right and wrong will be stoned. There is no love in his heart."

"My grandfather says Hillel is a very kind man," Jesus commented.

"And generous," John added. "He does not just teach about good deeds. It is his practice to feed the poor and patiently answer even the slowest learner."

"Be in the Temple after the high Sabbath." Like the voice of another person who was physically present and part of the conversation, the words of God were clearly spoken so both boys heard them. "Listen to the famous teachers. And, Yeshua, speak the words I will give to you."

"I will sit at the feet of Hillel before we return to Nazareth," Jesus audibly stated his response before turning his attention back to the teaching of Geber.

The sun had dropped behind the rugged hills that surrounded Jerusalem. In the twilight, Jethro, accompanying Daveed and Barabbas, crawled down the steep sides of the Kidron Valley. Looking back up toward the Temple, Jethro could easily see the silhouette of the fortress where Roman troops were always stationed.

"From the fortress, they cannot see into this part of the valley." Daveed pointed as he laid out the battle plan. "Jethro, you and your men are to set fires close to the wall of the fortress. You can expect the guards to leave their post when they see the smoke, so you will have to get away quickly."

"Meanwhile, I'll light several fires further out," Barabbas added. "Then after most of the soldiers are outside fighting the fires, I will shoot a fire-tipped arrow into the gate."

"That will be the signal for our attack," Daveed stated.

Sounds of shouting and singing caused the three men to abruptly stop talking and look down the valley toward the bridge that led from the Temple to the Mount of Olives. "The people, led by the elders, are going out to harvest and bring in the first fruits of the barley harvest." Daveed informed. Each man slowly released the breath he had been holding.

"All of these ceremonies," Jethro commented, "they mean nothing as long as we have to do them under the watchful eye of the Romans! God will fight for us!"

"If we climb out of the valley close to the road, we can join the crowd at the designated field," Daveed offered. "Then no one will wonder why we were wandering among the boulders and shrubs in this part of the valley."

Jethro and Barabbas nodded their agreement as they started the rugged climb to the road that ran along the top of the ridge.

"Has the sun gone down?" Three men with sickles in their hands stood in the middle of the barley field, ready to harvest but waiting for the crowd to respond.

Jethro, Daveed, and Barabbas stepped onto the road that ran beside the field just as the crowd responded, "The sun is down. Swing your sickles and reap!"

Immediately, the three men in the field bent to the task of cutting three sheaves of new barley, already tied, just waiting for a blade to cut the stalks. With more shouts and singing, the freshly cut sheaves were passed to the elders of the Sanhedrin, who then led the procession back to Jerusalem, back to the Temple where the grain would be threshed and ground into a measuring bowl of fine flour.

Boiled eggs, new greens, unleavened bread, honey, roasted almonds, and water to drink—Mary had prepared as festive a meal as possible for their last night in Jerusalem. She rearranged the baked-clay cups to make a place for her father. He would share this evening with them. In the homes of the well-to-do, there would be another lamb or a calf, but this would have to be enough for Zechariah and John, along with her family, she thought as she looked over the serving table. "The meal is ready." She stepped to the courtyard to call the men.

Jesus and John were the first to rush through the door, diving onto the cushions Ruth had placed around the table. "We're going to the Temple tonight!" Jesus announced. "We will watch the Levites thresh the first sheaves of barley and grind them into fine flour."

"There will be teaching tonight," John added. "Hillel and his disciples will debate the mysteries of the scriptures."

Helped by Joseph, Zechariah took his place at the head of the table. "The famous Pharisees are speaking of angels and the resurrection of the dead again," the old priest commented. "They speak of those things just to annoy the Sadducees."

"You know angels truly exist," Mary inserted her opinion as she poured each person a cup of water.

"And I believe there will be a resurrection of the dead," Joseph asserted.

"Yes, but you boys need to be aware. Some teachers love to debate more than they love to speak truth," Zechariah admonished. "Listen with discernment."

"Hillel speaks truth," Heli asserted as he rearranged his cushions before reclining beside his favorite grandson. "Jesus, I will go with you this evening and stay long enough to make sure you are introduced to the great rabbi Hillel. I want him to know you are my grandson."

"Tonight," Zechariah commented in a quietly challenging tone, "the famous rabbis and their disciples will debate the fine points of the law and the prophets until the measure of first fruits' flour has been fully prepared for the morning sacrifice."

"All night and well into the morning," John confidently inserted his information.

"You will not bait me into pretending I am still young enough to stay up all night," Heli responded to Zechariah's subtle challenge. "I will only stay long enough to have a few words with Rabbi Hillel and introduce Jesus. Then if you have room, I will come back here to sleep."

"Yes, Father. Sleep here," Mary responded as she placed a basket of unleavened bread in front of Zechariah. The old priest reached out and felt the basket, then the bread, identifying it with his hands.

"Tomorrow, after the morning sacrifices, the people from Nazareth are gathering at the Sheep Pool to begin the journey back to Nazareth," Joseph informed everyone at the table. "We will begin the journey when the sun is at its zenith." He noticed that Jesus nodded as he received the information, and his past experience assured him that no more needed to be said to his dependable eldest son.

"Do not forget the goats need to be milked and fed before you return to the Temple, and early in the morning, their pens need to be cleaned. Also, eggs need to be gathered," Zechariah admonished John.

"And your father needs some assistance as he prepares for the day," Joseph quietly added.

"I will not stay the night," John offered. "I will return with Heli."

"But I could stay the night listening to the rabbis and then join the group from Nazareth at the Sheep Pool," Jesus suggested.

"It would be good for the boy," Heli urged before Joseph could respond.

With a casual unconcerned nod of his head, Joseph agreed.

And Jesus just grinned in excited anticipation as Zechariah blindly broke the unleavened bread and blessed it.

"The secret things belong to the LORD *our God, but the things revealed belong to us and to our children forever, that we may follow all the words of this law.*[9] This law that has been revealed to us is the law that was given to Moses. There are no other words and no other prophets that reveal the will of God for our lives! So do not speak to us of other messages or messengers from God!"

"And stop constantly speaking of the resurrection of those who have died!" another man from the Sadducee benches shouted.

Sitting on the hard stone floor near one of the columns of Solomon's Porch, Jesus shifted his gaze from the young scholars who represented the viewpoint of the Sadducees to those men gathered around the great rabbi Hillel. By the dancing light of torches attached to the columns, Jesus studied each face, wondering who would respond.

Hillel leaned forward and tapped a serious young man on the shoulder. "Nicodemus? How would you answer?"

A little uncertainly Nicodemus rose to his feet. "God did speak to Moses on the mountain where he gave the laws, but that was not the end. He continues to speak to men through his prophets: *The former things have taken place, and new things I declare; before they spring into being, I announce them to you.*"[10]

"You are quoting from the prophets again," the Sadducee scholars scoffed. "Show us in the Books of Moses. Show us proof of the resurrection!" they challenged.

Again, Jesus searched the faces of those seated around the famous teacher and leader of the Pharisees. Who would answer? He noticed Geber was present along with some of his disciples. He was certain the Essene teacher had a convincing response.

The fiery finger of the Holy Spirit reached out, tapping Jesus on the shoulder. "Speak, my son. I have given you the answer."

In immediate obedience, Jesus rose to his feet.

Neither Rabbi Hillel and his disciples nor the learned Sadducees took notice of the young boy who stood waiting to catch the eye of one of the teachers.

"Do not wait for permission from men, from angels, or from demonic spirits," God admonished. "Just speak, for I have given you authority."

In a clear voice that had yet to find its maturity, Jesus answered, "It is recorded in the First Book of Moses. Our father Abraham took his only son Isaac up to the mountain to slay him as the Lord had commanded. Knowing that he must kill his son, he said to his servants, '*We will come back to you.*'[11] Abraham did not know the Lord would provide a ram. He believed God would raise his son from the dead. Even Isaac believed in the resurrection and proved his belief by cooperating with Abraham. Both Abraham and Isaac were as sure of the promise of resurrection as they were sure that a mighty nation would come from Abraham through the seed of Isaac."

Every eye was now on the plainly dressed boy who stood and spoke correctly but with the accent of the Galileans.

For the first time in his life, Jesus felt the pressure of numerous inquiring eyes. His human instinct demanded that he step back and then remove himself from the uncomfortable situation as quickly as possible.

But the Spirit of God firmly directed, "Do not hesitate. Continue."

"Because of his faith in a future resurrection, Abraham purchased a cave where he buried Sarah. The bodies of Abraham, his son Isaac, Jacob with his wife, Leah, all rest in that cave to this day. Each one insisted that he be placed in that specific cave to wait as a family for the voice of their Creator to call them back to life. Abraham, Isaac, and Jacob all believed the promise of the resurrection was for them and their descendants. They demonstrated their belief with their actions."

For a few moments, there was silence as the greatest minds in the nation considered the words of a boy who had not yet been brought to the bema of his synagogue. From the stunned Sadducees, someone challenged, "Where would Abraham have gotten such an idea?"

"In the First Book of Moses, you will find recorded the generations of the patriarchs. Adam, the created son of God, lived 930 years. According to the scrolls that contain our most ancient oral history, while Adam still lived, he passed on to the firstborn of each generation the promises of God, which included resurrection and restoration to the paradise that was before the first sin. This promise was carried by Noah onto the ark, and it was passed on to Abraham, who was a young man when Noah died."

"Step forward," Hillel said, beckoning with his hand. "I want to see clearly who is speaking."

Jesus stepped into the open area between the two groups of debaters.

"You are the grandson of Heli, the scribe from Nazareth," Hillel acknowledged the seemingly insignificant introduction that had been made earlier in the evening.

"From Nazareth?" someone sneered while another laughed.

"Most of my disciples have not delved into the records of our oral traditions. They are the writings that contain mysteries too deep to be included in those scrolls that have been designated as scripture for the people. Where have you studied?"

Politely, Jesus answered, "During his lifetime, my grandfather, Heli, has amassed a large number of scrolls: the Books of Moses, the prophets and psalms, as well as additional books of Jewish history and tradition. All of these are always available to me. As the Spirit of God directs, I study these scrolls."

"That is difficult reading," Nicodemus commented. "Most boys your age, especially boys from the villages, can barely read the portion they learn in order to come before their local synagogue to celebrate taking on the responsibility of manhood."

"God has blessed me," Jesus modestly responded.

"I would like to hear the boy read."

Jesus looked into the huddled group of Sadducees to determine who had made the request. His discerning eye caught the approving nods that were directed toward a very richly dressed young elder. "Yes, Joseph! Make the boy prove his scholarship," another elder exclaimed.

"Bring a scroll and a table to place it on," Hillel directed.

Immediately, two scribes hurried off to the Temple library.

Amazed, Jesus watched as a table was placed in front of him and a torch lifted from its holder on the column and brought close. "We have a scroll of the writings of the prophet Isaiah!" Hillel's young disciple named Nicodemus laid the heavy scroll on the table, and he, along with another disciple, began to open it.

"Are you familiar with Isaiah?" Hillel asked.

"Yes," Jesus replied. "Isaiah speaks of the resurrection after he explains that God's Anointed One will be a suffering servant." He turned to the men who were unrolling the scroll, "Do you know the place I am referring to?"

Both men exchanged slightly bewildered looks and then turned to their teacher, Hillel, but before Hillel could instruct them on how to find the passage that Jesus had indicated, Geber stood and approached the table. "I am familiar with the writings of Isaiah," he said. Bending over at one end of the table, the Essene teacher and former disciple of Hillel began to unroll the scroll while the man at the other end of the table rolled until near the end of the writings, Geber stopped and stood up straight. Looking Jesus squarely in the eye, he asked, "Can you find the passage you spoke of?"

Nicodemus pressed a pointer into Jesus's hand and then held the torch so it illuminated the columns of Hebrew script.

For a moment, Jesus studied the Hebrew script on the open scroll. Behind him, he heard a soft snicker. "The boy cannot read!"

"He has fooled the great Hillel!" a bolder Sadducee shouted.

"Do not let taunting spirits that speak through deceived men intimidate you," the Spirit of God instructed. "Read!"

A portion of the scripture seemed to be suddenly illuminated. The Hebrew letters appeared to Jesus like fire.

Swallowing his amazement, Jesus began to read, *"He was oppressed and afflicted, yet he did not open his mouth; he was led like a lamb to the slaughter."*[12]

"Who are you reading about?" Hillel interrupted with a probing question.

"The Anointed Servant of God," Jesus responded.

"The promised Messiah?" Nicodemus incredulously exclaimed.

"Yes," Jesus responded with the simplest and clearest answer.

"Let me understand you," the rich Sadducee named Joseph challenged. "Is this your interpretation of scripture? The Messiah who we are expecting to deliver us from the Romans will actually die like a Passover lamb?"

"Yes. But he will also live again," Jesus answered.

"In these Temple courts, men have been stoned for saying less offensive things!"

Jesus sensed that a satanic spiritual wind had suddenly blown through the columns of Solomon's Porch. He turned to see that an obviously important man had entered the scholarly circle.

In the spirit realm, the Holy Spirit, like a flaming sword, barred the onslaught of the spirits of Religion that always traveled with Rabbi Shammai. "Silence!" the Holy Spirit commanded. "You will remain silent before your Maker. This night, you will not speak through Rabbi Shammai or his disciples. It is the will of God that you hear and carry back to your evil commander all the words that are spoken by Yeshua, Jesus."

Huddled and intimidated, the spirits could only nod their acceptance of the divine mandate.

"Shammai, sit down and listen to this lad," Hillel invited. "He reads Hebrew as well as you do, and his interpretations will make your mind leap and your heart burn." The famous teacher turned back to Jesus. "Continue reading."

Jesus read, "*For he was cut off from the land of the living; for the transgression of my people he was punished.*"[13]

Under heavenly anointing, Geber abruptly interrupted the reading to make a comment that was directed to Rabbi Shammai. "There is no other way to interpret this passage. Isaiah is speaking of the death of the Messiah. Very specific things are going to be associated with this death." Then Geber, looking over the shoulder of Jesus, the boy from Nazareth, began to read, "*He was assigned a grave with the wicked, and with the rich in his death, though he had done no violence, nor was any deceit in his mouth. Yet it was the LORD's will to crush him and cause him to suffer... the LORD makes his life an offering for sin.*"[14] Is not the Passover lamb a sin offering?"

"I see your point," Hillel agreed. "Now let the lad continue reading. I like the pleasant sound of his voice, and I want to hear his commentary."

Obediently, Jesus found the place where Geber had left off reading, "*After he has suffered, he will see the light of life and be satisfied.*[15] The Messiah, after he dies, will live again," Jesus stated. "I can see no other interpretation."

"My Messiah, the one true Messiah will die and then live again," the Spirit of God insistently repeated. "Know this. Be certain of this fact!" With a fiery finger, the Holy Spirit wrote on Jesus's heart. "It is the desire of God that his servant suffer and die, but after this ordeal, the faithful servant of God will live again and be satisfied with the fruit of his suffering."

Geber stepped forward to add commentary. "And the Messiah does more than just live again. The Messiah brings righteousness to our land. His war is not with the Romans." Geber looked straight at Shammai and his disciples and then at the Sadducees. "He will attack the corruption that begins in this Temple and spreads to every corner of the land!"

"Corruption! Are you accusing us of corruption?" As a group the disciples of Shammai and the protesting Sadducees took several intimidating steps toward the table where Geber stood beside Jesus, a few stones sailed through the air. Geber dodged two while one struck his shoulder.

"Send for the captain of the Temple guard!" Hillel commanded. "There will be no stone throwing tonight!" Turning to Jesus, who seemed a little bewildered by adults behaving like poorly disciplined children, Hillel said, "Come stand by me, lad. They dare not throw a stone in my direction."

With a clatter of metal on leather, the captain of the Temple guard, along with several of his guardsmen, arrived on the scene, expertly taking their places between the rival scholars.

"Come with me, lad," Hillel offered. "We will go to my chamber next to the Hall of Polished Stones. I have scrolls there that I wish to share with you, and I want to hear your commentary on several passages."

As Hillel stood, all of his disciples stood. For a moment, Jesus hesitated, but then Geber caught his eye and nodded affirmatively.

At that moment, God spoke, "You are my son. I have brought you here to speak for me to the spiritual leaders of this nation. Go with Hillel. I have placed my words in your mouth."

Within the spiritual realm of that Temple, there was a sudden flurry of dark activity as the demonic spirits who had been restrained were suddenly freed to return to their Evil Commander with this message, "Yeshua-Jesus is in the Temple. He is teaching, and those who love the word of God are thrilled. Come and see for yourself!"

The women of Nazareth stepped off the road into the first campsite of their journey back to their village. Mary lowered her pregnant body onto the hard but welcome surface of a boulder that sat by the road. Her sister, Salome, immediately took charge of the children, sending her two oldest boys to gather wood and start a fire. Then she directed Mary's middle children to fill the waterskins. Turning to Mary, she asked, "Where is Jose?"

"On his father's shoulders," Mary answered as she pointed down the road toward the group of men that was approaching.

"And Jesus?"

"Probably with the men," Mary responded. "He spent the night at the Temple and said he would join us at the departure point. I never worry about Jesus. He is so dependable, but James!" She looked at her second son chasing Salome's boys while Ruth struggled to carry two full waterskins. "I wish Joseph would hurry," Mary sighed.

"The men are walking very slowly today," Salome commented.

"It's Jethro," Mary responded as she pointed to the approaching men.

"Haven't you noticed him moving from man to man? See? Right now, he is huddled with both Moshe and Joseph. I don't want my husband to have anything to do with whatever he is planning! And"—Mary turned to her sister—"Salome, you had better caution Zebedee."

Salome's eyes dropped as she replied, "Zebedee does not appreciate my opinions."

"Then I will ask Joseph to speak to him," Mary offered.

For a moment, the two sisters communicated with just their eyes. Mary's eyes offered silent understanding for the difficulties Salome faced while Salome's eyes cried out in painful longing for the respect Mary received from her husband. With one arm, Mary reached out and pulled her sister to sit down on the rock beside her. "When we were young, we didn't know what marriage would be like, did we?" Mary softly commented.

"No," Salome agreed as they watched the men step off the road and join their wives at the various little campsites the women had established.

Swinging their youngest sons down from their shoulders, Joseph and Zebedee approached.

"Has the meal been laid out?" Zebedee immediately demanded.

Before Salome could respond, Mary pointed to the basket of unleavened bread she had been carrying and said, "A fire has been built, and by the time you men wash, we will be ready to eat.

Without being asked, Joseph bent and lifted the basket, easily carrying it to their small campfire. Mary followed while Salome lifted her own basket of boiled eggs and spring figs. Then she fell into step beside her sister.

"Joseph is very kind to you," Salome commented as she watched her brother-in-law set the basket by the fire and then take both Jose and James down to the tiny stream to wash.

"I know," Mary answered as she knelt beside the basket. "And he has taught Jesus to be very thoughtful also." As she mentioned the name of her eldest son, Mary began to look around. "Did you see Jesus with the men?" she asked her sister.

"No," Salome responded. "I watched nearly all the men leave the road. Joseph and Zebedee were among the last ones."

"Joseph! Joseph!" Mary pulled herself up and ran to where her husband was washing. "Have you seen Jesus? Was he with the men?"

Joseph looked up. "He said he would be with us. I thought he was with his cousins. James?" Joseph turned to Zebedee's oldest son. "Have you seen Jesus anytime today?"

"No," the boy replied as he ran off to get some food from his mother.

"Maybe he is with my father," Mary suggested as she looked around for Heli.

"Heli was walking with Zerah," Joseph responded. "They usually camp together. I will find them." Joseph hurried off.

Anxious and frustrated, Mary walked back to the campfire where Salome was feeding her family. "I cannot believe we actually left Jerusalem without being sure Jesus had joined our group."

"Don't blame yourself," Zebedee admonished. "Jesus is nearly a man. He knew when we were leaving, and it was his responsibility to be there. You and Joseph are too easy on that boy!"

"I'm going back to Jerusalem," Joseph announced as he burst into the little group eating around the fire. "Something must have happened to Jesus. He never joined the group!"

"I'm going with you," Mary exclaimed. "Salome, will you take Ruth and the boys home with you?"

"We will come and get them as soon as we can," Joseph assured Zebedee, who was scowling and muttering something about irresponsible young men.

Hand in hand, half running, sometimes stumbling, Joseph and Mary hurried through the dusk and the darkness back to the city of Jerusalem. The white light of a full moon made it possible for them to reach the city gates by dawn.

"Mary, I will take you to Zechariah's home," Joseph offered. "You must rest."

"We will go there and ask if they have seen Jesus," Mary responded, "but I am so afraid for my son I could not possibly sleep."

A squad of Roman soldiers marched by, forcing Mary and Joseph to step back against the walled entrance to the city. "I cannot forget Bethlehem," Mary whispered.

"An angel warned us then," Joseph responded. "I have to believe God does not change. I have to believe if Jesus is in real physical danger, an angel will come to us again."

"It could not be that he was just disobedient," Mary spoke more to her own confusion and worry than to her husband. "He has never been disobedient or unfaithful."

Joseph did not reply.

The taunting spirits of Doubt that had spoken through Zebedee had followed the couple. Now they spoke again, "There is nothing special about Jesus. He is like all other boys, disobedient and unworthy of the trust you have placed in him!"

Instantly, Joseph felt a surge of anger. How could Jesus treat his parents in such an inconsiderate manner! The words of Zebedee kept running through his mind—"Jesus is nearly a man. He knew when you were leaving, and it was his responsibility to be there. Joseph, you are too easy on that boy!"

Without explaining or understanding his thoughts, Joseph gripped Mary's hand and began to forcefully pull her through the congestion of people and animals at the city gate into the twisted and busy streets of Jerusalem. Pushing and weaving their way through the crowded streets, they hurried straight to the home of Zechariah and John.

Ichabod settled himself in his usual place beside the Beautiful Gate. Immediately, he lifted his beggar's pot and, with his eyes, began to search the faces of those approaching the gate. If anyone made eye contact, he would raise his clay pot a little higher and pitifully cry, "Denarii?" He also searched for those who were regulars at the Temple and who frequently dropped coins into his pot. Noticing that the young elder, Joseph of Arimathea, was approaching, Ichabod tried to make eye contact, but the wealthy new appointee to the Sanhedrin was obviously in a hurry. He only paused momentarily to speak to one of the Temple scribes. Ichabod listened.

"Is the lad from Nazareth still in the Chamber of Hillel?" Joseph of Arimathea inquired.

"Yes," the scribe replied. "He has been there for three days now."

"After the first day and a half, I had to return to my estate," Joseph responded to the scribe's affirmative answer. "I could hardly tear myself away. I have never heard such in-depth commentary on the Torah and the writings of the prophets."

"Even Shammai has been silenced by the boy's responses!" the scribe exclaimed.

"I must return to that room." With a swish of his brightly colored robes, Joseph hurried through the gate to the chamber of the president of Judea's supreme judicial body.

Ichabod considered the conversation he had just heard. Three days! This was not the first he had heard of an amazing lad from the region of Galilee who was captivating the minds of both Hillel and Shammai. In his heart, there was a burning desire to slip through the gate, to go where the disabled were forbidden just this one time. He would like to see and hear the boy all the intellects of the Temple were discussing.

Clink, clink! Two coins were dropped into his beggar's pot. Ichabod looked up to see Nicodemus, a disciple of Hillel. "My master said to tell you he has not forgotten you."

Nicodemus started to turn away, but Ichabod called to him, "Is the boy from Nazareth still speaking to the elders and scholars?"

"The boy is amazing!" Nicodemus exclaimed. "He speaks with the knowledge and authority of one greater than Hillel or

Shammai. At the same time, he is a simple and humble child. Hillel has sent me on several errands, and I must hurry so I can return to sit at the feet of this child." Nicodemus abruptly turned and hurried toward the closest market where food vendors supplied the numerous visitors to the Temple.

"Denarii? Denarii? Ichabod continued his plaintive cry to be noticed and monetarily supported.

Dry-eyed and exhausted beyond the point of tears, Mary waited at the foot of the steps below the Beautiful Gate. For the second time, Joseph was walking through the Court of the Gentiles searching for Jesus. He had been to the men's purification pools. Together, they had searched Solomon's Porch, the area where the money changers and merchants haggled, the Women's Court, and the area of the offering boxes.

"God? Where is Jesus? Where is your son?" It was a prayer Mary had repeated countless times in the past three days. She turned to a woman who was about to ascend the steps. "Have you seen a boy about my height? He has dark eyes and dark wavy hair?"

The woman responded with an incredulous look.

"I know the city is full of boys who are my height and have dark wavy hair," Mary responded to the woman's nonverbal response. "But he is my son, and he is lost. His name is Jesus."

"Many boys are named Jesus," the woman replied. Her tone was kind but without hope.

"He is brilliant and wonderful." Mary struggled for words that would set her son apart from all the other boys in Jerusalem and in the Temple.

"We are from the area of Galilee. He is a simple boy wearing plain homespun robes," Joseph joined his wife.

"I don't know." The woman shook her head. "Speak to the beggar. He sits at this gate every day."

Discouraged and overwhelmed with the task of locating one ordinary boy, they slowly climbed the steps together, stopping in front of the beggar who sat beside the gate. With a reluctant sigh, Joseph took one of his few coins from the pouch in his belt and dropped it into the clay pot that was sitting at the beggar's twisted feet. "We are looking for our son," Joseph spoke to the beggar.

"He is about my height," Mary added.

"From Nazareth, in the region of Galilee," Joseph continued. "He came to listen to the rabbis."

"Your son is in the private chamber of the president of the Sanhedrin," Ichabod responded. "All the rabbis and scribes are talking about the brilliant boy from Nazareth."

"Where?" Mary breathlessly asked.

"Near the Chamber of Polished Stones is the chamber reserved for the president of the Sanhedrin. Ask one of the Temple guards." Ichabod picked up his beggar's pot and turned away, searching the faces of the people, trying to make eye contact.

Breathless and hopeful, Mary and Joseph hurried through the gate, stopping the first Temple guard they saw. "Where is the Hall of Polished Stones and the chamber of the president of the Sanhedrin?" they both asked simultaneously.

"Our son is there," Mary added in a pleading voice.

"Follow me." The guard turned and led them at a brisk pace through the Court of the Gentiles and then through the Court of the Women.

Alerted by demonic messengers that Joseph and Mary were approaching, Satan left his observation post within the chamber of the president of the Sanhedrin. There, in the presence of Yeshua, he had been restrained, but as he moved away, he sensed the Spirit of God and the warring angels were not moving with him. He was free to act!

"Jesus has totally disregarded his duty to his parents." Satan drew near to Joseph, speaking lies into the minds of the distraught parents. "You should be enraged at this youngster who has caused such a great disruption in your lives." And to Mary, he whispered, "Your son has been terribly inconsiderate, not to mention disobedient. He is as untrustworthy as any other child."

At the entrance to the private chamber of Rabbi Hillel, a crowd of learned men, with their students, filled the doorway and spilled out into the adjacent area. As they approached, Mary noted many of the men were very affluent.

Arriving at the back of the crowd, Joseph and Mary paused. In that moment, they heard the familiar voice of their son. "Jesus!" they both exclaimed. Without hesitation, they pushed through the scholars until they saw their oldest son standing behind an open scroll, beginning a commentary on a passage he had just read.

Mary gasped. Her hand flew to her mouth. She did not understand. She only knew Jesus, wearing his plain homespun robes, was standing before the greatest men in the land, looking them in the eye, speaking in a forthright manner—

"Stop and hear your son," the Spirit of God commanded. "He has not finished speaking all the words of his Father God."

"In the last Book of Moses, it is clear that this Anointed Servant of the Most High will be from one of the sons of Jacob." With pointer in hand, Jesus began to read from one of several scrolls that had been opened. "*The* Lord *your God will raise up for you a prophet like me from among your own brothers. You must listen to him.*"[16] Those are the directives from Moses. Then Moses goes on to give the directive that came to him straight from God, "*I will put my words in his mouth and he will tell them everything I command him. If anyone does not listen to my words that the prophet speaks in my name, I myself will call him into account.*[17]

"Our most brilliant king Solomon understood the Deliverer who was promised to Adam and Eve as they left the garden would actually be the Creator, the Son of God." With the confidence of an experienced teacher, Jesus moved to another table where several scrolls were stacked.

"Can I help you?" Nicodemus stepped away from his place near Hillel.

"The proverbs of King Solomon," Jesus identified the scroll he wanted. With the help of Hillel's young student, it was opened, and Jesus began to read, *"Who has gone up to the heaven and come down? Who has cupped the wind in the palms of his hands? Who has wrapped up the waters in his cloak? Who established all the ends of the earth? What is his name, and what is his son's name? Surely you know!"*[18] Looking up at the assembly of scholars, Jesus repeated, "Surely you know." Then he expanded on the scriptures he had read. "The Deliverer, the Anointed One that you are expecting, will be both the seed of Jacob and the seed of God!"

Unlike the rabbis who suddenly began talking among themselves, Satan understood those scriptures.

And just to make sure there was no doubt in the mind of the rebellious archangel, the Spirit of God flew in the face of Satan and announced, "The seed of Adam and the seed of God have come together in this boy to take back what was stolen in the beginning!"

Every energized cell in Satan's body longed to attack the boy who stood behind the table filled with scrolls, answering questions and giving commentary, but that boy was shrouded in glowing holiness. Warring angels with raised swords barred his access.

Shrinking back from the flaming face of Holiness, Satan muttered his protest, "The Earth is mine!" Then in a frenzy of misplaced aggression, he turned on the people in the crowded chamber. His evil eyes searched for a target, for someone he could use to attack the boy. Joseph and Mary stood by one of the columns. With a single evil thought, Satan dispatched Rage and Misinterpretation, two of his most effective spirits.

It took only moments for the demonic spirits to prepare his targets. Then the Evil One bypassed Mary and approached Joseph. "Do not let your disobedient son speak another word!" Satan hissed. "Restore your authority."

"Son?" Joseph's voice cracked like a whip, slicing through the anointed atmosphere. The bulky, muscular carpenter stepped forward.

Jesus stopped speaking and looked up into the deeply lined, seriously disturbed face of his father.

"For three days, we have searched for you." Joseph's voice was forceful and filled with accusation.

"Three days?" Jesus repeated as it dawned on him; he had been unaware of the passage of time.

The famous rabbi Hillel rose stiffly from his raised seat and slowly made his way to where Joseph stood confronting his son and waiting for a coherent explanation.

"Your son has an amazing grasp of both the Torah and the writings of the prophets," Hillel offered.

Respectfully, Joseph turned his attention to the most prominent rabbi in the land.

"Would you consider allowing your son to stay and be one of my disciples?" Hillel asked. "I will take him into my own home and treat him like a son. I promise, one day he will be one of the leading rabbis in this city."

The Spirit of God broke through the angry spirits that were attempting to steal all reason from Joseph. "You were warned in a dream," the Spirit clearly reminded. "When you returned from Egypt, an angel came to you in the night and said, 'Take the child and his mother away from Judea. Raise him in the region of Galilee, in the town of Nazareth. Let it be *fulfilled what was said through the prophets: 'He will be called a Nazarene.'*[19]"

"His place is with his mother and me," Joseph firmly responded as his anger diminished.

"Can't I discuss this with you further?" Hillel pressed.

"No." Joseph's response was short as he turned back to Jesus, indicating with a quick movement of his head that the boy was to step away from the table and stand by his side.

"Go with your father, Joseph," God directed. "Your work here is finished for now."

Without hesitation, Jesus obeyed.

"Your son is gifted," Hillel tried again. "Is there anything I can say to persuade you?"

"You can apologize for tempting a young man to forsake his duty to his family and his duty to keep his word," Joseph responded. "And after that apology, we will return to our home in Nazareth."

"I do regret the anxiety and the trouble you have endured," Hillel kindly responded. "But I do not regret that before my eyes close in the sleep of the dead, my ears have listened to your son speak on the law and the prophets and that through his words, my heart has burned with the fire of the Spirit."

With a firm hand, Joseph nudged Jesus to step over to his mother. At the same time, he bowed and properly stepped away from the famous rabbi.

"Son." Mary turned to Jesus. All her pent-up frustration burst from her heart. *"Why have you treated us like this? Your father and I have been anxiously searching for you."*

"Why were you searching for me?" Jesus asked. *"Didn't you know I had to be in my father's house?"*[20]

"Later," Joseph curtly directed as he pushed both his wife and son through the crowded entry. "We will talk about this on the journey home."

The dusty road between Jerusalem and Nazareth was unusually empty and quiet. For two days, there had been very little conversation as Joseph and Mary, with their son Jesus, walked, keeping a brisk, steady pace, only stopping to catch a little sleep and then moving on.

"Father," Jesus broke the uncomfortable silence, "remember you told me I must listen and then obey the instructions of my Father in heaven?"

Joseph paused and turned to his son. In an accusatory tone, he responded, "Your mother and I walked for one whole night to return to Jerusalem. We spent three days searching throughout the city and in every section of the Temple. I walked through every passage. I spoke to the Temple guards. I even asked a Roman soldier if any boys from the area of Galilee had been taken into custody."

"We were terribly worried." Mary scolded.

"The Spirit of God was speaking to me, telling me those things I was to say to the rabbis and their students," Jesus said, pleading for their understanding. "Everything God told me I said."

"This is my son," the Spirit of God whispered to both Joseph and Mary. "He has been obedient to me."

Joseph and Mary exchanged silent glances. Then Mary spoke, "From birth, you have been a boy who is full of surprises, unlike any other child."

"It is beyond my understanding, so we will speak no more of this," Joseph stated. "Only do not let your uncle Zebedee know that you got off lightly. He expects me to take the skin off your back."

"I will remain silent about this incident," Jesus assured his father.

"Joseph!" Mary protested. "I do not wish to remain silent. My son stood before the famous rabbis, and they were amazed by his scholarship!"

"Who will believe you?" Joseph challenged.

For a few silent moments, Mary considered her friends, the women of Nazareth who gathered at the spring to fill their water jars. In her mind she could see each face. In her heart, she knew they would hear her story and then behind her back make it the target of their jealous and mocking gossip.

"You are right," she spoke to Joseph. "I will just hide in my heart the moment I saw my son teaching the Jerusalem teachers."

Chapter 11

FANTASTIC EXPERIENCES!

*The one who comes from above is above all; the one who
is from earth belongs to the earth, and speaks as one from
the earth. The one who comes from heaven is above all. He
testifies to what he has seen and heard.*

—John 3:31–32

"This camel is a little small for the loads we carry," Toma
commented to Bohan as he ran an experienced hand over
the flank of a young female Nodab had picked from the herd.

"She is a sturdy animal," Bohan countered, "and she can carry
more than the male you have just selected."

"For both the male and the female camel," Toma offered as he
poured a pile of silver coins into the balance scale that had been
set up before the bartering had begun.

Bohan waited for his eldest son, Lazarus, to counter the weight
of the coins with standard weights and calculate their worth, then
he responded, "I expected a higher price. After all, a male and a
female together have the potential to birth a small herd."

Shrewdly, Toma countered, "Did you expect to sell six of your
camels in one day? I am purchasing six camels and establishing a
relationship that has the potential for regular purchases."

Bohan glanced at the four camels Toma had already purchased.
He had to admit it was a rare day when one man purchased six
camels. "I will accept your price," Bohan replied.

Lazarus added the silver coins to the other coins Toma had already paid. He picked up the bag of money and abruptly turned and strode toward the house.

Toma watched, stunned by the anger emanating from the man who walked stiffly and swiftly away from the camel pens.

"You will have to excuse my son," Bohan broke into Toma's thoughts. "He has things on his mind."

"He has me on his mind," Nodab entered the conversation. "Father? You and I have made peace with the foolishness of my youth, but Lazarus cannot stand the sight of me. Only when matters of business force him to be in my presence will he allow himself to see my face. I do not want to live with this tension." Nodab looked at Toma. "Once, you offered me a place in your caravan. Is that offer still good?"

"We can always use a man who knows camels," Toma answered quickly.

"Son," Bohan protested, "this is your home."

"I know it is my home," Nodab responded, "but it is best that I do not live here. Life on the caravan routes is good, and I will come through Bethany and see you often."

"I leave for Petra on the first day of next week," Toma informed. "I will not be back until after the Feast of Weeks."

"It is not required that a Jewish man go up to the Temple for the feasts if he is not in the land." Nodab looked at his father as he offered this small appeasement. "But it is required that we live as peaceably as possible. Therefore, I must go."

"When I return from this trip, there will be a wedding feast in Bethlehem," Toma offered. "I am getting married. I will send a messenger to invite you. You and Nodab, even Lazarus, if he will come, can spend the week celebrating with me."

"Joy? Sadness? I do not know which emotion to express." Bohan embraced Toma first, and then he responded, "We will come." Next, Bohan turned to his youngest son. "Go with Toma. He is a good Jewish man."

Jesus briefly glanced up from the new gate he was placing in the garden fence. His mother had just passed by on her way to gather fresh greens from the garden. She had passed by slowly, laboriously carrying within her the weight of her unborn child.

"Your mother's time of labor is very near," the Holy Spirit informed Jesus. "No human ever knows the exact time when a child will be born, but in the spiritual realm, the signs are obvious. In the kingdom of your Father God, heavenly messengers post signs to announce every significant event."

Considering the information that he had just received, Jesus returned to the task of attaching a leather hinge to the wooden post.

"Ohhh!"

His mother's sharp unexpected cry caused Jesus to drop his tools and run to where she squatted near the bushy mustard plant.

"Help me, Jesus." Mary reached up to grasp the work-toughened hand of her eldest son, allowing his sturdy body to take her weight as she pulled herself up. "Help me back to the house." She paused and grimaced as another contraction captured her body and temporarily immobilized her.

Jesus waited, supporting his mother's cumbersome body with his own strong and youthful muscles. When the contraction waned, they walked together over the rough ground.

"Tell your father to send the boys to stay with my father." Mary paused while another contraction rolled through her body.

Jesus waited, not exactly understanding the process of birth, but relating it to the time he had watched as their only donkey had delivered her foal. He remembered how the animal's normal behaviors had ceased until the birth had been completed.

They started walking again, and Mary continued with her instructions. "Send Ruth to the well to fetch Salome."

Jesus helped his mother into the curtained alcove that served as a sleeping chamber for his parents. He watched as she awkwardly lowered herself onto her sleeping mat. She paused there, grimacing and gripping the rolled edges of the mat. Then with a brief shooing gesture, she sent him out on the errands she had just laid out.

In the carpentry shop, Jesus worked beside Joseph. It was the time of the year when the farmers brought their tools to Joseph for new wooden handles, and each worked on a different farm implement. Through the heavy wooden door that separated the living quarters from the shop, they could hear Mary's labored groans.

"How long?" Jesus looked up from his work into his father's deeply furrowed face.

"Only God knows," Joseph responded with a heavy sigh.

In his heart, Jesus then asked, "Father God? How long?"

"Your brother will be born when the conditions are right. Tell your father, Joseph, Mary is to get on her hands and knees like a dog. Then his third son will be born. After you give this message, tell your father I am calling you to come up into the hills for two weeks. I have much to teach you. Then you will return to the home of your grandfather, Heli, until the time of your mother's uncleanness has passed."

"Father?"

Joseph looked into the serious face of his eldest son.

"God says the child, your third son, will be born when Mother gets on her hands and knees like a dog. You are to go in and tell mother and the women to do this. Then I am to go into the hills for two weeks of instruction from God. When I return, I must stay with Grandfather until the forty days of my mother's separation has been completed."

For a very short span of time, Joseph stood by his workbench contemplating the things Jesus had spoken. Then with two firm steps and one decisive motion, he swung open the solid door that separated the shop from the house.

Jesus could hear Salome and two other village women who were assisting his mother protest his father's intrusion. Then he heard Joseph direct, "Jesus said you are to help Mary get on her hands and knees like a dog. Then my son will be born."

"Jesus said?" Salome was incredulous.

One of the village women emphatically exclaimed, "Jesus is a twelve-year-old boy, and he has no business commenting on the ways of women in childbirth."

"Get out of here, Joseph," the village woman commanded. "Your child will be born on the birthing stool like every other child in Nazareth."

"No." From her prone position on the mat, Mary entered the discussion. "Do not tell my husband to leave. Get me up on my hands and knees so this child can be born."

Moments later, Jesus heard the first wails of his new brother. He then began cleaning up his work area.

Joseph stepped back into the shop. "It's a boy. What would you like to name him?"

Jesus thought for a moment and then said, "Simon, son of Joseph."

Joseph nodded. "It's a good Hebrew name." He stepped over to a corner of the shop and picked up his cloak, the one he wore when he worked in inclement weather. "Take this with you." He placed the cloak in Jesus's hands. "I'll see you in a few weeks."

Sitting on Joseph's cloak, near the top of the highest hill that overlooked Nazareth, Jesus could see every house, every field. The people, small as insects, moved through their daily routines. Suddenly, the voice of God filled the mind of Jesus.

"I will show you, while you are with me on this mountainside, many secret things, secrets in the town that lies at the foot of this mountain and secrets in my heavenly kingdom."

Immediately, Jesus saw Moshe, the tanner. Moshe was so close; it seemed to Jesus that he was standing beside him.

"Watch!" God commanded.

Curiously, Jesus studied Moshe. The man moved several large rocks away from the mouth of a cave. Then he saw the tanner look carefully from side to side before dragging a small wooden chest from the cave. He opened the lid.

"Gold and silver coins!" Jesus exclaimed.

"That pitiful pile of coins controls him," God announced. "Watch. See how he counts. He is holding each piece like it is more precious than a member of his family. My message for Moshe and all like him is, *Do not store up for yourselves treasures on earth, where moth and rust destroy, and where thieves break in and steal. But, store up for yourselves treasure in heaven… For where your treasure is, there your heart will be also.*[1] Be aware, *no one can serve two masters. Either he will hate the one and love the other, or he will be devoted to the one and despise the other. You cannot serve both God and Money.*

Therefore, I tell you, Jesus, *do not worry about your life, what you will eat or drink; or about your body, what you will wear.*[2] Look around you, *See the birds of the air; they do not sow or reap or store away in barns.*[3] I feed them. I am sure you know, to me you are of much greater value than those birds."

The vision of Moshe hiding his wealth faded, and Jesus found himself studying a flock of sparrows flying in unison and then landing to peck small seeds from the wild grass.

"Birds are marvelous creatures!"

Startled by a voice beside him, Jesus turned abruptly to look into the brilliantly glowing face of a bearded man.

"Flocks of ravens used to come to my hiding place by the brook that runs through the Kerith Ravine. Each bird carried a small piece of food in its beak. They would land on a rock beside the stream and leave the food for me to eat."

"Elijah?"

The bearded man with the glowing face smiled and nodded. "Before you left your heavenly home to come to Earth, I called you Lord Yeshua, and you called me the Fearless Charioteer."

Jesus chuckled, and then unexpectedly, heavenly memory exploded in his brain, and he exclaimed, "You love to ride along the walls of the Holy City in the chariots of God!"

"Ever since I stepped into the fiery chariot of God that carried me away from this Earth, over the gates of the Holy City, and up to the portals of the throne room, I have loved the chariots," Elijah admitted.

"I remember when you arrived," Jesus excitedly replied. "In my mind, I can see it! I can see the golden streets, the beautiful city and the sea of glass, the angels, and my Father's throne. I see the enormous houses he is preparing for those who are willing to live with him. *In my Father's house are many rooms!*[4] There is room for every person who has ever lived and every person who will live."

"It is your Father's desire that you live in the certainty of his provision," Elijah instructed. "When you are certain that your Father will supply every need, then Fear cannot bind you and Satan cannot ensnare you."

"How can I be certain of God's provision?" Jesus asked.

"By experience," Elijah answered. "In the writings of Moses and the prophets are recorded the stories of great men and women who experienced the provision of God. Even my story is recorded. And you will have your own experiences. God will allow you to experience deprivation so you can receive from his hand." Then abruptly, Elijah seemed to change the subject by asking, "Where is your food?"

Jarringly brought back to the reality of his humanity, Jesus replied with a little concern, "I did not think to bring any."

"That is good!" Elijah nodded affirmatively as he replied. "Your Father knows when you are in need and how to fulfill that need."

"And now, Seed of God and Seed of Adam, the chariots of the Holy One and the armies of heaven salute you!" Elijah abruptly announced.

One lone shofar sounded followed by a deafening blast of staccato trumpeting. With one sweep of his fiery hand, the Spirit of God swept aside the veil that separates heavenly and Earthly reality.

"The army of the Lord!" Jesus jumped to his feet.

Glowing chariots, blazing steeds, warring cherubs, and magnificent seraphs paraded before their Creator.

"More than twelve legions are at your disposal," Elijah informed Jesus. As the seed of God, you have the right to command them. As the seed of Adam, they will stand by and wait for orders from God or the Spirit of God to act on your behalf. You get to choose."

Seriously, Jesus considered his choice.

"I came to defeat Satan as the seed of Adam," Jesus finally replied. "I choose to live completely as the seed of Adam."

The last fiery chariot had stopped nearby. From the back of that chariot, a man stepped out and approached. As he walked toward Jesus and Elijah, he spoke, "Adam was given dominion over the Earth. He was given much more authority than men today exercise. You have all of Adam's authority."

Jesus's mind whirled with questions, but before he could ask the first one, the heavenly visitor was at his side, giving him all the information he needed. "My name is Moses, and I wrote the creation story as God dictated it to me." The tall thin man, magnificently bearded and white from head to toe, placed a fatherly hand on Jesus's shoulder. "Every day, Adam was visited by heavenly beings. Angels, Yeshua the Creator, the Spirit of God, even Father God spoke intimately with him."

"He was warned about Satan," Elijah interjected.

"He was instructed in the ways of God's kingdom because he had been charged with extending the kingdom so it would expand from the garden called Eden into the whole planet called Earth," Moses continued.

"And every day, he was learning by experience and instruction what it meant to extend the kingdom of God," Elijah added. "As the seed of Adam, you can expect that kind of instruction, that kind of communication from heaven. It is your heritage."

"My heritage," thoughtfully Jesus repeated the words of Elijah.

Moses commented, "Actually, it is the heritage of all mankind, but few desire it and fewer seek it. So ask your Father God for the full measure of your heritage as a son from the line of Adam."

"You know, Adam was a son of God made in the image of God," Elijah interrupted.

Then Moses continued, "*Ask and it will be given to you; seek and you will find; knock and the door will be opened to you. For everyone who asks receives; he who seeks finds; and to him who knocks the door will be opened.*"[5]

Nodding affirmatively, Elijah added, "Your earthly father, Joseph, is a good man who knows how to provide for his family. You can approach him with confidence and ask for a piece of bread. You know he will not give you a stone to break your teeth on. You can ask him for a dried and salted fish. He will not give you an unclean snake to eat. You can be sure if Joseph, who has inherited the sins of his fathers, knows how to give good things to his son, then your sinless and perfect Father will provide every good thing for you."

"Now," Moses said, "you have not eaten in four days. Your body is young and still growing. Father God does not desire for you to fast any longer at this time." With a beckoning gesture, Moses summoned an angel who laid before Jesus a silver pot of white flaky wafers. "Manna," Moses identified the food.

"And water"—Elijah placed a crystal cup in Jesus's hand—"from the River of Life."

After a long swallow of water, Jesus reached into the pot and began to eat. "It is sweet!" he exclaimed.

"This bread from heaven is my favorite of all that is available to eat in God's kingdom," Moses stated. "It reminds me of God's unfailing provision for his people during their wilderness journey."

As Jesus ate, Moses continued to speak, "I *used to take a tent and pitch it outside the camp some distance away calling it a tent of meeting.*[6] When I *went into the tent, the pillar of cloud would come down and stay at the entrance while the* LORD *spoke with me.*[7] Whenever you come up into the hills alone, the hills will be to you like the tent of meeting was for me. The glory cloud of God will surround you and God himself will speak with you. You must come to him."

"Come often," Elijah admonished.

Then both men stood and moved away from Jesus. Both stepped into the same chariot, and before the amazed eyes of the boy from Nazareth, the chariot rose in concentric golden circles faster and faster until it created a blazing funnel cloud that extended beyond the boundaries of the sky. Up, up through the swirling glory, the chariot swiftly glided out of sight, and the boy Jesus was left sitting on a hillside overlooking Nazareth, breathless and amazed.

The sun was dipping below the rugged hills. Twilight was overtaking the villagers, urging every family to gather within the walled compounds of their homes. Women quickly left the spring in the center of town, each carrying a jug of water for their family. Jesus could see each woman enter her own home and almost immediately light an oil lamp. The men of the village left their fields and urged their animals into thatch-roofed sheds attached to the back of their homes. Jesus turned his attention to his grandfather's home. He could just make out his grandfather, along with Zerah, entering the house. He was glad his grandfather had a friend to share the evening with. More movement caught his eye. Stealthy shadowy forms moved from boulder to shrub, then quickly crossed the road and entered the shop of Jethro the blacksmith.

"My son, you are right to observe. I want you to see men as I see them."

The Spirit of God suddenly opened to Jesus a window through which he could see inside the blacksmith's shop. Men were leaning over a map that had been etched with a sword into the packed-earth floor of the shop. Simon stood at the door, ready to warn the men if anyone approached.

"These men have not consulted you," Jesus responded to the unspoken prompting of Father God. "They are making their own plans."

"How do you know?" God asked.

"I can see the demonic spirits named Hatred and Bitterness. I can see Murder and Chaos speaking into the minds of the men who have gathered. Spirits of Religion and Self-Exultation seem to be overseeing the gathering," Jesus precisely articulated his spiritual observations.

"These are misguided men who have accepted a twisted interpretation of the scriptures. They believe the Galilean is the promised Messiah and that I have sent him to engage the Romans in combat. They are expecting the heavenly host to fight with them."

Jesus interrupted, "Will the angelic warriors fight with them?"

"No," God answered. "My angels and my Holy Spirit will spare as many lives as possible, but they will not participate in a battle I did not plan."

"Why are you showing me the things Jethro is doing?" Jesus wondered aloud. "Do you want me to be involved?"

"No, I want you to know without a doubt that you are the Messiah and the Romans are not your enemies. I have not sent you to free your countrymen from the Romans. You left your place in the throne room of heaven to defeat Satan and his demonic forces. Your battle is not a physical conflict. Your followers will not raise swords or make claims on earthly territories. You will drive demons out and bring the hearts and minds of men and women into allegiance to me. In that manner, you will build the Kingdom of God on Earth. That kingdom will grow and push against the kingdom of darkness until all the people of the Earth have made a choice. Then I will take the land and destroy my enemy."

"My mother will be relieved to know I do not have to fight the Romans," Jesus commented.

"There is going to be bloodshed at the Feast of Weeks. Your friend Simon will need you."

"I questioned the validity of the mission Jethro is urging the men of Nazareth to participate in. Now his son, Simon, wants nothing to do with me," Jesus responded as he remembered Simon's stinging words and the rejection he had experienced as they parted company on the road to Jerusalem. "Since that time, Simon has not even looked in my direction."

"Nevertheless," God replied with full knowledge of Jesus's hurtful experiences, "be prepared to offer undeserved loyalty and support. Stand by Simon when everyone else has fled to a place of safety."

"I will," Jesus said.

"When you return to your home," God directed, "there will be just one week before it is time to return to Jerusalem. During that time, make a leather-and-wood chair for Ichabod, the beggar who sits by the Beautiful Gate. Take it to him on the first day of the feast because he will not be in his place again for several weeks."

As God finished speaking, Jesus immediately saw a picture of the chair that he was to make. It was low to the ground, a tanned goatskin stretched between three pieces of wood. There were handles for bearers. The picture was enough. Joseph had taught him well, and Jesus was confident that he was prepared for this assignment from heaven.

"Jesus? Jesus!"

Mary came bursting through the heavy wooden door that separated the carpentry shop from the living quarters. "Where are your brothers?"

Jesus looked up from the leather skin he was attaching to the wooden support of a chair. "James and Jose were at the threshing floor this afternoon, adding their weight to the threshing sled," Jesus answered. "But after that, I did not see them."

"The goats need to be milked. The chickens have stopped laying eggs. The stalls are filthy!" Mary's frustration was obvious. Baby Simon, in a sling that rested on her hip, began to kick and grimace, then he broke into a full wail. Mary gestured toward the road and added, "Your father is with the rest of the village men—in Jethro's shop! What am I to do? They'll all die." She muttered under her breath as she began to pace and jiggle the baby on her hip. "If the Romans get word of any gathering, they will put an end to it with their swords." She stopped directly in front of her eldest son and asked, "What should I do?"

Jesus paused for a moment, waiting to hear a direction from Father God. Then he smiled and replied, "James and Jose are busy throwing the already threshed stalks of wheat into the fire. My Father in heaven just showed this to me." Laying his hammer on the workbench, Jesus then added, "Go feed the baby, and I will take care of the animals. The hens will be laying eggs by morning."

Mary stood nearly speechless, wondering about this boy who would be thirteen next spring. Ever since he had returned home after two weeks in the hills and another two weeks with her father, he had moved through each day with unshakable confidence. "What about your father?" As soon as the question left her lips, Mary silently rebuked herself. She should not be asking a child about adult matters.

"Father hears the voice of God," Jesus assured as he looked directly into his mother's eyes. "He will not align himself with the enemies of God."

Immediately, the cloud of Fear and Frustration that had been smothering her all afternoon lifted, and Mary turned and walked lightheartedly back into her home. She closed the door behind her and said to herself, "What an amazing child!"

"We will not pay taxes to Rome again!" The Galilean was speaking to the men of Nazareth. "We will run those Roman dogs away from the Temple Mount and out of the country! The attacks that will take place as evening falls on the fifth day of the feast week will be just the beginning of a revolt. It will spread throughout the land. Our immediate goal will be to draw the Roman troops away from the Fortress of Antonia and then to secure it for ourselves."

"Your plan may be premature."

Joseph turned to see that Zerah, the synagogue teacher, now stood up to challenge the Galilean. "Do you know the Essene scholars have studied the scroll of Daniel and have concluded that God and the heavenly host will fight for us in about fifty years?"

"The Essene scholars?" the Galilean scoffed. "Those water-weak men who wash all day and fast until they only have enough strength to lift a quill, dip it in ink, and copy from one scroll to another? They know nothing about war, and they care nothing for this land. If they cared, they would leave their cloistered community and join with the rest of the brave Jewish men who are ready to take up the sword in the name of God!"

Joseph watched as Zerah silently sat down and Heli rose to his feet. "When Moses came to Israel in Egypt, he brought with him the confirming signs God had given him at the burning bush. What confirming signs do you have to show us?" Heli challenged.

All the eyes in the room returned expectantly to the Galilean. "Signs!" he bellowed his red-faced retort. "Aren't the Roman crosses that line our highways signs? Our youth pressed into slavery?" He gestured toward Barabbas, who leaned against the closed door to the shop.

"You state facts," Heli responded, "but those are not supernatural signs. Every judge, prophet, and king of Israel has received a supernatural sign or an anointing—"

"Be quiet, old man," one of the Galilean's men spoke rudely.

Joseph then stood and, without apology, asked the Galilean directly, "How have you inquired of the Lord, and what answer have you received?"

Without responding to Joseph's question, the Galilean turned angrily to Jethro, "What is this?" He gestured with sword in hand toward the circle of men who filled the shop. "I thought you told me the men of Nazareth were zealous patriots? Do I have to slit their throats tonight because they heard our plans and are not with us?"

"No!" Jethro protested in alarm.

Jethro's brother-in-law, Daveed, quickly spoke up, "Those who will not participate will not speak of this night or of our plans. All are trustworthy."

"Then leave!" The Galilean spit his words through gritted teeth. "If you will not take a weapon and fight, leave this place now and do not speak a word to betray your neighbors lest their blood be upon your hands."

Without hesitation, Joseph stood. As Joseph approached the door, his eyes met the eyes of the escaped slave. Silent acknowledgment passed between them. Then with a respectful bow, Barabbas stepped aside and allowed the carpenter of Nazareth to pass. Joseph did not look behind to see who followed him into the night, but he sensed at least half of the men left Jethro's shop.

Satisfied with his decision, Joseph walked across the road and entered his own gate. As he turned to latch it, Mary came up behind him. "Jesus told me you would not stay with Jethro and you would not take part in the uprising he is planning."

"Jesus always knows, doesn't he?" Joseph turned and pulled his wife into his strong arms.

"He listens to his Father," Mary responded.

"Good," Joseph replied as he led his wife to their sleeping chamber.

Outside their sleeping chamber, Mary hesitated.

And Joseph stopped to hear what was on her heart. In the darkness and the sweet silence of their own home, they stood comfortingly close and confident in their relationship.

"I do not intend to go to Jerusalem for the Feast of Weeks," Mary stated.

Joseph nodded. He knew she did not normally travel with a baby as young as their newest child. "The boys can also stay home, except Jesus."

"Will it be safe for you and for Jesus?" Mary held her breath as she waited for her husband's reply.

"We will be safe if we leave the city by the fourth day of the festive week," Joseph answered.

"Would you consider not going at all?" Mary asked.

"God has called all the men of the land to meet him at his Temple on three specific dates. I must obey." Joseph felt his wife's body close to his own, and he did not miss the way her body tensed as he spoke. "Three times in my life, the angel of the Lord has visited me," Joseph continued. "He told me to take you to be my wife. He told me to take you along with baby Jesus and flee to Egypt, and he told me when to leave Egypt and return to this land. I believe that angel will be sent to direct me again if there is significant danger."

In response, he felt Mary's body relax and lean lightly into his own. He knew she also held onto those memories.

Chapter 12

THE FEAST OF WEEKS

My kingdom is not of this world. If it were my servants
would fight.

—John 18:36

I chabod carefully cleaned the oozing sore that had developed on his left hip. He winced at the sting of the disinfecting wine and then sighed in relief as fresh olive oil soothed the raw tissues. He knew it would probably be best if he did not return to his place at the Beautiful Gate until the sore had healed over, but the Feast of Weeks would begin in just two days, exactly seven weeks and one day after Passover. Already the pilgrims were pouring into the city. They were coming even from the most distant lands. In the morning, the city would be packed with faithful worshipers. The steps that led up to the Beautiful Gate would be so crowded that people could barely move.

He liked being part of the flood of humanity that surged up to and through the most ornate of the Temple gates, and he liked to listen to the Essene teacher Geber. The Beautiful Gate had become the place where the tall white-robed teacher sat and expounded on the writings of the prophet Isaiah. He disliked sitting alone in impotent idleness surrounded by the upper class luxury of his parents' home.

With jerky but self-sufficient movements, Ichabod pulled his tunic down to his knees. Then he looped his folded cloak around his neck and across his chest. Carefully, he lifted his left hip, and using his very strong arms as well as his pitifully twisted legs, he scooted like an injured bug out into the courtyard of his home. With an awkward buckling of his extremities, he settled onto the pile of cushions his mother had arranged for him near the cistern where rainwater was stored.

The late afternoon sunshine was comfortable. Discreetly, Ichabod adjusted his tunic and his cloak so he could expose his sore to the sunshine without being indecent. Then he looked around. The courtyard was pleasant, but so empty. One of the servants walked through. Ichabod watched as the young man glanced his way and then averted his eyes. Who could blame the servant for not wanting to see such a pitiful sight? It would be better to be sold into slavery than to be a cripple.

Ichabod imagined he could think the young man's thoughts. Thank you, God, that I was born a poor man. Thank you that I could attain the lofty status of servant in this household. And thank you, God of Abraham, that you did not turn away from me at birth and allow me to exit my mother's womb with twisted and useless limbs.

Why me? Ichabod looked up and silently directed his query to the mysterious God of his ancestors, who lived beyond the visible heavens. As usual, there was no response.

Sweet and heavy, the aroma of anointing oil drifted through the courtyard. Without turning, Ichabod knew either his father or one of his brothers had come home. They worked in the family business of compounding the anointing oil for the Temple to such an extent that the fragrance clung to their clothing and their skin. A slight breeze swirled over the courtyard wall, stealing the sweet fragrance away. Without turning, Ichabod knew whoever had been behind him in the courtyard had moved on to another part of the house.

Ichabod remained alone with his thoughts. Why me, God? What was my sin? Did my mother offend you? Why were my brothers, who do not speak your name with reverence, allowed to learn the secret formula for the precious anointing oil while I had to become a beggar?

The answer to his question came rolling through his mind in the form of a memory. "Every Jewish man must have a profession." It was his mother's voice on a late spring day very much like today, only years earlier. "You cannot enter the Temple or touch anything that has been dedicated to the service of God, so you will have to be a beggar."

Ichabod remembered his oldest brother's taunt, "Is that a profession or just a level of life?"

"It is a profession!" His mother had risen to his defense amid the haughty snickers of the male members of his family. "He will sit at the Beautiful Gate of the Temple every day!" she had declared with a fire in her eye that had silenced them.

Ichabod looked heavenward once more and whispered, "Thank you for my mother." He glanced over his shoulder to see her approaching with a small vial.

"Your father sent some myrrh." His mother knelt beside him and poured a few drops onto the sore that covered most of his hipbone. "He wants you to be able to sit on the steps during the feast. It will be a good time for begging."

Ichabod nodded his agreement. "The days have been counted. Only two remain. The sheaves of wheat are coming into the Temple from every part of this land."

"Your father suspects that power is about to change, and it may happen this week," Ichabod's mother quietly informed. "For the past three weeks, Hillel has been confined to his bed, unable to attend council meetings."

Ichabod nodded. He had heard that the aging president of the Sanhedrin was ill. He had overhead many of the councilmen expressing their genuine concern. He glanced at the vial of myrrh in his mother's hand and knew his father's gesture of concern was tainted.

"Your father wants—"

Ichabod interrupted his mother and completed her thought, "To align himself with the right people."

Dropping her eyes, his mother gave only the slightest nod to indicate that Ichabod understood every aspect of his father's request correctly.

"Tell my father power will shift to Shammai when Hillel passes on to the place where the righteous wait for their Messiah. His followers are the strongest, the most vocal, and they have the ear of the high priest. Shammai will be the next president of the Sanhedrin."

"You always know," Ichabod's mother responded. "And your father knows, in your own unique way, you are a very important man in the Temple, a kind of gatekeeper who hears every man's secret." A little smile played at the corners of her lips as she continued, "Some men would pay much to hear what you hear and to know what you know."

"They would not exchange their healthy legs for my useless ones," Ichabod replied in an acrid tone.

Once again, his mother dropped her gaze. Ichabod's shame was her shame also. She had no answers and no response for her son. Without another word, she moved away, back into her world of directing servants and maintaining a home.

Following the men from Nazareth, Jesus led the donkey that pulled the cart where each family in the small town of Nazareth had placed their first sheaf of wheat from their plot of farmland, along with a small assortment of other produce from their gardens. The first melons from Mary's garden were tucked in a corner of the cart under the sheaves of wheat. The chair that Jesus had constructed for the beggar at the Beautiful Gate was also in the cart.

Celebrate the Feast of Weeks with the first fruits of the wheat harvest. This is one of the three times a year all your men are to appear before the Sovereign LORD *the God of Israel.*[1] Jesus considered the scriptural command that sent them on this journey: five days of walking and four nights of camping each way. On this unusual festive occasion, all the women and children had remained in the village. There were no antiphonal songs. The impending revolt had stolen the joy and excitement that belonged to the occasion.

From his vantage point behind the men of Nazareth, it was easy to see the men traveled in two groups. One group walked with Jethro in purposeful energetic strides. The other group gathered around Heli and Zerah. They walked with the somber strides of men who had no choice but to go where they did not wish to go. Both groups of men turned the bend in the road, and suddenly, Jerusalem could be seen. In the afternoon sun, its walls dazzled even the most somber pilgrim. The men walking with Jethro let out a cheer. Jesus noted that his grandfather was wiping tears from his face.

Joseph slowed his pace and fell into step beside Jesus. "We will only spend two nights in the city," he informed his son. "We will take the wheat to the Temple. You may find your cousin John. At midnight, the Temple gates will open again, and while the priests are examining the offerings the people have brought, the rabbis will be teaching. I know both you and John will want to hear them. At dawn, the sacrifices will begin. The high priest will lift two lambs and wave them before the Lord. I am sure you will want to see that. Then two loaves of wheat bread will also be waved before the Lord. After that, there will be numerous sacrifices, those designated in the Books of Moses and the freewill offerings brought by individuals. At sundown, all those who are not remaining in the city with Jethro will gather at our usual camping place on the Mount of Olives. We will sleep and then exit the city at dawn."

Jesus looked into the serious eyes of his earthly father. He understood that Joseph was remembering their last journey to Jerusalem. "Only a directive from my heavenly Father will prevent me from being at our campsite by sundown on the second day," Jesus answered.

"I would not accept that response from James," Joseph gruffly replied.

"I know," Jesus responded.

"But I accept your honest reply," Joseph affirmed, then he picked up his pace and rejoined Heli and Zerah, who were deep in quiet discussion.

On the walls of the city, Jesus could see the heavenly troops. Silently, he accepted their salute, watching with curious interest as one of the seraphs flew from the wall and came directly toward him.

Invisible to the other travelers on the road, Ophaniel fell into step beside his Creator. "There will be no uprising," the heavenly messenger informed Jesus.

"That is good," Jesus quietly responded.

"The Roman authorities have found out about the plans, and soldiers are lying in wait, ready for the Jews to make the first move," Ophaniel continued.

"Can I warn them?" Jesus gestured toward Jethro and the men who were walking with him.

"You can, and you should, but most will not listen," the angel informed.

"What will happen to those who do not listen?" Jesus asked.

"Some will die," the angel answered directly. "Your warning is life to those who will listen."

In his throne room, God stood and made a proclamation that resounded through the heavenlies, "My son, Yeshua, speaks for me. Every word that comes from his lips is a word of life, and those who refuse to listen and act upon his words will lose their lives. Some will be given over to my enemy, and they will eventually make their eternal home in the lake of fire with Death and Hades. But those who die with hope for the promised Deliverer in their hearts will go to Sheol to wait for their deliverance."

"It is the word of the Eternal God," the seraphs above the throne shouted.

The cherubim who supported the throne responded, "The Eternal One has spoken. His words are true and everlasting! Amen!"

"Amen! Amen!" the seraphs began a chorus.

The beautiful beings rose up from the foot of the throne in magnificent movements of choreographed praise. All of heaven was excited because additional authority had been given to Yeshua, a boy, moving into manhood.

On the dusty road to Jerusalem, Jesus passed the rope by which he led the donkey to one of the sons of Moshe. Then he hurried ahead to Joseph, his father. For a brief time, they walked together, heads nearly touching as Jesus shared the heavenly warning. Then without hesitation, Joseph strode over to the men who walked with Jethro while Jesus quickly returned to the donkey and took the rope again.

As Jesus walked, he watched. The body language of the men was as easy to read as the gestures of the demonic spirits that hung above them. He saw Moshe hesitate and then step away from the group. A few others moved with him to walk with Heli and Zerah. His friend Simon turned, and Jesus caught his angry glance. In a rash moment, Jethro put out his hand and shoved Joseph in the chest. Reacting instantly, Joseph grabbed Jethro's wrist and held it just long enough to issue a final stern warning. Then he abruptly released his friend and stepped away from the group that was determined to disregard all words of caution.

As they approached the city gate, Jesus continued to watch.

The spirits of Insurrection and Death danced in excited anticipation while the angels on the wall above the gate wept.

Within the first mile marker from the city wall, all movement toward the city slowed as the population on the road funneled through the open archways into the narrow twisted lanes of Jerusalem. Each man retrieved his own sheaf of wheat. Some with stony determined silence, others with, "See you on the Mount of Olives."

"Simon?" Jesus called to his friend as he approached the cart with his father.

"Traitor!" Simon responded. "You didn't have to make up some story about angels telling you the Romans know and they are waiting for us! I don't believe a word of it. You don't see angels! They don't talk to you! You are just crazy and weird!"

Jesus blinked back his tears. He did not know what to say. How could he convince someone who was so adamantly determined to reject his message?

The cart was empty except for their own sheaf of wheat, a little food, and the chair that Jesus had made. "Near the Temple, the streets are too crowded for a donkey and cart," Joseph said as he placed a comforting had on his son's shoulder. "Take your chair to the beggar. I will take the donkey and cart to the home of Zechariah, then I will meet you on the steps in front of the Beautiful Gate."

Jesus knew his father had heard Simon's ugly words. The heavy comfort of his hand was appreciated. "I will be there," Jesus answered.

Above the chatter of the masses, Jesus heard a strong male voice. "*This is what the* LORD *says: 'Maintain justice and do what is right, for my salvation is close at hand and my righteousness will soon be revealed.'*"

Jesus pushed his way through the crowd toward the spot where Geber, the Essene teacher, stood close to Ichabod delivering the words of the prophet Isaiah to the people. At the top step that widened into a platform, Jesus approached the beggar who always sat there. As he drew near, the beggar fixed him with an expectant gaze and lifted his clay bowl.

"My gift will not fit in your bowl." Jesus lifted the low leather chair up onto the platform where Ichabod sat. "This is for you. God, the Father of all, desires that you sit comfortably. See"—Jesus placed his hand under the leather seat—"you will be about a hand's width above the stone steps."

"God, my Father?" Ichabod repeated in dumbfounded amazement.

"Father God," Geber restated as he stepped over to the place where Jesus stood next to the beggar. "I know this boy." Geber nodded toward Jesus. "He is filled with the Spirit of God. You can believe God sent this gift to you through this lad. So come, let me see you get yourself into the seat."

Jesus watched as the beggar used both his strong arms and his deformed legs to shuffle off of his mat. With a little lifting of his bottom, he rested comfortably in the soft leather of the chair. "Father? He could walk if you would say the word." Jesus directed his silent request heavenward.

"The time has not come for you to publicly heal the sick and cast out demons. That time is in the future," God responded.

With a small bowing of his head, Jesus accepted Father God's answer.

A disturbance on the steps caused the people to jostle and press against each other. Jesus looked up to see Shammai and his disciples ascending the steps as a unified force, thoughtlessly pushing the people aside. Upon reaching the top step, the famous teacher paused within a few feet of Geber. Looking the popular Essene teacher in the eye, he said, "I have just come from the home of Hillel, your powerful protector. Within a few days, he will go to the place of the righteous dead, and I will take his seat as president of the Sanhedrin. My first act will be to bring you before the court. I will try you for speaking against this Temple and its functions."

With merely human senses, it was easy to see the snickers that passed among Shammai's disciples. With divinely opened eyes, Jesus could see how the evil spirits moved and carried those snide snickers from person to person.

Instantly, there was a heavenly response. The air crackled with the divine presence of the Spirit of God. Jesus felt the warmth of his presence before he heard the Holy Spirit speaking forcefully through Geber, "*Because the Sovereign LORD helps me, I will not be disgraced... He who vindicates me is near. Who then will bring charges against me? Let us face each other! Who is my accuser? Let him confront me! It is the Sovereign LORD who helps me.*[3] I can walk in darkness because God is my light, but you must provide yourselves with flaming torches, *so; go walk in the light of the torches you have set ablaze. This is what you shall receive from the hand of the LORD: You will lie down in torment.*"[4]

"Say no more!" Shammai took a step back, then quickly removed himself from the intimidating Spirit of God that was like a wall of fire between himself and the Essene teacher.

Again, Geber turned to the people and resumed teaching. "Do not concern yourselves with evil men. The word of the Lord through the prophet Isaiah is, *There is no peace... for the wicked.*[5] *Hear me, you who know what is right, you people who have* God's *law in your hearts: Do not fear the reproach of men or be terrified by their insults. For the moth will eat them up like a garment; the worm will devour them like wool. But the righteousness of Almighty God will last forever.*"[6]

In his heart, Jesus felt a stirring, and in his mind, he heard the voice of Father God. "These words have been spoken this day for you. Never fear the reproach of any one."

In silent acknowledgment, Jesus momentarily bowed his head. When he looked up, Geber was gazing directly into his eyes, and he was so moved by the Spirit that to the divine eye of the son of Mary, he glowed. "Who will believe what I now say? The Anointed Messenger of the Lord is being taught by God. He is growing up before the God of Abraham *like a tender shoot... He* has *no beauty or majesty to attract us to him, nothing in his appearance that we should desire him.*"[7]

Geber paused and made eye contact with the people who had pressed close to listen. "We have seen God's Anointed One, but his appearance was ordinary so we did not worship him. When the time comes and God reveals his messenger, you will be surprised. You expect a splendid royal warrior. Instead you will see what appears to be an ordinary man who has been rejected and experienced painful sorrows." Turning back to look directly at Jesus, Geber continued his prophetic utterance, "The messenger that God has promised will understand heartbreak and death in the most personal terms."

"Through my own words," God announced, "through heavenly messengers, and through the Spirit-filled mouths of men, my son, Yeshua, will be confirmed and built up in his spirit so that he is prepared for all things."

At that moment, Joseph pushed through the crowd. Bypassing Jesus, he went directly to Geber. "John, son of Zechariah, has sent me with this message. His father, the aging priest, did not get up from his bed this morning. When the lad went in to assist him, he found that his father's breath was gone."

Before Joseph could continue, Geber turned to his disciples and said, "Go to John, the lad who is a Nazirite. Perform all that is necessary for the burial of his father because his vow forbids that he touch the dead. Then bring the lad to me, and together we will go to our brothers in Qumran." Geber then turned back to Joseph. "I know you are family. These plans were made before the fact of Zechariah's death."

Joseph agreed, "They are good plans."

"Father?" Jesus started to speak, but he could not finish his thought.

Bursting out from the Court of the Gentiles through the Beautiful Gate, a squadron of armed Roman soldiers began roughly pushing the people off the steps. "No more gatherings! By order of the governor of the land of Judah and the Roman Empire!"

Urgently, Joseph shielded Jesus from the shoving soldiers. The crush of the frantic crowd prevented them from descending the stairs, so they found themselves huddled between the outer wall and the backside of the Beautiful Gate. The beggar was also there, tumbled and bruised. In anxious silence, the trio waited for the melee to flow down the steps and into the streets of the city.

Somehow, Geber and his disciples managed to move with the fleeing people. Soon after the top step cleared, Temple servants hurried to Ichabod. Lifting him in the chair Jesus had made for him, they carried the beggar away from the Beautiful Gate.

Joseph then took Jesus by the shoulders and guided him down the steps into the street. "What has happened?" Joseph asked the first man who would pause long enough to respond.

"Men from Galilee were attempting an uprising," the man responded. Then he paused and looked directly at Joseph, "You're from Galilee! Your accent betrays you. Be careful to whom you speak. You may be accused."

"Jethro?" Jesus whispered his concern.

"Who have they captured, and where have they taken them?" Joseph pressed the man for information.

"The men were caught placing weapons in the passages beneath the Temple," the man continued. "They were taken to the Fortress of Antonia. You can be sure that after sundown, they will be tried. The sentence will be carried out at dawn."

Both Joseph and Jesus gasped.

Responding to their alarm, the man added, "A few escaped."

"The soldiers are looking for Galileans, aren't they?" Joseph assumed aloud.

"Yes," the men agreed. "So take your son and leave the city."

Like so many others, the man turned and walked quickly away from the Temple. Now there were more people hurrying away from the Temple than coming toward it. Joseph and Jesus stood in the street with the crowd passing them on both sides.

"What should we do?" Jesus asked both his earthly and heavenly Father simultaneously.

"We'll go to the Mount of Olives," Joseph responded. "The men from Nazareth will gather there. Then we can see who is missing."

Jesus did not receive a direct response from heaven, but the peace he had with his father's directions was sufficient assurance. They were responding correctly.

Night fell on the solemn group of men from Nazareth. They huddled against the rough bark of the ancient olive trees. Too fearful to light a fire, too distressed to sleep, they waited for dawn, hoping that Jethro, Simon, Daveed, and Ezra, son of Samuel, would walk into camp. Just before dawn, Zebedee, with his sons, James and John, came into camp. He wanted to be sure Joseph and Jesus were safe.

Then the sun rose, and the men could hardly believe their eyes. The bridge between the Mount of Olives and the city was lined with Roman soldiers.

Terror grabbed the heart of every man on the Mount.

"Yeshua!" God spoke into the mind of his son. "Turn away from the bridge and look down into the valley."

Jesus pulled his eyes away from the awesome might of Rome. Immediately, he spotted some movement in the tall grass that grew between the boulders in the valley.

"Simon!" Jesus knew instantly it was his friend attempting to make his way to the encampment. Pausing just long enough to direct Joseph's attention to the boy who was struggling through the rough terrain, Jesus dashed down the mountainside with Joseph close behind him.

Joseph reached Simon first and scooped the boy into his strong protective arms. "Where is your father?" he asked as he pressed the boy against his chest.

"The Romans," Simon sobbed. "They caught him and took him away. Last night, there was a trial."

"What are they going to do to him?" Jesus asked.

"Don't ask." Joseph tried to signal Jesus not to probe into all the distressing possibilities.

"The Romans will crucify Simon's father," God revealed the heartbreaking facts.

Emotional agony like physical pain rolled through Jesus.

"Put aside your own pain," God instructed. "Care for your friend."

"Look!" A shout went up from the men standing near the top of the Mount.

Jesus and Joseph both looked up. They could see two Jewish men forced to stumble across the bridge. The crossbeams that would be attached to the upright posts at the place of execution were strapped across their shoulders.

Simon started to turn his head to look, but Joseph quickly pushed the boy's face back into the folds of his robe. "Let's get up to the men of Nazareth," Joseph urged as he helped Simon to his feet, guiding him up the boulder-strewn incline. Jesus led the way while Joseph made sure his own body blocked Simon's view of the road.

At the camp, the men were gathering their belongings. Moshe breathlessly returned from the point where the road met the bridge. "It's Jethro and his brother-in-law, Daveed. I did not see Ezra, but I heard one man say they had another Galilean imprisoned."

A collective groan went up from the men.

"We had better leave before we are taken in for questioning," Moshe added.

"I cannot leave my father." Simon's young voice brought every man to a standstill.

For the first time, the men noticed Joseph coming toward them holding Simon firmly within the circle of his right arm.

Moshe ran forward with both arms extended toward the boy. "You cannot help your father. You need to return home to your mother."

"I will not desert my father!" Simon angrily wrenched himself away from Joseph, but he was only able to take a few desperate steps before Jesus, along with a few of the men, caught and subdued the boy.

As Jesus held his friend struggling and sobbing in his arms, his own eyes locked with the eyes of Joseph, his father. "He cannot leave his father," Jesus communicated.

And Joseph nodded his understanding.

"Jesus and I will follow at a distance," Joseph announced. "The rest of you return to our village."

"It is too dangerous!" Moshe exclaimed.

"Son"—Heli took several steps toward Joseph—"Mary will be very concerned."

"Tell her to sit with Jethro's wife. Assure her. I will return with both boys when everything pertaining to this matter has received the necessary attention."

The rest of the men were already moving down the incline toward the road that would take them home. They were going back into the city and out through a gate on a road that did not pass by the place of crucifixion.

"Go on." Joseph gestured toward Moshe and Heli. "I will be careful." He turned to Simon and Jesus. "Come, boys." Taking one under each arm, they began walking slowly toward the road that led north, to the place of execution.

What do I say? Joseph silently addressed the God who had spoken to him very clearly on a number of occasions. How do I explain to these boys that I am helpless? I cannot prevent this execution. I can only hope to offer comfort to Simon and to return him safely to his mother.

"In a way, I am as helpless as you," God spoke through his Spirit into the heart of Joseph. "I have limited myself by allowing man to make choices that have consequences. Jethro chose to be involved in this revolt, and he refused to heed every warning. I could not undo the consequences for Adam and his dear wife, Eve. Neither can I undo the consequences for Jethro."

The place of execution was in sight. Close to the road, two posts planted in the rocky soil stood upright, almost touching a large rock shaped somewhat like a skull. Ominously, the gray-and-white rock overshadowed the heart-wrenching place.

The soldiers, with their prisoners, had arrived. Two large signs that read Insurrectionist were placed on high ledges that had been carved into the strangely pocketed rock. Joseph could see that Jethro and Daveed were flat on the ground. He saw a soldier carry some iron spikes and drop them on the ground near the men. This was too much for Simon and Jesus to witness. He, a grown man, did not think he could watch.

Joseph stopped walking and turned both boys around so they could not see. He urged them to the side of the road, pushing them down so all three huddled together with their backs to the dreadful scene.

"What is going to happen?" Simon asked in a quivering voice.

"Your father is going to rest with all the faithful sons of Abraham," Jesus quickly responded.

"You mean he is going to die," Simon sobbed. "They are going to kill him."

"I wish I could tell you that is not going to happen," Joseph answered as he pressed the boy into his own body with all his strength. "I wish I could stop the soldiers, but—"

Suddenly, the air was filled with pleas for mercy and pleas for a quick death. The heavy hammer slammed against the head of an iron spike, and one of the men screamed. Joseph moaned. The boys sobbed and shook. Each strike, hammer against spike, set off a new round of screams and sobs, wails and moans.

"My father, my father," Simon wailed.

"My friend, my friend," Joseph moaned.

"My Father? My Father? How can you allow such suffering?" Jesus sobbed his grief-filled question.

"My heart is breaking," God responded. "I am sobbing with you."

"What can you do?" Jesus asked.

"Both Jethro and Daveed are sons of the covenant, so they will wait with Abraham, David, and all those I love. It is a pleasant and protected waiting."

"What are they waiting for?" Jesus asked as he struggled to see beyond the tragedy of the moment.

"These two men and all those who are in covenant relationship with me are waiting for my Righteous Son to take the keys to the gates of Sheol away from my enemy. For now, both the righteous and the wicked wait in the place of death, but the day is coming when you will break down the gates and my righteous ones will follow you to our heavenly home."

The flaming hand of the Holy Spirit suddenly pulled aside the veil that separates the spiritual realm from the physical world so Jesus could see the place—a deep valley. A river ran through the middle of the valley. One side was green and pleasant, the other side burned and barren. "This is Sheol, the Place of the Dead," God explained. "The gate is at the mouth of the river."

The hammering had stopped. Only the clattering of metal against leather and then the measured steps of the soldiers could be heard as most of the squad returned to their fortress beside the wall of Jerusalem. When the soldiers were well down the road and around the bend, Joseph said to the boys, "Wait here. Do not leave this spot and do not turn around until I return." Then he pushed Simon into Jesus's arms and climbed up onto the road.

Joseph could see only two soldiers had been left to guard his friends on their crosses. The soldiers had moved a short distance away to a bench that had been constructed just for those left to guard the dying.

Cautiously, the carpenter from Nazareth approached. "Oh, Lord, have mercy," he prayed as he walked.

One of the soldiers looked up.

Joseph could tell he was Syrian. "Lord, do not let his natural prejudice be aroused."

The soldier stood and placed one hand on the dagger attached to his leather girdle. "Do you know these men?" he asked while nodding curtly toward the crosses.

"One man is my neighbor," Joseph answered. "He came to Jerusalem to celebrate the feast with his son. The boy is with me." Joseph gestured toward the two boys huddled on the side of the road. "The boy wants to say good-bye to his father."

"Insurrectionist?" the soldier still sitting on the bench sneered his accusation.

"Neighbor," Joseph countered. "I have his twelve-year-old son with me. He needs to say good-bye to his father while his father can still speak."

"You have a father," the Holy Spirit reminded both soldiers. "If your father was on his deathbed or on a Roman cross, wouldn't you want to comfort him?"

The soldier who was standing nodded silent permission.

Then before Joseph turned to get the boys, he made one more request, "Can you give the men something for their pain?"

"Vinegar mixed with gall," the soldier replied.

"Do it please," Joseph said as he turned to hurry back down the road to get the boys and bring them to the foot of Jethro's cross.

What can I say? How long should I allow the boys to stay? Mary was right. I should have tried harder to dissuade Jethro from this Zealot foolishness. "Jesus, Simon, we can go to the foot of the cross," Joseph spoke as he approached the boys. "Simon," Joseph said the boy's name as he drew him securely into the crook of his arm. "Your father is in pain. Try not to add to his distress. Assure him. Tell him you can run the blacksmith shop and you can care for your mother."

As they approached the crosses, both soldiers stepped silently aside. Simon broke free from Joseph's protective embrace and flung himself into the dirt at the foot of his father's cross. At first, he just sobbed. Then he looked up into the strong face he loved and said, "I will never forget all the things you taught me."

"I will care for your son and your family." Joseph stepped up to steady Simon and look into the face of his lifelong friend.

"Tell my wife..." Jethro gasped then continued, "to go..." He gasped again before finishing, "to her brother in Cana. And Simon—" There was a long shuddering pause as Jethro's muscles went into uncontrollable spasms. "I love you...Now... you must...leave this...place." There was another long pause in the conversation as Jethro struggled to breathe. When he could speak again, he said, "Joseph, take...my boy...away. And do not let...that traitor, Ezra...return to...Nazareth."

"Yes, my friend," Joseph spoke as he pulled Simon up from the ground, away from the crosses.

He could hear Daveed, crying, gasping for breath and saying to the soldier who stood beside him, "Just kill me...Use your spear...and end...my...life."

Half pulling, half carrying, Joseph, with the help of Jesus, moved Simon away from the crosses. They found a place down the road where they could not hear but could still see the men on the crosses. Together, they waited without food or water for five nights and four days.

Jethro's wife and daughter found them there. When the soldiers removed the bodies from the crosses, they buried both Jethro and Daveed.

Chapter 13

A Wedding in Bethlehem

*The kingdom of heaven is like a merchant looking for fine
pearls. When he found one of great value, he went away and
sold everything he had and bought it.*

—Matthew 13:45–46

"Over here." Barabbas led the way into the blackness of a
cave in the Judean wilderness not far from Jerusalem.
He pointed to a level area, and the men following him carefully
lowered the body of their leader, Judah the Galilean, onto the
hard rock surface.

"He's still breathing." From a kneeling position beside
their would-be messiah, one of the men informed his fellow
revolutionaries, "We need some water and some wine. Maybe we
can clean the wound. Possibly, he will survive."

"You two." Barabbas tapped two men on their shoulders. "Go
find water, wine, and some food." Then he turned to another pair
of men. "Locate Ezra, son of Samuel. The Romans should be
releasing him soon. He is the one who sent word of our mission
ahead of us, and he was one of the witnesses at the trial. Make
sure he does not return to his home and his wife."

Muttering their mutual agreement along with their bloody
plans for revenge, two more of the Galilean's men exited the cave,
leaving Barabbas with two other rebels to care for their fallen
leader and make plans for the future.

"We need a fire and a lookout." Barabbas set the remaining men to work. Then he knelt beside his fallen leader. His eyes had adjusted to the darkness of the cave, but even then, there was only enough light to see large shapes without details. Without seeing, he pushed aside the blood-stiffened robe that covered the Galilean's wounds. With his hands, he began to feel, starting at the man's shoulders and moving down across his chest and abdomen, trying to assess the extent of his injuries.

The wound Barabbas found with his fingers was abdominal, a clean slice across the width of the lower belly. The ex-slave considered the location and size of the wound and then concluded that in spite of the bleeding, if the blade had not penetrated too deeply, Judah the Galilean could possibly recover. Under his probing fingers, Barabbas felt his leader move. Then he heard a soft moan.

"We have carried you to a safe place," Barabbas informed his commander. "The men have gone for supplies."

"How did the Romans know?" the Galilean whispered.

"Ezra, son of Samuel from Nazareth," Barabbas responded. "He sent word ahead and told the Romans to wait for us in the passages under the Temple."

"I should have killed every man in Nazareth who was not with us," the Galilean responded through gritted teeth.

The face of the carpenter of Nazareth filled Barabbas's mind. Not every man, he silently protested before gruffly informing, "Ezra will not return to his home in Nazareth. I have sent two men to meet him on the road."

"Good." It was a weak response, a final response. The Galilean slipped into unconsciousness and then into final oblivion.

Slowly, the gates to the Place of the Dead opened. The angels of God that always stood by the entrance to the verdant side of the river covered their faces and wept while their demonic counterparts triumphantly carried the soul of the Galilean into the barren bowels on their side of the valley. "One more messiah to add to the dung heap of misguided souls that are the property of Satan," the evil angels tauntingly chanted as they literally tossed the spirit-being of Judah the Galilean into a massive wasteland filled with hopeless souls.

"Toma! Toma!" Joseph called as he pushed his way through the crowd of well-wishing neighbors that surrounded the bridegroom. "We are two days late because the road from Nazareth to Jerusalem has a Roman checkpoint for every day's journey." Joseph gave his cousin a manly embrace while jovially asking, "Do you have any wine left? I am parched!"

"Kheti is overseeing the wine," Toma responded as he led Joseph, followed by Jesus and James, to the banquet table. Indicating a seat beside two unfamiliar men, Toma said, "Let me introduce you to Bohan. We purchase camels from him. And this is his son, Nodab, who is one of our camel drovers."

Kheti interrupted the introductions by hurrying over with two cups of wine. "Joseph, how good to see you. And, Jesus, you are almost as tall as your father!" He placed a cup of wine in the hand of each before turning to James and saying, "I will bring you some of the children's wine."

"Kheti is thinking about retiring from the caravan routes," Toma informed those closest to the table. "In Petra, he sold all of our trade goods, every camel and every donkey!"

"I had to," Kheti jumped into the story as he handed James a cup of wine diluted with water. "I was in Petra searching for gemstones when a merchant approached me with the largest, most perfect pearl I had ever seen. When I laid my eyes on it, I knew I had to have it. When I heard the price, I knew it would take everything I owned!"

"And some of what I owned," Toma interjected. "You could not believe my surprise! When I arrived in Petra, there was Kheti sitting on the steps of the red stone temple that faces the market place, not a camel in sight."

"It was a pearl of great worth, and selling all that I had was a small price," Kheti protested.

"Where are you keeping this pearl?" Joseph asked.

"In a safe place," Kheti quickly responded.

"Even I have only had a glimpse of this gem from the sea," Toma stated.

"Will you sell it?" Bohan asked. The gleam of a shrewd merchant was in his eye.

"Never!" Kheti exclaimed. "I would rather be a drover, working beside your son, than give up this pearl." Then he looked at Toma with a bit of a challenge in his eye and added, "This next trip, I will be one of your drovers! After all, at one time, you were one of my drovers!"

"How can I turn down a man with your experience?" Toma jovially accepted Kheti's offer. Then he added, "But don't get me in trouble at the tax collectors' booths. You were bribing tax collectors so they would not give our little six-camel caravan more than a quick glance, and doing it right in front of their Roman guards."

"Romans! Romans everywhere!" Bohan exclaimed. "Between here and Bethany, everyone is being stopped. Everyone is being searched!"

"For weeks, the Romans have been scouring the countryside for the Galilean," Joseph explained. "There was an attempted uprising—"

"We heard," Toma and Kheti answered almost simultaneously. "The soldiers believe the Galilean was injured and that he might have to be transported by wagon or cart. That's why they are all over the roads."

"Yeshua?"

Jesus looked up toward heaven.

"Step away from the table, and I will speak," God instructed.

Jesus set his half-emptied cup of wine on the table and moved into the shade of an olive tree.

"My kingdom is not a kingdom of the world. It is not an earthly government that men fight to control. My Anointed One will not raise a sword or lead armies into battle because the kingdom is already his. He will merely allow people to get a glimpse of this kingdom. And then those who are worthy will react like Kheti when he saw the pearl. They will give up all that they own, even their lives, to have it. Once they own it, they will never sell it because there is no price great enough."

"Who is part of your kingdom?" Jesus asked.

"Every person who has submitted themselves to my will. Every person who hears my Spirit and obeys, completely disregarding the cost," God answered.

"The cost to rule an earthly kingdom is high!" another voice warned. "How much greater the cost to rule a heavenly kingdom?"

In the warm afternoon sun, Jesus shivered. He recognized that malevolent voice. It was Lucifer, the angel he had seen falling from the golden walls of the Holy City. Then suddenly Jesus was remembering Jethro and Daveed on their crosses. Their moans, their pleas for a quick death ran through his mind like it was an event of the present and not the past.

"The boy has seen enough!" God's voice cut across the demonic vision like a blade of white lightning.

Jesus slumped weakly against the tree and closed his eyes. When he opened his eyes, Kheti was pushing his cup of wine into his hand.

"You look like you have had too much sun," the experienced caravanner commented. "Take small sips and rest. Soon you will feel better."

"Oh, Elesheva, you are a beautiful bride!" Mary exclaimed as she slipped into the group of women that surrounded Toma's new wife. "You look just as young and beautiful as you were at your first wedding!"

All the woman laughed, and Elesheva's sister commented. "It is the same veil."

"So much time has passed, so much has happened," Elesheva responded. "I do not feel young, neither do I feel old. I think I just feel like a different person."

"With a new family!" Salma, the wet nurse, laid the just-fed baby Seth in Elesheva's arms.

"Oh, your new son!" one of the women exclaimed. "You are blessed: a good husband and a healthy son all at the same time."

"He reminds me of your sweet little Kefa," Mary whispered.

"I know," Elesheva quietly responded. "The Lord has looked upon me and seen my emptiness. He has filled the void in my heart."

"There will be more than this little one," Mary predicted as she pulled little Simon from the folds of her robe.

"Mary, how many children have you had since you left Bethlehem?" Elesheva asked.

"Well, there's Jesus, my oldest. He is sitting over there under the tree." Mary pointed as she spoke.

Then she heard one of the ladies comment, "He was the only boy-child to survive the slaughter. There are no boys his age in the village of Bethlehem." Immediately, there was a responding buzz of hushed comments.

Mary's eyes darted from face to face. Some of these women had lost their baby boys to the Roman swords. She fidgeted uneasily with baby Simon, who was sleeping in her arms, and then she quickly tucked him into the sling that hung from her shoulders.

"I believe we are close to the same age," Elesheva broke into the uncomfortableness of the moment. "When I see that you are still having babies, it gives me hope for many more children." Then very kindly, she added, "I'm glad the soldiers did not get your Jesus."

All the women stopped talking for a moment, their eyes resting on the adolescent who sat under the olive tree.

"He is a well-built lad," one of the older women commented, "but he does not resemble his father, Joseph."

"I can see my father's features in his face," Mary carefully answered. "But Joseph has passed on to him so many character traits and skills. He does not know how to do all the things a master carpenter can do, but those he has been taught, he can do as well as any grown man. Joseph and I are proud of him. Now James, he looks like Joseph, and then there is Jose, my four-year-old, and Ruth, who is such a help—"

"Mary, you could have children for another ten years," one of the older women announced.

"*Sons are a heritage from the* LORD, *children a reward from him,*"[1] Mary replied before stepping away to slow James and Jose down as they ran among the wedding guests.

"Our gift! Our gift for the bridegroom and his bride!"

Joseph's shouting drew the women out of their conversations and turned their attention to the donkey cart. Joseph and his son Jesus lifted a smoothly polished tabletop and then a pair of supports from the cart.

"It is beautiful!" Elesheva exclaimed as she hurried over to run her hand over the smooth wood surface.

"Thank you, Joseph!" Toma exclaimed.

"Don't thank me," Joseph responded. "Jesus did all the work. It will not be long before he will be the master carpenter and I will rest in the shade."

"Ichabod?"

Looking up from his solitary reclining position near the fountain in his parents' courtyard, Ichabod saw his mother approaching.

"At this time, when power is shifting in the High Court, your father has sent a petition requesting that the remuneration our family receives for compounding the incense and the anointing oil be increased. He desires for you return to your begging post by the Beautiful Gate and be especially aware of conversations between members of the court."

"Father should have petitioned while the great Hillel was still alive and presiding over the court. Hillel was always far more generous than Shammai," Ichabod responded.

"Nevertheless, bring your father some names, families that would enjoy a special fragrance and then speak up in favor of higher remuneration," Ichabod's mother urged. "You will be returning to the Beautiful Gate on the first day of the week?" she questioned as she quickly glanced at the diminishing bruises that covered his twisted legs.

"I will be there," Ichabod bitterly responded, "sitting in my chair and looking more pitiful than usual."

John finished his solitary meal and placed his wooden bowl on the floor beside the mat on which he sat. For a long time, he stared thoughtfully, looking out through the opening of the cave that he shared with Geber. Except for the companionship of Geber, he was usually alone: too new to the Essene community to dine with the members, too new to be present when their "secret" knowledge of angels and healing arts was discussed.

From the elevated level of this isolated cave, John could see a vast expanse of parched and rugged Judean wilderness. Below, a few hand-watered spots of vegetation indicated there was life outside this cloistered Essene community. In the distance, a thin line of color suggested freshwater could be found, but John knew it was just an illusion. Geber had told him the Great Salt Sea was not far away. Its water was only good for producing minerals.

He sat back down on his mat and thought about stories his father had told him: the angel beside the altar of incense, the day his cousin Mary had come to visit, and the birth of his cousin Jesus. They all seemed like such distant memories. He wondered if he remembered them correctly. Even the last Passover when he and his cousin Jesus had shared so much—it seemed like another world, another life.

"John, son of Zechariah?" God called his name, and the voice of the Almighty echoed, bouncing majestically from wall to wall within the cave.

Immediately, John knelt, facing the entrance to the cave and Jerusalem, the city of God on Earth. With his hands stretched out above his head, he bent over until his face touched the rock-hard floor of the cave. In that worshipful position, he waited.

"Look out. What do you see?" God inquired.

Without lifting his head or opening his eyes, John saw once more the Judean Wilderness that surrounded the Essene community in Qumran. "A desert," John answered in his mind, "a wasteland where nothing grows."

"It is the place where you will grow," God responded. "It is the place where I will instruct you until you are of age to join the community of the Essenes. Then you will leave their company to be the *voice of one calling in the desert, prepare the way for the* Lord; *make straight in the wilderness a highway for our God.*" There was a brief time of silence. Then God spoke again. "See those deep valleys? In the souls of men, there are deep valleys of sin. Your words will be so Spirit-filled that *every valley shall be raised up.* See those barren mountains? In the minds of men, there are mountains of resistance to truth. As you speak the words that I will give you, *every mountain and hill will be made low and the rough ground shall become level, and the rugged places a plain. And the glory of the* Lord, the promised Messiah, *will be revealed and all mankind will see it. This has come to pass because the mouth of the* Lord *has spoken it.*"[2]

When Geber entered the cave, he sensed the weighty presence of the Spirit of God. Then he saw John stretched out on the floor of the cave like those serving in the Court of the Priests during the time of intercession. It was then he understood. The boy knew greater spiritual secrets than the mystical teachings of the Essene community. Quietly, without disturbing John, Geber lowered a large jar to the floor. Out of its mouth protruded the linen-covered scrolls he had brought for John to study. In respectful silence, the Essene teacher sat and waited through the night. At dawn, John sat up on his knees, and then he rose to his feet. In silence, he walked to the pool for community purification. Geber followed, like a student walking in the footsteps of a famous rabbi. Those who sat at Geber's feet for instruction stared in openmouthed surprise. Then they quietly fell into step behind their teacher.

At the steps that went down into the cool pool of water, every man paused as John removed his clothing and stepped down into the pool. His hair that had never been cut, covered his naked buttocks. Deliberately, he walked down the stone steps into the pool. Quickly, he ducked under the surface of the water. When he came up, he announced to Geber and all his disciples, "I have washed, but am I clean? I am only clean if I have first repented and turned away from my sins."

A distant shofar sounded and then another. The faint sound of repeated shofar blasts came from the little village close to the Essene retreat. "It is the Day of Trumpets!" John announced. "Will you heed their warning and turn your hearts completely to God before you wash? Only then will you be clean."

Geber turned to his disciples and clarified, "It is not the outward washing we do so many times in this place that makes us acceptable to God. It is the conscious choice to regret those things in our lives that are displeasing to God and then to decide not to do them again." Geber turned to John, who still stood in the waist-deep water. "For some time, I have known God reveals himself to you and expounds upon the Torah and the prophets, but my pride would not allow me to seek instruction from a boy. Forgive me. I will humbly sit at your feet and hear what the God of Abraham has revealed to you." After saying those words,

Geber removed his white robe and walked down into the water. Stopping in front of John, he ducked completely under the water.

"Place your hands on his head," the Spirit of God urged.

As Geber emerged from beneath the water, he felt John's hands on his head and heard him pronounce, "Now you are clean!"

Chapter 14

MANHOOD RECOGNIZED

*And Jesus grew in wisdom and stature, and in favor with
God and men.*

—Luke 2:52

Ichabod adjusted his position in the leather chair the carpenter's
son from Nazareth had made especially for him. This was his
second chair. When the first chair had become worn almost to the
point of being unusable, suddenly the apprentice from Nazareth
had appeared with a new chair.

Ichabod recalled the face of that kind young man—tan and
healthy, relaxed and cheerful. The beggar ran his hand across the
leather on his chair. After two years of use, it was now worn and
smooth, stretched to fit the oddities of his contorted body. He
knew it would last another year or two.

The beggar turned his attention back to earning his wages.
With a practiced eye, he surveyed the people on the steps. It had
been a slow day. Most people were working in their fields and
gardens, not planning on a trip to the Temple until after the last
trumpet blast of the daily trumpets for the final month of the
year. There would be one day of silence, then the next day would
be filled with trumpets and shofars announcing the beginning
of a new year, a ten-day season of repentance, and the final
harvest feasts.

When that time came, there would be a good crowd. Ever since the new governor, Valerius Gratus, had arrived from Rome, there had been such a military presence in Jerusalem during the feasts that no one had dared attempt an uprising. So the people, though annoyed by the presence of so many foreign soldiers, felt safe enough to bring every family member.

The experienced beggar turned his head to observe two important councilmen from the Sanhedrin as they strolled through the Beautiful Gate. Ichabod recognized both men immediately: Simon the son of the great Hillel and Gamaliel, Simon's son and the grandson of Hillel. There, on the top step, within an arm's length, they paused to continue an obviously serious conversation. Their body language conveyed an urgency that caused Ichabod to incline his head so he could hear their conversation.

"Since Governor Rufus was recalled to Rome and his successor Valerius Gratus took up residence in Caesarea, he has made the feasts the most difficult time of the year," Simon commented. "Already, three thousand Syrian troops have been stationed in the city. They are standing shoulder to shoulder on the wall of their fortress. Every day, they are staring disrespectfully down into the Temple courts."

"We have a full month until the Day of Trumpets, and already, the governor has left his residence in Caesarea and moved into the Fortress of Antonio that overlooks the Temple," Gamaliel informed his father. "We approached him, Joseph of Arimathea, Nicodemus, and myself. Very respectfully, we requested the garments for the high priest. He laughed at us!"

"Laughed!" Simon exclaimed. "You made a serious request. Doesn't he understand? The priestly robes are old and worn. They have to be repaired, and that takes some time. The high priest has to wear them from the first day of the trumpet until he removes them to wash before entering the Most Holy Place on the Day of Atonement!"

Tersely, Gamaliel answered, "We explained that some pieces of fabric probably need to be replaced before the Fall Feasts, and the procurator replied that he would release the garments when he had selected the high priest who was to officiate! He also indicated that we could expect some changes in leadership within the Sanhedrin—possibly a new president!"

"I will speak with Shammai. We will write a letter of protest and send it to Rome," Simon protested. "We were to be allowed to govern ourselves!"

"Remember, you are writing to a new emperor. Caesar Augustus has been dead for four years, and Tiberius is ruling now. Gratus was his first appointment to Judea," Gamaliel warned his father. Without glancing at the beggar, the two men then walked down the steps together.

The gentle waves of Galilee steadily lapped against the rocky shore at Zebedee's fishing anchorage. Up on the beach, removed from the reach of the wavelets, Jesus held a piece of wood in place while Joseph secured it into the hull with iron nails. Five more pieces of wood, cut to fit precisely in a hole where rotten wood had previously endangered the life of the fishing vessel, were stacked nearby.

"Joseph?"

Jesus looked up to see his Uncle Zebedee approaching.

"Is this boat going to be ready to go out tonight?"

Joseph stopped hammering and looked up, allowing enough time for Zebedee to approach before answering with a definite no.

"No?" Zebedee roared back. "I have a fishing crew that has been idle for two days!"

"And you have a fleet of boats that could sink in the middle of the lake because you have not replaced the rotting wood!" Joseph countered. "When Jesus and I finish this section of the hull, there is another spot where three planks need to be replaced. If you had called me before the rot had spread, then it would have just been a matter of replacing a board or two. I have practically rebuilt this hull, and you have two more boats that need my attention."

"Your wife was with child, and my wife had to go stay with her. I was doing women's work instead of tending to my fleet," Zebedee grumbled his excuse.

"Which child?" Joseph quickly responded. "This wood has been rotting since before Simon was born!" With the toe of his sandaled foot, he nudged a plank he had removed from the hull and watched it crumble. "You need to thank God your fishing crew did not drown."

"You're a carpenter, not a fisherman," Zebedee shouted back at the top of his lungs, "so don't lecture me on my trade! Fishermen have to take risks. It's part of the job. If we don't fish, we go hungry!"

"Well," Joseph replied in an even and unruffled tone, "if you are fishing tonight, you will have to take your chances with the boats I have not had time to work on."

With a loud huff and a lot of muttering, Zebedee turned on his heel and strode away.

As Joseph set back to work, he said, "Son, I want you to pay close attention to how I have shaped the planks and how I am fitting them so there is a watertight seam."

Jesus nodded, indicating his understanding while he continued to hold the plank so it fit securely into the groove in the board above it.

"It is time for the grapes and the olives to be harvested. I know we only have a few vines and two trees, but it is an important harvest for our family. Your mother cannot do it alone, so I do not have time to stay and repair the other boats in Zebedee's fishing fleet." Joseph continued talking to Jesus while he worked. "I want you to stay here in Capernaum with your uncle Zebedee. You can finish the repairs on his boats."

"Zebedee is a hard man to work for," Jesus responded candidly.

"That I will not deny," Joseph replied, "but under all his angry shouting, he is a fair man."

"He is a fear-filled man," Jesus countered.

Joseph stopped working and looked at his son, waiting for further explanation.

Jesus responded to the question in his father's eyes. "When I look into Uncle Zebedee's eyes, I see spirits of Fear. They are Lying spirits. They tell him unless he makes people feel afraid of him, something bad will happen."

"You can really see that?" Joseph asked incredulously as he considered the truth of his seventeen-year-old son's statement. "You are right. Zebedee does try to intimidate people so they will be afraid to do anything other than what he suggests." After another pause, Joseph asked, "Do you think you can work with him?"

"You have shown me it is best to remain calm and give him straight factual answers," Jesus responded.

"And," Joseph asked, "what has your heavenly Father shown you about dealing with demonic spirits?"

"God has shown me the faces of many demons and how they work to control and make people harm themselves as well as those around them. When I see them, I am never to back away. Instead, I look at them squarely through the eyes of the person they have ensnared. Usually, they will immediately become silent. Kindness often disables them. Only the strongest spirits will attempt an attack."

Joseph shook his head as he tried to comprehend. "I am sure you know it would not be wise to speak of such things to your uncle Zebedee."

Jesus chuckled as he imaged his uncle's thundering response. "I will remember and adhere to your advice," Jesus answered.

"Then after we finish repairing this boat, I will leave and return to Nazareth. Do all the repairs you can do until one week before the Feast of Trumpets. At that time, come to Jerusalem. We will meet at the Beautiful Gate for the first trumpet blast."

"Jesus? Jesus!" Like a massive thunderstorm, Zebedee strode from his anchorage to where Jesus was completing the repairs on the last of his fishing boats. "Is this boat going out tonight?" he thundered.

"Yes," Jesus answered. "Just have your crew move it into the water."

"James! John! Bring the crew!" Zebedee called. "We are taking four boats out tonight."

"Can I go fishing on the lake tonight?"

Zebedee turned around abruptly to face his nephew. "You must be pretty sure of your work if you want to sail with us."

"I am sure the boat is sound," Jesus replied. "I have never been fishing all night on the lake." Jesus looked directly into the eyes of his uncle. He could see the spirits of Fear, silent and quivering.

"Go on this boat with James and John." Zebedee pointed to the fishing boat the men were dragging toward the water. "You can sleep most of the night, but when they pull in the nets, give the men a hand. You are a strong young man, almost ready to open your own carpentry shop. The crew will appreciate the help."

"Thank you!" Jesus cried as he ran to lend a hand to the men who were moving the boat.

The sun was setting as four boats slipped away from the anchorage in front of Zebedee's home. Sitting in the bow of one boat, Jesus turned and watched as the breezes from the lake filled the square sail. He felt the wind suddenly take charge and the little boat immediately picked up speed.

"How do you like this, Jesus?" his cousin James called from his place near the man who controlled the rudder.

"It's more fun than hammering nails into the hull," Jesus answered. Then he laughed at the sheer joy of feeling the wind in his face and the waves beneath the hull. He watched the coastline until darkness made it indistinguishable from the water. By then, the little boat had found its anchorage for the night.

By torchlight, the crew threw their heavy nets over the side. Then they settled down to wait. The day had been long; Jesus curled up in the bow of the boat. He could see the stars. It was a cloudless night. All over the lake, he could see tiny dots of light. Many boats were out fishing tonight. Zebedee's boat rocked rhythmically in the cradle of the waves. Jesus slipped into comfortable sleep.

From a boulder-strewn cove, Satan and Raziel fixed their evil eyes on the small fishing boat where the apprentice carpenter slept. They could see Michael and his warrior angles had surrounded the vessel. Unless those guardians from the throne room of God withdrew their protection, there was no chance an attack would be successful. Throughout the night, Satan and Raziel watched, but the heavenly guards never moved from their watchful positions.

With a disgusted shrug of their massively evil shoulders, both fallen angels turned their attention to another of Zebedee's fishing boats.

Swaddled in the gray mists of dawn, the fishermen hauled their nearly empty nets back into the boat.

"Zebedee is going to tell you to go find another fisherman who will pay you wages for empty nets!" Raziel shouted.

Every man on the boat trembled inwardly.

"Zebedee expects full nets every morning," one crew member warned.

"He cannot hold us responsible!" another protested. "How are we to make the fish swim into the net?"

"You are responsible because you cast the net in the wrong place," Raziel encouraged their fear and self-reproach.

"The fish you need are lurking in the cove," Satan threw out a destructive suggestion.

"Sail into the cove and cast your nets in the shadows of the boulders," Raziel repeated.

As one man, the crew responded to the satanic commands, lifting their stone anchors and setting their square sail to move Zebedee's wooden fishing boat into the rocky shallows of the cove.

On both sides of the boat, all the nets were cast, and to their amazement, they quickly filled with fish. Joyfully, the men began to haul in the heavy nets with their load of wiggling fish. It was an exciting moment when the bulging nets broke the surface and hung on each side of the boat, ready to be manually hoisted over the wooden sides of the boat. No one noticed that the stone anchors were not holding. A sudden breeze caught everyone off guard and sent the bow of the boat grinding onto a solid protrusion of land just below the water's surface.

The men felt the bow hit and then hold fast in the mud. While most of the crew held their precious catch, two fishermen jumped out into the knee-deep water to push the boat free. As they pushed, they felt the new timbers that had been put into the boat scrape against the rocks. They dug their heels in and pushed again. Unexpectedly, they heard the snap of the weathered wood that was next to the freshly installed planks as the boat was forced against an immovable rock.

"We're taking on water!" one of the men in the boat hollered in alarm as he stuffed pitch-covered rags into a hand-sized hole in the side of the boat. Water steadily poured around the temporary patch of tarred rags and gathered ankle-deep on the floor of the boat. The men abandoned their fish-filled nets, allowing them to sink back into the shallow water. With the weight of the nets removed from the boat, the vessel immediately rode higher in the water, causing the hole in the hull to be above the waterline.

"We can make it back to Zebedee's anchorage, but we will have to leave the nets and the fish behind," one man stated the obvious, and everyone silently agreed. The sail was carefully set, and they cautiously moved into deeper water, sullenly skimming through the morning mists toward their home anchorage.

"What are you going to tell Zebedee?" Satan challenged the brooding men. "You have no fish. You have lost two nets and put a hole in his newly repaired boat!"

"Zebedee allowed a boy to do a man's job!" Raziel suggested. "And he did a poor job. Look at the new boards near the hole. You can pry a few of them loose. Zebedee will never see the hole in the weathered wood. He will just see that whole timbers have come loose and floated away."

One of the fishing crew began tearing at the newly-fitted boards next to hole. Without discussion, everyone on the crew understood the plan, and all hands assisted in removing and tossing overboard several pieces of wood that were above the waterline and around the hole. Now the burden of their risk-taking and miscalculation would fall on the carpenter's apprentice, the nephew of Zebedee. Everyone heaved a collective sigh of relief.

"Jesus! Jesuusss!"

Lightly, Jesus jumped over the side of the fishing boat and waded toward the shore to meet his red-faced bellowing uncle.

"I lost two nets full of fish! The new boards that you put in my boat came out, and my crew nearly drowned!"

As the last words left Zebedee's mouth, Jesus felt his uncle's hot breath on his face and saw his uncle's bulging bloodshot eyes only a finger's length from his nose. All around him, he could feel the presence of Mocking spirits, Angry spirits, Taunting spirits.

"Zebedee has no right to talk to you like this. You know you did a good job on his fishing boats. As a matter of fact, the boat in question was repaired by your father! Be a man and tell him to get out of your face!"

"Be my son and answer wisely," the Holy Spirit countered the satanic suggestion.

"I take responsibility for both my work and my father's work," Jesus calmly responded. "Take me to the boat."

Zebedee abruptly turned on his heel and led the way to the spot where a shamefaced fishing crew loitered around a boat with a good-sized hole in the hull.

"Lying demons are present," the Holy Spirit warned.

"I know," Jesus said as he ran his hand over the freshly splintered wood. He straightened up and pointed to the splintering. "It took a lot of force to create this hole." He looked his uncle in the eye and waited for a response.

Zebedee bent over and looked at the place where the boards had been torn from the side of the hull. "I have never seen that kind of damage on a fishing boat before," he admitted.

Jesus glanced at the men who were standing around. He could tell by their body language that they were nervous, and in the spirit realm, he could see the Lying spirits that were hanging on to each man.

"Why don't you admit that you just did a poor job of repairing this boat?" one of the men suddenly accused.

"My father and I repaired this boat together," Jesus responded. "Neither of us did a poor job."

"This is the boat both you and Joseph worked on!" Zebedee turned to look suspiciously at his crew.

"I can replace the missing boards," Jesus quickly assured his uncle. "This boat will be ready to sail in a few days."

"Meanwhile, I will need new nets!" Zebedee never removed his smoldering suspicious gaze from the guilty faces of his crew. "You will spend those days making new nets!" he bellowed.

"The nets are in the rocky cove on the other side of the point," the Holy Spirit informed.

"My uncle?"

Zebedee turned to face his nephew.

"If you will send James and John in a boat over to the rocky cove beyond the point, you will find your nets."

"You know this to be a fact?" Zebedee asked in amazement.

"Send your boys and see what they bring back," Jesus tactfully replied. Then he turned to the men, completely disregarding the fact of their maturity and his own youth. "Haul the boat out of the water," he directed.

And the men moved as if the order had been given by Zebedee himself.

"Uncle?" Jesus fell into step beside Zebedee as he strode angrily away from his anchorage. "How many fish do you think you lost today?"

"Maybe a hundred," the master fisherman replied.

"When I have finished repairing your boat, I will do my best to replace your loss," Jesus offered with confident assurance.

In midstride, Zebedee stopped and turned to Jesus. "How are you going to replace the fish I lost?"

"Every evening and in the early morning hours, I will wade into the lake and cast a net until I have replaced the fish you have lost," Jesus answered.

"I did not ask you to replace the fish," Zebedee blustered. "I should not even ask you to repair this boat again. Those men are lying! I don't know what they did during the night, but a corporate lie is written all over their faces."

"Nevertheless, you need the boat, so I will repair it," Jesus responded with genuine warmth. "And I will replace the fish." In his uncle's eyes, he could see the spirits of Fear shriveling, not disappearing but weakening.

Unexpectedly, Zebedee threw his fishy-smelling arm around Jesus's shoulders. "Your father, Joseph, is a good man, and you are very much like him."

"Yeshua, my son?"

In the darkness, Jesus recognized the voice of God.

"Do not wait for dawn. Wade into the water and cast your net into the darkness."

Immediately, Jesus responded. Wearing only a fisherman's loincloth secured with a sturdy knot, Jesus stepped from the shore into the predawn shallows of Galilee. The water was cold and black. He could not see; he could only feel the rocky lake bed and the water slowly rising to his knees as he took cautious steps away from the shore. As the water reached his thighs and tugged at the piece of linen that was his only clothing, he stopped and lifted the lightweight casting net from his shoulders. Hoisting it and repeating the overhead circling and swinging motions that James and John had taught him, he blindly threw his handheld net into the darkness. He heard the hemp hit the water. With his hands on a line that attached the net to his waist, he sensed with his fingers when it settled beneath the surface.

"Yeshua, you are my net, firmly attached to all that I am," God spoke again. "I have thrown you into the blackness of Earth so you can catch men and women and bring them back to me. Call them. Call them to me. They will come."

Still holding onto the net, Jesus focused on the words of his heavenly Father. So often, when God spoke, it was not direct and immediately clear. Instead, an interpretation was required.

"Speak to the fish," the Holy Spirit repeated the Father's directions. "Say 'Come to me, all you fish that swim in darkness.'"

Without questioning, Jesus repeated, "Come to me, all you fish that swim in darkness."

Instantly, he could feel that the net was suddenly heavy with flipping tails and flailing fins as desperate fish writhed within its confines. Hand over hand, Jesus pulled on the line that attached the net to his own body. The net was not moving, so Jesus had to follow the line, walking chest-deep into the blackness, into water that was indistinguishable from the moonless sky. Groping underwater with his hands, Jesus grasped two sides of the bulging net and brought them together. Working with the natural buoyancy of the water, he raised the net from the stone-covered bottom and began hauling his catch to the shore. By the time he stepped into waist-deep water, he was straining every muscle in his young body to bring the overfilled net into shore.

"Father?" Jesus called out as he continued to struggle with the net. "There are so many fish in my net! And it is so difficult to bring them to shore!"

"Son, all of humanity is sightlessly drowning in dark water. So many! So many!"

"Father?" Jesus gasped. His foot slipped, and he fell into the water, but his hands never released their grip on the net. "The load becomes more difficult to move as I near the shore!"

"It will take everything you have to bring humanity out of the dark waters that separate them from me. Do not forget the effort of this day."

Sharp rocks cut his bare feet. The coarse weave of the net rubbed and burned through the palms of his hands, but Jesus did not release the net. In his soul, he realized this ordinary task had turned into one of his Father's object lessons. He could not allow himself to fail.

Gray fingers of light reached skyward from behind the rugged mountains on the eastern side of Galilee. They forced the darkness to recede and hide in the caves of the western hills. With one last effort, Jesus brought the net full of fish onto the shore. He dropped the hemp mesh, and the net fell open. Some of the fish spilled out onto the ground. Jesus dropped to the ground beside them, tired but satisfied, enjoying the sweet fishy odor of a fresh catch.

On the horizon, he could see the silhouettes of fishing boats returning from a night of dragging their nets in the dark water of the lake. Behind him on shore, the wives of the fishermen were setting up racks to dry the catch. Jesus saw his aunt Salome with young Benjamin. "Aunt Salome," he called. "I have brought in the first catch of the day!"

Salome looked over to where her nephew was sitting on the ground beside a throw net and a heap of still-wiggling fish. "Ladies!" she called to the other women. "The first catch is in! Let's get started!"

The women with their baskets hurried over, gathering up the fish and exclaiming over the size and number of fish that the seventeen-year-old carpenter's apprentice had brought in.

Jesus watched them hurry off to the drying racks.

"Step into the water and throw your net again."

Jesus knew the voice of Father God, so he quickly rose to his feet.

"Haven't you learned anything from your uncle and cousins?" spirits of Doubt and Earthbound Knowledge countered. "Fish can only be caught between dusk and dawn, when they cannot see the net."

Pushing Doubt and Earthbound Knowledge aside, Jesus picked up the net again. With the early-morning light illuminating the entire lake, it was easy to wade into the water and cast the net as far as the cord attached to his waist would allow. He saw the net hit, float momentarily, and then slowly sink. There was a sudden churning as fish swam directly into the net, quickly filling it one more time.

"Feed the fishermen," God directed.

"They need meat for their bodies and food for their spiritual minds," the Holy Spirit added.

Jesus understood. The net was not as full as before, so he quickly brought it to shore. He gathered sticks and scraps of wood and then built a fire. Next, he turned to the task of scaling and gutting the fish. By the time the wood had become a bed of glowing coals, Zebedee's boats were tied to their mooring posts. The women were carrying baskets full of fish from each boat to the drying racks, and the men were spreading the nets out to dry.

"Uncle Zebedee? Uncle Zebedee?" Jesus called his uncle. "Bring the men over when they have finished. Their food is ready!"

Zebedee stopped barking orders for a moment and strode over to the burning coals and roasting fish. "Where did you get these fish?" he bellowed in an accusatory tone. "Did you take them from one of my boats?"

Before Jesus could answer, Aunt Salome came running up. "He caught them with a casting net," she breathlessly informed. "One whole rack was full of drying fish before your boats even approached the anchorage," she added.

"And this catch," Jesus asserted, "is for you and your crews, who must be very hungry after working all night."

"You must have been throwing that net all night!" Zebedee exclaimed in openmouthed amazement.

"Just twice," Jesus responded. "The Spirit of God directed my net."

"You cannot be telling the truth!" Zebedee exclaimed. "I have fished with a casting net, and I know how many casts it takes to bring in all these fish."

"Zebedee," Salome softly but insistently pushed herself into the conversation. "I, along with the wives of the other fishermen, filled one whole rack with fish from one casting. I saw the net, full of fish, with fish spilling out onto the ground. This is his second casting. I saw him haul it in."

"Are you supporting his impossible story?" Zebedee turned on his wife.

"He is Joseph and Mary's son," Salome replied. "You have said Joseph is a trustworthy man and that Jesus is just like his father. Mary has told me many impossible things that have happened for Jesus. Now I have seen the impossible with my own eyes." Without allowing Zebedee to reply, Salome turned and walked away, leaving her husband to come to terms with the impossible.

"Well, the fish are ready to be eaten." Jesus turned away from his uncle and began pulling roasted fish from the coals, tossing them into the basket Salome had left for him.

"I smell coal-baked fish!" Jesus looked up to see his cousin James, along with several men, approaching. Down near the boats, Salome was directing the men toward the fire and the roasted fish. They were coming, full of hunger and smiles.

Zebedee was still bewildered, standing there struggling to believe his eyes and not the demonic protests in his mind.

The men were eating, squatting on their heels around the basket of baked fish near the dying coals of the morning fire. Quickly, Jesus made the short trip to Zebedee's home and brought back the one scroll he had brought with him from his grandfather Heli's library, the ancient historical book of Joshua. Careful to properly care for the scroll, he threw his cloak on the rocky ground then laid the rolled parchment on top of it. He opened the scroll to the first columns of Hebrew script.

"Read to us, Jesus," one of the men requested.

"And then explain it," another suggested.

"Yes, sometimes I don't understand the ancient Hebrew," a familiar gruff voice stated.

Jesus looked up to see his uncle Zebedee standing over him, admitting that like most fishermen and tradesmen, his understanding of traditional Hebrew was limited.

Squatting on his heels and using a clean fishbone as a pointer, Jesus began to read, "*The LORD said to Joshua,... 'Moses my servant is dead. Now then, you and all these people, get ready to cross the Jordan River into the land.*¹"

As he read, the men finished their morning meal and settled back to listen. Even Zebedee made himself comfortable on the ground, transfixed by the clear, pleasant voice of his nephew, "*Be strong and courageous, because you will lead these people to inherit the land I swore to their forefathers to give them. Be strong and very courageous. Be careful to obey all the law my servant Moses gave you; do not turn from it to the right or to the left that you may be successful wherever you go.*"²

James felt a little shiver run along his spine, then he heard the man behind him whisper, "When Jesus reads, it seems as if God is right here speaking to Joshua." James nodded.

"Do not let this Book of the Law depart from your mouth; meditate on it day and night, so that you may be careful to do everything written in it. Then you will be prosperous and successful. Have I not commanded you? Be strong and courageous. Do not be terrified; do not be discouraged for the LORD *your God will be with you wherever you go."*[3] As Jesus continued reading, the words that he read seemed to glow like the coals that were still burning among the ashes. In his heart and in his mind, God seared his command, *"Be strong and very courageous. Be careful to obey all the law."*[4]

Jesus stopped reading and looked up at the men. Every eye was on him. Not one man moved or seemed at all distracted. "Did you understand what I read?" Jesus asked. Then he quickly summarized the text in the local dialect of Aramaic. Heads nodded affirmatively as each man heard and understood completely what they had previously only understood in part.

"Jesus?" his cousin John spoke up. "There are so many laws in the Books of Moses. How can a man keep all of them?"

"There are more than six hundred laws in the Torah," Jesus answered, "and the disciples of Shammai try to turn those six hundred laws into a thousand!"

Everyone laughed.

"Be strong and courageous to resist laws that are made by men. The law is the instruction of God for man. He does not mean it to be burdensome," Jesus responded. Then he continued, "Every man does not have more than six hundred laws to remember and obey. Some laws are just for the priests, and some apply only to women. Some laws are for married men, and some are only for those who own property. Do not concern yourself with those things God has not given to you."

"My nephew speaks with more wisdom than a Jerusalem rabbi," Zebedee proudly announced.

Flashing his uncle a smile of appreciation for such rare praise, Jesus continued, "Rabbi Hillel, who was once one of the great teachers in Jerusalem, said that all of the law can be observed if one loves God above all else and then loves all men like one loves oneself. Then the law will be satisfied, and God will be pleased."

From the throne room, God added his blessing, "Well-spoken, my son!"

It was the last day of the religious year, a day of silence and anticipation. Ichabod sat in his usual place on the uppermost step near the ornate arched doors of the Beautiful Gate. With a practiced eye, he studied the few worshipers who were ascending the steps to enter the Temple.

It had been a slow day. Most people were in their villages, burdened with the pressing tasks of harvest. For the next two weeks, they would remain hard at work, taking only a day to go to their local synagogue to observe the Feast of Trumpets and, ten days later, another day for the Day of Atonement. Only as the Feast of Tabernacles approached would the steps to the Temple become crowded with farmers bringing the first fruits of their produce to the Temple. Ichabod glanced down into his nearly empty beggar's pot, then he consoled himself with the thought that the Feast of Tabernacles was not far away. That was usually a generous time. Many lighthearted pilgrims would climb the steps and willingly bless a crippled beggar with their shekels.

On the wide dusty street below, Ichabod suddenly recognized a face. It was the carpenter's son from Nazareth, the kind lad who had given him the chair that he sat in every day. Over the years, the boy had grown and changed. Now he was looking more like the man he would become than the boy he had been. Ichabod watched as the young man walked purposefully toward the steps that led to the Eastern Gate where Ichabod sat. Effortlessly, he bounded up the stairs, stopping beside the beggar.

Ichabod looked up. "I did not expect to see you in Jerusalem for the early Fall Feasts."

Jesus grinned the genuinely open-hearted grin of a young man without burdens. "Normally, I would be taking our grapes to the winepress, but my father wants to sell a piece of family property in Bethlehem. He can only sell it to kinsmen, so we are going to Bethlehem to see if a cousin or an uncle would like to purchase it. Then with the price of the field, he plans to set up another carpentry shop in Capernaum by Galilee. I will live there with my cousins and run the shop. Mostly, I will repair fishing boats."

"Your father must have great confidence in you," Ichabod responded a little wistfully.

"My father has three sons younger than I. He wants to make sure he can train all of us to be carpenters and have places for us to work."

"Your father sounds like a good man," Ichabod commented.

Jesus nodded and changed the subject. "How's your chair holding up?"

"It's worn but solid," Ichabod replied.

Jesus looked the chair over with a craftsman's eye. "Soon, the leather will need replacing. I should be able to make another chair for you and bring it next year at the Feast of Weeks."

After quickly scanning the faces of the people near the foot of the steps, Jesus squatted easily on his heels. "I will wait beside you," Jesus offered, "unless you think my presence will deter those who would normally drop coins in your pot."

"Stay and wait," Ichabod responded.

Jesus glanced at the sky. "I see two faint stars—when the official watchers see one more star and the new moon, it will be the beginning of a new year."

Suddenly, behind them, both men heard a commotion and proclamations coming from the Temple courts. "Make way! Make way for the messengers of the New Moon!" Four men with flaming torches, accompanied by members of the Temple guard, rushed through the open gates, running without hesitation down the steps and across the bridge that led to the Mount of Olives.

"They are going to light the signal fire," Ichabod informed. Some of the runners will continue on to inform the next town that the new moon has been seen and the New Year is beginning."

From the highest point of the Temple, there was a sudden blast of silver trumpets and ram's horns. From their perch on the uppermost step, both Jesus and the beggar could see the torches being put to the signal fire. It blazed against the early evening sky.

"How many times have you seen the signal fire lit?" Jesus asked Ichabod.

"I don't know," the beggar responded. "On the first day of every month, as soon as the new moon and the first three stars of the evening have been officially sighted, the fire is lit."

"It only burns for a short time," Jesus commented as he accurately repeated the words Father God was speaking to him. "One day from this spot, you will see a signal fire lit, and it will never burn out. From that fire, you will see other fires ignite, and those fires will never be extinguished."

"The whole world would soon be ablaze!" Ichabod chuckled as he shook his head at the absurd comment the lad from Nazareth had made.

"No, men's hearts will be ablaze," Jesus responded with a certainty that sent shivers of premonition through the beggar's body. "You will hear it, and you will see it," Jesus affirmed. "You have never walked through this Beautiful Gate into the Temple courts, yet you know everything that happens inside the Temple walls."

"I am a cripple, an offense in the face of God. I am not allowed to enter the courts of the Lord." Ichabod's voice was edged with bitterness.

"At this moment, God is stacking the wood, preparing his signal fire. On the day he lays the torch to the kindling, you will see and hear things that have never been heard before, and as the flames leap from the kindling to the wood, you will leap from this spot, running and dancing through the street. On that same day, you will walk through this gate and be allowed to worship in the Temple courts."

"Jesus!"

At the sound of his name, Jesus turned his attention to the street. At the bottom of the steps, his father Joseph beckoned for him to join him. Immediately, Jesus jumped up. Throwing a farewell grin and a sincere shalom over his shoulder, he bounded down the steps and fell into step with his father.

Servants from Ichabod's home arrived very shortly after the lad from Nazareth left. They lifted Ichabod in his chair and carried him down the steps and through the streets to his home in the upper city. Ichabod was almost unaware of the route he traveled. The boy's words burned in his heart. They made no sense to his rational mind, but they burned in his heart.

Together, father and son worked their way as quickly as possible through the always crowded Jerusalem streets, out the Dung Gate, past the ever-burning refuse of a crowded city. From his carpenter's satchel, Joseph pulled a small handheld oil lamp. Using a small horn of oil, he filled the lamp and then set a linen wick. "It will be completely dark soon," Joseph commented while quickly stepping over to one of the fires that burned close to the road. He lit a dry twig and then the linen wick. A tiny flame drew the oil through the fabric.

"That will be enough light for our feet," Jesus said. He took the lamp from his father and held it so a tiny circle of light illuminated their feet. One step at a time, they could view the path all the way to Bethlehem.

The burning Valley of Hinnen was soon behind them. The new moon gave no light. Only the little lamp showed where each could safely place his sandaled feet. "This reminds me of the night you were born," Joseph reminisced. "The night was dark. My lamp had run out of oil. Your mother and I were traveling this very road. Everything that could go wrong had gone wrong." Joseph shook his head as he began to list the mishaps of the journey: the difficulty of traveling against the Passover traffic, Roman soldiers forcing them off the road, a stone in the donkey's hoof, and then the start of Mary's labor. "You were born in the stable behind that house." Joseph pointed to a small home where only one light burned in the window. "One of the Temple shepherds probably lives there now." They passed the house, hurrying on to the home Toma had made with his new wife, Elesheva. "You don't remember when we lived in Bethlehem," Joseph continued sharing the past with Jesus. "I built your mother a house on the old foundation of the home that had belonged to Boaz, the husband of Ruth, to their son, Obed, and later to Jessie, the father of King David. The house that I built still stands by the field where your ancestor Ruth followed behind the harvesters. I am hoping Toma or his uncle will want to purchase both the house and the field," Joseph shared his plans with Jesus.

"Are you sure you want to sell such an important piece of property?" Jesus asked.

"If I sell it to Toma or uncle Shaul, it will stay in the family. Beyond that, I am not concerned about keeping the property. What I am concerned about is your future and the future of your brothers. There is not enough work in Nazareth for two master carpenters," Joseph continued. "But in Capernaum, fishing boats always need to be repaired. I have spoken with Zebedee. He agrees."

"How does James feel about this?" Jesus asked.

"I imagine he will be a little jealous," Joseph admitted, "but he needs at least four more years as my apprentice before he will have enough skill to work on his own. With you in Capernaum, there will be more work for him, more opportunity for him to become experienced."

They arrived at the gate of what used to be the home of Jabek. "Shalom?" Joseph called. "Is my cousin Toma and his wife, Elesheva, home?"

The gate opened immediately. Elesheva stood in the doorway with a small lamp in her hand. "Oh, Joseph! Jesus! What a surprise! Come in and spend the night. Then in the morning, you can go on to Bethany. Toma is there looking for donkeys to add to the caravan." She stepped aside so her husband's cousin and nephew could enter.

Joseph noticed that the silhouette of her body beneath her robes was that of a woman very close to her time of delivery. "God has blessed this home," he commented.

Elesheva beamed, "Yes, the Lord, blessed be his name, has filled me with joy and hope for the future. Toma, Kheti, and Nodab are purchasing caravan animals from Bohan of Bethany, but Toma does not plan to take this next journey. He is going to stay in Bethlehem until after our child is born." Elesheva looked directly at Joseph. "Tell Mary my good news."

"Mary will rejoice with you," Joseph replied.

"Last night while you were resting before our meal, I directed my herdsmen to separate the two—-year-old donkeys from the herd, so it would be easy for you to make your selection," Bohan commented as he led Toma and Kheti, along with Nodab, to an old barn near the edge of his property.

"I used to play in this barn," Nodab commented as they stepped into the musty old structure where shafts of sunlight streamed through holes in the roof. "But it is now in need of repair!"

"It needs to be totally rebuilt!" Lazarus harshly forced himself into the conversation as he joined the group. "I have only recently reacquired this property. For many years, it was not for sale, and when I was finally able to buy it back, this was the condition of the barn." His statement was ripe with pointed accusation, and every man understood that Lazarus the elder brother had no intention of making peace with Nodab for the follies of his youth.

Quickly deflecting more potentially ugly statements from his elder son, Bohan moved to the closest donkey. "Toma, Kheti, look at this strong animal. Nodab, lead it out into the sunshine so they can get a good look at him. Lazarus, let's bring all these donkeys out where they can be examined."

Pulling pieces of rope from pegs along the wall, each man threw a rope halter around the neck of an animal and led it out of the barn. In the back of the barn, Bohan reached for a rope hanging from a peg that was wedged between a stout wooden supporting beam and the stone wall. The rope seemed to be stuck on the rough splinters of the beam, so he gave an extra hard tug. At first, there was a slight trembling in the beam. Then dirt and thatch poured down from the roof. Suddenly, the wooden beam splintered and broke. The rock walls on either side of the beam crumbled, and Bohan was suddenly buried in the rubble.

"Father!" Lazarus and Nodab shouted in alarm as they rushed back into the still-crumbling structure. Kheti ran for the servants while Toma began moving the rocks and timbers that now blocked the entrance to the old barn.

Wailing, loud and insistent, greeted Joseph and Jesus as they neared the estate of Bohan, the large-animal merchant. Jesus spoke the truth that both his earthly and heavenly fathers already knew.

The gate to the estate was open, and no servant stood nearby. Only a group of women, obviously professional wailers, stood near the house, shrilly bemoaning this family's tragedy. With trepidation in their hearts, Joseph with Jesus walked into the unfamiliar courtyard of a very wealthy man. "What has happened?" Joseph stopped a servant who was hurrying by.

"Bohan, my master, has been crushed to death. The wall of an old barn collapsed and buried him. His eldest son, Lazarus, is also injured," the servant responded.

"Is Toma the caravanner here?" Joseph asked.

"He is with Lazarus in the main house. You can go in," the servant said as he rushed off to complete his errand.

"Son, wait here for me," Joseph said as he stepped toward the entrance to the house.

"Father God, speak to me about this situation," Jesus prayed as he moved toward a quiet corner of the courtyard.

Before God answered, a girl of marriageable age stepped away from the mourners and walked purposefully toward him. Her face was veiled, and her body shook with sobs. "I saw that your father carried a carpenter's satchel. Have you come to build the bier to carry my father's body?" she managed to ask between sobs. "I do not know whether to tell you to construct one or two. My brother Lazarus, they tell me, is severely injured." The girl choked out her information. "My older sister, Martha, has instructed the servants that I am to stay out here with the mourners. She thinks I cannot help, but I can tell you where to find the wood and the tools."

"My father and I are carpenters," Jesus kindly responded, "and we would be willing to help—"

"Jesus! Jesus!" Toma came running out the door of the house. "Come, come quick!" He pulled Jesus away from the girl and back into the house with him.

"My son," God spoke. "The older man has been welcomed into the rest of the righteous. He will wait until you take the keys of death from our enemy, but it is not time for his son to die. If this man's son were to die at this time, he would become the property of Satan for eternity. Touch his body. Every place where you lay your hands, I will bring healing to this man. But because it is not time for your public ministry, demand that everyone leave the room."

Urgently, Toma pulled Jesus into a crowded sleeping chamber. At first, Jesus could not see the injured man. He only heard his labored breathing interspersed with low groans. While Toma pushed Jesus through the family, servants, and friends around the injured man, Jesus searched the faces in the room. He recognized Nodab, and then he found his father, Joseph.

"What is this?" A young woman blocked Toma as he tried to bring Jesus close to the bed. "Who is this boy? My brother's injuries are not a spectacle for every person who travels through Bethany!"

"You don't understand," Toma responded. "This boy, the carpenter's son"—he nodded toward Joseph—"can help your brother. I have seen—"

Joseph interrupted, "My son has a special relationship with God. There have been times when he has prayed, and God has intervened miraculously."

"But I cannot pray in this room filled with people," Jesus stated. Then with authority that amazed every person in the room, he said, "Leave the room!"

Toma and Joseph responded first, urging Martha and her husband to send everyone watching by the deathbed into the courtyard. Then Martha added her authority to the request, "Leave the room. I want to be alone with my brother."

Politely, the crowd filed out until only Martha and her husband remained with Toma and Joseph.

"I must be alone with your brother," Jesus unwaveringly restated God's instructions.

Joseph and Toma responded by urging Martha and her husband to step outside.

When the door to the room had been closed, Jesus moved over to the dying man.

"Every place where you lay your hand, healing will be given to this man," God repeated.

Without hesitation, Jesus placed both hands on the man's chest, and immediately, he heard the man's breathing become normal. Jesus then moved his hands along the man's shoulders and down both arms. As Jesus moved, he felt surges of healing run through his body, down his arms, and out through the palms of his hands. His hands burned like fire as he continued to run them over every surface of the man's body. Jesus felt broken bones snap back into place and blood circulation return to normal. Finally, he rested both hands on the man's forehead, and Lazarus, the eldest son of Bohan, opened his eyes.

Then it was that Jesus saw Anger, Bitterness, Resentment, and even Murder glaring out at him.

"This man has invited us to make our home in his soul. Only he can put us out. You have no authority over us," the demonic spirits confidently announced.

"Lazarus?" Jesus spoke the man's name. "Is there any place in your body where there is still pain?"

"The pain is gone," Lazarus said as he came to a sitting position on the edge of his bed and began looking around the room, slightly puzzled. "I was at the old barn bringing out the donkeys…My father?"

"He is dead," Jesus responded gently. "Both of you were injured when the barn collapsed."

"Nodab?"

"He is waiting outside this room with my uncle Toma, my father, and the rest of your family and friends."

Rage immediately manifested. "My father is dead because of that worthless son!" Memory flooded his mind. "I will drive him from this estate!" Lazarus leaped to his feet and began looking around for clothes. "He is no longer part of this family! To me, he is a dead man!"

Deliberately, Jesus stepped between Lazarus and the tunic that was draped over a nearby chair. "You are the dead man," Jesus said as he looked directly into the eyes of the enraged man.

"Your father has gone to rest peacefully in the paradise God has prepared for the souls of the righteous. He will live again, but you, with murder and unforgiveness in your heart, can never enter the peaceful rest of the righteous."

In the depths of Lazarus's eyes, Jesus could see the demons trembling. Lazarus was also physically trembling.

"My brother robbed this family. He took half of our fortune. He broke my father's heart. Because of his irresponsibility, my life has been totally dedicated to rebuilding this estate. Finally, I have purchased the last piece of property to totally restore this estate. My last purchase included the barn, which would have been in good repair had it not been sold to fund Nodab's follies. Before I can undo this last monument to the foolishness of my brother, it falls on my father and kills him! Nodab is responsible for my father's death. How can I just forgive him?"

"You only need to say the words, and God will do the rest," Jesus instructed.

"I forgive—those are powerful words," Jesus urged. "With those two words, you can free yourself from all the Anger." At that point, Jesus's voice became gentle and knowing. "The Rage and the Anger are actually painful, aren't they?" Placing his hand over the heart of the bare-chested man, his dark young eyes locked with the eyes of Lazarus, a man at least ten years older than himself. "Free yourself from the torment you are feeling," Jesus urged. "Just repeat after me—I forgive Nodab."

Jesus looked deeply and unflinchingly into the eyes of Lazarus. He viewed a moment of internal struggle, a space of time when the primary demonic spirit of Unforgiveness tried to assert his control. But Unforgiveness found himself immobilized, bound by the unyielding holiness of the carpenter's son.

"I…forgive…Nodab." The words came out of Lazarus in a shuddering whisper, followed by a torrent of tears.

Jesus, with his spiritual eye, saw all the demonic spirits flee as Lazarus slumped weakly into a sitting position on the edge of his bed.

The door to the sleeping chamber suddenly burst open. "I will not wait any longer!" Martha announced as she rushed back into the sleeping chamber to see what was happening to her brother. Abruptly, she stopped! Her hand flew to her mouth in amazement. Her brother, nearly naked, was sitting on the edge of his bed!

After her first wave of joyful amazement subsided, Martha's strong sense of correctness took over. "Find Lazarus some clothes!" she directed any male within the sound of her voice. Then she quickly turned and left.

Weak-kneed and laughing, she leaned against the wall in the courtyard. Relief, confusion—Martha hardly knew what to feel. Suddenly, the mourners pressed around her. They began to wail, louder than before. "Stop! Stop! My brother is well!" Martha announced as she grabbed her younger sister, Mary, by the hand and pulled her away from the mourners and into the house.

Martha's husband was the first man to reenter the room, followed by Toma, Joseph, and all the others. Only Nodab remained outside the room, but close to the door. All eyes immediately went to Lazarus, a man obviously no longer suffering. All eyes then went to Jesus.

"This is the work of God," Jesus simply responded to the questions in each man's mind.

"Where is my brother, Nodab?" Lazarus asked.

All eyes then shifted back to Lazarus, and once again, he was the center of attention.

"I am here." Nodab stepped into the open doorway. Taking a deep fortifying breath, he approached his older brother. "I rejoice to see you have recovered. At the same time, my heart breaks over the death of our father." As he came face-to-face with his brother, Nodab could not make eye contact. Silent tears began to fall. "The foolishness of my youth follows me and continues to bring tragedy to this family." Nodab choked on his words as he began to sob. "Forgive me, my brother." Nodab, once a proud young man, now dropped down on both knees at the feet of his elder brother.

The Spirit of God moved into the room, breathing compassion into the elder son of Bohan.

Lazarus was surprised by the tenderness he suddenly felt for his younger brother. Without hesitating, he reached down and pulled Nodab to his feet and then embraced him. Both brothers wept together for their father and for all the years they had been estranged.

Toma and Joseph, with Jesus, quietly slipped out of the room, allowing the brothers their time of reconciliation. "We could build the bier." Jesus suggested.

Joseph nodded while Toma stopped a servant to offer their assistance.

It was nearly sundown when Lazarus and Nodab stepped into the carpentry shed on their estate. Together, Jesus and Joseph were securing an axle and two wooden wheels onto the flatbed of boards that would carry Bohan's body to the family gravesite.

"We're finished," Joseph announced.

"My father's servants would not have had the skill to complete this bier so quickly," Lazarus stated. Then looking first at Joseph and then most directly at Jesus, he said, "Thank you. I do not understand what you did today, but I know I owe my life to you."

Running his hand over the smooth boards that made the bed of the bier, Nodab commented, "This is fine workmanship."

Joseph responded, "It is the work of my son. He represents me and all that I have taught him. Today, I declare to you, he is a master carpenter, and soon he will have his own shop in Capernaum."

In the heavenly throne room, God stood and announced, "This is my son. He responds to every word I say. On Earth, he represents me and all I have taught him. His work is my work! This is my son!"

Index of Characters

Biblical Characters

Abel
The second son of Adam and Eve; he was killed by his brother Cain. (Genesis 4:1–12)

Abraham
An ancestor of Jesus. (Genesis 11–25)

Adam
The first man; he was created by God and placed in the Garden of Eden. (Genesis 2-4)

Barabbas
The criminal that Pilate freed at Passover when Jesus was crucified. (Matthew 27, Mark 15, Luke 23, John 18)

Beggar at
the Beautiful Gate
Fictionalized as Ichabod, the crippled son of Asa, the Temple perfumer. (Acts 3)

Cain
The firstborn son of Adam and Eve; he became the first murderer. (Genesis 4)

David
A king of Israel and ancestor of Jesus (1 Samuel 16–2 Samuel 24, 1 Chronicles 11–29, Matthew 1)

Elijah	Old Testament prophet who went to heaven in a chariot of fire (1 Kings 7, 2 Kings 2)
Esther	The queen of Persia; she saved her people, the Jews, from annihilation. (Esther 1–10)
Eve	The first woman; she was created by God from Adam's rib. She was Adam's wife and was the first to fall into sin. (Genesis 2–4)
Heli	Grandfather of Jesus, one theory is that the genealogy in Luke is actually the genealogy of Mary. (Luke 3)
Herod Antipas	A Son of Herod the Great and ruler of Galilee (Matthew 14, Luke 23)
Holy Spirit	Third person of the Godhead.
James, son of Joseph and Mary	The brother of Jesus (Matthew 13:55)
James, son of Zebedee	Possibly a cousin of Jesus, one of the disciples, the brother of John (Mark 1, Mark 9)
Japheth	The son of Noah (Genesis 6-10)

Jesus	Son of God and son of Mary (the Gospels of Matthew, Mark, Luke, John)
John, son of Zebedee	Possibly a cousin of Jesus, one of the disciples, the brother of James the disciple (Mark 1, 9, 14)
John, son of Zechariah	John the Baptist, a cousin of Jesus (Mark 1,6; Luke 1,7)
Jose	Brother of Jesus, son of Joseph and Mary (Matthew 13:55)
Joseph	Carpenter of Nazareth, husband of Mary, earthly father of Jesus (Matthew 1, Luke 2)
Joseph, son of Jacob	An Old Testament type of the Messiah (Genesis 37-48)
Judah, son of Jacob	An ancestor of Jesus (Matthew 1:3, Genesis 37-48)
Lazarus	Friend of Jesus who lived in Bethany, fictionalized as the elder brother in the parable of the prodigal son (John 11)
Martha	The sister of Mary and Lazarus of Bethany (John 11)
Mary	The mother of Jesus, wife of Joseph (Matthew 1-2, Luke 1–2)

Mary	The sister of Lazarus who lives in Bethany (John 11)
Michael	A prince of angels who fights the forces of evil (Daniel 10, Revelation 12, Jude 1)
Moses	A deliverer chosen by God to lead Israel out of Egypt (Exodus, Numbers, Deuteronomy)
Noah	An ancestor of Jesus, builder of the ark (Genesis 6–9)
Peleg	An ancestor of Jesus who lived during the building of Tower of Babel (Genesis 10:25)
Salome	The sister of Mary and the wife of Zebedee, this relationship is theorized by comparing the two scriptural passages about the women who were with Mary at the cross. (Mark 15:40, Matthew 27:55–56)
Satan	Once a heavenly angel named Lucifer. He rebelled and became the enemy of God, also called the Evil One or the devil. (Job 1)
Shem	A son of Noah, ancestor of Jesus (Genesis 6–9)

Simon the Zealot	A disciple, fictionalized as a childhood friend of Jesus (Acts 1:12–14)]
Xerxes	The king of Persia (Esther)
Yeshua the Creator	Yeshua is the Hebrew name for Jesus; in this story, it is used as the heavenly person of Jesus.
Zebedee	A fisherman married to Salome; his sons are James and John; possibly the uncle of Jesus (Matthew 4:21–22)
Zechariah	The father of John the Baptist, a relative to Mary the mother of Jesus (Luke 1:36–80)

Fictional Characters

Abigail	The wife of Ezra, son of Samuel
Ahaz	The son of Moshe, the tanner of Nazareth; childhood friend of Jesus
Asa	The father of Ichobod, perfumer for the Temple
Baruch	Shepherd of Nazareth
Benjamin	Youngest son of Zebedee and Salome, cousin of Jesus

Bohan	Father of Nodab, Lazarus, Mary, and Martha of Bethany, large-animal merchant
Daveed	A Zealot, follower of the Galilean, brother-in-law of Jethro, the blacksmith
Debir	An Egyptian and head drover for Kheti and Toma's caravan
Elesheva	Jabek's widow, wife of Toma
Ephriam	A man in the Essene community in Jerusalem who owned a donkey and cart
Ezra, son of Samuel	A man who lived in Nazareth, husband to Abigail
Geber	An Essene teacher
Harim	The son of Moshe, the tanner; boyhood friend of Jesus
Jared	The owner of the olive grove and press on the Mount of Olives
Jethro	The blacksmith of Nazareth, a Zealot, father of Simon the Zealot, friend of Joseph
Joram	Priest and friend of Zechariah

Kheti	Egyptian owner of a trading caravan; Toma is his partner
Moshe	A tanner in Nazareth, friend of Joseph
Nodab	The fictional name for the prodigal son and fictional brother of Lazarus of Bethany
Obal	The husband of Salma, the wet nurse
Ophaniel	A guarding angel
Raziel	A fallen angel, second in command to Satan
Salma	The wife of Obal, wet nurse for baby Seth
Salmon	The owner of an olive grove in Nazareth
Seth	The adopted son of Toma
Toma	Joseph's cousin, coowner of a trading caravan
Uncle Shaul	Uncle of Toma and Joseph who lives in Bethlehem
Zerah	The teacher of the synagogue school in Nazareth

Historical Characters

Antiochus Epiphanes	A Syrian king who tried to force the Greek culture on the Jewish nation about 175 BC
Archelaus	The son of Herod the Great, who became the ruler of Judea when his father died. That position was taken from him by Rome in AD 6, and he was sent into exile.
Aretas IV	Nabataean king from 9 BC–AD 40; Herod Antipas married his daughter and opened trade relations with his nation.
Galilean	A Zealot and messianic figure who led a revolt against Rome about AD 6.
Hillel	A well-known first century Jewish rabbi; he lived from 75 BC–AD 15. He founded the rabbinical school of Hillel in Jerusalem.
Judah Maccabee	The hero of Hanukkah who defeated Antiochus Epiphanes
Shammai	A well-known first century Jewish rabbi; he was the head of a rabbinical school in Jerusalem.
Varus	The Roman governor of Syria

Biblical References

Chapter 1

1. Genesis 4:3
2. Genesis 4:2–5
3. Genesis 4:6–7
4. Genesis 4:7

Chapter 2

1. Psalm 119:9–12
2. Luke 1:35–36

Chapter 3

1. Psalm 82:1–2
2. Psalm 14 1–2
3. Psalm 101:7
4. Genesis 4:9
5. Genesis 4:9
6. Genesis 4:10
7. Genesis 4:11–12
8. Genesis 4:13–14
9. Genesis 4:15
10. Genesis 4:16
11. Genesis 4:17
12. Deuteronomy 10:18
13. Isaiah 1:2
14. Micah 6:8
15. Proverbs 31:8–9
16. Psalm 113:5–7
17. Lamentations 5:1–3

18. Isaiah 1:17–18
19. Leviticus 24:21
20. Joshua 23:6–7

Chapter 4

1. Psalms 121:1-4
2. Psalm 121:5-8
3. Psalm 19:8–9
4. Daniel 11:31
5. Daniel 11:32–33
6. Proverbs 30:4
7. John 3:16
8. Genesis 3:15

Chapter 5

1. Esther 4:15–16
2. Esther 5:1–3
3. Luke 3:23–24
4. Luke 3:24
5. Luke 3:25
6. Luke 3:25
7. Luke 3:27
8. Luke 3:27–29
9. Luke 3:29
10. Luke 3:29–31
11. Luke 3:32
12. Luke 3:32–33
13. Genesis 37:26
14. Genesis 37:26
15. Genesis 37:27
16. Luke 3:34–35
17. Exodus 20:4
18. 1 Chronicles 16:8–12

19. Genesis 11:8
20. Luke 3:35-36
21. Job 17:25–26
22. 1 John 4:1
23. Luke 3:36–37
24. 1 Peter 5:8–9
25. Luke 9:62
26. Luke 9:62

Chapter 6

1. Proverbs 22:1
2. Proverbs 22:3–4
3. Proverbs 22:2
4. Isaiah 46:9, 11–13
5. Psalm 51:1
6. Psalm 51:2–3
7. Psalm 51:4
8. Psalm 51:6–8
9. Ezekiel 16:4–5
10. Ezekiel 16:6–7
11. Psalm 30:5
12. Deuteronomy 28:58
13. Deuteronomy 28:59
14. Psalm 78:37–38
15. Malachi 2:17
16. Malachi 3:1
17. Malachi 3:3
18. Luke 1:13–15
19. Luke 1:19
20. Luke 1:16–17
21. Malachi 3:5
22. Exodus 20:15

Chapter 7

1. Proverbs 11:2
2. Genesis 3:24
3. Luke 15:18–19
4. Luke 15:22
5. Luke 15:23
6. Luke 15:24
7. Luke 15:27
8. Luke 15:29–30
9. Luke 15:31–32

Chapter 8

1. Psalm 48:1–2
2. Psalm 48:2–3
3. Psalm 48:4–5
4. Isaiah 62:6
5. Isaiah 62:7
6. Matthew 26:52
7. Isaiah 62:10
8. Isaiah 62:11
9. Isaiah 62:12
10. Joel 2:1–2
11. Psalm 27:13–14
12. Zephaniah 1:12–13
13. Zephaniah 1:4–5
14. Zephaniah 1:7
15. Psalm 68:5–6
16. Psalm 113:1
17. Psalm 113:2
18. Exodus 12:3, 6
19. Psalm 115:1
20. Psalm 115:9
21. Psalm 115:12

22. Exodus 12:7
23. Exodus 29:13
24. Psalm 116:1
25. Psalm 116:3–4
26. Psalm 116:4
27. Psalm 116:15–17

Chapter 9

1. Genesis 22:7–8
2. Genesis 22:9-10
3. Genesis 22:11-12
4. Genesis 22:13–14
5. Isaiah 53:7
6. Isaiah 53:11
7. Exodus 6:2, 5–6
8. Psalm 24:3–4
9. Exodus 2:23
10. Exodus 3:7
11. Psalm 78:43
12. Psalm 78:44
13. Psalm 78:44
14. Psalm 34:8
15. Psalm 34:8
16. Psalm 78:45
17. Psalm 78:45
18. Psalm 78:45
19. Psalm 78:46
20. Psalm 78:47–49
21. Job 38:24–25
22. Luke 1:76–78
23. Malachi 3:1
24. Malachi 3:2-4
25. Malachi 4:4–5
26. Exodus 12:29

27. Exodus 12:30
28. Exodus 6:6
29. Isaiah 52:9–10
30. Psalm 136:10–15

Chapter 10

1. Isaiah 40:6–7
2. Isaiah 35:4
3. Isaiah 35:4–6
4. Genesis 35:2–3
5. Exodus 29:36
6. Malachi 3:1
7. Malachi 3:3
8. Isaiah 59:1–2
9. Deuteronomy 29:29
10. Isaiah 42:9
11. Genesis 22:5
12. Isaiah 53:7
13. Isaiah 53:8
14. Isaiah 53:9–10
15. Isaiah 53:11
16. Deuteronomy 18:15
17. Deuteronomy 18:18–19
18. Proverbs 30:4
19. Matthew 2:23
20. Luke 2:48–49

Chapter 11

1. Matthew 6:19–21
2. Matthew 6:24–25
3. Matthew 6:26
4. John 14:2
5. Matthew 7:7–8

6. Exodus 33:7
7. Exodus 33:9

Chapter 12

1. Exodus 34:22–23
2. Isaiah 56:1
3. Isaiah 50:7-9
4. Isaiah 50:11
5. Isaiah 48:22
6. Isaiah 51:7–8
7. Isaiah 53:2

Chapter 13

1. Psalm 127:3
2. Isaiah 40:3–5

Chapter 14

1. Joshua 1:2
2. Joshua 1:6–7
3. Joshua 1:8–9
4. Joshua 1:7